PEBBLES
from the POND

A Teacher's Story

ROBERT WESLEY CLEMENT

Pebbles From The Pond
Copyright © 2024 by Robert Wesley Clement

All rights reserved. No part of this publication may be reproduced, distributed, or transmitted in any form or by any means, including photocopying, recording, or other electronic or mechanical methods, without the prior written permission of the author, except in the case of brief quotations embodied in critical reviews and certain other non-commercial uses permitted by copyright law.

ISBN
978-1-962868-44-0 (Paperback)
978-1-962868-45-7 (eBook)
978-1-962868-43-3 (Hardcover)

Pebbles From The Pond

Dedication

After completing four books and receiving positive feedback on my writing it became time to give credit where credit is due. The years I spent in the classroom and as an administrator needed to be acknowledged.

PEBBLES FROM THE POND is a work of fiction but the characters inhabiting the story are mostly true. Certainly the students I taught brought this narrative to life.

The years I spent in education and particularly the five years I taught in Embden, Maine was a time when the community truly engaged with their children's learning. I was allowed to take learning from the written page and draw from the world around the pond.

This story celebrates the hundreds of parents who made our job as teachers a whole lot easier.

One parent in particular stood out and though we have now lost her, Jeanelle Creamer stood up for every student in the school, I call her earth mother.

A special lady in my life, my wife Carey, has been a constant source of encouragement. Finally my son Khristian and daughter Shellee, you keep rooting me on; thank you all.

Table of Contents

INTRODUCTION

Imagination is a word that conjures up *fairy tales, flights of fancy* and *creative problem solving*—celebrated in literature, film, and in the market place. Who among us hasn't heard or read the four fateful words, <u>Once Upon A Time.</u> A trip into a world that lulled us to sleep or left us restless. In a school setting students are encouraged to use their imagination when they write, draw, paint, compose, or construct.

My own story writing has used characters that defy gravity and the reasoned mind to allow the reader to move beyond the accepted and expected.

In the real world, right here on good old Terra-Firma, faced with the unknown, the unseen, the silent —in darkness that changes sounds and shapes of the most ordinary into all the bad things that go bump in the night—imagination is not an ally.

When the sky shrouds itself, hiding your most trusted spirit guides—the moon and stars—that same imagination can leave you breathless, nearly paralyzed, your five senses fueling your fear.

PROLOGUE

My fading perfume is losing its battle to an overpowering scent of fear—a smell like wet wool—a disturbing smell. My pores emit a vapor that clings to my shirtsleeves. Sweat is running down my chest inside my shirt. Every imaginable warning sign is flashing in my head, every alarm bell ringing out. This can't be good. My mouth goes dry, trying to swallow my fear; useless. Then there is the dark. So thick I can taste it. Blackness, the great quantifier, the back drop of a hundred childhood nightmares. *Where am I?* I sense I'm in difficult terrain not easily traveled even in full light. My chest feels as if a terrific weight has been placed upon it. A shallow breath is all I can manage. In my mind I hear a phrase I have used dozens of times—half kiddingly in most situations but not now, it's screaming now. There's no other way to express it—**I'm scared as Hell**.

Sitting with my back against a tree trunk, I shrink into the bark, trying to make sense of everything. There is an absence of sound. I sniff the air but only smell myself. I strain my ears. All I hear is my heart thumping and pounding. The silence is deafening. Finally, I manage a deep breath. Peering into the blackness I conjure up the worst outcome imaginable. I touch my legs. They're scratched and bleeding. My arms are torn and sore

"

from squeezing through the undergrowth. As I strain my mind to capture meaning from this nothingness, my mouth sends a foulness down my throat that increases with each breath. I reach for anything that might bring recognition. Or a way out. My eyes ache. I take more ragged gasps of breath. They mix with my thumping heart. Another long raspy shuddering sigh leaves my lips, and becomes a quiver running the length of my body. I look up for my spirit guides. They are nowhere to be found. Backstage somewhere, behind an ebony curtain.

CHAPTER ONE

Group Learning

August 1980. I park my car in the grass. I had been advised not to park on the tar, 'those kids use every bit of the parking lot to extend what they view as their outdoor playground. Don't get off on the wrong foot,' I was told, 'they will eat you alive.'

I was early on this first day of school but had wrestled overnight with the haunting dream that seems to appear whenever I'm taking on something new. So up early, stoked with coffee and anticipation, mine is the second vehicle to park on this patch of grass. Through the windshield I view a canopy of trees standing at the edge of an athletic field, the leaves a regal emerald green. Still August. My experience in New Hampshire tells me it won't be long before a blush of embarrassment will creep into the picture. Driving to Embden nearly every morning during the past two weeks I gaze into a panorama of mountains, some with famous names, others simply a reminder of the power of nature. As a group, they show their faces around nearly every turn of my drive in—none sporting a beard of white as yet, but soon. That thought brightens me, for I am a skier. Not knowing what the day will bring, I sigh. I remove my hands from my new security blanket, the leather-wrapped steering wheel, reach across to gather my three canvas totes of learning materials, and manage to kick the door closed without having to put the bags down on the wetness. *First success,* I sigh. Actually, I find myself sighing quite often these days. It's my way of summoning my next step when not quite sure where that next step might be landing. I look back once more at the little red sports car I have splurged my savings on after getting this job, two years old but new to me. I smile. Safely on the tar parking lot I bend to put the sum of my learning down and reach for the keys that will open the glass doors to my future. I lurch backward as the door pops open and come face to face with a woman wrapped in an apron that goes to her shins.

"Good morning, my name is Darlene, I'm chief cook and bottle washer here," a hand extended with a big smile at the end of the sentence. Just past that smile a smell of fresh baked bread. The aroma heavenly.

"I'm Melody Standish, call me Melody." I take that hand and reply, "That bread smells delicious."

"I heard we had a new lady Principal," Darlene says, "And I like your name. Let me help you get that gear aboard and settled, then you find your way back here into the kitchen. There is a pot of coffee brewing and that bread you're smelling is yeast rolls—you have to have one—sets the direction for the day." She winks and smiles and then says, "Oh yeah, you'll need a quarter."

I look at her quizzically.

"For the coffee." Grabbing one of my totes she follows me down the corridor. Welcome back posters greet me on both sides, created by the two teachers who will teach a total of six grades in two classrooms in this building. We exit through the rear door of the school and cross a tarred space used by the older kids for basketball. Two basketball hoops hang from rectangular plywood on each end of a makeshift court. No painted lines, the grass and one wall of the school serve as out of bounds it seems. New white cotton nets have been attached to the rims since I was here last but the paint on the plywood could use some fresh makeup. That might be a good project for a kid.

"See you in the kitchen," says Darlene. As the door to the main building closes behind her, I am left at the door to a metal double wide trailer. 'Growing pains,' I was told when shown around after signing on. 'We'll need a building project soon.' I look once more to my surroundings. Early morning wetness covers everything. The roadway stands maybe thirty yards away to the west. The school property near the road is secured with a rail fence. I notice what looks like a bunch of sticks woven and filled with stones under one of the wood fence railings. Kids playing here over the weekend probably. To the east a large field is inviting the morning sun to breakfast, just now clawing its way through the tree line causing the wetness to glisten. A back-stop for baseball stands with its back to the parking lot and at the other end of the field a smaller version for girls' softball. Within the week soccer goals will claim their season on this field. The grass needs mowing but soon a lined soccer field will emerge. 'These kids live season to season,' another nugget of wisdom I had been given in the two weeks I have been aboard. My mind wanders, *Boundaries both visible and the ones we set for ourselves seem to govern our lives. I will be coaching a team that hasn't won a game in the recent past.* I sigh once more. *May have to expand those boundaries a bit.*

Flipping the light switch my recent efforts to make this room my sanctuary adorn the walls. I smile, relax, and sigh. I have spent the larger part of the past two weeks in this room, sandwiched between meetings with the other administrators and the two teachers I will be working with. I look at the bulletin board created days ago and it seems to convey what I hope is a positive beginning. Using a picture of a stop sign, a railroad crossing, and a beating heart, a message is written below each picture:

Stop Sign —Stop!
Railroad Crossing—Look!
Beating Heart—Listen!

After getting the students settled, my plan is to use this bulletin board to begin establishing classroom rules. I will ask students to write this very first morning. Use their imagination. How might these pictures and words set a direction for the way we work with one another?

This will be their first writing assignment and it will reveal a lot about the students. How do they respond to a task? Who shows the ability to write a complete sentence, convey a clear thought? How many will at least make an honest attempt?

I also know that developing mutual respect is the engine that will drive this train. We will all dance the dance the first few days but, in the long term it will be my job to convince them I have something to offer. I have some ideas to promote that.

Part of this past two weeks has found me combing through each students' record and viewing what success and failure has looked like. I viewed copies of year-end grades and school attendance. I am armed with at least a snapshot of what I'm facing. Then the real pictures looked me in the eye. School pictures. Since they first entered the education process. Tonight, I will go through each response, reconnect with their school record and individually give them feedback. I want the students to know everything they write will be reacted to. There will be no busy work, no handouts to merely fill time. Hopefully, collectively, our classroom rules will take form from their own ideas, possibly using my three words on the bulletin board as a template.

On my desk is the faded magazine I found in the closet in the main building that houses supplies. As I conduct my daily business, the article on teacher deportment dated 1915 should keep me grounded. I open to the page that offered the rules a teacher was expected to follow. Rules that had nothing to do with teaching ability. My finger touches each headline:

You will not marry during the term of your contract.

I can probably live with that one.

You will not travel beyond city limits without permission.

You are not to keep company with men. *That just might be a deal breaker.*

No riding in a carriage or auto with a man other than a father or brother. *Oh dear me.*

You may not smoke, wear bright colors or dye your hair, but wearing two petticoats is expected.

Sweep the floor, build a fire in the stove by 7am. Scrub the blackboard daily. Be home by 8PM. if not at a school function.

And we think women teachers of today are under scrutiny, I just shake my head.

I look around the room, sigh once more and silently cheer myself on. *You can do this.* The remaining walls have poster pictures of people who have persevered to become pioneers for all sorts of causes. A woman, an Indian chief, a scientist, three men, a girl. These pictures have no legend that describes their efforts. Some of our reading will include people on these posters. When a student needs a prompt, I will introduce a brief history of one of these images and encourage a research effort.

This little school, set within walking distance of a cold water pond serves as the heartbeat for the town. I have been hired to serve as principal of the building and teach all subjects for three grades, 6th-7th-8th. In about an hour from now, thirty-two of the kids arriving on one of four busses will find their way to this mobile classroom they will call home for a school year of one hundred and seventy- five classroom days.

Day one has arrived. *But first that cup of coffee and a yeast roll.*

Darlene is not alone, my two fellow teachers are in conversation when my nose leads me to the kitchen. One of the ladies is a veteran teacher.

"K-2, that's me," says, Mrs. Poulin, silver haired with a ready smile. I met her two weeks ago. We shake hands again this morning—her hand as warm as fresh yeast rolls, ready for the day. Been there, done that, her warm hand implies.

Miss Nichols, a newbie to the district and the profession as well, nods looking lost. I take her hand, cold as the door to the mobile classroom. I wink, "We got this."

"Are you ready for this, ladies?" Mrs. Poulin asks, raising her coffee cup. "These kids run the gamut from gifted, to not terribly interested." She bites into a yeast roll, "Fortify yourself."

I stare into my cup and muse for a moment. This is my third teaching job. *I might be new here but I have learned at least a thing or two about how a school runs.*

I drop a quarter on the counter, "Let me grab a yeast roll. Darlene you tell us how all this really works."

Darlene smiles. She has seen Principals, teachers and students come and go. Almost shy about giving advice—never-the-less she is being asked. She takes a sip of coffee and looks out the window into the early morning light. She turns, "These kids like to help. Find little chores in your classroom that need doing and share the wealth." She wags her finger, "Don't ever play favorites. These kids might not all be the best readers but they can read a lie and favoritism like it was April Fools' Day." She takes a sip, "Feed them what they need. Add a little sugar when you can, and lots of air—let them breathe—these kids need to breathe." She drained her cup. We nodded, clonked cups and toasted the truth.

Teaching 101 had just been prescribed, and so it begins with the arrival of the first bus. As each bus enters the drive—lights flashing—stopping just outside the entrance, I stand waiting. Students begin spilling out. I announce my name and offer a hand to each as they exit the bus. Shy glances, quick nods, not ready to meet my eyes, but each one hears my name. Mrs. Poulin standing inside at her classroom door ushers her k-2 students to a cubby with their name already in place. Students she has taught in the past who have now moved on, happy to see at least one familiar face—hug her on the way to their new challenge further down the hall.

To the children entering her classroom she admonishes, "Find the seat with your name on it, that's your first bit of schoolwork, then sit down. There is a little picture puzzle on your desk you can try to solve while we wait for the other children. The brightly colored pencil is my gift to you. When everyone's here we will go onto the playground and I will give you a tour of the places you can play."

Miss Nichols waits at the door to her classroom and introduces herself to the grade 3-5 students as they wander in. Veterans now, with more experience than the lady shaking their hand, they know the drill. Even with a new teacher some things wouldn't change. They find the cubby with their name, stash their new binders, pencils, snacks, and for some, bag lunches. They then line up to be dismissed to the playground. Our aide Mrs. White is on duty out there. She hadn't made it in time for a kitchen coffee but has her own Styrofoam cup offering a little steam to the morning. She keeps the students corralled until all the busses have emptied. Most of the kids know one another but many have not seen their school friends over the summer. Little knots of conversation and laughter are taking place. New clothes and a smile in place at least for now.

After going through the awkwardness of a first day and two new teachers on site as well, the inevitable whispering, giggling and posing is taking place. Today marks the beginning of slowing down, quieting from a summer with few reins. When all the busses are accounted for the bell rings and we enter our classrooms.

In my room the boys settle in like day old snow—slumped in their seats. I call names from my class list and everyone is present for this first day. Some answer loudly—here—others simply raise their hand. I sigh. Thirty two names called, seventeen girls and fifteen boys, each with their own back story. I straighten, time to probe a little.

After a slightly longer introduction than the handshake at the bus I present the writing assignment. I point to the bulletin board. I ask them to try to include one example of how they used each of the three words written on the board over the summer.

"No I don't mean the time you crossed a railroad track on your way to fish or a ride into North Anson or Madison and had to cross those tracks with your parents," I kid. "So give these words a little thought in your response. Did you stop doing something this summer that you had always done? Like teasing your younger brothers or sisters' maybe? Just kidding, you wouldn't do that." I winked. "Did you look at anything differently, like how a summer job you didn't think you would like turned out ok and you put money in your pocket?" Heads nod. "Did you listen to someone's advice and find out they were right and saved you from screwing up? Did you listen to any new music?" I moved about the room. "Do your best. If you can't come up with anything just tell me about your brothers and sisters. Write about one fun thing you did over the summer. Tell me anything you feel comfortable sharing that will help me get to know you better—a favorite sport, activity, book, movie, song—anything really." The class collectively sighs. I smile.

As heads lower to the task, several look to the window as if to summon strength from this sunny morning—this first morning. Everyone seems to be pushing a pencil, the youngest following the lead of the elder statesmen to their right. I catch the eyes of a tall boy, Waren I believe. I check the newly formed seating chart. Yes it's Waren. He doesn't break eye contact, he gives me a tight little smile. I nod my head slightly and lower my gaze.

We don't have a gym or auditorium so at 9:30 we march in a line to the k-2 classroom in the main building to set some school rules. Pretty standard stuff. We three teachers had put together a list of what we felt we needed to maintain order. We didn't share that with the students. We asked Gary, one of the eighth grade boys who seemed to be holding up the back wall (Mrs. Poulin had recommended him earlier) to man a chalkboard and serve as the writer of the rules. The older girls stand at the opposite wall as if a game of Red Rover is about to start. When we ask what rules we need to make the school run smoothly the younger kids look up with wide eyes as older brothers and sisters politely offer up ideas. We get more than we had hoped for and in the process democratically elect a committee to set up what a violation of these rules might look like and a list of possible consequences.

Gary, the boy at the board, offers up some sound advice. "I think you teachers should plan the consequences, I don't want to be blamed by my buddy Aaron—for keeping him after school." Everyone laughs at that but we see the wisdom of the statement. Aaron's face goes red as everyone looks at him, but he clearly loves the attention.

We end with twenty rules that will be posted in each classroom. The new committee will meet and draft a list of possible consequences. We teachers will choose from among this list, add our own if necessary and finalize them. Our list of Consequences will be posted as well. *No surprised looks when the hammer comes down.*

I spend the remainder of the morning of this first class day with students handing out text books. Remembering Darlene's admonition I call on as many students as possible for the task— and a task it is. Thirty-two students in three separate classes each with their own textbooks for English, Reading, Social Studies, Science and Math. *Are they serious? Can't be done!* We need a break by 11:30 and I declare a first day recess. "Don't think this will happen every day. But the way you act and respond in class will certainly add to the possibility." I give them a little smile. *I am already trying to win the boys over, no better enticement than an unexpected recess.*

Recess goes well. Pickup basketball with a knot of boys and girls who set their own rules of play and administer them without violence. Others choose to walk the school boundaries sharing gossip. Jump rope is still in vogue for six grade girls it seems, Hop

Scotch as well. When a basketball goes errant and ends up on the lawn near the fence no one shows any interest in retrieving it. They grab another ball and continue to play. The bell signals lunch and I ask a boy to go get the ball. "I'm not going after it." He pauses, "ask Troy, he's brave."

I look around and the entire class has gone in to eat. I sigh. The lawn is dry now, I walk to the fence reach down to grab the ball. In that moment a pair of bronzed weathered hands appear reaching for that same ball. I look up and meet the eyes of an old man who is clearly Native American. The man merely nods his head and hands me the ball. I open my mouth to speak. That little nest of rocks sit smooth and polished like birds' eggs. I am about to ask the old man what they mean.

He holds up his hand. "I am Henry, we will meet in time." With that he is gone.

I look closer at the rocks. They rest in a nest of sorts, twigs, interwoven—definitely man made. I put the ball back in the portable, turn off the lights, lock the door and go to lunch.

Lunch is macaroni and cheese, green beans and those delicious yeast rolls—applesauce for dessert. Two of the eighth grade girls help serve. Darlene developed and posted her rotation of helpers for the first month. 'If one of them is acting up in class I don't want them,' she had told me. 'They won't like having to meet my eyes from the other side of that line.' She stood up straight, her 5'2" looking a lot taller, 'Nobody likes to disappoint the cook!' She had smiled this morning when she handed me the list but I knew she was serious. I am about to ask Darlene about the old man when the bell rings.

I spend the afternoon meeting with each of the three classes separately, my aide Mrs. White keeps the others busy outdoors. Let them breathe Darlene had said.

Looking for in-put on what they felt had worked well in their classes the year before, I ask, "How did the teacher get around to each of you?"

Shy smiles, these kids aren't about to speak badly about their past teachers. Several squirm, not comfortable. "OK, let's try this a different way, do we have any aspiring teachers in here?" Several hands go up. "Any nurses, or firemen, or lawyers, or business owners?" Half the class raises their hands. "What do these professions have in common?" Hands go up and the proper responses, while expressed in various ways, share a commonality—helping.

"I agree with all of you and that is the way we will be working with one another this year. I can't help each of you individually, all day every day, but you can help each other. Tomorrow I will show you how that can work. You have one assignment for tonight which is to read the story on page twenty for sixth graders. Seventh graders your story starts on page thirteen. Grade eight, page nineteen. No writing for this one but I will be asking questions tomorrow. I have chosen a story for each grade that exemplifies what helping might look like."

After meeting with each class and assigning the story for that class we gather as a group so I can announce: "That's enough for today. Hand in that writing assignment I gave you this morning then let's hit the tar. I think I can out shoot everyone in this room. And you jump rope people—I can jump through the alphabet game twice without stopping—so get ready. And Hop Scotch; don't even get me started." Everyone is giggling and smiling, trying to figure me out.

When the last bus winks its tail lights I have said good night with several high fives thrown my way. One seventh grade girl Fawn, whispers, 'you smell good Miss Standish.'

That last recess gave me some credibility with the athletes at least. We four adults stand there looking like we wouldn't mind being just whisked away to wherever; to have our day end when we reach a bus stop. We all sigh then, *must be contagious,* I think to myself. We go into Marie Poulin's classroom to debrief.

Mrs. White excuses herself. "My day does end when that last bus hits the road so I'll see you ladies tomorrow."

A little bird has seated itself on the window sill and can be heard chirping, flitting from one open window to the other as active as the kids we work with. Marie reassures us that this multi-level teaching can work and given time we will figure it all out. "Just be strong and assured in what you are doing, and show you care." Two more birds land and we stop for a moment just to watch their antics. When they fly off Marie continues, "Embden has strong parent involvement and overall they are very supportive." she clears her throat, "Some of the strongest challenges will come from an ever changing school board and whatever new teaching or testing gimmick is the current rage," she quiets for a moment. "And then there's the Elementary Supervisor," she pauses, starts to speak then pauses again. "I'll let you figure him out on your own." She looks in the direction of the kitchen, changing the subject. "Darlene nailed it. Be firm, fair, forgiving, and throw in a yeast roll now and then," she laughs. "Let's get out of here and breathe ourselves."

When I open the door to my little sports car at 4:15, it is stifling. I open the windows and sit facing the tree line I had seen in a very different light hours ago. When the cooling breeze enters the interior it seems to be reinforcing the message from the kitchen. I take my first deep breath of the day. *Right on Darlene and Marie.*

CHAPTER TWO

Life At The Top

The twenty five minute drive back to my apartment has a very different feel from my—nervous don't know what to expect—drive in. I have taken an apartment on the third floor in the town of Skowhegan. That decision still has the jury out. The mountains and the water seem to be calling me. As the rubber hits the road I notice things I missed in the early morning light eleven hours ago. Looking into the yards of students and residents of the district, I see mostly well-kept, working folks' homes. Having spent the day with thirty-two kids I have broken bread with—I now take an interest in my surroundings—now it is personal. My student's live here. Kids are out, all ages, dogs chained or running along as part of the activity. Bicycles propped up against porches, one lying on a lawn and several in use. I move to the centerline as I pass two boys armed with fishing poles. They wave to my back window—I toot. I can't identify them with ball caps pulled low but their size suggests they were in class. I think they recognize my car, it had been a magnet at various times during the day. A logging truck headed in the opposite direction loaded and leaning has me hugging the ditch. Bumpy road this five mile stretch. Embden road transitions into the outskirts of North Anson with little fanfare and I soon find myself at a stop sign marked by east- west Route 16. To my right The Corner Store stands surrounded by vehicles. I had stopped in several times over the past two weeks and it seems to offer a little of everything, from fast food to very good cuts of meat all served up with a ready smile. With a gas pump out front the store is ideally located to snare traffic headed for recreation— my recreation—Sugarloaf Mountain, a forty minute drive to the west. Another option, Saddleback—is up there somewhere as well, though I haven't ever skied it. Good college team memories from skiing Sugarloaf. I squeeze the wheel excited about the prospect of future weekend skiing. The Appalachian Trail is in those western mountains, also a draw—hence a busy store. Across the road from the store the Carrabassett River—barely carrying any water, dotted with boulders—slowly makes its way east. I turn left onto Route 16, and cross a railroad track with a trestle to my right spanning the Carrabassett. Shortly another stop sign has me looking at downtown North Anson. A printing company across the street along with an antique store of some sort and further to the north a grocery market, anchor what is considered the center of town. To my immediate left a garage is doing business. The fire department building stands silent. My head is on a swivel— to my right a telephone company. I pat the wheel and move on. That right hand turn finds me quickly crossing a bridge over the Carrabassett River. The river will disappear a short distance east, mixing its history with the mighty Kennebec. I accelerate, my engine responds as Route 201A stretches out. I glance once into my rearview and the bridge I crossed disappears but my mind fixes on the name for the district high school, Carrabec. These two waterways that have a visual and physical connection to all five towns now mesh in the name. Each of the five towns in the district has their own elementary school housing students' k-8. These five schools compete with one another in sports as well as the annual spelling bee competition. They come together in the spring though, for a shared concert, each school sporting their own unique colored t-shirts. Embden School has historically been the smallest in population but is enjoying a growth spurt just now.

The mighty Kennebec reveals itself for the first time to my left as I travel the five miles along route 201A to the town of Anson. Vast fields of Cattle Corn—soon to be cut and used to feed milking cows—turn their tassels toward the late afternoon sun. I notice that people corn is being sold from a farm stand across from a cattle barn. I spot a metal box that shows the honor system is still in vogue in rural Maine. Crows are visible in twos and threes, cruising above the corn. My windows are closed and my air conditioning is on high so I can't hear them but I can visualize their beaks moving. Complaining over everything and anything. A group called a murder is just leaving a large tree screaming I'm sure their claim to this bounty that follows the river. Suddenly I think of the short story by Edgar Alan Poe, The Raven, and smile. *You really are a teacher aren't you Melody. Suddenly I get it, these guys scream like bloody murder. Where I come from we called them ravens but I think they are pretty much the same bird. I'll have to check that out.* I come out of my reverie and notice a wood mill on my right, the parking lot dotted with cars. Piles of hardwood logs laid out like Lincoln logs visible to the side and rear. A metal pipe coming from the building spews sawdust onto an already huge mound. Further south around a long curve, on my left, small islands of rocks appear in the middle of the Kennebec. Hemmed in by wooden cradles placed there in a time when logs and later pulpwood floated down this river.

I checked out this oddity the first week I spotted them. These rivers with so much history are possible research topics for students in our social studies class. In the town of Anson my little sports car gets a wave from someone washing a fire truck in front of the Anson Fire Department. I put on my left turn signal to cross the Madison-Anson Bridge—the Kennebec River under my tires. The river is quiet, peaceful, not making waves in a geographic boundary the bridge span forms. The bridge divides more than just towns. I had no idea the extent of the divide and the rivalry of the two towns and by extension the two school districts at that time.

Main Street in Madison starts with a paper mill to my right that uses the power of the river to generate electricity in its effort to keep the economic blood flowing through the town and beyond. The mills reach—just like the river feeding it—begins way up stream.

Fathers of children in a dozen little towns are impacted by the mills economic ups and downs. Paper Mills all along the Kennebec River that spans half a dozen counties have provided opportunity for independent men to make a living on their own terms for a hundred years. *Another research paper maybe.* Anson Stick to my left is another business that has a full parking lot on this late summer afternoon. I don't know what they produce as of yet but I'm sure I'll find out. Several places to eat enter my field of vision. An Insurance company, a department store, Christopher's Wholesalers, a hardware store, garage, and then a stop light. Going straight through the light puts me on Route 148 for the next five miles when another stop sign will send me south on Route 201. For the third time I have snapped on and then immediately off my radio. Still haven't caught a song. Within minutes I am in downtown Skowhegan. My apartment is on Winter Street, a left turn. My apartment is on the third floor of a house that has seen better days. Once owned by a well-to-do businessman it's clearly beginning a slow sag. Left to a son who has not kept himself in good repair the house seems to mirror his approach to life. The ground floor is vacant. Bet there is a story there. An old lady and her husband inhabit the second floor. In our two chance meetings, watching their painful exit down those stairs I wonder how they ever navigate their flight up. Passing their doorway I pause, I have lived here for just a month and consider myself a private—mind my own business person—ahh, but if walls could talk.

It's well after five when I turn the key and fondle the glass knob to my three room flat. I take a breath, the long brass key I carry in my purse is used only when I am gone for the day—'too trusting by half,' my Mother says. When the door opens I am hit with what's called passive solar. The warming afternoon sun has overheated the place. I immediately open all windows. Then I open the door to my bubble—it's what sold me on the place—a glassed in porch just off the kitchen. Eight feet wide and twelve feet long with glass on three sides, perched thirty feet in the air. Sunsets have been beautiful from up here. Examining the world through my own private lens serves as a calming influence on me. The window on each end has been left open and a breeze makes its way from one window to the next. I breathe. As the air washes over me I can smell a little of the effort I exerted on the black top court followed by my jump rope routine. Frankly I stink. If I allow myself the luxury of sitting down to read or relax, the mental tiredness of a day spent with kids will define my evening—I will immediately fall asleep. I jump up and do five jumping jacks, *let's add to this smell.* Grabbing my trusty sneakers that have spent the day patiently waiting, airing out from my run last evening, I change up. With my sneakers tied in a double knot I run down my steps not pausing to hear how my down stairs neighbors are handling this beautiful evening. I'm out the back door and headed left towards North Avenue, staying on the sidewalk. A grey squirrel crosses in front of me. I have to change my gait to avoid him. "Look both ways little guy," I say aloud. Turning south towards town within a half mile I reach and cross Route 2 then bang a left towards Coburn Park. I enter the park on the right and immediately feel I've entered a different world. I discovered this treasure during my first week on one of my runs. Flowers and plants and solitude appear immediately. To my right and down a long decline the mighty Kennebec appears once more, miles from where it guided me home. It sits forty feet below but seems to be quietly tracking me. It seems my life here is going to be defined by water. I complete the circuit and exit the park. I turn right as images of my family enter my mind and replace the river, memories becoming the flow that moves my feet. Descending a steep hill, the river reappears for the next mile of my run along Route 2 east, but I am lost in thought and it barely registers.

The rhythm of my run puts Mom and Dad and me on a mountain slope. I have barely learned to walk but already can navigate a beginners ski run. They are still out there in Park City, Utah. I see the side of the mountain with our cabin perched there looking out over things, much like my new glassed in observatory. We skied out our back door. I suddenly shift gears—both my pace and my focus—and I am at college in the east, studying and skiing in New Hampshire. My endless journeys down those slopes with the wind in my face, I dreamed of who I might become. The freedom I experienced during those years coupled with a vivid imagination left me with a degree in literature and little else. I emerged as a frustrated writer of children's stories who is still waiting to be published. A file folder full of disappointment has not deterred me. I did take several teaching methods courses—thankfully—so in the real world, in the light of day I am a teacher. Based on what I experienced today I should be able to gather a wealth of material for a future story—lots of characters in this class. I haven't given up on being published.

My first two teaching gigs were in private schools, parents with money, kids' with big plans. 'Be smart,' my parents said, 'have a fallback plan in case this writing doesn't pan out.' So now armed with a Principal's certificate as well as my teaching certificate I find myself in Maine both as a teacher and first time principal.

One of the first things I noticed in moving here is the distance between things. Unlike New Hampshire and Vermont where I skied and hiked, here you look into the mountains from fifty to a hundred miles away—nothing is in your face till you get to your destination.

The hills are the same though I am reminded as this hill on the Malbon's Mills Rd. has my heart rate increasing with the effort. I had turned left off route two east a mile ago and headed back towards town. I have covered approximately three miles by the time I hit flat ground and have found through years of running that at three miles I find my personal Nirvana. The final two miles of my run I'm fairly floating above the ground—my mind continues floating as well. A left onto the Dr. Mann Road takes me back to the edge of town—upper North Avenue. My mental trip complete and within a mile of my apartment I pick up the pace for a half mile sprint. A right turn onto Winter St. signals a time to slow, beginning my cool down. Reaching the steps to my apt. I stretch out my limbs using the steps, breathing deeply, savoring the feeling that is going through me. When I climb my stairs for the second time in the past ninety minutes it's with a lightness that seems to lessen the squeaking of each stair—like I lost twenty pounds on my run. From the door in the hallway on the second floor the squeaking hasn't lessened. Either they are both deaf, hate one another—maybe both—or this is what true love sounds like in your seventies. Man those two need to go for a run—or at least a walk—something!

An hour later I have showered and smell much better. I hug myself. I make a sandwich throw a few chips and a pickle onto a paper plate and get myself a glass of icewater. Munching while watching the last remnant of day disappear from my perch on the porch, I sigh. Another beautiful sunset. I gather my plate and glass and go in to re-acquaint myself with the boys and girls I met this morning.

The kitchen table is going to be my workstation I have decided and glancing at the clock on the wall, this place of business is going to be open for at least the next three hours. First things first. I put on an easy listening instrumental album—good-old-around the-campfire- guitars—baying to the night. I grab an Oreo, pour a glass of water and empty a tote.

As I pick up the first student's paper, I match it up with their picture from their folder. Most of the student responses are fairly rote renditions of the model I provided. They all love their dog, most mention a sibling and for the boys at least, fishing, swimming, and riding bikes seemed to have dominated their summer. A few mention haying and outdoor chores. One is an aspiring mechanic working in his dad's shop. Their references to Stop, Look and Listen mirror what I suggested but that's to be expected—If everyone knew everything there would be no need of me.

The girls write with just a touch more flair and their summer passed with friends as the only constant. Some are into reading, (that's a plus), babysitting, helping with housework, day trips to the lake.

Two hours later I am reading the last paper. I study his picture. He's a boy who had remained very quiet all day. I had noticed him, he had studied me. Not surprised his paper is on the bottom. It's clear from the lack of yearly photos he has not been in Embden for all of his schooling. Though tall and slim he didn't play basketball today but rather stood at the edge of activities. The other boys didn't react in either a positive or negative way to his presence. No one invited him to join in now that I think of it. The look he carried on his face was one of bemusement—in his own world it seemed. This is what he wrote.

Did you notice a grey squirrel hanging around outside our classroom all day? He stopped and watched. He looked lost. Maybe he missed everyone over the summer and enjoyed listening to all the chatter. He could be climbing trees swinging from the branches playing in the breeze. Instead he sat just off the tar watching us. It makes me wonder. By the way did you discover that nest of smooth rocks yet? You look nice in blue. Waren

I studied the writing, this boy has a flair. So different from how anyone else had reacted to the assignment. *Was he talking about himself and using a squirrel to send the message? Hmm, this kid definitely notices things though.* Having taken what seems like a dozen or more writing classes, words like Metaphor, and Narrative enter my head. These terms will be introduced along with many others over the course of the year; it seems Waren whether he realizes it or not is way ahead of the game.

I stretch and yawn. I muse, *I'll have to ask Mrs. Poulin about those rocks.* I check the clock, 9:43pm. I put the three different colored class folders to the side and take a final look at the mimeograph masters I will run off early tomorrow morning. One for each class. I broke the school day up into segments. In the two weeks before school started I quickly figured out a traditional teaching approach was not going to work. When I watched the number of text books delivered today those thoughts were confirmed. I had let my imagination take over and had come up with a template; a plan that I had hinted at today.

I looked at the mimeographed master for the eighth grade that was altered slightly for each class. Each time segment will have the day's lesson attached for each day of the week.

The weeks schedule will be handed out to students on Monday morning. Grades six-eight will have lessons and assignments for each subject on their desk when they arrive. While I focus on one class the others will be expected to read react and respond to the lesson in front of them. Mrs. White is in my room to help for two of the class periods then she leaves to help Karen and Marie.

The (helping) part of our discussion today will ask the most capable and motivated to assist their classmates when they need it. I expect eighth graders to help six and seventh graders as well as their peers.

Capable six and seventh graders will be called upon to work with their classmates as well. And where I can combine classes to teach to the entire thirty-two at once, I will surely do that. Will this work? I sure hope so.

I walk out onto the porch and view a calm clear evening from thirty feet in the air. The street lights sit just below my porch window offering silhouettes for the trees lining the street. Bats flit from one shadow to another, and suddenly I smell a skunk. A grey squirrel appears like a ghost on the window ledge, looking me right in the eye. I think I nearly stepped on him earlier. I think of Waren's story and I swear the tight little smile I had seen this afternoon is being worn by this little furry creature. From my own little bit of native heritage—though it had never seen much exploration—I point and call him by his Indian name—Miko. This darkened little bubble has me pretending I control all that is below. Well maybe not all. The skunk smell permeates the porch, I hold my nose and close the windows, the porch door, and retreat to my bedroom where I close that window as well. The skunk smell is dissipating by the time I complete my bathroom duties. I reopen my bedroom window, a night breeze thanks me by rustling the curtain. I sigh once more, offering up silent selfpraise for what has seemed a good first day. No more reading tonight, my latest mystery novel rests on my night stand. The last thing I remember is snapping off my lamp and pulling the covers up around my neck—waking only when the radio alarm sounds five am.

CHAPTER THREE

Her Name Is Eliza

When the bus that traveled the Western Shore Road and the Wentworth Road picking up students of all ages arrived on that first morning in late August, the high school students aboard transferred to a bus that would take them to the high school. The remaining students exited last and moved toward the building. An argument between the drivers of the late arriving bus and the bus waiting for the high school students became heated. I heard the commotion but was busy shaking hands with the late arrivals and directing them to their classrooms. *I wonder what that is all about. Probably a man thing.*

Three new kindergartners from the last bus to arrive look lost as they enter the first day of the next thirteen years of their lives. Mrs. Poulin who has already sent the rest of the kindergartners to the playground asks a second grader on his way to his classroom why their bus was late. "Evan was late picking us up. The boy rolls his eyes and spreads his hands, "Just like always," he finished.

Marie Poulin rolled her own eyes. Evan, who doubles as the building janitor and bus driver and according to him—Jack of all trades—had some growing up to do in Marie Poulin's estimation.

The first and second graders on the late bus knew the drill and after putting their things away went out to join their classmates. Mrs. Poulin assisted the three remaining kindergartners in finding their seat and locating their little rectangle of space on the wall. One of the three seemed awed by everything in the room. She wandered the rows then fingered the long row of children's stories that lined the shelf that ends with a pencil sharpener. The little girl studied this strange machine, slowly turning the handle, a big smile transforming her features. She raised her eyes and looked at the posters on the wall. Pictures of animals, with letters beneath stymie her but she silently tries to decode them. Mrs. Poulin approaches the girl, she has a name tag for the girl. "You are Eliza DeBloise, right?"

The little girl nods. Marie reaches down and sticks the name tag on her shirt. "I'll teach you how to read all those posters yourself this year but if you would like I will read some of them to you right now. They are kind of funny, see what you think." When she finishes she walks Eliza out to meet her classmates. Thus has begun the education of Eliza DeBloise.

Getting Down To Business

It's cool this morning—mid-fifties but seventies again by mid-afternoon the every five minute weather announcement proclaims. Sunny as well, the radio barks before offering up a rare song between morning gargle and canned announcements. My first cup of coffee is riding shotgun warming me inside and out. My little sports car is the only love of my life at the moment and I actually talk to it on the way in, squeezing the leatherwrapped wheel and offering praise to how it hugs the road. My radio alarm woke me up at 5:00 am and the white noise hasn't lessened. Just one song broke through the chatter in the time it took me to get from Skowhegan to Madison. *I'm going to buy some cassette tapes for the player I haven't yet had installed*, I promise myself as I twist the knob to off. Silent smoke is billowing out of the giant stack at Madison Paper, mostly steam and not much smell. Several houses along the river seem to have taken up smoking as well, the occasional wood stove already making its presence known. The fog hovering just above the water offers a warming blanket to the river beneath. *How can the same route provide so many different looks,* I muse. Of course I'm a pin up girl for trying new looks and wardrobe changes since leaving home so there you have it I guess—new looks, new opportunities.

I turn into the school yard on this late August morning knowing there is a three day weekend coming up in two days, Labor Day. Darlene watches me approach, ready to open the door. The smell of a new batch of yeast bread washes over me as the door opens—much like the fog on the river that followed me to work. A sweet spicy smell rides the coattails of the yeast bread. I raise my nose. Darlene notices.

"I made us a little treat with some left over dough. Let me take that travel cup and re-fill it while you're putting things away."

"Darlene you're going to put pounds on me."

"I wouldn't worry, those kids will work off anything I put in your belly," she laughs.

When I get back Darlene has a cinnamon bun all buttered for me. We sip coffee exchanging small talk but I finally had to ask, "What's the story with Waren Stiles?"

"Well that didn't take you long," Darlene says softly, eyeing me—her own eye's twinkling. "Do you have a week?"

"He wrote an odd response to the writing I assigned, even his name is spelled differently. I thought it was a typo when I saw it on my class list—so yeah I'm curious."

"Well," she pauses as if she needs to compose this story—get it right, "He's been with us since sixth grade. There is supposedly a younger sister but a lot younger I'd guess." She pauses again. "He lives down near the end of the pond on the west side. I have never seen him away from school. Never met his family. They live off on a little dirt path, away from the water. Within a quarter mile of Camp Deveraux."

"What is Camp Deveraux?" Then I hold up my hand, "Never mind, tell me about Waren?"

"He's got to you already hasn't he? He does that to people. He's like a bird in flight with no destination, he lights and leaves, he's everywhere and nowhere. I can honestly say I don't think anyone knows much about Waren except Waren, and I'm not even sure about that." Then comes the warning, "His teacher last year, your predecessor," she smiles, "did I say that right?" She looks right at me, "He was completely undone by the boy."

'He unsettles me,' "the teacher told me and this was a man saying this, a big man at that."

I peer up over my cup, "I think he was comparing himself to a grey squirrel in his writing." It was quiet in the kitchen for a moment, both alone in our thoughts.

I swallow the last bite of my cinnamon bun as Marie Poulin arrives.

"Marie can you tell Melody anything about Waren Stiles?"

Marie puts down her carry-all and reaches into the cabinet for a cup. She seems to be framing her answer even as she pours herself a cup of coffee. "I have never had the boy in class so if you're asking me if he's capable, I can't answer that. He appears very intelligent. I would say he seems different, more closed than most of his classmates. I don't believe he's said a dozen words to me in the last two years. He's always polite and respectful though."

"He's never volunteered in the lunch room so that tells you something about not having a need to fit in. He does his own thing." Darlene seemed stymied by the boy as well.

We looked like three coffee cups sharing a conversation, "It was a different piece of writing from anyone else's that's for sure. I always like a challenge. I'm sure it will be fine," I utter as I drain my travel mug, rinse it in the sink, drop a quarter in the jar, and head for the door. I turn, "Darlene can I pay by the month it might be easier. I don't always have a quarter on me."

"All donations are kindly accepted in whatever form they arrive," kids Darlene, winking and smiling broadly.

The pledge of allegiance finds everyone in attendance and alert. Every desk sports an agenda of what will be happening during the two remaining days of this week. I glance at the purple stains on my fingers, the mimeograph machine much less cooperative than the students I am teaching.

Mrs. White collects lunch money and takes attendance, recording it in my grade book. At months end I will have to re-enter that data into the official register that goes to the state. The amount of money given to the district depends on accurate attendance records. That had been the subject of my very first encounter with my elementary supervisor. He explained it all as if he were addressing a child.

As I sit with the sixth graders, having passed back their writing, I invite them each in turn to expand on what they had written. I glance around the room, the other two classes seem to be reading their handouts, or opening a text, following the lesson plan—so far so good.

I make eye contact with Waren, he gives me that same tight little smile. I am reminded once more of Mikos' visit last night.

Thursday passes without incident. I settle in for the night after a shorter run around the town's outer most streets. I spoon a bowl of homemade spaghetti. I turn on the lamp on the porch and between bites open an eighth grade literature book. I want to find stories that might interest the entire class. Most had read the story assigned last night but little excitement had been generated. I plan to find some stories we can read and discuss as a room, no grade distinction. The younger grades will follow the lead of the older students. The girls I don't worry about, they will read whatever is assigned. The boys!!!—not so much!

When I met with Waren at my desk to ask about his writing he seemed evasive. When I suggested to him that it seemed he was using a squirrel as a way of explaining how he viewed the school, that tight little smile reappeared. I didn't mention his compliment on my clothing.

"Why would you think that? I just saw a squirrel doing his thing, that's all."

"Well I thought it was creative never-the-less." I continued, "I write children's stories and you have given me an idea for a story, so thank you Waren." Waren hadn't responded, he simply returned to his seat. When we made eye contact later I swear his tight little smile had loosened.

I sigh, *why am I thinking of Waren? I need a story that will set the tone for the year,* I muse, as I flip through the literature book provided for the eighth grade. Suddenly I recall that a commonality in the boys' responses was hunting and fishing. And the girl's know about hunting and fishing as well, from their own experience or through a brother or father.

I recall a story I had taught in that school in New Hampshire. I go back to the table of contents and there it is. It seems maybe this book is a hand-me-down from the high school. It certainly is not new. Most of the boys in all three grades had remarked on their hunting and fishing adventures—I revisit the story. *Is it too much?* I reread the beginning. *I think this might work.* If this works I'm home free with these guys. *How are the girls going to react?* I look at the vocabulary in the story and it seems they could all navigate it with help. *Is the theme too mature?* I begin mentally planning the written activities that could go along with the reading. This might also be an opportunity for some community involvement. I'm excited. I rise to look down from the porch and study the ground way down there. No skunk tonight, no squirrel either but the bats are still swarming appearing and disappearing in the streetlights. My mind shifts to the long weekend ahead. I just might explore what this little town of Skowhegan has to offer after dark—besides skunks squirrels and bats. I sigh and hug myself.

Following the written plan, Friday offers a time segment for special programs. Some of these programs will be put on by the district, some I will initiate. Since it's the first week, there isn't a program for today so I wing it. "Let's all walk down to the fish hatchery," I announce. Darlene had given me the idea this morning over coffee and made the call. Mr. Murphy who works there has agreed to give us a tour and explain how it works.

Several groans emerge, but I can't tell from where or for what reason. "It's another beautiful day to be out doors but if you would rather I use the time for book learning I can arrange that," I smile. "Learning takes many forms you know." Sighs follow—but no groans—option one seems to be garnishing some new recruits.

"Ok then, we have to stay in line till we get there, agreed? Mrs. White will be at the rear I'll take the lead. No running, screaming, or jostling for position. Sixth grade you will be directly behind me, then seventh, then eighth, Ok let's go on the tar and line up." When I look back to check our progress I see Waren is anchoring the line walking about three steps behind everyone else.

The quarter mile trip is uneventful and I for one learn a lot about the raising and distribution of hatchery fish. Native brook trout apparently is not the norm in Embden Pond unless you get lucky. We all received a hand-out with some basic facts: There are 6500 lakes and ponds in the state of Maine. 1200 of those are referred to as <u>Principal Brook Trout Fisheries.</u> This designation means they are not usually stocked. A goodly number not stocked in the last ten years offers a further designation as <u>self-sustaining</u>. 120 are classified as <u>remote,</u> no planned road or entry within a half mile of the water. The fish we see swimming below us in cement pools are fed a grain like mixture. They will be trucked to various lakes and ponds and released—thus the term, <u>stocked.</u> Each student is given a handful of grain pellets and they take turns gaining the attention of the fish who all scramble to the feed as pea sized nuggets hit the water. They are laughing. Occasionally a nugget reaches an unsuspecting victim in the audience. That particular activity stops when I give them the glare. When we re-gather after the feeding frenzy one girl asks, "Is Embden Pond stocked?" several boys snicker at this, I hush them.

"Yes," the hatchery employee answers, "Everything from Salmon, Trout, Bass, and Pickerel—several other lesser known species as well. The State owns Embden Pond. It's Deep and cold. Deep and cold is good for lots of different kinds of fish." Mr. Murphy takes a mental break and looks among the students, "Hey Troy I didn't see you there. PJ. Is that you? You need a haircut." Realizing he's not alone with the boys he apologizes, "Sorry about that, these two are in here half a dozen times in the summer trying to get me to tell them where I stocked fish in the spring," he laughs dismissing us. "Anyway have a good walk back, I hope the tour was helpful. And have a good Labor Day weekend." He put his hand to his chin, "You know Ma'am the community is putting on a barbecue at the school and fireworks over the water Sunday night if you are looking for something to do over the long weekend." Darlene had given me this same invite over coffee this morning.

When I fire up my little sports car on this Friday afternoon I have gained further knowledge of this quaint little town that isn't really a town in a traditional sense. There is no main street or a down town or even a sidewalk. It's clear the school is the biggest magnet for community involvement. Embden Pond—now that is a whole other community.

Miss Nichols and I talked at the end of the day and have agreed to meet at a local watering hole in downtown Skowhegan for our first social soiree.

Just as the street lights begin to hide the stars above and the bats begin to swoop the night I exit my third floor flat. The stairs creak as I descend. I am past the door of the second floor apartment when a voice reaches my back.

"Young woman, do you have to get up so early every morning, I feel your feet hitting those stairs and it shakes the whole place. I can't hear you but I can feel you."

I turn, "Hi there, I'm Melody. I've noticed these walls and floors are thin, maybe we can all walk softer and turn down the volume a little." I offer my hand and a smile. A confused look follows but the hand does reach mine—slightly hesitant—not sure what he might be agreeing to.

"I'm Ed. Ed Cronin, my wife Edith and I, we've lived here for seven years." He was breathing hard after a full sentence. His false teeth slid slightly, he seemed embarrassed by that and clamped his mouth shut. He had very little hair and his glasses perched on the end of his nose.

"Well glad to meet you Ed, I feel like I already know you and Edith. Have a quiet evening I'm going to explore your town for a little while."

Watching me intently he remarks, "Hmmph, that won't take long." He turns and on his way back into his apartment says to my back, "not much good happens after dark in this town if you ask me. The missus and I see flashing lights going up the avenue half the night on weekends."

I turn, about to descend the stairs, "Well maybe this will help—I don't have to get up as early on the weekend so you should get a good night's sleep for the next couple of nights. Good night Ed. It was good to finally meet you." Ed Cronin is cupping his ear and has a confused look on his face. I don't think he heard a word of what I just said.

I began whistling. *That went well*, I think to myself.

The Old Mill Pub hanging over the banks of the Kennebec River seems like it might be a good place to meet people. I walk a mostly down-hill trek of maybe a half mile. Karen is standing just inside the door, waiting for me. The smells of fried food and the sounds of music and heightened voices immediately puts me in a festive mood. We are ushered to a small table on the second floor and both order a local ale. Karen is six years younger but she is drumming the table to the beat so it seems we share the same taste in music—and beer.

An easy listening guitar reaches across from the little balcony that is being used as a stage. The man's voice is gravelly but he's in tune. It's obvious this is not his day job—though it's nice and relaxing. A line I had heard, *you sound better than you sing,* enters my head and I chuckle then find myself humming along. I always have trouble with the words but I recognize the tune of most songs I listen to. It's Friday night and the work-week is over. Without a word or explanation I high five Karen. We both raise our mugs in silent toast. We did it. We got through the worst of any new job—the beginning. I study the crowd over my beer glass. Mostly couples up here I notice but I'm pretty sure I don't want to be down those stairs bellied up to the bar to meet a guy that way. We both order a pub burger and fries, and another ale. Then we talk school—go figure. Half way into my second beer for some reason Waren enters my head and I ask Karen if she has met him at noon recess.

"Can't say I have," she offers and just like that it's left at that, my mind flitting like those damn bats.

By nine pm. the music has stopped and the rest of the evening will be dominated by patrons entertaining themselves with their shared stories, their raised mugs, and voices. I yawn. I'm ready to call it a night. Karen offers me a ride and I take it. When she lets me out I thank her for both the ride and the evening. She promises to check out some other venues for future excursions. "I've heard about this place called the Solon Hotel. Live bands and good food. A little bit wild I'm told, but a good time."

"Sounds like a plan, see you on Tuesday morning. Goodnight. By the way I might go to that barbecue on Sunday at the school, a good chance for folks to meet the school Marm. Maybe I'll see you there. Anyway have a good weekend."

As I am about to climb the two flights of stairs a flashing light and screaming siren are climbing the avenue. *Sorry about that Ed,*

I think to myself. But at their landing I don't hear a peep from my neighbors to the south. There is a light blinking on my message machine as I enter the darkened kitchen. I hit the bathroom then return and push the button. My mother's voice emerges wondering where in the world I can be when she has taken the time to call? I sigh, "Mother, Mother, morning will be soon enough." I shake my head, mumble to myself and head back into the bathroom to remove the remnants of hamburger from between my teeth.

Chapter Five

Heart Strings

Saturday morning I am just entering my street after a five miler over what I've mentally labeled my, *park and river run* when I see lights flashing in front of my building. There is a town cruiser and an ambulance both idling in the roadway with no one in the vehicles as I jog past. I enter my drive then move to a tree at the side where I lean against the trunk. I am cooling down, sweating like a pig, my eyes stinging. I wipe away the sweat with my shirt. As I am stretching against the tree the door to my building opens and a man holding one end of a stretcher emerges. I wipe more sweat away. The other end enters my vision with a person lying motionless between the two men. They place the stretcher on a dolly and make their way to the ambulance parked on the street. There is a rise to the drive and the dolly picks up speed as it follows the grade. Sudden shouting between the two men reminds me of two bus drivers in a disagreement at the school recently. As the stretcher is being placed in the back with an attendant, a quick thought crosses my mind, *those flashing lights don't always get to the top of the avenue.* Just behind the dolly is Ed Cronin, crying and wringing his hands as halting steps try to get to the stretcher. I quickly surmise it must be his wife Edith. A police officer has appeared and runs down the drive, reaching and placing a hand on Ed's shoulder. He steers a protesting Ed to his cruiser. "You need to calm down sir, while I call this in."

I haven't moved from my spot by the big oak that anchors one side of the driveway. Ed has been placed in the rear seat of the cruiser and looks through the back window. He finds my eyes, a look of hopelessness and helplessness mixes with tears coming down his face. He disappears behind two large hands, his head bowed.

No one but Ed has noticed me yet. Engines roar, a siren sounds, lights flash, then all goes quiet. I can't help but think again of what Ed had said about lights flashing all weekend long. Neighbors disappear back behind their curtains. *I'm thinking maybe I need to call the building owner, though his interest in the place seems marginal at best.* I walk up the drive and when I get to the entrance I see yellow tape blocking my way up the stairs. Someone must think this is a potential crime scene. The cruiser with Ed in it is starting up the street. "How in hell am I supposed to get to my apartment?" I shout to the disappearing black and white. *I guess I do need to call the owner—there is another way to the apartment from the first floor—in an emergency only I had been warned.*

'You'll have to call me to unlock the down stairs door though, so please don't have any emergencies,' the landlord had implored. As I am remembering that conversation while pondering all this, another cruiser pulls up and several officers emerge. I am sitting on the steps leading into the house still bathed in sweat when they approach.

"Do you live here?"

"I do."

"I take it this is not a single family dwelling then?"

"I live on the third floor and am actually trying to figure out how I get there." I point. "There is yellow tape blocking my entry."

"That's what we are here to check out. We'll be as quick as we can but it might take a while. There's a photographer coming to take some pictures. Sorry. By the way do you know these people?"

"Only in passing their door in the hallway."

"Anything you noticed about them, did they fight?"

"I never witnessed a fight. I heard loud voices at times but I'm not sure you would call it fighting."

He was a handsome guy standing there in his uniform and I looked a mess. I was reluctant to introduce myself looking like this. He didn't give me the opportunity to just melt away however, he held out his hand. "I'm Sergeant Luke Harris, and you are?"

"Melody Standish," I offer rising. "I've just finished a long run so forgive my appearance."

"No sweat," he grins and winks at me.

I catch his little word play and find myself smiling back.

"I'm a runner myself. Anyway do you have any idea what could have happened here?"

At that moment his partner hollers to come check this out and I am left standing alone again.

The sergeant looks back and I read his mind. "Not going anywhere"—I point to my saturated running gear, then the tape. The Sergeant nods and smiles.

When the Sergeant emerges he writes down what I have to offer of the couple on the second floor. All the hollering and accusing I have heard in the last month is certainly going to suggest a long hard look at what might have happened. I try to minimize what I have heard from below. He tips his hat and shakes my hand once more. He gives me the look and says, "I know where you live. I'll be in touch." *More word play maybe.* "Your entry should be open in a couple hours, I have to get back. Nice meeting you Melody."

I continue to inhabit the outside steps wrestling with my next move. The decision is made for me when ten minutes later the owner of the store—so to speak—arrives. One of the neighbors must have called. He parks on the side of the street and just sits there staring at his building. It's like he doesn't want to get out and face any of this. Several minutes pass. I can see his mouth moving. Finally with what seems a herculean effort he opens the car door and morphs into-an oversized sofa of a person. *Wow*, I think to myself, *I don't remember him being this large—course I only met him once sitting behind a table.* He lumbers up the driveway nearly blocking a morning sun that frames and exaggerates his girth.

He navigates what must feel like a hill and after catching his breath, a wheezy voice asks, "So what happened here?"

"No clue Mr. Belson. There are still people taking pictures inside so you can ask them I guess."

He rubs his grizzled jaw. "Damn place is more trouble than its worth."

"Could you open up the back way in, I'd really like to clean up?"

He fumbles through his ring of keys, layer after layer of them mirroring the weight he has gained in the years he's acquired the doors these keys unlock. Finally he pulls two keys off the ring. "Here, these two should work. The silver one opens the main entrance on the first floor and that brass one will open the door to the back stairs. That same one will work for both inside doors." He is spent already. Melting before my eyes, sweat beginning to glisten like he had accompanied me on my run. He clearly is not going in. He sheepishly clears his throat, "Might be quite a mess in there. I haven't been in since the last tenant trashed the place—just locked the doors. Damn renters." He looks me right in the eye. I am one of them. He turns and I watch him take little baby side steps on his way down the drive. Straight ahead would not have ended well.

I watch him all the way into his car which goes to one knee to accept his weight. He gives me a feeble little wave of the hand and an even feebler smile. Then he is gone.

I move to the front steps and open the door to the first floor. Mr. Belson could not have prepared me for what struck first my nose then my eyes. With two senses assaulted I can feel a little of the man's pain. Through ripped and torn blinds and curtains the sun is poking its head into corners where litter, trash, broken shelves, trashed furniture, graffiti and torn wall paper toast the day. The smell seems to be a combination of body rot that is embedded in cushions and from a sink and counter piled to the cupboards with dishes of half eaten dried and rotted food. The refrigerator with the door hanging on one hinge, its mouth full of rotten who knows what-all, hides its shame in the shadows. The two rooms I need to navigate to get to what I surmise is the entrance to the back stairs is a health and fire hazard. *I'm living above all this,* comes to mind. How can human beings be this callous? How could the landlord not have gotten this cleaned up? In frustration I pull my sweaty tee shirt up over my nose and fumble with the key. There's no going back now I tell myself. The door creaks. No light comes on in the entry when I flip the switch. Utter darkness. I take one of those little baby steps I had just recently witnessed. My mind fills even as my eyes empty into the darkness. Every scary image I have ever conjured enters my head as I take that first step upward. A spider web makes contact with my face and I panic. My own breath deserts me. Insects are attached to that web and they rub against my skin, one is on my eyelids. I scream aloud as I bat it away. Panic travels the length of my body, I am in full shiver, flailing now, nearly losing my balance. I take a pinched breath through my nose and lock my mouth. My heart begins to race. I grimace, cringing, reluctant to put my hands on anything, batting the air in front of me. My eyes are useless and nearly shut anticipating further assault. My hands sweep the real and imagined like a windshield wiper. I cringe. Magazines and papers stacked a foot high line the steps. They slip and slide beneath my feet forcing me to grab the wooden rail. I cringe again as what sounds like dried seeds crunch beneath my feet. My hands find grit from whatever is attached to the railing. Turn around my mind tells me. I suck in a small breath as if through a straw. Determined now, the only way out is up. I hold my breath for the distance of this first flight. For just a moment a battle scene in a war movie fills my mind. I charge upward. There is a small diamond shaped, grime covered stained glass window on the landing between the floors. I manage a breath as a glimmer from that window frames my next effort. I find the key hole. I breathe again and lower my head refusing to acknowledge what is in my path. I plunge upward. There are less obstacles on the steps but just as many cobwebs and spider webs descending, crisscrossing from the bannister to the wall. When the key fits and opens the lock on my first attempt, I push inward sending the table and plant I had placed there crashing to the floor. Ignoring the plant and overturned table I explode into my kitchen, gasping, wearing a smell on my skin that mixes with sweat—fear. I tremble and shake all over while stumbling to the bathroom. I don't dare look at myself in the mirror. I can feel spider webs and dead flies clinging to my hair. I sigh and take a series of deep breaths trying to calm myself. I sit on the toilet to keep from blacking out. I turn on the cold water put my mouth to the faucet then manage to gargle, rinsing and spitting several times. Involuntary shudders continue in spasms. I breathe in, I breathe out. Slowly a curtain of normalcy rises up from my toes. I sigh. I feel like I just ran a consecutive five miler, I'm exhausted. For a full five minutes I remain seated there numbly tugging and pulling dead flies from my hair and placing them one by one in the trash. Alive and safe my sense of humor will not be denied and I begin the old game, he loves me he loves me not. With each removed dried body I am regaining control. I mumble to myself. This has all been a little too much. When the hot water in the shower hits my face the smell of dove soap washes over me, for some reason that smell brings tears. I scrub my hair. Always a Breck girl, I rinse, and scrub again savoring the smell. Toweling off, I rub my skin red, sighing a whole bunch of times and slowly, slowly, I'm back. Caressing each limb adding moisturizing lotion, I examine, take stock, I am indeed whole.

Fortified with a bowl of oatmeal with cinnamon and blueberries swimming in milk, I sit on my porch with a cup of coffee. I am wiped out. Looking down from my perch my car sitting there all by itself, cruisers and ambulance gone, I can almost believe this didn't happen. But it did happen. Ed's wife left here in an ambulance. Ed left here in a cruiser. You just scared the bejeesus out of yourself getting up here. I'm looking into the bottom of a cup I can't remember emptying. I need to call my Mother.

"You just caught me dear, your father and I were about to do a late morning ski. Where were you when I called?"

My mother and I have what can be called a—love hate, never say what you mean relationship. I have learned to fill in the blanks which probably aggravates things but I can't help it. I probably get that from my dad who has learned to navigate my Mother's biting personality. She means well but her delivery is atrocious.

"Here in Maine on a Friday night, with a work week under my belt, I felt I owed myself a little celebration. So Mom, I was celebrating."

"Oh. Were you by yourself dear, have you made friends? There never seems to be anyone in your life—well, since that one boy anyway."

The last two hours descend on me like black flies and I bite back.

"His name was Lars, Mom, you do remember Lars don't you? You should."

"He wasn't the right boy for you and you know it. I could tell the minute he walked in the door."

Thinking of the doors I just passed through I can't let it go.

"Maybe if you had given him another minute before you poked and probed you would have come to a different conclusion. He's a successful Doctor today Mom, In Vermont, two kids and a dog I'm guessing."

"Well I didn't mean anything I just wanted to know his intentions that's all."

"Water over the bridge now, Mom, that was six years ago. What did you need?"

"Well nothing I suppose, I just wanted to hear my daughter's voice."

"You did that."

"Whatever do you mean?"

I can't have this conversation right now.

"That was my voice Mom, the one who told you I'm not able to come to the phone right now but if you leave your name and number I will return your call." I sigh, "I'm returning your call Mom, why did you call?"

"You seem a little upset dear are you sleeping properly, did you party too long last night?"

My mind returns to the last hour or two and I really, really don't want this conversation. But I did call. Stupid me. "I'm fine mom what did you need?"

A long silence fills the line and I can visualize my Mother struggling to remain civil. "It's your father, I think he's ill."

"What do you mean, ill? Has he seen a doctor?"

My mother who never has to struggle to explain herself, struggles, "It's not that kind of illness," she searches for words, "well honestly, I think," she pauses again, "no I'm sure," *I can picture her nodding her head into the phone,* "he's lost his mind."

"Can you be a little more specific? You are talking like my students write."

Her next words seem to come from deep within a darkened tunnel, bouncing off a maze of walls reaching my ears one echo at a time.

"Odd hours… strange calls… new smells… full of energy… won't listen… wants to sell the house and the business—I think he plans to leave me."

I am about to answer when she continues, her voice now small and scared, in a voice I hardly recognize. "What will I do dear, I have no one and you have moved so far away?"

"Are you sure of any of this or are you just imagining? Have you confronted Dad?"

Suddenly my mind fills with what has possibly taken place a floor below me and the image of my parents twenty years from now in the role of Ed and Edith screaming at one another all hours of the day and night fills my thoughts.

"He refuses to sit down and talk about anything these days, can you talk to him?"

I am softening ever so slightly.

"Of course I'll talk to him. So you two are still skiing with one another it seems, that's a hopeful sign at least."

"Hmmph, he takes one trail I take another and he skis so fast I might as well be on my own."

"Well, Mom I'll call dad tonight. I'll pin him down and see if he sounds like he's lost his mind."

"Thank you dear, you're such a sweet girl. I miss you, you know."

"I know. I'll call you tomorrow. Go do what you do best Mom, ski." I sigh. I hang up the phone. It's then I hear gravel crunch and look down. There is a cruiser back in the yard. I watch an officer get out of the vehicle. He looks up and waves.

"I'm coming up," he says.

I scramble to get into jeans and a collar shirt, there is a knock at my door.

Luke Harris is standing there with his hat in his hand. I study his uniform then look past him, remembering the alternate route I had taken a short time ago. I shake my head and have to chuckle. Then I sigh.

"Good morning again. Am I that funny looking?" His eyes are twinkling.

"Come in, no I was just thinking I could have used your light about an hour ago.

He looks at me oddly.

"It's a long flight, I mean story," I chuckle again, *at least my sense of humor has returned intact.* "Come on in."

CHAPTER SIX

The Wanderer

Twigs snap, last year's leaves rustle, the scuffing of boots on rock shout to the birds now taking flight. This late summer day finds Daniel reaching the western edge of Maine. The leaves haven't turned yet. From his hikes in a different set of mountains, Daniel knows Maine will take the lead in an east to west ripening of apples and blushing leaves. He plans to witness it all. Walking through shaded tunnels of deep green foliage, dappled sunlight teases then retreats. A giant boulder looming twenty feet in the air offers respite for this weary traveler. He leans against its warmth, removing his back pack—rummaging. First fingering the little postcard sized painting, always on top— laminated and wrapped in cellophane. He studies the drawing. His constant companion for many years—his sanity really. A rare smile reaches his lips. A bag of peanuts and trusty water bottle appear in his hand in the manner of a rabbit pulled out of a hat. He looks at his surroundings, *so you have left civilization*—he snorts - his

44

life has been anything but that. This arduous journey, covering hundreds of miles and half a dozen states, is covering twenty years as well. As much as possible Daniel has traveled beneath a canopy of evergreen, birch, maple, poplar, and an assortment of vines. Ever present brush like week old whiskers is a constant irritant adding to the forest's visage. Daniel sees himself much like that brush and undergrowth—a nuisance—avoided if possible. Tolerated, walked through, past and over without comment or recognition when necessary. He leans into the rock, the sun warming and softening his memories. He breathes deeply. He has made his way to Maine. He began life here and it's the one place where he has ever felt truly found, safe, understood, and nearly normal. This might just be his last chance to rediscover himself. When returned to Maine twenty years ago to attend a summer camp after living in a city in Pennsylvania for six years, a man influenced his life. This man gave him hope. Reaching even further back he vaguely remembers another man who had been an important part of his childhood. It was this earlier memory he would be trying to revive on this trip. He removed the tablet he sketched on and sniffed the air, his body smelled of the woods and of himself—a pungent mixture. He studied a number of the sketches that chronicled each day of his trip. It seemed the lines softened ever so slightly as he edged ever closer to his destination. His illustrations of leaves, vistas, rocks and animals becoming more recognizable. At Coburn Gore, Maine's border, a sign had directed him to the last state on the Appalachian Trail. He studied the sketch of the sign. An arrow and mileage sign. Pointing the direction of home.

Getting here from Pennsylvania Daniel walked a series of days on parts of the AT. When he ran out of food he left the trail and ate and slept in small towns. He had not committed to finishing this journey totally alone until his last hitch on a tarred road had turned out badly. The remainder of this trip would be done in solitude and as much as possible, off road.

This time of year there would be few thru hikers heading north or south and the weekend warriors you might meet were anxious to get it done and get back to their day jobs—a quick nod of the head would send those chance meetings on their way. Forgotten glances before they registered. At least he hoped that was the case. The boulder warm and inviting, subtly mesmerized him. He washed down a last handful of peanuts and despite the unforgiving hardness he dozed.

When he woke the sun had rearranged this out-door living room. The walls now freshly painted in darker hues and the ceiling now multi-colored, and dotted with punctuation marks of clouds, shapes used over the years to describe his behavior. He checked his watch for the time. Shaking his head and twisting his neck he removed the kinks and cobwebs. He stood up and stretched his six foot frame, each part of his body claiming attention. His feet were sore, his back ached and his butt felt asleep. He rubbed his grizzled face, re-set the stained ball cap on a greasy head of shoulder length hair and breathed in deeply. Mentally preparing himself for a walk of several more hours he took a first step. If he was lucky enough to find off trail shelter that would be a plus. If not a small tarp and sleeping bag would at least keep him dry. He filled his lungs with the afternoon then gathered himself, adjusting his baggage. Walking along he mentally did the math. He had enough food for maybe three or four days, with any luck that should be enough. He had no map but had planned his destination, Bigelow Mt.; had a little sketch of it in fact.

He could visualize this trip from beginning to end. From Bigelow he would leave the trail and find his way to Embden, Maine. It was there he hoped to find his Indian grandfather, Henry Strongbolt.

CHAPTER SEVEN

The Grilling

My little Mazda seems to have the route memorized now and I find my mind allowed to work overtime on the drive up to Embden on this sunny Sunday afternoon. Twenty four little hours and my whole world has turned upside down. Luke, the officer who I will have to say right up front, is downright handsome, told me Ed is in custody and probably will be for a while. The evidence points to an argument. While most probably an accident it ended with his wife down the stairs. Edith the wife, is in intensive care and has not regained consciousness. So I'm living alone in this big old house. A house that seems to be slowly swallowing itself from the ground up. My little nest on the third floor the only remaining normalcy. The noise those two made was over the top but at least there was someone else in the house. And my *mother*—I'm calling dad tonight. What am I supposed to do? And did I just meet a keeper a day ago? With no effort on my part the little Mazda has the school in its sights, *you are a quick learner*, I tap the leather covered steering wheel, *you keep this up and I might have to give you a name.* At the edge of the school property the lawn has disappeared—pickups and cars have covered it. The parking lot appears full and I begin a U-turn to park on the roadway when I see a sign and a roped off parking space. **SCHOOL MARM** it says. A caricature of a woman with a stick in her hand standing over a student's desk, drawn in color crayon, sits below the words. Someone has already penciled in Dwayne's name as the student. I have to chuckle. The parking space is looking out over all the action. *Put your game face on Melody, you are about to meet the parents.* Barbecue smoke is rising at second base, or rather where second base will be in the spring. There must be a hundred and fifty people gathered. Tables hug first base line loaded with bowls of casseroles, baked beans, salads, a large tin of Darlene's yeast rolls and platters of cookies. Sitting there behind my windshield I continue my sweep of the situation.

A McDonalds cooler anchors the end of one table and a knot of men near a pickup seem to be nursing cans in coozies—obviously Sunday suds. Recognition waves begin and multiply amid grins and wide smiles. I am sure the story of the teacher in a little sports car has reached the kitchen table. Balloons float, strung along the backstop. Kids and adults have a pick up soccer game going. Half the soccer field has been claimed, using orange cones for goals. The high grass covers their footwear but they all seem to be having fun. Younger students are running everywhere but on the soccer field, already admonished as too little I assume. They are too busy playing to have noticed me as yet. Darlene—ever my savior it seems—wanders over and greets me at my car door. "Well I'm glad you made it. Your supervisor is here and the Superintendent as well, not to mention the three board members from Embden." She smiles and winks, "You just passed your first test—didn't even need to be quizzed."

I look at her, confused.

"You are on time."

I smile and nod.

The afternoon becomes a ritual of hand movements. I'm Mom to so and so, kids running by saying, 'hey,' little waves of recognition, me putting something into my mouth. For a time the kids capture me and I join in a soccer game. Karen and I more than hold our own in the deep grass. When we finally beg off, those still playing nod with an athletes respect. Darlene stays within shouting distance not deserting me and for that I'll be forever thankful. I see the old Indian on the periphery of all the activity. He does not introduce himself.

Superintendent Hatch stays long enough to be noticed and is then off to another celebration in a different town. 'Have to please them all,' he tells me while shaking my hand. Says he's already hearing good things. My supervisor..., well he is a different beast. Short and wide with a loud laugh he lives on the lake. He seems to be enjoying himself, yukking it up with his neighbors. He seems to know everyone here. It's not till well after four pm. that he makes his way to me.

"How were your first three days?"

I am about to tell him some of my ideas when he spots someone and excuses himself. He never finds his way back.

I give Darlene the reader's digest version of what has happened since I said goodnight on Friday and beg off the fireworks. "Don't blame you a bit." She pauses, "you know if you think you might like to spend the winter on the lake and not rattle around in a big old house, a lot of people close up their places right after this weekend. Some would love to keep them open and make a little tax money."

"You're right, I'm not excited about rattling around in that big old house, as you call it," I smile, "but let me think on it."

"I'll nose around see what's available for a fair price then you can decide if it makes sense."

Several of the older boys who have been oohing and ahhhing my car all afternoon approach me and ask for a ride sometime.

I just smile. An older gentleman has been eyeing me and not my car from a distance. He reminded me of Waren, sneaking glances. I have caught his eye more than once. He looks to be Native American, several shades darker than myself. He makes no attempt to speak and when I look around a short time later he has disappeared. Waren comes back to mind. He's not here.

The crowd slowly thins out and I'm ready for a nap. All the comfort food has me yawning, which I try without success to stifle.

Settled back in my little car, the sun looking directly into the eyes of those waving good bye I back out and head to that big old house. I sigh, yawn, and sigh once more. I catch Marie out of the corner of my eye as I look back one last time. Realizing I hadn't had the opportunity to talk to my colleague, I tap my brake. She waves me away. Her gesture assures me we will catch up on Tuesday over coffee and yeast rolls. I pat my stomach which actually hurts from a burger, a hot dog and pasta salad. And two chocolate chip cookies. Right now I can't even imagine I'll be hungry by Tuesday. The last of the day's rays follow me home. I settle for a few minutes on the porch and witness twilight seeking its fifteen minutes of fame, wrapping fingers around all solids, squeezing the color out of them before the real deal—darkness—claims the night. There will be no need for after dinner exercise tonight I tell myself. The yellow tape may be gone from the second floor hallway but silence hangs outside the door like a funeral shroud. I pour myself a glass of cold water and re-settle on the porch. It is indeed silent. I am indeed in this house all by myself. All the food I ate has made me drowsy and I give in—I'll just close my eyes for a moment.

It's after midnight when I wake and make it to the bathroom to brush my teeth. I am stiff from the position I slept in on the porch and maybe a little from soccer. I groan and struggle to get out of my clothes, not bothering to shower. A cool breeze enters my bedroom, curtains flaring ghost like. The sheets are cold, I shiver and pull the covers up to my chin, not ready to close windows on summer just yet. I hug myself and I dream.

When I wake I find the dream has stayed with me all night allowing just enough to escape with my waking to have me worrying about my mother and father. In my dream—my childhood in that cabin on the side of a mountain—has me as an adult analyzing the only conversations I remember having with my parents. They involved either learning to ski, improving my skiing, taking ever more difficult trails, or celebrating the ribbons and trophies I won. I don't recall praise for my school grades—being home schooled, good grades were just expected. Every milestone that didn't have to do with skiing was just an expected outcome. It's taken me thirty-two years to ferret out that my parents are Shallow Hal Inc.

Maybe it is all that has taken place below me that's triggered this revelation. Ed and his wife maybe love one another enough to be angry with how time, age, and infirmity, has damaged their relationship. Helpless to the physical and mental challenges they are going through they lash out at the person they love most in the world. So sad. I don't know this to be true but after a night of dreaming I believe this.

My parents never argued that I ever heard, or even raised their voices. The sound of skis swooshing through fresh snow would better describe the tenor of their conversations. Red faces, tanned bodies and smiles stemming from a successful trip down the mountain, that's what I remember. Wine glasses raised, and toasts made, with the looming mountain the center of our existence.

My father was successful in business, that I know, but I couldn't tell you what he did beyond long phone calls directing traffic. He left for a week at a time every other month and he brought me back every conceivable newfangled ski improvement that hit the market. The morning after arriving home we would hit the slopes with him coaching me through the instructions. Poles changed, skis changed, boots changed, even the clothing I wore—though they were always gender neutral. I never had friends—we didn't even have a dog. No grandparents either. If you don't know, you don't even know what you've missed.

I do remember I was more than ready to leave when age and education offered me the ticket. My parents were forever disappointed that I chose to attend college in the east. At least I thought they were. Now I'm not so sure. I was Home Schooled by a mother who followed the curriculum that was state mandated and that was the extent of it. There were field trips, no frills, or side trips. No trips into town to get my hair done, or my nails done, or even a shopping trip to a mall. I lived in jeans and flannel and my father trimmed my hair. 'You need to keep it short for skiing,' he'd say as he circled my stool sitting in the middle of the kitchen. When my breasts arrived, my mother reminded me that 'they are simply little mountains, moguls really, just ignore them.' That statement constituted my home schooled course in sex education.

Was I loved? Yeah kinda, sorta—like you love the skis and boots that allow for a successful run. I think I was a comfortable accent piece that validated their relationship—a been there- done-that union—with me as living proof. Now that I think back on it, I think they wanted a son.

All this, running through my mind before coffee, has me sighing up a storm. The smell of that coffee brings me back to the morning. It's bright and sunny again. "Yes," I shout through my porch window. I'm not running alone this morning. Luke during that first conversation asked if he could show me a route he runs. I sip coffee between bites of a few tablespoons of cereal. I don't want to run on a full stomach. The seeds and nuts I'm crunching make me think of how Miko the squirrel might enjoy my breakfast as well. I raise my cup, "Here's to a successful run, may it be the first of many." Suddenly I realize I am being my father and I lower the cup quickly. *No I am not Shallow Hal,* I reassure myself silently.

An hour later, Luke's truck enters the drive way and after he shuts off the engine I hear the strains of Dan Fogleberg rising to my window seat. He's singing one of my favorite songs, *Leader of the Band*. I wave and take the stairs two at a time inhaling the words I can still hear in my head. As I pass the door on the second floor I think of what happened here. I sigh.

They say women are attracted to men in uniform but this guy—this guy—he looks just as awesome in a pair of shorts and a green running shirt. His dark hair is hiding under a Boston Bruins hat. "So where are you taking me this morning officer? I hope not directly to jail." I offer all this to his open window. "Do I dare get in?"

Luke laughs, "We haven't even reached GO yet my lady. If you kick my butt on this run however, I may have to reconsider—I have a little pride you know. Get in," he says with a grin as he opens the passenger door.

"This isn't going to be a board game officer just a leisurely jaunt through the woods, so no worries." *There's that phrase again.* My classroom passes before my eyes and I smile, sliding onto the cool leather. I sniff the air, Luke smells as good as he looks. I sigh.

"Okay don't forget that when those competitive juices kick in." He backs out onto Winter Street and the adventure begins.

"We'll park this rig in a barn yard on the way. I know the owner so it's fine." Dan Fogleberg's voice had been lowered when I reached the truck but is now raised a notch. *Run for the roses* reaches my ears. *How appropriate is that?* I think to myself.

"Hey, maybe you can help me decide on a tape deck installation officer. Which are the most popular on the black market?" I laugh.

"I actually possess the skill necessary to put one in for you, so that begs at least another meeting." He adds, "No matter the results of today's finish. By the way, I like your hair in a pony-tail."

Even his eyes are smiling, *and oh what white teeth you have Sergeant Luke.*

We head south on Madison Avenue and take a right onto what is called the River Rd. I mentally tick off each landmark. "Is that still the Kennebec River?

"Yup, it shows up at various points all the way to the next town, Norridgewock. On the other side it follows Route Two to the same town."

"That's how I came here—on Route Two—from New Hampshire, a month ago. The Kennebec River seems to be stalking me Sergeant, can you help me with that?" Luke looks at me quizzically.

"This river follows me on my runs here in town. Then in my car from Madison to North Anson. And then I add raising my voice, introduces me to its cousin—the Carrabassett. And there's this beautiful pond just a sprint away from the school. Its water, water, everywhere it seems—even the name of the school district—**Carrabec**—**keeps** two rivers in my head."

"You have quite an imagination Miss Melody Standish, are you a writer?"

"Oh, I like your detective skills Sergeant—in fact I do write, children's stories."

"You'll have to show me something you've written," Luke smiles, and quickly takes a right turn onto Beech Hill Rd. "Well we won't be running along the river today, just a long gravel road through the woods." After the length of a song, and the silence that follows, Luke takes a left onto the Red Barn Rd. We park in a farm yard looking out over fields and woods with a gravel road splitting the dense foliage. There are cows milling around the fields, some with birds riding their backs. A stretch of corn imprisoned in barbed wire seems to be a property line. An open barn with various farming machinery surrounding it speaks of full days of work here. A muddy pickup—a working man's truck-sits off to the right of a farm house with smoke coming out of the chimney. Firewood sits in an open shed with the barn serving as one wall. I raise my eyes to the hills. Green still dominates but color will not be denied, just a hint softening the look, like eyeshadow.

"Double tie your sneakers Luke I won't fall for that old trick of—wait up—my shoes untied." Luke grunts, smiles and hands me a water bottle. While I'm guzzling, Luke has left the truck and is fifty yards ahead before I get the cap back on. "Hey no fair, wait up."

Luke runs in place, "Did you just say—wait up?" He winks and we begin our run with gravel crunching beneath our feet. We settle into a pace that allows us to talk and Luke tells me where this road goes.

"It actually ends up in Madison on what's called the Ward Hill Rd. You travel past the Madison end of it every day. We'll jog up to where it intersects and head back. Out and back it's not even four miles. That's about all I run these days."

The road is shaded and smells that ride the wind tickle the nose at intervals, subtle smells that are gone before you get your mouth open to comment.

There are no vehicles out here so we run side by side doing our own thing in tandem. Measured breathing and sidelong glances replace conversation as we pick up the pace on the return trip. When we arrive back at the truck, we high five each other knowing it was a successful first date. The ride back is quiet. No music competing with the thoughts we are both carrying in our heads. Finally I break the silence.

"Would you like to see my view of things, from my perch on the porch? I'll make you a late morning coffee."

Luke chuckles, "Now that's a line I haven't heard before. What I'd really like sometime, is a ride in that little sports car, but for today the coffee sounds great."

We trudge up the stairs and pause at the door of my now missing neighbors. "Tragedy really," says Luke, "I don't think there was any intent, just frustration. Hearing loss we know. We found parts of three different hearing aids. But Edith wasn't wearing one. It's in the report. Muddled minds maybe and not enough money to pay the bills. The guy wouldn't stop talking, he's a mess. We haven't located any immediate family. Ed swears there's a sister-in-law but he wasn't sure where. I don't think the lady will leave that hospital alive. No kids to take charge. Poor old guy is going to end up God only knows where."

When we're settled on the porch with coffee, I offer my take on what happened. "Don't take this as a statement but all I ever heard was hollering. I couldn't make out conversation but I can tell you they were not happy down there. Lack of hearing was definitely an issue. The one conversation I had with him he was basically reading my lips. So what caused it I couldn't say but it's sad how two people who have lived together all those years could get to that place."

"In my view it mostly comes down to one word, MONEY. A huge percent of the time everything that happens around my job involves money. Stealing, burglary, domestic crime, even accidents where the person falls asleep at the wheel. Why? Because they are working two jobs—it's all about the money." Luke sighs. "Ed said they couldn't afford proper hearing aids and those they had actually made things worse. So the conversations got louder and louder and the frustrations that must cause changes everything."

We both sighed. Our conversation turned to our work, both happy with our job. Luke rose. Ending with assurances that there will be future runs, we exchange phone numbers and a hopeful hug. I have a good feeling this could lead somewhere promising. I hear those stairs creak then Luke's truck roars to life. Silence follows. I need to put my game face back on. I need to call my Dad. But first I need to shower. My head wrapped in a towel and still stalling, I heat a bowl of Dinty Moore Beef Stew. I scan the pages of a fashion magazine. I realize I am stalling. Ok I sigh. First that phone call I need to make then I'll grab my planner and set about lesson planning for the next four days. Nobody answers in Park City. I leave a message for Dad to call. That squirrel is back walking along the window ledges peeking in each window, making eye contact. Waren comes to my mind and I realize he has stayed on the periphery of my consciousness since day one. I haven't caught him making eye contact again though.

Next week's planning will offer opportunities for individuals to emerge from the masses. The chapters in Math are pretty straight forward, I can tweak them as necessary. This reading thing I want to get right. For me reading is everything. If I can inspire some life-long readers I will have done my job here. I revisit the story I have chosen that all three grades will read together. It's titled **The Most Dangerous Game**. On the surface the story might seem too gruesome and advanced but I am going to take it slow and make sure we are discussing all the hidden messages that surface. We will read it in class. Before we begin though we will read a more innocent story, Bambi. A children's story but with clear messages as well. Can't wait for the first reaction to this choice. Hopefully by the time we finish **The Most Dangerous Game**. It will become clear to students how different authors present their view to the reader in startling different ways.

CHAPTER EIGHT

Settling Into A Routine

By the end of the first week of September—four straight days of classes—the students have me figured out. Yes I have a sense of humor, yes I can be led off topic, yes I can whip them in a game of basketball, and yes I really can kick ass with a jump-rope.

I am figuring the kids out as well. New ideas emerging from how these kids interact. Even the playground is showing me the ebbs and flows of relationships. It's obvious that hormones are wreaking havoc as I watch the group dynamics change on a daily basis. In class at least the seating plan for who sits next to who does not change. I'm finding the more physical the outdoor activity the more settled they return to class. Oh yes, I am learning as much if not more than my students.

Group reading will be at least one area I deviate from established curriculum. More to follow maybe as I see kids making connections. When I announced that we were going to read the story Bambi in class, heads went up, eyes rolled and a few snippets of laughter emerged. I ignored the snickering. *They will eventually see the method for my madness.* I hand out seven literary terms and their definitions. "Your job will be to point out how these terms are used in the story."

The terms: <u>Foreshadowing,</u> an author's use of hints or clues to give the reader an idea what might happen next. *I had recently witnessed that in my conversation with my mother. And if what happened downstairs from my apartment wasn't an example of foreshadowing, then I better give up being a teacher.* <u>Imagery,</u> words or phrases that appeal to one or more of the five senses that help create a vivid description for the reader. *Well meeting Luke had reached two of my senses and I am hoping for more.* <u>Climax,</u> the highest point of action in the story. <u>Mood,</u> the atmosphere or feeling an author creates in a piece of writing. *Meeting Luke has certainly lightened my mood.* <u>Character Trait,</u> the quality of a character; what are they like. <u>Irony,</u> a situation where the opposite of what is expected to occur takes place. <u>Fable,</u> a brief story usually with animal characters providing a lesson or moral.

Most of the students had either read the story of **Bambi** or seen the movie. We read the story aloud. I took a neutral tone in the questions I asked the students to react to. I was pleasantly surprised by the depth of the answers. Some of the literary terms seemed obvious, others I had to point out. A good beginning. Next week's lesson plans will include additional literary terms that will help us dissect all stories going forward. Then I will introduce **The Most Dangerous Game**. Can't wait to see what paths that story leads us down.

It's not until Friday afternoon that the nest of stones surfaces again. Once again it's an errant basketball that sends someone scurrying towards the rail fence. I'm not part of the game, rather, just milling about when I see the boy pull up short and begin to return to the game empty handed.

"Hey Raymond get that ball will you?"

"Nah it's okay we have more."

Raymond, please get the ball, someone has to and you are the closest."

"I'd rather not, Troy will get it."

"I'm not asking Troy, I'm asking you."

The boy starts slowly back towards the fence but stops several yards away. "I'm not going near there Miss Standish, Troy will get it, just ask him."

In fact Troy has begun walking toward the fence when I touch his shoulder. He looks me in the eye.

"I'll get it. No worries ma'am, not a big deal."

I sigh, I don't want an argument on a Friday afternoon but I do want some answers. "Ok get the ball but then I'd like to speak with you."

"No problem. Be right back," says Troy in his soothing unruffled way. From what I've seen of Troy so far not much gets to him.

I walk him away from the noise and ask him about this nest of stones that is to be avoided at all costs.

"Nobody knows how they got there. My older sister whose a senior in high school told me about them when she was here. All I know is they disappear when school gets out for the summer and they are back when it starts up again. Supposedly if you touch them it causes bad luck. So everybody avoids them like the plague. That's all I know."

"But you don't seem scared of this curse, why's that?"

"My dad."

He sees I'm looking for just a tad more explanation.

"My dad says, 'It's not the truck that's sitting in a yard that will get you it's the one you can't see just yet—the one down the road around the corner.' My dad runs a trucking company. He's pretty clever. So I don't worry about those little stones laying there. Better chance I'll get hit by a truck." He shrugs and walks off.

The bell rang just then and we all got ready for dismissal.

After the kids left I wandered in to Marie Poulin's room and asked her about the stones.

"They were here when I came seven years ago. I think we all just take them for granted now. Every class adds their own little twist to the history and legend. I've looked at them before. All smooth like they had been in water for a long time, from Embden Pond or some little stream I'm guessing. Some local having fun with us I suppose." She continued, "Troy is right, they do disappear when we go on summer vacation. I come in from time to time over the summer and the little nest is gone."

"Has anyone ever removed them during the year, you know, to see if they re-appear?"

"I don't think it's ever occurred to anyone to do that. Why would you want to tempt a supposed curse?" she smiled, but I think she was serious.

"Well thanks for the insight. I am about to put on my sneakers and run a couple of roads in the area I heard about this week. I'll see you on Monday, Marie."

All week I have waited for three things to happen. One, my father to call back, and two, for Waren to reestablish contact like he did that first day. It almost seems like he's avoiding me. If I look up he's looking down. If I'm on one side of the grounds he's on the other. I sigh. With my head down and my shoes laced and tied, I don the a baseball cap and wave good night to Marie and the night janitor who lights up with a big smile. Oh well I went one for three. Luke called.

I exit the school yard and turn left onto the Embden Pond Road. This will be a quick little run—a little pick me up—before I head home. I glance left there's that little nest of stones. The literary term <u>external conflict</u> jumps into my head. (Me being the character those stones being nature.) "I'll figure this all out,"

I chuckle aloud and set my mind to my run. I see the right turn onto the Creamer road and take it. A gradual uphill climb becomes a significant hill. My heart rate slowly rises as I climb this dirt road, the second line of a triangle. Birds are sitting on the wires questioning why a sane person would be trudging this hill when you can just fly over it. Their laughter has me thinking of writing a story about a talking bird—I chuckle to myself. *Just start a story Melody quit talking about it.* I am plenty warmed up, my heart rate has elevated in direct proportion to the incline. The ground levels off and I raise my eyes and notice things. Golden Rod hugging the ditches, enjoying the last few days before they fade like last night's dream. Purple plants I still don't know the name of, has me mentally guessing. The silence of the woods on both sides of the road screams at me. A blue sky with a wisp of clouds so thin I can't conjure up an image, just hangs there, silent as well. The rhythm of my heartbeat slows into my comfort zone. I sigh. Ahead a stop sign appears and a power line, its three strands of wire like ruled paper facing a reluctant writer. A tar road rises in the distance. When I reach that ribbon of black I turn right and a long downhill marks the third leg of my run. Wentworth Road, right where it's supposed to be. Heat coming off the tar warms my legs. Shortly I'm cruising down a long hill that flattens out. Another stop sign becomes visible from beneath over hanging branches. My triangle nearly completed I turn right once again and the school re-emerges to my left. My little sports car has been patiently waiting on the grass along with one other vehicle, a muddy raised up 4x4 red pickup. After a quick trip to gather my things and a trip to the bathroom in the main building, I stand at the water fountain. It's quiet. The night janitor is toiling away emptying waste baskets. He appears then disappears into a class-room. I am usually gone before he arrives from his afternoon bus run. The sound of a vacuum breaks the quiet. I pass a classroom and give him a thumbs up. He smiles and waves. Earphones over a ball cap, he is moving to a beat I assume is music—keeping the sucking sound at bay.

His name is Evan and he drives bus twice a day, then serves as the building custodian. I still haven't asked him about the argument he had with another driver on that first morning.

The drive home happens with no consciousness on my part. Luke is taking me to hear a local band tonight that is playing in Waterville. Several of his friends play and sing in the band we'll be listening to. When he called and asked me he said he dabbles with drums and plays a very weak saxophone. 'Kinda like singing in the shower,' is the way he described his musical talent. I am excited to be with adults. Sitting on the porch trying to entice the only living thing here besides me, my new little friend Miko the squirrel, to come join me using a piece of bread. Long stares and furtive little head turns but Miko does not approach. All the while I am going through my wardrobe in my mind. I take an extra- long shower then try shaping my hair in different styles. I settle for what I think is a wholesome look. I decide on a simple skirt and blouse. Luke hasn't seen me except in running shorts. Luke arrives at 6pm. His radio shuts down with the death of his engine. I can hear his feet pounding the stairs. A quick knock and an, "out here," brings a six foot specimen into view.

He looks at me with those deep blue eyes and nods his head. "Wow, you clean up good teacher lady."

Using a feigned southern school Marm voice I answered, "Well thank you neighbor, you're looking mighty fine yourself this evening."

Luke laughed, then got serious.

"Edith, your neighbor from the second floor has passed away." He paused briefly, "I don't think Ed is going to be charged, but that's not my call. Anyway the mess continues." Then he brightens, takes my hand, "On a more positive note, there's a new little Mexican restaurant that has opened in Waterville. So-o-o," he dragged out, "I thought maybe we could try it then hit that bar my buddies are playing in." He smiles, "Also I have been researching tape decks for your vehicle. I just have a couple of calls to make, so-o-o, a middle of the week meeting perhaps? I was thinking maybe a little run—a little barbecue—you watching me play mechanic—all at my place of course."

Ed crying out of the back window of the cruiser reaches my mind even as I hear Luke. I shake my head in resignation, *not my issue I tell myself.* I'm still wool gathering when Luke touches my arm.

"Hey you with me, you look like you just left the building?"

"I'm sorry Luke, it all sounds like fun to me. Count me in." Here comes that sigh. "I just can't get those old people out of my mind." I give Luke a big hug. I'm still holding on when my Father suddenly enters my head. I shake it from side to side. "Get me out of here Luke," I fairly shout, pushing away yanking the door open and taking the steps two at a time.

It's a quiet ride to Waterville each of us lost in our own thoughts, letting whatever events that filled our past week drain ever so slowly away. Jim Croce's album, **I got a name** serves as a conduit.

When we pull into the parking lot at the restaurant Luke shuts it down—what he calls turning off the ignition—he touches my hand. We walk in arm in arm.

The food is good, the margarita even better. Luke tells me a little about these friends of his between bites from the bowl of chips and salsa that precedes the meal. He's met them since moving here, one is a fellow officer. He sits in with them when someone can't make a rehearsal. "I refuse to play in public, so don't even ask," he admonishes. I hold up my hand in mock surrender.

It's dark-dark by the time we reach the bar where the band is playing. A neon sign announces the bars' name, **Getting It On**. Laughter and loud music welcome us in and in darkness that nearly matches the outdoors we squint to find the table where several of the player's girlfriends and wives are sitting. Introductions all around and then we settle in to hear them play.

The band plays a mixture of soft rock, country, and even a couple of bluesy ballads. Luke closes his eyes when a horn joins in, perhaps envisioning his best shower performance ever. We dance a slow one, my head finds Luke's shoulder—a good fit. He introduces me to the guys during a break and the wise ass comments—all in good fun—dominate the conversation. I can tell these guys care about one another and I am a little envious. The ladies seem to share the same easy comradery. I nod to myself, *I might make some girlfriends here, though none volunteer that they are athletes. Girly girls, that's ok too.*

When we get to my place, Luke leans in and kisses me. I liked it. Then I kiss Luke, he seems to like it as well. I look out the passenger window up at a quarter moon, the silhouette of the trees, some hazy stars. The old house looms in the half light—suddenly appearing a little spooky—and I know I don't want to spend the night alone. The street light stares blankly offering no opinion.

I look into his eyes, "I'm not usually this forward Luke, but stay with me tonight. I'm not promising more than a wild make-out session—if you can live with that—climb these golden stairs. By the way I don't do handcuffs." I laugh out loud.

Luke chuckles, he gently pushes me away and studies my eyes from a distance. Now that I've voiced my offer the street light seems to brighten, subtly adding just the right light for the occasion. He studies me. "You don't appear to be one who makes rash decisions young lady so I'll take you up on your offer. If I get out of hand you can ban me to the porch to cool off. Or cuff me to a chair."

We cuddled and kissed for an hour or more. Laughing about the evening and giggling over some observations we had made about one of Luke's friends and the girl he had with him. Then it was back to some kissing, slowly exploring. Then we slept.

The morning found me looking at the back of Luke's head. I shifted to get up and make coffee but a body turn and a strong arm brought me into his embrace. In the light of day we finished last night's suspended slow dance. It was wonderful and gentle and caring and unforced. The last parts of the puzzle were joined, we smiled. Thinking back to the precaution Luke had taken before we joined as one, I just had to ask. "So Luke were you a Boy Scout?"

Luke spoke, "Actually yes why do you ask?"

I just smiled.

Luke rose. "I'll just hit the john then make coffee. You wrap yourself in that blanket and join me on the porch when it's ready."

Waited on already, I love the thought.

I heard Luke opening and closing cupboards and drawers. He didn't ask for help in finding anything. The new sounds had me thinking about poor Ed, *what would become of him?*

After a breakfast of eggs and toast and a second cup of coffee Luke told me he had to work tonight so he would call me tomorrow.

"Say Luke, find out more about what's going to happen to Ed and when the funeral might be. I should probably go. I doubt there is any family. Anyway, find out what you can, ok?"

"You are a good lady Melody, I'll follow up." He winked. "That was the best eggs and toast I have had in a long time—maybe forever." We both smiled reading between the lines and a healthy hug and kiss sent the man off to fight crime.

I took a shower and then played with my hair in the mirror thinking it might be time to shorten it a little. Since leaving home I had grown it out and worn it long—in defiance I guess. I saw a style in a fashion magazine recently that might look good on me. Suddenly some new clothes might be in order as well, nothing gender neutral. I started humming, not a sigh in sight.

I stretched myself out on the little day bed on the porch and was thumbing through the magazine trying to find that hair style, when the phone rang. It was my Father.

"Well there you are daddy, you finally got off that hill. How is Mom?"

"Your mother is your mother. Did she tell you to call me?"

"I could lie. But yes, she said you were acting strangely and she was worried you were losing your mind."

My father chuckled, "Melody I'm sixty years old. I simply want to do some new things, see some new places—get out of Dodge so to speak. Your mother wants no part of that. She says she's comfortable in the old so there must be something wrong with me if I want change. She's calling it a mid-life crisis and it will pass." He sighs.

I have to chuckle, maybe this sighing is hereditary.

"You know we don't argue so these two opposing pieces of ski tow rope have been gentle tugs up to now. How do I get her to understand this ski vacation we've been on for forty years is ending?" I clear my throat about to respond though I have no idea what I will say.

"Hear me out. In just over three weeks all ties to a work schedule will be over. I am heading to a little town in Florida that a client told me about. Did you even know that I paint? Well I have, since you left. I took a few lessons and if I must say so I have a little talent. I'm going to hang out on a beach and create pictures that tell a story that I hope to interest tourists in," he pauses. "I haven't told your Mother all this yet. Honestly I don't see the point. She doesn't listen, never has. I have arranged for her to keep the house and she will receive a generous monthly income. But hear me Melody, in three weeks I am a gone goose."

"Dad," I started.

Once more my father took over, "So rather than me calling you, maybe you can call your mother. Somebody needs to get through to her about all this before it's all done through lawyers from a distance." He still didn't give up his end of the mouth piece. "I'm sorry but I've got another call I need to make. I'm looking at a little place one street back from the ocean with an apartment over the top. Love yuh. Let me know how you make out. I'll call in a week or so to keep you updated." I sat there, not in shock or disbelief but rather thinking, *I can't believe they lasted this long.*

I spent Saturday night going over the student's written responses to Bambi. It was easy to find the hunters in the group and their initial responses from the first day of reading in class doubled down on their conviction that hunting provides food for the family. By the end of the story on Friday though, **Bambi** was getting a lot of love from even the mighty hunters of the group. Most of them had found other examples from the literary terms. None of my questions were designed to provoke any particular response but rather to tell the story from the view of all the players in the forest. One last piece will be the showing of the movie in class and a general discussion of how a movie and a written story differ. Then I will introduce some new literary terms before we begin, **The Most Dangerous Game**. I will be curious to see if they find places where these terms apply in a very different way. And will anyone pick up <u>foreshadowing,</u> in the title. Vocabulary words and a spelling test will emerge from words they have not seen before. They will be asked to use these words in a sentence. The story should take three class days to complete. I am anxious to find out who can see beyond the words on the page. Hidden meanings, what greater truths is the author trying to share. It's one of the lessons good stories and literature evoke.

Sunday Luke calls. He's going to sleep-in this morning he's got to cover for a fellow officer tonight. The funeral is Tuesday at 4pm. He tells me if I'm going he'll go with me. Ed is staying with that sister-in- law who showed up on her own. She appears to be in worse shape than his wife was—hearing wise at any rate—so that is not going to last. Luke's parting words, 'I miss you already and I'll pick you up at three-thirty on Tuesday.'

CHAPTER NINE

Two Funerals and A Shroud of Mystery

I called my Mother on Sunday night and just as dad had predicted, she wouldn't listen. It was a short conversation ending with sighs on both ends with no real discussion of the issues. "Bye Mom, I love you." I hung up wondering what she would do when the lawyers got involved.

The house joins me in a sigh as the wind outside picks up. My only companion, Miko, the little squirrel is glued to the window ledge on the porch. This afternoon I left some crumbs out and I see they are gone. "Hang on little Miko," I caution as the moving branches with little oak dusters attached reach for the windows as if to remove film from the panes—*the better to see you my dear.*

The school calendar I have pasted to the inside cover of my planner offers a basic framework for the year. I find I'm beginning to change it already in my head. The next five weeks with one early dismissal day included—will be the longest stretch of uninterrupted learning in the first half year. When Columbus Day arrives in October, students will be cheering the man for more than just discovering America—he brings on his voyage a rare three day weekend. I also notice the first school board meeting is scheduled for this Tuesday evening, September 9th. As the school principal I am obligated to attend every month. This month it's being held at the high school. I have never met the full board. My fellow principals will be there. I have met them briefly in several team meetings that I mostly sat through as a silent participant, everyone busy with the start of a new school year. First time as a principal, so I'm not sure what to expect.

The little squirrel has my attention again. He has moved to the window nearest me and is looking through the screen, seemingly right into my eyes. "No you can't come in," I baby talk him, asking if he liked the treat I left. He ignores me and jumps on a swaying branch.

I move to the kitchen to complete the week's lesson plans. As I thumb through Science and Social Studies texts looking for common themes that might allow me to combine classes in those subjects, the reality of the task ahead of me is daunting. I think back to my earlier teaching at the private school in New Hampshire. *When had the students seemed the most engaged?* I mentally flip through the hundreds of lesson plans I had prepared over those years. It never seemed that reflection was as important as right now. The classes had been small, the students motivated. I had been allowed the luxury of working with students—one on one—each and every day.

Like a yellow highlighter underlining the important parts of a sentence, the phrase, <u>when they made their own discoveries and connections</u> reaches my consciousness. I think of the past two weeks and look for a commonality the students share. Darlene's admonition to, 'let them breathe' adds the yeast to a recipe I am concocting in my head. I made a decision then and there to make the outdoors our classroom whenever possible.

Science becomes the next textbook I dissect. The trees and flowers, the earth and sky, the pond and hatchery, the farms, the birds and animals. As the chapters and their lessons and concepts slide through my fingers my mind is racing ahead to the opportunities for active learning this little community provides. *Don't get ahead of yourself, Melody* I caution my racing heart. *Let's take one topic and apply it and chart the result. Let's be scientific about this.*

All five foot seven of me stands before the class for the pledge of allegiance. I am more relaxed than at any time since taking the job. On every desk is the first example of what I am officially calling, *active learning*. In my head I call it, *Darlene's Directive*. Hand on heart we pledge loyalty. Within the first hour a student has looked at the week's lesson plans and raises her hand. The rest of the class is engaged in a math assignment. I walk to her desk. "What does this Science assignment mean? I'm trying to get a head start on my work."

"Good for you Rachel, you are the first to discover our new approach to your Science book. It will mostly take place outdoors. Right after lunch we will discuss it then go outside and plan our first lesson together."

Rachel looks at me quizzically, but a smile reaches her lips.

"I will walk you through it. I think you'll like the plan. Your own ideas will be a strong part of how we attack that Science book."

Recess has me changing out of my dress and flats. A baby blue Nike sweat suit and black New Balance Sneakers transforms me into a competitive beast. A Carrabec ball cap sits atop my raven black hair and shades the part of myself I am most proud of—hazel eyes with flecks of blue. The loyalty I am pledging to the high school by wearing the cobra hat hopefully will be noticed by the kids and carried home to older sisters and brothers at the high school. I have already become a first pick for the daily recess basketball game. The first two weeks of school with this physical crew have shown that it makes sense to stay in my sweats for the remainder of the day. Most days, hopefully, there will be two more opportunities to be physical. Now if this active learning thing takes off we'll be out doors even more often.

The afternoon finds us sitting on the set of bleachers, the sun streaming down—breathing—as Darlene would say. "Ok let's look at the science lesson." Everyone is armed with a pen or pencil and a tablet of paper or notebook. The janitor who doubles as one of our bus drivers has a co- worker helping him assemble the soccer goals out on the field. Eyes stray to the tug of war going on out there. The boys are snickering. I move so that I am in front of the show that is going on in the field. I make eye contact. "OK listen up. In a few minutes I am going to dismiss you in twos. Your assignment is to walk the playground and fields and write down what you see. Really take a look around. Look up. Look down.

What do you see that is natural—and what is manmade? You have half an hour. Chart everything. We will go back inside and catalogue what we found and decide what branch of science fits best for your discoveries. A good part of your science curriculum is out here, we just have to identify it" I stretch my arms embracing this outdoor classroom. "Wouldn't it be cool to be able to put that book away letting the outdoors be our lesson plan?"

Heads nod. Mumbles emerge, I can tell some of the boys view this as another recess. The girls will set them straight. I send them off in twos. I have paired some eighth graders with sixth graders I have paired boys with girls. I used my powers of observation in making these pairings. It's amazing what taking kids out of their comfort zone will do. The never be caught dead talking to an eighth grade girl mindset of a sixth grader changes completely when its teacher directed.

While they are flitting around like bees I approach the janitor. I kid, "Are you boys done fighting, or do I need to give you detention?" Both men look down sheepishly. One more little barb, "And don't either of you tell me the other one started it?" Then I offer my hand. "Will these be ready this afternoon? We have our first practice scheduled for 2:30." I noticed the two moving at a snail's pace when we were at lunch.

"We just got the goals this morning Miss Standish, that's asking a lot. The fields need to be mowed, laid out and lined. Nets attached. That's a week's worth of work and we have five elementary schools to get set up before the first game," Evan complained. Then he thought of something else—a kicker they call it. "Me and Jerry here we have to get back to the bus barn and drive our routes as well." He took off his ball cap and wiped some imaginary sweat from his brow.

"Is this the first field you're setting up?"

"Yes ma'am it is, so you see what we're up against."

Thinking maybe I can create an ally here I offer a suggestion, "Tell you what, you get those two goals together and I'll see that the field is mowed, laid out, and lined." I smiled, "How does that sound?"

Jerry wiped his gi-normous paw on his trousers and offered his hand again swallowing my hand in a hardy grip. A giant smile accompanied the hand. "Really pleased to meet you, and thanks. Works for me how about you, Evan?"

Evan was giving it some thought. "You sure you know how to run that tractor, we don't need no accidents that will come back to bite us?"

I assured the men if they could get the goals assembled, between myself and the class we'd get the rest done. "Some of these boys look pretty handy." With that I strode back to monitor my charges. I looked around.

I smiled to myself, everything seemed to be going off without a hitch, the students were becoming actively involved in their own learning, little complaint and new friendships emerging as well. All except **Waren**. I couldn't recall who he was paired with but when I saw him wandering around alone I looked at my chart. I find the girl doing just as I asked. "Kathy? So how is it that you and Waren are not working together?"

"Waren said he prefers to work alone."

"And you took him at his word?"

The eighth grade girl who had spent the past two years in the same classroom with Waren raised her eyebrows. "His word is his word, he don't waste any either." She turned serious, "Are you mad at me?"

"Kathy, I'm not mad at you, I just needed to know the lay of the land. If you know what I mean?"

She smiled, "My father talks like that—in little riddles but I know what you mean. You're going to talk to Waren, right?"

"Your father is raising a smart daughter. You just write down what you can on your own, and no worries, its fine."

Kathy pipes up, "You're sounding like Troy Miss Standish." She wanders off. I find myself blushing. I'm supposed to be the vocabulary builder around here.

I found Waren at the far side of the double wide pre-fab classroom we called home. He was crouched, facing away from me holding something in his hands. He was making a strange noise. Was he crying, or praying, or something else entirely? I stayed back and watched. He got to his feet and walked to the edge of the woods and placed something in the undergrowth.

I opened my mouth to speak but for some reason I couldn't—it seemed like an invasion of privacy. For that same reason I needed to see how this was going to play out. I slunk back to the playground, utterly confused, baffled, and bothered by what I had just witnessed.

I herded the students all back inside and asked Mrs. White to start the process of recording what the students had written down. I went into the bathroom in the main building and splashed cold water on my face. I needed to compose myself. How do you address something like this?"

When I returned, a long list of possible science lessons had been identified.

I kept my eye on Waren for the remainder of the day but he never made eye contact. He seemed to be whispering to himself, his lips making quick little movements. *God he looked just like Miko just then.*

When school dismissed, the seventeen students who had signed up to play soccer changed up and were busy kicking one of three balls around as I made my way onto the field. I whistled them to the bleachers. Waren wasn't among them—*for some reason I felt secretly glad of that.* We went through a series of drills and then scrimmaged for twenty minutes. These kids could run flat out forever and they actually passed the ball to one another, girls and boys. I mused, *maybe this might just be fun.* The grass was way too high but for a first day it worked. I told them of my plan to take charge of our field. Heads nodded as student's volunteered rakes.

When all the students were gone I wandered over to the patch of woods where Waren had placed something. There was nothing there—odd.

I had joined the kids for their soccer scrimmage and they worked me hard. I was getting a little stiff in the knees—*maybe I'll take a break from a run this evening,* I told myself as I rubbed away the stiffness. Lowering myself to the leather seat and sighing, I checked off another successful day. On the way home I saw a tinge of color emerging in the mountains and foot hills to the west. *It wasn't wishful thinking on that run with Luke, fall is coming.* For a skier those colors—while beautiful—simply whets the appetite for what will follow. I smile. The feeling in my knees reminds me, you pay a price for those flights down the mountain. I'm lost in thought till the river to my left suddenly looms dark as if preparing for an oncoming storm of winter. The cloud passes the river sparkles and I think, *don't get ahead of yourself girl.* I squeeze the steering wheel, turn on the radio and turn it right back off again—talk about a storm cloud—they are still trying to sell me something I don't want or need. Hopefully Luke will have some info on that tape deck for my baby. As I enter Anson I shift gears and the day is before me again. On the negative side I had to postpone playing the movie, **Bambi.** I should have checked out the condition of the projector first I guess. I called the high school and they are shipping one out that works with a bus driver in the morning. Finding I have the ability to think on my feet though— that's a good thing. Having planned the week ahead allows for these little mishaps to occur and simply move forward. Today we did two math lessons instead of one. All worked out, *no worries,* I can hear Troy in my head. The Science class seemed to be well received, so yes, it was a successful day.

Trudging the stairs—my knees still complaining about the rigor I just put them through—the squeaking of the stair treads gives voice to my complaint. Ed enters my head on the way past his door. I shake him away. During a long hot shower, Waren comes back to mind. While I'm eating a little pasta on the porch the grey squirrel lands with a light thump taking that two foot plunge from the tree limb to the window sill. *What was Waren doing?* I muse, *He seemed to be grieving or chanting over something?*

A slice of bread that has passed the use by date doesn't seem to discourage the little guy and he munches away. I speak aloud to my furry friend, maybe he can help. "Waren, a boy in my class seems to care about one of your cousins, Miko, but he doesn't seem to like anyone else. What's up with that? Maybe you can make a call for me." I chuckle, "You like that bread huh? Well there will be plenty more where that came from." The phone rings, *Are you phoning in your thoughts little guy,* I laugh as I go inside to pick up, It's Luke.

"Hey lovely lady just checking in."

"If you are fishing for a, hi there handsome, consider it done."

Luke laughs.

"You will have to wait till Wednesday to show me the tape decks you found. I forgot that right after the funeral I have to get ready for my first school board meeting. So we're on for the funeral, then on for Wednesday night—you're cooking. I have soccer practice so I won't be home till after five. I'll call you when I get here."

Luke tells me he misses me. I like that.

"I Miss you too. If you aren't too busy, pop up for a minute. If not I'll see you tomorrow afternoon."

The squirrel was gone as well as the bread when I got back to the porch.

I corrected papers for an hour, wrote down some additional literary terms to use with the new story **The Most Dangerous Game**, and by the time the lights came on in the street I was ready to call it a day. Luke hadn't popped in so I got into my pj's and fell asleep in the first chapter of **Salem's Lot**, a horror story. *Don't blame the book*, I told myself as the book, my eyes, and the lamp surrendered to the night.

Evan delivered the projector to my classroom along with the mail. I signed the receipt for the delivery on this cooler than normal Tuesday morning, in the first full week of September. We spoke briefly and I sent him to the kitchen for one of life's little rewards. His parting words, "I think you just might work out Miss Standish."

Today Bambi left the pages and landed on screen. We talked briefly about movies versus books. The girls seemed to see more romance in a movie, the boys just thought it was easier to view a movie than read a book. Anyway I love this movie and the kids did too. Even the mighty hunters seemed moved by the plight the animals found themselves in. The term <u>foreshadowing</u> became an instant hit and after we discussed how it was used in the movie, students were using it to predict all manner of things. We also talked about <u>fables</u> and students volunteered a number of them they had read. *I love these guys.*

When I went to join Mrs. White on the playground at noon recess a knot of kids had gathered at the end of the mobile classroom.

Sam, an eighth grader, had found something that everyone insisted on seeing—before jumping back with hands raised. Sam had placed whatever it was in a ball cap and was scaring the girls.

"Sam let me see what you have there?"

"It's just a stupid dead squirrel Miss Standish, it was laying right by the edge of the woods. Probably a cat got it." "Show me where you found it." Sam walked to the area where Waren had placed something yesterday afternoon. But I had checked and there was nothing there before I left work after practice.

Tim, one of the eighth grade boys, used the occasion as a foreshadowing opportunity. "I think there's more to this than just a cat." He looked around to see if other students were paying attention. They were. "I think we'll find out what really happened in the next chapter," he kidded. Everyone laughed.

One of the sixth graders suddenly piped up, "We have to have a funeral." Clapping and comment followed. That did it, every one added their voice to the idea and like I said earlier—I can be taken off task.

Back in the classroom I decided to make this a teachable moment. "I am actually going to a funeral this afternoon," I said from the front of the class. "How many of you have ever attended one?" This discussion occurred after noon recess. Four of the students raised their hands. I invited anyone of them to share their experience. One had held a funeral for a family pet that had died. Another spoke of an older family friend. One girl spoke solemnly of a friend who had died in a fire when she lived in Winslow, Maine. "Everyone cried, there was lots of music and her picture on the casket watched it all taking place from the side. I still think about her. It was terrible."

"Thank you for sharing Abby, it is terrible when a young person dies. That is not supposed to happen. And when it does it turns the world upside down."

Those who had attended a funeral where the person was really old had not been too emotionally affected but watching their parents tear up had saddened them. In my mind I was thinking ahead to who we might ask to be our first guest speaker. I'd have to get written permission from home first, but it might expand on this teachable moment. We'll see.

I continued, "The funeral I'm going to is for an elderly Lady. It is sad but we temper our grief by knowing she had a long life." I walked among the rows of students framing my next sentence carefully, "Now we don't know how old this squirrel was but let's assume he was old and had a good life. So no tears." I smiled.

Chuckles rose, heads nodded, and we set about planning the funeral for later this afternoon. Waren never said a word and refused to take part in the planning. He did say aloud, "I won't be going to the funeral."

"I respect that Waren, but I know you cared about the squirrel, you even included it in your writing."

Suddenly a different Waren emerged, his face darkened and his eyes clouded, "Somebody in this class hit it with a rock or something. It didn't die of old age." He looked around the room— fire smoldering in his eyes—he got up and stormed out of the classroom. The metal wall shook with the slamming of the door.

I sent someone into the building to get Mrs. White to cover the class and went in search of Waren. I hoped he hadn't left the school grounds—that would require disciplinary action.

I found him on the bleachers staring off into the distance. I walked up and sat down beside him. He refused my request to talk but did agree to come back into the classroom after he had a chance to cool down.

He returned within a half hour but didn't speak. He walked to his seat and put his head down. There were no comments from his classmates. The somberness in the room was fitting as we gave the squirrel a royal sendoff completing it with a song all the students knew—**You are my Sunshine**. Two of the older boys, Tracey and Fred, were chosen to bury the squirrel at the edge of the woods. Sam protested. "I found him, I should bury him."

I sighed. "OK Sam, go with Tracey and Fred."

The day ended with plans for tomorrow afternoon.

"I have scheduled the soccer practice for tomorrow as a work session. We will mow and line the field. We will kick the ball around if we have time. This is our field we will take care of it. If you are a walker and you volunteered a rake, bring it to school with you." Heads nod. Team building.

The day finally ended without further incident. Students' K-5 lined up in the main corridor waiting for their bus number to be called, while the walkers -of which there were a dozen—were allowed to stay on the playground until all the busses are on the road. Grades 6-8 joined the walkers, waiting for their bus to be called. I sent Mrs. White to the playground to monitor dismissal.

Marie handled the orderly exit to the busses from inside the main building. I sat at my desk. I pondered what had happened in the classroom. I thought of the school rules we had posted and agreed to—*had Waren broken one, and did I need to discipline him? Would my response be a test that the other students are waiting for me to correct and grade by disciplining the boy?* I sighed, put my things together and when the students were all gone went in to say goodnight to Marie and Karen.

I have a second funeral to attend and a school board meeting. I hope they are not equally somber. The ride home revealed no waving fields of tasseled corn, no sounds of cocky crows reached my ears. No bicycles had appeared in front yards, no yelling or screaming kids. Truthfully I was lost and muddled in all that had happened and had seen nothing but the centerline in the road.

When we got to the service, which was held in a church on what's known as the Island in Skowhegan, there were only five cars in the parking lot. Ed was standing at the casket and was holding onto another older gentlemen when we walked in. We sat in the second row, the church was mostly empty. The reverend went right into bible passages which indicated he didn't know the lady either. The entire service didn't take but ten minutes. We walked to the front. The casket was closed. We shook hands with Ed, offering our condolences. He held my hand and then began to weep. He looked so alone and confused. My heart went out to him. I squeezed Luke's hand. If I could feed a stray squirrel then I should help an old man.

"Where are you going to live, Ed?"

He sighed deeply, tears still in his eyes. "I want to go back to my apartment, but I don't think I can manage it on my own."

My mouth moved but I'm not sure my brain engaged. Luke's eyes widened and he looked at me with a raised brow.

My Judgement Is Called Into Question

When we got back to my apartment Luke followed me up the stairs. He had been quiet since the funeral service ended.

He held his hat in his hands, "I know you have to get going to that school meeting but please think about what you're doing. It's not too late to change your mind."

"Luke, he has no one else."

The hat turned slowly as if wringing out the words, "I don't know you well enough to be giving you advice, just think it through, that's all." He looked deep into my eyes, "In my business, emotion and quick decisions lead to bad endings. Every day I could get caught up in the despair if I let myself." The hat settled on his head.

"I have to go Luke, thanks for going to the funeral with me. I promise to sleep on it, I haven't committed yet." I walked towards him. "Give me a hug and wish me luck in front of my bosses." I watched the hat disappear down the stairs, sighed twice then followed.

I was the first person to arrive. The smell of coffee washed over me as I entered the library. A tin of Molasses cookies and a tray of Brownies sat there teasing my taste buds, I realized I hadn't eaten. I poured myself a cup, adding a little cream, all the while eyeing the cookies. I snuck one.

Everyone seemed to arrive at once, laughter and small talk ushering them through the door. I selected a seat in the second row of upholstered chairs set up like a movie theater. Fourteen chairs surrounded three rectangular tables arranged in a horseshoe pattern in the front of the room. Thirteen representatives elected from the five towns and their chief prosecutor, (the Superintendent) hired to administer district policy, looked out over the library and the arranged chairs. When the clock showed 7:00 pm. the gavel struck and within thirty seconds all were in their seats with bright shiny faces giving the coffee pot and refreshments a brief respite.

All board members were here tonight on this first meeting since school started. Introductions all around with head nods then down to work. The Superintendent summarized the opening of school and addressed problems that had surfaced. "I believe we are going to need an additional bus. We have twenty new students—all bus students—that we had no prior knowledge of. We have eight new high school students and twelve elementary, seven of those in Embden." He looked up from his notes, "The upside is we are growing, with new revenue for each student we add. While the board considers this request—in the interim—we are going to add an additional Embden bus run. The Embden busses are all at capacity now."

He looked up once more from his notes, "Other than a stove going down at Mark Emery and a tractor in Anson that refuses to start, it's been a smooth beginning. I thank the Principals and the Supervisor of buildings and grounds and transportation, all seated in the audience, for that. Good job team." A polite round of applause followed. He moved slightly to his left as if turning a page. "I would also like to formally introduce Melody Standish the new Principal and teacher to the board members. Melody will be teaching grades six-seven-and eight at Embden." He chuckled as he checked his watch. "Actually she's been at it a while now. Please take the time to introduce yourselves at break. Stand if you would Melody."

I rose self-consciously.

"Melody comes to us from a private school in New Hampshire where she enjoyed a good measure of success. She introduced a reading and writing curriculum that within two years moved grade level reading scores in her school to the highest in the state. In addition her writing class saw several of her students published— so a warm welcome for Melody. We are fortunate to have found her." Board members and the audience as well, applauded. He smiled then, "For all you skiers in the audience, I believe Melody could give you a lesson on the slopes." Light laughter followed. "Melody would you care to add to your resume?"

I looked toward the board then back at my fellow administrators and the twenty or so citizens filling the four rows of chairs. I cleared my throat and began. "I am pleased to be here in your community. My first two weeks have been enlightening to say the least. With thirty-two students spread over three grades I won't have any difficulty sleeping that's for sure—and I don't mean in class." Everyone laughed.

I shifted gears, "I would like to invite parents and board members to visit the school. If you give us a heads up before coming, Darlene in her kitchen is a great first stop. She is a terrific baker." Light laughter moved the dialogue, "I'm looking forward to a good year of learning for the students—and myself." I sat back down. My Elementary supervisor caught my eye and his look signaled we would be talking at break. His look told me he didn't like something someone had shared. Perhaps on the way in.

I watched the interaction of the board as they went about their business. For tonight at least all seemed in accord and the agenda produced no soundbites. The Supt. seemed pleased. A committee was formed that included the bus supervisor to research a bus purchase and a report back for action at the next meeting. The Elementary Supervisor made his report. Very by the book I might add, and we moved to break.

I found a molasses cookie that was just my size. I refilled my Styrofoam cup and walked to a display of books near a window. Board members did in fact seek me out and welcome me aboard. It felt like a receiving line.

That older gentlemen the one with long snow white hair, and weathered leather skin I had seen twice before now, stood aside offering no conversation. A rounded hat sporting a feather turned slowly in his hand. His suit was wrinkled but clean. A tie seemingly made with leather strips was held closed with a turquoise slider. I thought of Luke standing like that in my apt. needing to speak his mind. The old man waited until I was by myself and approached.

"Good evening young lady welcome to Maine. The real Maine I mean." He put out his hand. "My name is Henry." His was the voice of a thousand stories all told around fire and smoke, a lot of it inhaled the huskiness indicated. His skin was several shades darker than my own, age spots dotted and mapped his life's journey on gnarled hands. His grip was firm, lingering, as if inviting me into his soul. Our eyes met and I found myself mesmerized, looking into an ancient volcano—dormant but not dead.

"I live on the water with snowdog." The smell of dried leaves, moist soil, smoked fish and falling water all came to mind in that instant—smells so strong I could taste them on my tongue.

The message he had come to deliver was sent through those eyes in this first greeting. He nodded twice and followed up in a measured tone—as if part of a chant. I was briefly reminded of the sounds Waren had made.

"You stand tall—you look firm—you will be tested—your resolve must hold fast—I live on the water—you can find me."

My mind raced. Talk about foreshadowing.

He took my hand once more, it was electric. With the release of my hand, like a wisp of smoke he seemed to disappear.

I tried to catch my breath, when I looked up the elementary supervisor had filled his space.

"So Miss Standish, how are the cookies?"

I looked down at the half-eaten cookie, still digesting Henry. He was apparently an Indian Elder of some sort. I shook my head, my mind slowly leaving an ancient cave—this new message arrived in a clipped tone.

The words and tone suggested a mixed message. I looked up. *Smart ass eyes, and from the tenor of his voice the reference to a cookie was going to be the only sweetness in this conversation.*

Moving right to the heart of things he said, "One of the Embden board members tells me you are teaching a children's story in your reading class."

I held up the last bit of cookie then popped it in my mouth and drained my coffee. My mind looked back into Henry's eyes, it seemed to settle me. "The cookies are delicious." I paused, "That is what you asked me isn't it?"

Flustered—his hands began to shake—Wayne T. Folsom— already known to school personnel by his initials, W-T-F. I hadn't caught on at first when I heard several of the Principals refer to him this way. Darlene with a blush of her cheeks cleared it all up. My new boss reddened. "So the cookies are good, excellent." He gritted, "about that children's story, is that accurate?"

Marie Poulin had warned me he was a control freak. 'Try not to rile him, just listen, nod your head then do what you think is right.' She had chuckled then, 'the man is so full of himself he could never imagine an opinion differing from his own might surface.'

"Honestly sir, I don't think I can fairly explain in the five minutes we have before the meeting resumes. "But," I smiled, "I would be glad to bring you my lesson plans," *I actually just said that. Calmly, Thanks Henry.*

He didn't react to my suggestion but simply ploughed ahead, "Did you teach a children's story to your classes?" He followed with a whispered, "You know, you weren't my first choice, my second either for that matter." The words, "Private School indeed," slipped out under his breath. He smiled, thinking his words provided a sting that would render me helpless. All they did was odor the air. I didn't rise to the bait.

"Yes I did." I opened my hands to reveal there were no hidden cards that would change this hand.

He simply stood there, he didn't know where else to take this, he had emptied his gun.

I offered once more to expand on the topic when time allowed.

"My office at four pm. tomorrow," he managed.

"Can we make that 4:30?" I have a soccer practice to run."

He was reeling now but obviously needed the last word. "Make that 4:15." I shook my head in the affirmative. He didn't disappear as Henry had, rather, he slithered into his seat. I was reminded of the older boys that first morning in my class. No not like my boys, they had melted, he definitely slithered. I chuckled to myself. I watched him talking to himself. *Good old Marie, I'll have to buy her a cup of coffee, one for Henry too if I ever see him again.*

As the meeting moved on to minor topics I found myself reflecting. *In the span of two weeks six males had entered my life who seemed to be asking something of me. Luke, maybe my new shining knight offered all sorts of possibilities. Old Ed, alone and needing assistance, would I be the right fit? Waren, a troubled young man with anger issues, is he reaching out to me through his actions? Henry is a mystery, but he approached me for a reason. My father seems ready to finally do something he's always wanted to do, is he seeking my approval? And now my elementary supervisor who seems ready to question my motives with no investigation. Is there a hidden agenda there?*

I rode home in the darkness of a rural Maine September night. It was cooling down and I turned on my heater. Six very different scripts filled my head. I turned on the radio and three songs played in a row—without interruption—yet I heard none of them. As I entered my yard the call letters for the station reached my ears followed by the catchy name, **The River**. *Seems water is in my life to stay.*

The house was dark, the stairs creaked and echoes of my footsteps followed me through the door. A solid red light under my phone indicated I could ready myself for bed, 5:00 am would come around at the same time no matter how many hours of sleep I had. I didn't even think about opening my book. The last thing I saw was the time, 11:14 pm. Dreamed all night, can't remember any of them, no nightmares at least, I always remembered those.

***

I looked around the room as attendance is being taken and note Waren's seat is vacant. First day anyone from my classes has missed school. The picture story, **Where in the world is Waldo?** enters my mind for a moment, then both Waren and Waldo disappear from my mind. I walk the four aisles of students handing out the story **The Most Dangerous game**, written by Richard Connell. This story will demand my full attention.

"We are going to start the day with group reading in class, all three grades. "If you are uncomfortable when called on just say pass. This is a very powerful story and some of it may be a little difficult for you, that's why we are reading it together. Team story," I pipe up which brings smiles. "This story is usually taught in high school but as a group we're going to take this journey together. Stops along the way will give the opportunity to share our emotions. We will identify some of the literary terms you have come to recognize, and add new one's as they emerge. I will throw in a little vocabulary when it makes sense. When we have finished I hope you will begin to see the different points of view that literature offers. Every author you read will use different styles but if you read carefully and keep an open mind you'll discover common themes. **Bambi** and **The Most Dangerous Game** could not be more different and even the intended audience would seem at odds, yet we will find examples where the stories mirror one another. Two of the new terms we will explore are <u>comparison</u> and <u>contrast.</u> The remainder of the new terms are on the back of the last page."

I laugh, "I'm sure these two new terms will be used in a myriad of ways in our class once you use them a few times. Literature is the most powerful medium in the world and it can take you anywhere and immerse you in worlds and situations that you could never conjure up on your own. Ready for a trip?" I walk up and down the rows making eye contact. "The reason you are getting this story in pieces is I don't want anyone reading ahead. First I will explain <u>comparison</u> and <u>contrast</u> using the last story we read, Bambi."

After giving examples and inviting students to discover others we were ready.

Let's begin shall we?" I find a chair for myself and ask Grace to begin. Students are given several paragraphs to read, stopping at natural breaks of dialogue, or when I interrupt. This story will hold their interest I am certain. When I stopped for the day, before the story took on the most troubling tone, groans of complaint arose. They were already intrigued. "See you're hooked. That's what a good writer does. You are left wanting more, right to the end. "That's enough to absorb for today. Tonight you will be looking for comparisons and contrasts between Bambi and the passages we just read." I'm handing out a sheet of questions to do just that."

Later when Science class met we looked at the commonality of observations the students had found in their outdoor search. And the winner is, the leaves, just beginning to change color. A visual departure from the summer color green the students had unconsciously walked beneath, around and through for the past five months or so. Every group had listed them in their walk. We formed teams—two teams from each grade. With the topic decided on, each team was tasked with brainstorming what they would like to research about leaves including their changing colors and all its implications. We would all report back tomorrow.

Our very busy day ended with Soccer practice.

The tractor mower was sitting at the edge of the soccer field. To the side lay three bags of white marking chalk, a reel measure, stakes, a large ball of twine, six rakes and a little metal push cart with a narrow opening for the chalk. Obviously the janitor was taking me at my word. The field had not been cut in some time so raking would be the hardest part. My team of seventeen were on the bleachers awaiting my orders. Steve spoke up, "Haying this thing might be easier." Laughter followed.

"I agree, but it's not an option. Here's what we're going to do."

When we returned to the bleachers at 4:00 pm the field had been mowed and raked into long lines of freshly cut grass. The side lines had been measured, laid out, and lined. Roger's father at the farm located next door to the school had agreed to scoop up the freshly cut grass. Tomorrow we would mark the center lines, the end lines, and the penalty areas at each end.

"This is your field, gang. You own it, let's make it as difficult as possible for any team to come here and claim a victory. Tomorrow I'll show you how our defense will do just that. Dismissed!"

I gathered my things—powered up my rig—a phrase Luke used in starting his truck, and took in the scenery on the way to the office in Anson. Indeed to my mind the world was brighter than yesterday. Colors of fall were emerging at every turn. The mountains had added blush to their cheeks, intent on being viewed in their best light. Several of the players were still on the road, their bikes hugging the side of the pavement, the rakes they had managed to carry had me thinking if they crashed it might be my bad. Michael waved furiously, his bike wobbled and I held my breath. I suddenly felt secure in how I was working with these kids. I felt Henry's hand on mine guiding my steering. I put on my game face as I went to battle my boss.

He was cordial I'll give him that. He couldn't hide his tone however and though in the end he agreed to give me some time, I could tell I would never make him a believer.

"I'm a curriculum man through and through. Follow the teacher's guide you can't be faulted. I know you had some success in your past school, but this isn't Kansas, Dorothy, and this isn't Oz. If I get more complaints we will need to meet again and it will become my way or the highway."

"I don't think he heard a word I said," I muttered to my little car as I gripped the wheel envisioning a physical approach to reasoning. One thought did emerge, *if I'm not his first or second choice and yet I got hired, who really is in charge here?* I smiled at that.

After a nice shower, I put on jeans and a tee-shirt, tied back my hair and splashed on a scent that seemed outdoorsy and skipped down the stairs. On the quick ride to Luke's I realized that I truly did believe in what I was doing as a teacher and would not allow myself to worry anything to death. "I am Woman, watch me roar," I sang aloud.

Luke welcomed me with a warm hug and a lingering kiss. He grabbed a plastic container and invited me to follow him out back to the charcoal grill where a card table with a bottle of wine served as centerpiece. "The potato salad is store bought I confess but I got the corn at a farm stand and I steamed it myself. He poured us both a glass of wine and we toasted one another without speaking. What to do about Ed didn't come up until well after a burger, two ears of corn, and the last sip of my second glass of wine.

"Have you had a chance to think about it?"

"Actually yes, I plan to go and see him this weekend and then I'll know. No emotion, just examine the possibilities." I sighed. "I have a confession to make as well. The old house I'm living in, well let's just say it's too big and empty, I'm thinking about moving to Embden Pond for the winter and spring. Would that pose a problem for you?"

"Not at all," then he seemed to falter. He stammered, his face twitched, "I may be looking at a change of address myself."

I looked at him, waiting for the shoe to drop.

It came out in a gush like a garden hose turned on from a distance and a rush to reach the working end. "My cousin is a lieutenant in a medium size city in Arizona, the area is growing and they are looking to increase the size of their police force, he says with my background I could join as a detective." He sighed.

I didn't speak.

"I haven't decided and it's still in the talking stages but I have to be honest with you. It's a lot more money and more chance to advance my career."

"It sounds like possible changes for both of us, so-o-o," I kidded dragging things out like he did at times trying to soften the subject, "I shouldn't waste your time teaching you to ski this winter." I smiled but it was a fraud. Inside my head the wheel of fortune spun with a different name attached to each of six prongs.

To be honest the rest of the evening was strained. We small talked through the fading light but there was a different feel to my climb when I reached my apt. I went out on the porch, the stars were emerging through darkened skies. The street lights were hindering what I needed to do. I slipped on a jacket and got into my car. I drove to Coburn Park and eased my little sports car to the side of the road. The gate was locked but a pedestrian can enter at any time. It was dark. I found a bench and sat down. No street lights in here to mask the heavens. I wished on a star then found my spirit guide, Ursa Minor. Funny I hadn't thought about Little Bear since I was a kid skiing under the stars with my father. Dad was Ursa Major or Great Bear as it was called. For one winter we nicknamed one another, Great Bear and Little Bear. Then like a night that slowly pales with clouds hiding those stars the game receded into memory. Sitting there I sighed up a storm.

Back in my apt. and in bed I thought back to every one of six recent conversations. Each one had unfinished business attached. Enough mystery for tonight, the lamp clicked off with conviction.

Gathering Storm Clouds

The campsite—more of a lean-to that kept only the harshest elements at bay—was fifty yards off the trail.

Daniel opened his sleeping bag then checked the time, 9:06 pm. He sat on a rock watching the stars emerge and found the various famous formations, his favorite was the Big Dipper. He remembered a story his mother had told him years ago about how it landed in the cosmos. 'Your father actually told me this story when we were first dating. There is a lot to learn about your father and your heritage, someday maybe you'll meet the man who knows the whole story.' His mother was no slouch herself in the story department. She could create an alternate ending for most of the children stories read to him at night. This ability served her well in the first few years after she lost a husband, and Daniel his father.

It seemed a bare recollection of his father remained and the memory of his grandfather had faded as well. He had been happy back then, that much he remembered. He started school in a brand new building. He was riding a bus. His grandfather was beginning to teach him things about his uniqueness. Then his father died and everything changed. Soon he was living in a different place far from his grandfather. This was the one story his mother could never seem to conjure a satisfactory ending.

He looked up to the stars. He breathed the night air. Pure. Stars dotted the blackness, he felt small in their presence but good about the distance he had traveled today. He would be leaving the mountains tomorrow and find his way to the lake. The one person in the world who might save him lived near there. *I hope to God he's still with us,* he thought to himself. He took a pill, washed down with a swig of water and saluted himself. "Down to one," he said aloud, toasting the one day left in the mountains and the single pill he allowed himself, small victories. The outdoors seemed to be the one place where he emerged from the fog of life—the one place he could calm his inner demons.

***

Miles away on the bank of a little stream that enters Embden pond in the most subtle of ways, Henry Strongbolt gazed at these same stars. A night sky that told in its twinkling pulses of light of a time when his people roamed the waterways and the land beneath his feet. There were few left standing to share the stories his forebears told over open fires but Henry would never forget. Others before him had marked their history with figures etched in stone in the mighty Kennebec to the east. Chronicled chapters of his people's story drawn on nature's chalkboard. His last name was his constant companion. A reminder of the legend of **The Thunderers**, seven brothers who created the lightning and thunder throughout the world. Tonight was calm and his thoughts turned to the season before him. An evening meal of corn and squash was settling nicely. He rose and stretched, breathing in the coming autumn. So many of these seasons he had roamed this world formed by **Tolba** and **Moskwas**. Lately his bones complained of the walks he took daily. He rubbed his knees and spoke aloud to them, "You complain with my first steps when I have yet to clear my mind. You return to my campfire at days end to ask if I have reached my destination. I hear your voice. Ahh I feel your voice." He chuckled to himself, rubbing the ache vigorously. Tonight, Henry seemed to feel the cosmos closing in on him, the pulses of light seemed more intense. Powerful forces on the loose speaking to him of a coming storm, not winter white, rather a disturbance of man-kind's making. His memories of man-kinds' transgressions were not filled with joy, but rather sorrow and regret. He rose from the little bench that served as his observation post—a resting place that allowed him an unobstructed view of the pond. He rubbed his knees once more. He drew in a deep breath and disappeared into the darkened canopy of fur and spruce and pine. His companion, Snow Dog who had remained silent found his place about four yards to Henry's rear awaiting any command that might reach his ears. Henry was invisible here, his small log cabin would have to be stepped on to be seen. **Miko**, the pesky squirrel was nearly squashed as he darted into Henrys' path. Snow Dog sniffed but ignored the squirrel and followed Henry to the camp. *Going to get cold tonight*, thought Henry as he closed the door. Snow Dog settled himself on the little steps and looked into the heavens. He had ancestors speaking to him as well.

After a restless fitful night I rose to the first serious frost of the season which had placed a blindfold on my windshield. I shivered and turned on the Defrost. Sitting numbly, cold air washing over me moving my hair, I wait for the world to appear. A poem I had read somewhere reaches my mind. It was titled <u>*FROST.*</u>

<u>Two nights ago you placed your cold hands on my window leaving your prints.</u>
<u>In the morning you tried to bite me.</u>
<u>Last night I watched you begin your measured march.</u>
<u>While I slept you licked my window.</u>
<u>This morning my window is covered in a vanilla frosting.</u>

Last night's nightmare intrudes. I shiver again. Another thought, *I think my damn supervisor caused my bad night.* The air warmed. First a little circle and then with the swipe of a wiper my vision clears. I shake away the boogey man, breathing in deeply. Backing into the street, smoke and furnace exhaust rises from chimneys sending out a clear signal that fall had arrived overnight. The grass wears wedding white that will turn a shimmering silver when touched by the magic wand of the morning sun. Garbage cans stand sentinel at the side of driveways this first day of a new week. I hum to myself, following the roadway with little to catch my attention. In Madison the high school and just to its west the Junior High stand waiting for their day to begin, cars already in their parking lots. Vapor rises from both sides of Madison Anson Bridge. Plumes from the exhaust stack at Madison Paper are furiously exiting like the last smoke of a condemned prisoner. Further on in North Anson, tail pipes offer visual proof that the engine hasn't stalled while their owner fuels up with a breakfast sandwich or pastry and coffee at, The Corner Store.

My second favorite season has arrived. Training runs in college with teammates—my first team mates really—produced several friends that have endured. I plan to call one of them over Columbus Day weekend, maybe plan a ski outing not too long from now.

Karen is already in Darlene's kitchen when I park and enter. I set down my bag. "Coffee this morning I presume, I see you don't have your travel mug with you," offers Darlene.

"Yeah, a little late this morning, I didn't sleep well. My mind was spinning all night."

Karen cuts a roll from the square and butters it. She places it on a napkin and hands it to me. "This will fix you up boss."

I laugh, "Thanks, by the way Darlene, have you found me a place to live on the lake?"

She raises her cup in triumph, "How about a choice, I have two possibilities. One on either side of the lake. One east side, one on the west. Each has three bedrooms and a single bath. The one on the west side has an additional room that is off the kitchen. It is not heated but could be used if necessary."

"And the price difference?"

"Here's the deal, the one that's closest to the school is five hundred a month, open till the first week of July. West side is a little more, but for me personally I would like the seclusion. It gets the morning sun. There is a little stream near it. Six hundred, but if you can move out for a couple of weeks in August you can have it for as long as you want. Both are furnished."

"You have been busy, can I see them both?"

"I have names and numbers to call. Glad to have you as a possible neighbor, neighbor. I don't live on the lake but I do house calls," Darlene laughed.

Karen speaks up then, a bit guiltily, "I would invite you to live with me but my little place barely has room for me and Jake."

We raise our eyes. *Possible gossip.*

"Jake is my dog."

And on that note we all chuckle and go to work.

There is an apple sitting on my desk. I have to smile. *Someone has been sleeping on my desk,* I laugh to myself, recalling Goldilocks and the Three Bears. Wonder who put that there? I pick it up and smell it. The apple is warm. *Must have happened after practice last night.*

The class register does not lie. It is the official record kept by each teacher and submitted to the state at the end of the year.

Waren's absent again. Third day in a row is duly entered. Today I will have to make a call. I need to do this all official-like.

Math is math, but I do try to spice it up a little by using everyday items the kids might identify with. I'll admit I am not a math fan so in this instance my boss will be pleased, I'm following the curriculum.

Everyone is starting the homework that follows the lesson. This gives me the opportunity to ask Mrs. White to watch the group while I go in to call my Supervisor. He is out supervising I'm told but he will get back to me I am assured. *Oh well I did my due diligence in the matter,* I nod to myself and go back to face the beast called Social Studies.

But first let's just take a commercial break—(in educational jargon that's called recess.)

The grass glistens, the frost gone but not forgotten. Still a nip to the air. The boys though are down to their tee shirts already. A pile of outer coverings spread out on the edge of the grass, as colorful as the autumn leaves soon to dot this same grass. Basketball rules at recess. Wandering groups of kids waiting their turn to play don't let a little moisture stop their travels. Suddenly a trio come running. Still a distance away, "Miss Standish," the girls are gushing in unison. "The squirrel is gone! The squirrel is gone!"

I hold up my hand, "Slow down girls." I point to Kirsten, "Say that again, slowly."

The three girls arrive at the same time. Coming to a sliding stop as if trying not to overrun second base. They all began to speak at once.

"Girls, let Kirsten speak. Please!"

Kirsten, the tallest of the girls takes charge. She breathes in, then out, then begins. "Someone dug up the squirrel from where we buried him."

The hollering has attracted a crowd. The basketball game has stopped. The ball even now rolling, hitting the building and reversing across the tar to the wet grass. Jump-ropes have gone slack. Marbles have stopped moving. I feel like the inviting end of a magnet with all my little iron filings gathering.

Thirty-one voices, all thinking it is their turn to speak their lines on stage have me raising my arms in surrender. "PLEASE," I shout, "let's all calmly walk and take a look shall we? There is plenty of time to raise a conspiracy theory."

They look at me with furrowed foreheads. Silently asking, *what did she just say?* But they did quiet. When we reached the little mound of stones and dirt, indeed it has been disturbed, and the little squirrel is indeed missing. Eyes circle the grave. Confusion, suspicion and anger are the words beginning to give voice. I hear a whispered, 'I bet Waren did it.' Heads nod. I keep my mouth shut. I will address this in the class room, *another teachable moment perhaps.* Within five minutes the games have resumed. Suspicions are cast but the worm of truth is left to be nibbled away at rather than gnawed on. Unless a new ripple of evidence surfaces the matter mostly forgotten in a behind the back dribble or an obvious but rarely called foul. For other students the alphabet is being recited with kids' names attached to the spinning rope.

When we are all back in the classroom I shovel the dirt, putting the matter to rest. "I'll bet you have all been accused at one time or another of something you didn't do. Am I right?" Eyes cast downward but heads nod. "I'll bet you didn't like it one bit. Waren isn't here to defend himself so let's keep our opinions to ourselves. Let me handle it." I raise my brows and look stern.

"Okay, on to social studies shall we."

Social studies is not a favorite for most kids, and the first several weeks have produced more stifled yawns than any other subject. The eighth graders are studying **United States History**. The sixth graders must master Geography. And the seventh, **World Cultures**. Wow. I am following the curriculum for now but I'll end up searching for commonalities that allow us to plan at least some whole class lessons. Right now I'm just shaking my head as I move from group to group, directing traffic.

Lunch is Spaghetti with meat-sauce, green beans and the beloved yeast roll, all washed down with a half pint of milk—white or chocolate. Oh yeah, and canned applesauce.

Not a lot of conversation as the students eat at their desks. A hungry lot, the boys seem to inhale their food. I check in the office, no return call from my supervisor.

I am a little excited to begin the reading this afternoon. I hoped the kids were making connections. After listening to the comparisons and contrasts the kids had found and documented, I had to smile. **Bambi** had done its job. I hand out the next section of, **The Most Dangerous Game.** We will continue with the story after I give a quick review of what we read yesterday and introduce the first vocabulary word of the week, <u>palpable</u>. I put the word and definition on the board. "Copy this down. I think it adds to the mystery: <u>you can almost *touch* it though it's not solid; *hear* it yet it makes no sound; *see* it though it takes no form.</u> Let's look back for a moment to how it's used in the story. Can you feel what Rainsford was experiencing? Good writing puts you there, inside the character's head." Heads up—eyes focused—they appear to be listening.

"Philip will you pick up where we left off? Philip read of Rainsford finding himself in the water after falling from the boat. In this second day of reading pistol shots off to his right have moved him to the rail. He loses his balance. Perhaps the earlier conversation with his shipmate had affected him more than he imagined. At any rate he is in the water. He needs to find his way out of this mess and he strikes off in the dark waters, in the direction of the pistol shots. He hits land and drags himself out of the water, exhausted. We stop the reading.

"Do we have to stop now Miss Standish, this is getting good?" asks Kathy.

I smile. *Hmm excitement replacing sighs that's a good thing I think.* I charge ahead. "Let's put some of these literary terms to use shall we. Anyone see another example of <u>Foreshadowing</u> surfacing?" I chuckle, "No pun intended. Or <u>Irony,</u> find any of that yet?" Several hands are raised. I call on the wrong one. "Miss Standish, you know you talk funny sometimes." A pause. "But you're likable." Eyebrows rise in nearly every seat.

Off task but I had to respond. "Thank you Troy, I guess." I left it right there. "So Troy did you pick up any examples of foreshadowing or irony in today's reading?"

"I just figured he was going to drown. Guess he didn't. I was wrong."

The class burst out laughing. I laughed along with them. When we settled, I started again. "Well as Troy said, Rainsford didn't drown. What are some possible scenarios we might see as the story continues? Could you write an ending if the story stopped here?" Nearly everyone raises their hand. "See, you all have an idea of what you could do to end this story. That's what good writing does, it hooks us. Do you see now why I have been parceling out this story in small chunks?" Several heads nod. "Each day we will be making discoveries. These discoveries will be made as a group." I switch gears. "Your assignment for the next thirty minutes is to plan out and begin writing your own ending for this story. Go back and reread what has been exposed. Use your imagination. The ending should be at least a thousand words. I know that sounds like a lot but really it's not. By the way what's a brier?" Dwayne raises his hand.

"It's a pipe, right?"

"Yes it is, any pipe smokers in here?" I kid.

Mark raises his hand, "My mother puffs on a Corn Cob pipe when we go camping. To keep the damn black flies away."

Everyone laughs and gasps at the use of the word damn, but I ignore it because usually Mark is the quietest kid in the class. He actually volunteered a response. "Thank you for the insight Mark on how to prevent a black fly attack. I just might get me one of those." Everyone laughs.

"So we will begin now and tomorrow we will use class time to finish. I'm available now to help you brainstorm if necessary.

I will collect your stories on Monday and we will finish the story in one reading." I move around the room. "Then we will see who came closest to what the author wrote. We may have some budding authors in here, who knows? Any way have fun with it. It's your story to finish. Start by revisiting **The Most Dangerous Game**. Even the title should be sparking your imagination."

We held our first real soccer practice today. The farmer had taken away the piles of grass so we had a full hour of practice after getting the remaining lines marked out. I had promised a defense that would keep our opponents out of our goal and I did just that. I also told them that from now until the season ended, recess would provide us an additional half hour of practice a day. "That team—is what's called an edge—two and a half extra hours a week is going to bring Embden its first championship ever." They hooted. "Now give me three laps and get out of here."

A lone parent sat on the bleachers watching the activity. I walked up to introduce myself. I held out my hand. "I'm Melody Standish, do I have your son or daughter in my class?"

"You do."

"Oh." Are you comfortable telling me who?"

"I'd rather not, just consider me the parent of all these kids, I love them all."

I later learned her name and she became a friend but in all the time I spent in Embden, to my mind she became, Earth Mother. She attended practices, games, concerts, board meetings, was very involved in the Parent Teacher Organization, the spring fair. She headed fund raisers for uniforms, and could be found from time to time sipping coffee with Darlene in the kitchen. The woman was amazing but never wanted attention drawn to herself.

I checked my classroom, no new apple had appeared this afternoon. I locked up and went into the building. The janitor had returned from his bus run and was pushbroom sweeping the corridor. He stopped when he saw my silhouette framed in the door glass. "Hey, Miss Standish. You did a good job with that field, care to try my floor duties," he kidded.

I laughed, "Well thanks for that but I would hate to be the cause of your unemployment."

He looked confused, then startled. When I broke into a grin he caught my drift and smiled.

"Anyway, you had a call while you were on the field. It was Mr. All-knowing, returning your call, he said." When I furrowed my brow he corrected himself. "Sorry, it was the ELEMENTARY SUPERVISOR, you know W-T-F," then he smiled. I feigned ignorance. When I didn't rise to the inside joke he shrugged his shoulders and continued, "He said he would try in the morning. You could stop by this afternoon, his day doesn't end until six pm. He made sure to add that."

"So tell me how you really feel about my boss."

"I'll just shut up now. But if he comes in here again and takes this broom out of my hands, after twice taking over my mop, showing me how it should be done. Well you won't have to worry about you causing my unemployment."

On that note I skipped out to my car, singing, *you are not alone, not alone, any more.*

***

Forty miles away, Daniel Bradford left the mountains.

***

Three miles up the western shore of Embden Pond, Henry Strongbolt was gathering fire wood for the winter. It would be cold again tonight, though he could smell rain, possibly by tomorrow afternoon.

CHAPTER TWELVE

Autumn Arrives In All Its Majesty

The Calendar is a blur· My day planner is filled with notes, some accomplished, others abandoned when a teachable moment surfaced. The classroom and the thirty-one kids who keep me laughing and my head above water are my sanctuary. That being said, Columbus Day could not have arrived at a better time. Fall rains had arrived and trying to keep these guys busy during in-door recesses was like herding cats. Chess was introduced. Checkers. They tried to teach me cribbage but my mind was so muddled trying to direct traffic they gave up on me. In addition Waren hadn't returned. Cold rain was the least of my worries.

***

It had all begun three weeks earlier with a home visit. My boss determined after connecting on the phone to have a meeting. In our meeting he decided we should go together to find out why Waren was not in school. He was waiting in his sleek sedan when the school emptied. I nodded through the glass and got into the passenger seat. "Now when we get there let me do the talking Melody, I have been doing home visits for a long time and you have to be firm."

"Have you met Waren? Or his family?"

"Can't say I have but, it doesn't matter, like I told you—just follow the curriculum." He smiled his arrogance.

Okay then, I nodded to myself.

Waren lived on the western side of the lake in a little trailer just a hundred yards up a dirt road to the left of the water. The leaves had changed outfits but the vibrant colors couldn't disguise the squalor that sat in their midst. Twenty-five feet long at best and maybe eight feet wide with castoffs of every description ringing the outside walls. I for one did not wish to leave the car, *not inviting.* It was clear a little child lived here. A broken dolls carriage and a red pail and yellow shovel lay where they had last been used. A lawn mower sat pushed up against the woods. What use it could ever serve in this rutted dirt covered yard gave it reason to hide its face. The little grass that existed skirted white plastic five gallon buckets dotting the open space, placed haphazardly as if charged to catch the rain. The trailer, colored a weathered faded green—with what had probably at one time been a white accent strip was stained and pocked with rust colored acne. A storm door stood above a single step. The screen door fronting it was torn and hanging at an angle never to be closed again. I took this all in as I imagined Waren having to face this every day. *No wonder he's angry.* My boss though, he had a curriculum to follow and was out the door with enthusiasm. A big black and tan dog rounded the corner of the trailer. The dog hadn't announced his coming and was salivating a possible rare find. About to follow his own curriculum strategy a voice brought him to a screeching halt. Waren appeared. Waren walked forward putting a hand on the dog's head. Wayne T. Folsom, the dog just a foot away, had lost any color he might add to the season and was both breathless and speechless.

"This is Pete." Waren reached down and rubbed the dogs head. "Good thing I was home." He raised his eye brows at the elementary supervisor. "Who are you, and what do you want?" It was only then that Waren spied me through the window glass and barely nodded. I nodded back, I had no intention of getting out of the car. My boss tried to gather himself as he eyed Pete warily. The dog growled deep in his throat as they made eye contact. "He won't bother you none…. that is…. unless I'm threatened," Waren dragged out.

Wayne T. Folsom cleared his throat and stroked his tie, "I'm not here to threaten you young man merely to find out why you aren't in school."

"I've got things to do."

"What about your studies, you need to be in school?"

"I'll get back when I can. Best I can offer."

"You do realize you have to go to school?"

"There are lots of things I have to do. School is somewhere on that list."

"I'm the Elementary Supervisor," he huffed and puffed.

"It's my job to see that you get an education."

Waren had to chuckle, "Oh I'm getting an education alright. Yes sir, I am surely doing that."

"So when do you think you might get back?"

"Maybe in a month or so. He gestured to the trailer, "After I get this place ready for winter."

"Are you here alone, I'd like to meet your parents?"

Waren stiffened. Pete noticed and growled deep in his throat. "You're getting into my business now. Let it be.

I'll get back when I can." Pete echoed his master by growling once more.

Needing the last word no matter who the audience, Wayne T. Folsom finished with a flourish, "Well I'll give you a week to get winterized and then I'll have to refer you to the Supt. and school board for further action." With that he brushed his hands in finality and reentered the car.

I watched Waren turn and slap his thigh, Pete rose to follow.

"Well there, that should do it," I dead panned.

Obviously not a student of literature my boss missed all the foreshadowing and a half dozen other literary terms that had just been heaped on him.

He set his posture to stiff and backed out of the yard.

On the home front I had met with old Ed and he was now Goldilocks, sleeping in my bed on the third floor of an apartment I am soon to vacate. I am sleeping for the next couple of weeks on the porch. On the upside Ed has made friends with Miko and entertains himself by watching the squirrel gather his winter's provisions. Another good thing. Ed likes to read. Which is very good thing because I don't have time to spend hours of small talk in the few hours I have to myself. I have promised to bring him some books. There is no TV. I don't think Ed could understand it anyway—hear it possibly at a high volume—but understand it, nope. I gave him the book I kept wanting to start, Salem's Lot, but he hasn't gotten very far. I think he might like Zane Grey westerns better. I am mostly immersed in staying ahead of my students and feeling sorry for myself in the romance department so Ed is left to entertain himself. He likes to cook, so in that area I am already seeing an unexpected upside. Luke is leaving to take that job. He did manage to put in a tape deck and we still talk but its tapering off to just phone calls. I'm going to miss him.

If I'll do the shopping Ed will see to it that I get, 'at least one good square meal a day,' he tells me. He's a good old guy—cooked food smells are comforting—and the building doesn't seem to make the same ominous sounds when Ed is there to absorb some of them. I have found that it's best to be facing Ed if I want him to understand me. He can hear sounds but he has a hard time with the words if he can't read lips as well.

***

We finished **The most Dangerous Game** with students high fiving one another when the General met his demise. Hunting took on a whole new meaning and terms like <u>irony, climax, theme,</u> and <u>narrator</u> became part of our—<u>lexicon</u>—another term I threw in for good measure.

The science lessons are moving along nicely, the outdoors certainly is keeping the kids from nodding off. At the end of this first unit we are going to hold an open house for parents with different groups presenting in a number of ways what they have been studying.

So with all this going on I didn't need to get (the call.)

Of course I wasn't home and Ed can't hear that particular sound which is probably just as well. 'Melody this is your father, your mother has injured herself, call me when you get this message.'

We won the first two games of the soccer season by playing the defense we worked out. Both games found our competitors knocking on our door countless times but we didn't let them in. Both times they had become frustrated and added their last line of defense to their offense and we beat them back to their own goal. Eric a seventh grader is the fastest kid on the field and we lulled the enemy to sleep and Eric struck like a cobra—the mascot for the High school. Two one goal wins has me singing up the stairs. "Moving on up, to the west side," I belted out, changing the words to suit my soon to be new digs. I opened the door and Ed's first words are, "Your light is blinking." He pointed with a stirring spoon, I could smell spaghetti sauce. It was warm in here the porch door was closed and the windows were steaming up. Home Sweet Home.

I opened the porch door raising windows slightly then returned to listen to the message. I dialed my father immediately, my mind expecting the worst.

"She's going to be okay, she took too many sleeping pills; an accident she says."

"Who found her?"

"No one. She called me after she woke up vomiting and disoriented. I think she was sending me a message. I can't even confirm that it happened. Would you call her again, she needs to get a grip?"

I sat there in stunned silence and for whatever reason those starry nights out on the slope came to mind. Suddenly I needed a dad, at least the memory of one when we actually communicated. "Dad do you remember when you were Great Bear and I was Little Bear, that one winter?"

"Of course I do, you'll always be my little bear. We had some wonderful times way back when. Why? Your class studying the skies?"

"No, I met this old Indian guy a while back and he has me thinking about the little bit of our heritage that you knew and told me about. Remember the squirrel that haunted us and got into things? Well I have a Miko just outside my window. And don't be shocked. I have a man living on this side of the glass."

My father started to speak but I stopped him.

"He's an old man dad, older than you, and he can't hear—not because he's not listening—he's nearly deaf.

I have so much to tell you but I can't do it now. I will call mom. What I can offer I have no idea but I'll try. I'll call you in a few days. Actually it will be at night. Good night, Great Bear."

I drew comfort from the one sided conversation and from sitting across from old Ed who puffed up when I complimented him on his *secret sauce*. He had told me he was going to fix dinner tonight and right about now I needed that comfort food.

Later Ed was sitting on the porch in the glow of the light from the kitchen. I had just finished the dishes. I could just make out Miko outside the glass. Ed was talking to him. He had placed some of the garlic bread from tonight's dinner on the ledge and was feigning an Italian dialect. I like this old man.

I sat down, sighed and called my Mother. She answered on the first ring. "It was an accident honey, so don't even begin."

"Well hello to you too."

"Sorry but I'm sure your father has given you all the gory details by now, and I'm sure he embellished."

"Actually, he didn't. He's just worried."

"I'm fine. In fact I have made a decision. I think it's time I got out of here myself. How would you like to have your mother back in your life?"

I was speechless. I mean I was utterly speechless.

"Don't answer me now, just think about it. I could cook and clean for you and we could get close again."

I was speechless. I mean I was utterly speechless.

"I'm calling your father to discuss all this and hear exactly what he's suggesting and offering. Then I'll get back to you. Honey I'm fine, this was just the wake-up call I needed. I'll call you in a week." With that said she hung up.

Do I need to add I was utterly speechless?

***

Two weeks went by and Waren didn't return to school and my mother didn't call. So a negative and a possible positive. Unfortunately, in math terms that adds up to a negative and if I may add, I'm a positive person.

The bulletin boards in the hallway reflected the changing season. Halloween had come and gone. Now Turkeys and pilgrims lined the corridor announcing our next vacation and family gatherings.

The suggestion came from W-T-F. Not wanting to appear weak and with few real alternatives he suggested perhaps I should tutor Waren until he finishes his winterizing. He did not seem to want to involve his boss the Supt. or the school board. His suggestion was more of a command as you can well imagine. So here I am once more having to save someone. There is no phone at Waren's so my little car is finding its way through nearly extinguished color. As if torn from a picture, with just a frame of bare trees remaining, the road accepts a warming blanket of oranges, reds, yellows, and browns. I pull into the driveway, the rutted dirt path also newly decorated. Pete is waiting, sitting on his haunches, laughing at the toy auto that just showed up. He yawns. This is going to be way too easy. He raises himself, about to come investigate, when Waren steps out and with a slap to his thigh brings Pete back to his side. I wave through the windshield. Waren gives me a little wave back. It is then I sense more than see, another person. Where he came from or how he got here I have no idea, but Henry is standing at my passenger window.

CHAPTER THIRTEEN

Leaves Are Falling Down Down Down Red and Yellow Golden Brown

It was just after three when I passed the little school on this bleak November day. Low hanging angry darkened clouds seem to be brushing the treetops removing grime. Fingered branches scrape dirt and dust as the clouds rush off stage. Children are in a field kicking several balls around. I hear a whistle and watch a woman wearing a ball cap, hair sticking out a little hole in the back, gathering kids to her side. I hear laughter. I pause. I went to school here many years ago. I liked it here before everything changed. I mop my brow. I could use a drink of water and the toilet but its best that I remain invisible at least for now. The road ahead bends to the left. I spent three summers on the pond just up ahead, and though that too was years ago it still looks mostly the same. My mind wanders frequently—residue from the pills I am trying to eliminate I suspect. In fact much is different. The set of buildings I'm returning to are abandoned. Closed up. Camp Deveraux is no more—well except for me. I have reclaimed a little of the past. I have been here for weeks now and still I have not found Henry. This troubles me.

***

With practice over I am about to go to meet with Waren for the second time. I sit in my car looking out over the now silent field. I sigh contentedly. The season passes through my mind. Our team is 7-0 with a victory over Madison Jr. High yesterday. Today I couldn't get the smile off the kid's faces. **No worries** has become the teams' mantra. Gary, Troy, PJ., Steve and Eric, made that first sign that all the classes, k-8 have copied in one way or another. The younger students hearing of the exploits of their older brothers and sisters are coming to the games with their parents. Suddenly Embden Elementary is the place to be. The whole town seems to be infected with the excitement. The P.T.O. is selling bumper stickers with NO WORRIES the message. We start the play-offs next week as the number one seed which gives us a bye in the first round. When I explained that to the kids, Gary put it into perspective for everyone. 'That means we are already 1 and 0, team… SO', and he raises his arms foreshadowing the expected group response. 'NO WORRIES!' The atmosphere in the school is if off the charts. Parents can't say enough good things about the smiles their kids are bringing home with them daily. Success in sports is the dessert that accents a good meal. Well right now Embden Elementary is eating, high off the hog-as the saying goes. Today we held a school rally with the team dressed in their uniforms while the student body on the bleachers watched them practice, cheering when a shot hit the net.

Gazing out my passenger window as I start the engine, I am suddenly reminded of that first meeting with Waren. I was shocked but in some way secretly pleased when Henry appeared at my car window on that first visit to Waren's hide-away.

On the roadway I pass a man who is carrying a sack on his back and sporting a walking stick. He looks to be about my age, though a full beard and long hair makes it difficult to say for sure. I study him in my outside mirror for a moment before he disappears. Possibly someone who has wandered off the Appalachian Trail, though its late for that I would think.

Henry reenters my head as the lake darts in and out of my vision. He lives near the water he had said the first time I met him.

The first ten minutes of that first visit with Waren was spent with me talking to both sides of my car. Henry, a listener, nodded in the right places. Waren is a bright boy but stubborn. It took those first ten minutes of negotiating to get my door open and the three of us moving to a four foot reel. Its previous life spent carrying telephone cable—now serves as a make-shift table placed behind the little trailer. Pete sniffed me. He made eye contact as well. After deciding I was harmless he lumbered away to his next assignment. When I saw where I was being led I was glad. I did not want to go into that building. The back-yard, a ten foot clearing, not a lawn, with a little path into the taller trees was ringed with blackberry bushes and poison oak or Sumac. I can't tell the difference. Just stay out of it. It smelled nice out here though. Freshly cut and stacked wood smells. A cooking smell wafted out the open window above the table. Occasionally smoke found its way off the roof and entered the conversation. Wooden crates served as chairs. I could only imagine what lay just inside those tin walls. Henry seemed to be studying me. I placed my tote on the table and handed Waren a new three ring binder and several pens and pencils. I folded my hands.

I began by telling him we missed his presence and hoped he would be back soon. He looked at Henry but did not answer. I handed him a paperback I hoped he would enjoy reading and report on.

"This book **The Outsiders** is going to be your reading class for now. I have listed the literary terms we are using and I want you to look at the story and find parallels to your own life Waren. Start a journal of what your days look like and then compare it to what the main character in the story is going through. By the way the teller of this story is a fourteen year old boy like yourself." Waren looked at Henry but did not speak. Pete back from chasing a rabbit watched over all this with his tongue lolling but offered no comment.

On I mushed. "We are using the outdoors as a way to study both Science and Social studies. Remember we started that the last day you were with us. You missed the open house. I smiled, "But I brought some pictures." I handed them to Waren, he studied the pictures of various science projects that had emerged. He looked at Henry but didn't speak.

"The kids seem to like the way we are learning. The parents are saying good things." *I'm dying here throw me a rope Henry.* Henry looked at me and smiled with his eyes. *Focus Melody.* "So again, use your imagination and your surroundings to write about what you find. I have listed possible topics for you to expand on." I turned my head, *this time I won't think it I'll say it,* "Henry, perhaps you can help him with this." Henry nodded, a smile reached his lips. *That's a good sign.*

"Your math book is straight forward, just do the work necessary to insure you understand the concepts. I will collect and correct and grade things on a weekly basis. Hopefully not too many weeks go by before you are back with us."

Waren looked at Henry but did not answer.

I was ready to go, but had to ask, "Are you living in here all alone?"

Waren looked at Henry but did not answer.

I left it at that.

***

Today when I entered the yard there was no smoke coming out of the little chimney. Pete didn't round the corner ready to gobble up a visitor. The screen and storm door to the little place had somehow been straightened and closed. I walked around back and there sat a plastic bucket, cover in place, on the table. A hand scribbled note was taped to the top. <u>You will find my homework inside. Leave any work you brought for me in the bucket. Please close the lid tightly. Waren</u>

I shouted out his name to the trees but he was not around. I sat down at the table and in the late glow of a November afternoon I read what Waren had written about the first three chapters of the story. *This kid is clever, he shows insights and makes connections most grown-ups don't.* I go back to the first words of his message, his words: <u>This table I am sitting at as I write to you Miss Standish is my office. Do you see the irony in its former life as a lifeline to the world? The telephone cable that coiled itself around and around and around delivered messages that changed people's lives. See I'm learning.</u>

<u>Ok to the story, good choice on your part, it's holding my interest.</u> No other comment.

A baggie of leaves is accompanied by a brief poem that provides a narrative of understanding seemingly too deep for an eighth grader. Below is Waren's Science report.

<u>Too brief they stood above the ground</u>
<u>Danced in the wind until one day found.</u>
<u>Death came not by change of season</u>
<u>But rather man-kinds' reckless rhyme nor reason.</u>
<u>The trees that wore these emerald capes</u>

<u>Were felled in swath's offering no escape.</u>
<u>Rutted trespass form open sores</u>
<u>Headless victims to the wild bulls gore.</u>

In poetic form Waren had explained the challenge of environmental science. He did not pass judgement he merely documented what he saw.

This kid takes my breath away. There has to be a way to help him find his way in the world.

I put the weeks work in the bucket as instructed. I feel like I am casting a bottle with a message into the briny deep hoping it will find its way ashore. *I have no idea where this is going to go but I have a feeling Henry is going to do a lot more than nod his head before this year is over.* As that thought leaves my head I am struck by another. *Did I just have a foreshadowing moment?* The sky is darker still and it smells like rain. I speed up hoping I can get a run in before it starts. I have been carefully putting together a collection of tapes I can play when I am traveling these roads. Carol King's Tapestry album is playing and assures me, <u>You've Got A Friend</u>. The message light is on when I walk through the door. Ed is waiting patiently, the table is set and I smell onions frying. He's hungry I can tell by the way he's pacing but he won't eat without me. I sigh. No quick run for me. He looks at me expectantly, "The message can wait Ed," I smile, "Let's eat, I'm hungry."

Ed smiles.

Ed, between little bites described his day. Dozing, trying to track Miko's movements, reading, a peanut butter and jelly sandwich for lunch. "Bring me another Zane Grey story Melody, He's the best." He points to a crossword puzzle half finished. "I'm stuck on that. Do you have the answer sheet?" The blanket on the recliner indicates where he had done his dozing. "A cat was walking around down there today, skinny and mangy looking, Miko was teasing him by running back and forth across his path."

"I'll talk to Miko about that."

Ed smiles.

I hand him a copy of The Outsiders and explain the kids are reading this. He smiles again. "I want to know what these kids are learning, I never finished High School. I learned to read using Comic Books."

I nod as Ed moves to the easy chair and rise myself to retrieve my message. There are two of them. First my mother. The message was upbeat, sounding nothing like the lady I had talked to last. I dial her number. "Hi Mom what's up? You sound happy on the phone."

"You aren't going to believe this honey but I found a man."

I swallow my tongue, but manage, "What are you going to do with this man?" I try to keep it light.

"Why honey as quick as I can shed my current last name I'm going to marry him."

"You are not bringing him here with you to live with me are you?"

"Oh God no, that was just me feeling sorry for myself. This man lives just over the mountain. I met him on the last run of the day. Prophetic don't you think?"

"What does Daddy think?"

"Who cares, not his business. He was throwing me out like an old shoe anyway."

She went on to give me the gory details and I sat there shaking my head.

"I'll keep you in the loop honey."

I sigh. *She's on something. Almost schizophrenic her voice rising and falling like a bad connection.* Suddenly Waren is back in my thoughts. *That damn telephone cable.* My next message is Luke.

"I leave on Saturday I called to see if we could meet to say goodbye. Who knows what the future might bring?"

Before calling back I have to clear my head. The comings and goings, additions and subtractions, I have to do a mental tally. *Mother is not coming. Luke is going. Ed is here. Waren missed our lesson. Who knows about Henry? My supervisor doesn't like me. We are moving from this place. The landlord would like to subtract me completely. This seems to be the new math for sure.* Ed calls me to the porch. He has Miko sitting on his shoulder. *When did Miko become a roommate? I need a run, dark or no dark, rain or no rain. Full stomach be damned. Lots to think about. My head is spinning.*

The street lights are on and wood smoke is drifting down as the approaching storm squeezes the air out of the evening. I will do just a two miler I decide, all under artificial light. I turn my mind off and let my feet take me where they will. I am into my run for a mile or so when I

pass my landlords house. The shades are pulled but the lights are on. Ed told me the guy is a hoarder. I don't know about that but our conversation about me breaking our contract tells me the guy has definite problems.

It was just two weeks ago when I found the leak under my bathroom sink and called him. He gave me another run-around. "Put a plastic bowl under there. I'll get to it."

It was then I told him I wanted to move.

"We have a contract, you will owe me for three more months or so."

I decided to gamble a bit. I want to meet face to face. Your place or mine. We settled on my place. We stood like two idiots in front of my apartment building. His opening words already breathless looking up, "I'm not climbing those stairs"

"Ok. I have a list of things that either are not working, just plain broken, or leaking that need your attention. You have promised since I moved in to fix them." Then I play the hole card, "I figure I owe you a month's rent at most. The first floor is a fire hazard. Maybe I should tell someone. I have an old man staying with me, you know."

You could see the turmoil churning. First his feet shifted like he was on a small boat then his knees buckled slightly. By the time the storm of uncertainty became visible at the neckline he had turned a bright red and I feared a stroke. Clearly this was a man who had lost touch with himself, his surroundings, and his possessions.

He mumbled, "Too many fire codes to follow anyway." He sighed, "That lady falling got me in all kinds of hot water. Police and Fire in and out of that apt." He threw up his hands. "I'm just gonna sell the place. Close it up for the winter and sell it in the spring." His face sagged, he had indeed given up. "Give me the month's rent and clear out." He began to cry.

Sorry but I just couldn't find it in myself to console him. *What is wrong with these people?*

Just as I turned back onto Winter Street the sky joined my memory of that meeting with my sobbing landlord in what turned out to be a real tear jerker.

CHAPTER FOURTEEN

Dancing Leaves

"Miss Standish can we have a dance?" The girl looked at me expectantly.

I looked up, it was Shelley. "I hadn't really thought about a dance. Why don't you explain how this would all work?"

"Well," she began, "first we create a theme." She held up her hand and two fingers appeared. "Then pick a date—since it's still fall, maybe an autumn ball or something like that." A third finger joined its neighbors. "We make decorations and refreshments, get a DJ." Her eyes lit up. Her hand was displayed like a child tracing the colored Turkey brought home and displayed on the refrigerator. "Then we get the word out to the other schools and everybody just shows up." She shrugged, both hands open in appeal, "So, will you chaperone, Miss Standish?" A big hopeful smile shaped her finish.

I had to smile, "You certainly make it sound simple. Let me speak to the other principals and I'll get back to you. We want to make sure no one is already planning one. If so I will find a date that's open. How's that? We do have reason to celebrate don't we?"

She smiled.

I finished my lunch and walked my tray into the kitchen. Time to consult with my mentor. "So Darlene tell me how these dances work."

Darlene smiles. "Oh so they finally got up the courage did they? They've been pestering me for two weeks. I told them just ask her for crying out loud." She turns, "I'll fill you in over coffee in the morning. By the way, Date filled molasses cookies and brownies will be in the fridge for tonight's meeting. I'll have the coffee pot all set up as well."

"Darlene you are amazing."

She shrugs, "I know."

Classes were moving the calendar. Soon the outdoor learning would have to move indoors. It was a gray, cloudy, and very windy day. Walking back to the classroom I took the scenic route behind the main building. The soccer nets were being dismantled by the same two men who had put them up. As they worked in tandem folding the nets in the wind, still jawing at one another I might add, I looked back on the season. The teamwork the boys and girls displayed all season long nearly brought home the gold. We lost in the championship game to Mark Emery School. The kids handled it well but felt it was unfair for Mark Emery to add a new player who had just moved into town. The Mark Emery coach just threw up his hands in a what- are-yuh-gonna-do manner—but he couldn't hide the smile behind his eyes. The new kid made all the difference, scoring both goals in our 2-1 loss. We did have a penalty kick that would have tied it but it hit the post.

We have a runner-up trophy though, that is proudly sitting on my desk.

Two weeks till basketball season and I will be coaching the girls. We have enough players for a girls' team for the first time in recent years. Mrs. Poulin agreed to coach a cheering squad and

Miss Nichols is coaching the boys' team. Of the thirty-one kids in the class—Waren still not in attendance—only three kids are not playing or cheering this winter season.

As for the education taking place daily. I am teaching US History through a paperback series by **John Jakes, The Kent Family Chronicles**. I have read the entire series in the past and they are part of my personal library. Ed is beginning to read them too. I truly enjoy how Jakes makes history come alive.

When the flyer announcing the Grants arrived in my school mailbox I hadn't thought much about it. It was when I was trying to find ways to combine curriculums that I remembered local grants were being offered by the local teachers association. I wrote a three page minigrant and received seven hundred dollars to purchase student copies of the John Jakes series up to the civil war. Thankfully two social studies teaches were part of that leadership group awarding the grants. I am spending evenings going back through each title highlighting the passages that mirror the classroom texts. My goal is to give the students the relevant history but in a way that seems more personal. From the text book I will include portions that allow me to quiz and test. What I am attempting to do is breathe life into a history that most kids see as an old dusty attic complete with spiders. The first book in the series titled, **The Bastard** seems to be working. I sigh. In my head I am still wrestling with how to combine World Cultures and Geography. *There has to be a way.*

It is just before the days' dismissal that Mrs. White whispers in my ear. She takes over the class and I go into Miss Nichols classroom. She points out the boy and I signal him to come with me. He has written a note that was confiscated by Miss Nichols. In the note he threatens to shoot a fellow classmate. This is a fourth grade student who has not had any discipline issues to my knowledge. I find his folder and ask him why he wrote the note, as I scan his record.

"He picks on me all the time. I'm sick of it, nobody does anything."

"Have you spoken to Miss Nichols about Stanley picking on you?"

The boy nods. "She said she will watch him and if she sees him being mean she will talk with him. But Miss Standish, Stanley is sneaky. He gets me in the bathroom when no one else is looking."

"What exactly does Stanley do to you?"

"He calls me names and he says things about my family too." Then Louis describes the physical abuse. "He pokes me in the ribs and pulls my neck hairs when no one is watching."

"How long has this been going on?"

"It just started a little while ago." Louis looks up confused. "He used to be my friend."

"So why do you think he's doing this now?"

Louis put his finger to his lips, thinking—maybe for the first time—about how this all got started. "Well my sister was going out with his older brother and she broke up with him. Maybe that's why."

"Is that it? Was it a bad break-up? Was Stanley's brother angry with your sister? Did he say things that got other people involved? Like your parents for instance?"

Louis Simpson thought this over. His finger returned to his lip. "Well, I heard my dad on the phone once with his dad and there was hollering."

I mulled this over. "Well Louis you can't threaten people. I'm going to have to talk with your parents. But I will also talk with Stanley and his parents. We might all have to sit down and work this out. I'm not going to do anything until I can get both sets of parents to come in. Promise me you won't write any more notes."

Louis promised and walked back to his class while I looked up the two phone numbers.

I filled in Miss Nichols just before we pulled the shades on the day.

The janitor was just returning from his afternoon bus run as I was leaving the building. He walked right up and asked me if I had found an apple on my desk a while back. My mouth opened. I was about to answer when he popped the question. "Are you seeing anyone?" "No," I answered. He simply turned on his heel and entered the building whistling. *Oh great*, I thought.

Tonight the board meeting will be held at our school. Ed and I are living on the lake now and in the two weeks we've been here I have seen a dramatic change in the lake, as well as a change in Ed. The lake is mostly chalkboard gray now with windblown whitecaps scribbling warnings to batten down the hatches. The trees are threadbare, their garments in tatters. Ed has adopted a recliner that looks out over what is quickly becoming a barren bleak landscape. He is anything but bleak. "I can see white in those mountains, like vanilla frosting. His eyes smile. "I can't wait for ice on the lake and snow on the ground. That will change everything. I always liked winter." He stands and walks to the window and looks down his eyes searching. "I found a family of squirrels to watch." He looks back at me. "I sure do miss little Miko, though."

"Well you can't invite any Embden squirrels to dinner, at least not inside. Speaking of which, what is for dinner, Ed?"

Ed puffs up, proud of his effort in the kitchen. "Shepard's pie and apple crisp for dessert. How does that sound?"

"Works for me." I add to his good feeling. "You are amazing Ed."

"That's what my wife used to say." Then tears up. "I really miss her."

I walk over and ruffle his nearly hairless head. "Of course you do, you two had a wonderful life together, don't forget that."

Ed nods and moves to the cupboard for plates. His teary eyes avoiding mine.

As I ready myself for the board meeting, Luke crosses my mind. I haven't heard from him since he left. And what's up with the janitor? I don't need another man in my life just now.

On my way to the board meeting I see a man on the road way. He is wearing a back pack and headed in the opposite direction.

It's dark but the hair and beard remind me of the man I saw a few weeks back. Not much foot traffic in Embden so I am curious.

When the Supt. arrives, before the meeting begins, he reminds all the principals of the team meeting in the morning. "Donuts or cookies are on you, Melody."

"But there is no store in Embden."

He looks at me, confused. "I thought you lived in Skowhegan? I was looking forward to a Dunkin Donut. Where are you living?"

"I'm on the lake now. I'll have cookies ready, I just need to make a phone call." The supt. eyes me strangely. *Keep him guessing,* I think to myself as I walk to the little office to call Ed. Thankfully Ed is near the phone and picks up on the third ring. I have to fairly shout into the phone but Ed gets the message.

Henry is in attendance tonight but he makes no attempt to talk with me. He seems to be on a gathering mission. He listens to everything that is said but offers no public opinion.

The supervisor of buildings and transportation provides the only drama of the evening. "Someone has been breaking into the kitchens in three of the schools, stealing food. Flour, sugar, butter, frozen Hamburg, hot dogs, baked beans, canned vegetables." He tries to lighten the message. "Seems like we've become someone's supermarket." No one around the table is smiling. He clears his throat and continues, "No pry marks so we're not sure how it's being done. Not a huge amount taken but the mystery is how they are getting in." If it continues and we see a pattern we might have to set a trap. Some kids probably." The board buzzes with little pockets of conversation. Everybody has a theory. Calling the Sheriff is bandied about.

Darlene hadn't mentioned it to me so I'm assuming it has not taken place in Embden.

Henry seems to be taking special interest in these violations. I watched his eyes. Stoic he remains but I just felt like there was something there. Something Henry knows that we don't. At the break, Henry gets up and leaves without a word. *Odd.*

Various committees report out. Negotiations with the teachers over salary seems to have bogged down. The head of the bargaining unit made a presentation to the full board. He had an overhead of salary schedules for five districts our size. Our starting salary and step increases were well below the median he points out. Heads nod but not a single board member chooses to address the issue. The board chairman simply notes that negotiations are on-going and we all hope for a good result.

When I got home chocolate chip cookies with walnuts were cooling on two racks. Ed had gone to bed. I snuck one, they were good. I actually began writing a children's story in long hand. I begin with the title, MICO OF THE FROZEN NORTH. Ed has me thinking again about squirrels. Maybe there is a story there. But it's late and I'm tired. I put down my pencil. *Rest little Miko I will begin building your world, maybe tomorrow night.*

A dusting of snow overnight greeted another gray morning. I sit in Ed's chair and gaze out over the black water sipping a cup of coffee, nibbling another victim. There is no wind. The world has become a snap shot frozen in time. Barren would be the color of choice if such a color existed. This is the first morning I can remember that I would like to just stay curled up inside and read and maybe bring Miko to life in my writing. These kids have certainly given me enough material. All I have to do is turn their stories into an animal fable. Sitting there numbing it, a rabbit jumps out of the still life. He hops out of the trees and down to look out over the pond. He twitches his ears, shakes his head and hops right back to the tree line. He seems to be echoing my feelings. *A good day to spend where it's warm and dry hippity hop. Ah but duty calls.*

The roadway is a little greasy as I make my way to the team meeting in North Anson. I praise the traction of my little sports car but what happens when there is six inches of the stuff covering the road? Cause for concern. The meeting goes smoothly with the elementary basketball schedule approved and passed out. The

Supt. forms a committee to look at the reading program and I volunteer to serve. The team agreed Embden can host the first dance. The kids will be pleased. The Elementary supervisor has been strangely quiet but seems to eye me whenever he thinks I'm not looking. Strange man. On the way out he tells me he will be in sometime soon to perform an evaluation. I nod.

The same man I had seen twice previously is on the road walking in the direction of the school. He has his thumb out. I stop.

"I'm only going as far as the school but if that helps, hop in." The man places what looks to be a back-pack of groceries on his lap and closes the door.

"My name is Melody and I'm the new school Marm here-a-bouts," I kid, watching the road, keeping things light.

The man does not speak, merely nods.

"Are you from the area? I think I've seen you on the road several times before."

"The school will be fine."

"Excuse me?"

The man appears weary, of what I can't tell. The day, the ride—life. He looks older up close—worn out.

"Letting me out at the school will do just fine."

As we round the corner and reach the edge of the school property, the man actually speaks. "Those little rocks, what do they stand for?"

I am startled, "I… I I'm not sure, really."

The man nods, "you can let me out at the edge of the drive."

I pull just inside the entrance. The man manages to exit, "Awful little car Miss." The rest of anything else that might have followed is swallowed by the glass.

Shaken—I decide to stop in to see Darlene before going to class. "Darlene how long do you remember those rocks being out there?"

Darlene takes a sip of her never ending cup of coffee. "Well I've lived here for fifteen years, and people have talked about them for at least that long, so maybe even longer than that." She thinks for a minute. They seem to weather the winter. "If you want to talk with someone who might have an idea, ask Henry Strongbolt."

My eyes widen.

"His family has lived near the lake for generations. Why are you asking now?"

I shake my head trying to clear my mind. "Not sure myself Darlene, just getting a funny vibe about those rocks and the curse and all that." I sigh and head to class. Mrs. White is just finishing up reading the underlined passages of the first book of the **Kent Family Chronicles**. In **The Bastard**, Philip Charboneau has landed in America after being denied his rightful inheritance in England and nearly killed. He has learned the printing trade which gets him introduced to Ben Franklin. He changes his last name to Kent. He will go on to be part of the Boston Tea Party and eventually take part in the Revolutionary War where General George Washington honors him for his bravery. The narrative allows us to view history through the eyes of living breathing characters which seems to be holding the kids interest.

I thank Mrs. White for covering the class. There is a note on my desk. Dwayne was caught throwing spitballs and Mrs. White is leaving the consequence up to me. I actually feel pretty good about it. First time I have had to be away from the building for any measurable time and spitball mania is as bad as it got. I'll let Dwayne wash the lunchroom dishes while we play basketball, he'll hate that. I call him up to the desk.

"Dwayne let me see your hands." He holds them up. "You think we can get them cleaner than that?" He looks at me puzzled. "Darlene is going to need some help with the dishes this noon time, both lunches, how about it?"

Dwayne is about to protest when the light comes on. He looks sheepish. "Just having a little fun Miss Standish."

"Doing dishes can be fun, so have fun at lunch Dwayne." We make eye contact, enough said.

I address the class. "I have an announcement to make after lunch that I think will please you. So plan on a different afternoon schedule."

The news that we will be hosting the year's first dance brings shouts of joy. I had noticed several eighth grade girls sporting rings around their necks. When I innocently quizzed one of the girls about her new jewelry addition I learned a lot about small towns. All these boys in class are like brothers. These kids have shared classes for years. 'We meet kids from other schools when we play sports or do festivals. We would never date a boy from Embden.'

Stupid me!

I immediately assign different groups to organize, advertise, select music, plan refreshments, and decorations. I move from group to group offering suggestions and tempering the ideas when necessary. I see team work continuing to emerge and the kids are actually listening to one another's ideas.

The snow is all gone and a sleepy afternoon sun has yawned and stretched and finally emerged from under the blanket of clouds as I once again head to tutor Waren. November comes in many guises. I hope Henry is there. I need to pick his brain.

Smoke is coming out of the chimney, a good sign. It looks like we might not be communicating by bucket this week. Waren opens the door and holds up a cup of what I assume is coffee. He points to it and I nod my head. The reel table has a centerpiece this week, a bowl of apples. That's a good sign as well. It is Henry who rounds the corner with a steaming cup. "I added a little milk, no sugar am I right?"

"You are correct Henry, how did you know?"

"I have seen you running."

"So from seeing me out running you surmised no sugar?"

Henry nods. "A fall apple would suit you."

"Well once again you seem to know me better than I know myself." I grab an apple and take a bite.

Henry nods.

"Listen, before Waren joins us, can I ask you a question?"

"Let your query ride the breeze, I will try to capture the little bit which remains in my memory."

This man is way deeper than me, I think to myself. Ok here goes. "What's the story on that nest of rocks?"

CHAPTER FIFTEEN

Rocks, Water, And Madness

Daniel stands bent over. Waste wood hidden by foliage across the road from the lake gathered. A buffer of scrub trees hides a recent logging operation. Smells of fouled earth and the sourness of wood de-composing meets his nose as he leans down hacking at usable pieces. A deodorant of pine sap does its best to mask the befoulment. Vast piles of branches, some with a six inch circumference are left to rot providing a treasure trove for a hunter gatherer. Daniel chops and fills his canvas tote with sticks of a size that ignite a fire and larger ones that will sustain it. The little camp ax—sharpened during long evenings staring at the walls—strikes with a purpose. The Deveraux camps deserted now for some years provides a perfect hiding place. A cold afternoon breeze sends his breath cascading, inspiring rhythm to his ax blows. A machine like effort finds Daniel reflecting. He has been hiding in one way or another since a kid. With each stroke of his ax the years chip away. He glimpses times of desperation, suicidal thought, anger, animosity, and anguish. Like a movie in reverse broken into rhythmic small clips, he pauses the reel when his mind arrives back in this very place. He rises, sweat on his brow. He looks around as if for the first time. Twenty years have passed since that first summer. At least a dozen diagnoses mark those years, along with prescriptions, both verbal and medicinal. Offered up at face value to help sort out *'what's wrong with Daniel?'* Faces emerge as well. Some well-meaning some just plain full of bullshit and pomposity.

With the wood gathered and delivered—the one time he's been warm today—he sits this early afternoon in a one room maintenance shack with light from a single window illuminating the pages of the book on his lap. The sweat from his earlier effort drying now, chilling him. He shivers but chuckles to himself as he opens the book. *The librarian might miss it but the kids sure won't.* **I Never Promised You a Rose Garden,** a book found in the beam of a flash light, on a night of foraging.

Though clad in a woolen stocking cap, thick sweater pulled over a flannel shirt, wool socks and heavy boots he feels chilled. It will be an hour or more before he can light a fire. His wardrobe purchased for ten dollars from a thrift store, back and forth he rocks trying to generate heat. He is well into the story now. The one theme in the story that resonates is the girl seeming to create an alternative universe. Daniel nods, he has thought since the age of eleven he himself was not of this world. When invited to participate in the formal social events that come along with Jr. High, Daniel found no joy in any of it. Adolescence brought with it anger and confusion seeping into his pores mixing with the smells of young adulthood. New smells that seemed almost toxic. His vision during that time seemed to change focus as well. He began to see only the topic sentence of a paragraph rather than the underlying descriptions and reinforcement of the written word.

His day became a series of topic sentences. Much as a scratched phonograph record sounds like an extended stutter. In his mind he could hear what others were thinking. Every measure the world puts in place for life's journey was coming up short. Mirrors offered no reflection. Smiles no reaction. Past friends shook their heads and dissolved. It was at the end of that first year with hands raised in surrender that his mother found a time out—if not for Daniel—at least one for herself. That fall when things began to change with her son, she at first laid to arriving adolescence. She said in the beginning—humorously, 'Some kids get zits others get zapped in a different way. What you are feeling Daniel is normal. Just get out there and have fun.'

Nothing felt like fun to Daniel that autumn. The leaves as they burst forth in color seemed to literally be on fire. Daniel could smell and taste the smoky flavor of Elm and Maple, Oak and Birch. And it didn't end with the smell. That fall everything seemed to be covered in a haze that accompanied the smells. His ears became hypersensitive, the sounds coming out of the mouths of the kids at school became deeper and dragged out, more adult like. His teachers' directions were muffled and distant as if they were speaking through a tissue. The wind entered his ears like a locomotive out of control. A full month after entering this new world he realized someone was talking to him in his head. Not only were they speaking but they were hearing and smelling, tasting and touching. Daniel studied himself in the full length mirror after a bath. *Yes his body was changing. He was thinning out and little hairs were sprouting under his arms and around his privates. Do all kids feel the way I'm feeling? These things I'm feeling are they sprouts too? Are other kids hearing voices?* Embarrassed and confused by it all, Daniel did his best to ignore the voice. He even kidded to himself, *at least I don't have the zits.* One of his teachers who was not ignoring it all called his mother. Mr. McIntyre, his science teacher observed that the kid he'd gotten a heads up on from an elementary teacher and friend, had said Daniel was a born scientist and artist. 'He's going to make you look like a genius,' he'd been told. Well this boy had not arrived as advertised. He seemed to have no interest and was not even doing his homework. "Yes I know Daniel is going through puberty. It happens to about ninety percent of my students every year, but what's going on with Daniel is much more extreme. He doesn't seem to hear me when I speak. If he is hearing me then he's choosing to ignore me. We have an important Science project coming up. It ties together everything we've been studying this year. If Daniel doesn't take this seriously he will be well behind. Kids are avoiding him in class and the hallways. You might want to have him see the school counselor."

Seeing the school counselor began a twenty year odyssey of arm chair quarterbacking—the what—why—and how—Daniel was feeling, acting, and acting out. Various medicines, pills and prescriptions were added, diluted, deleted and ultimately dismissed along the way. Over the course of twenty years he sat with psychologists, psychiatrists, school counselors and medical doctors. That first autumn and winter the only voice that reached him was the voice in his head. That voice seemed to be directing Daniel to a different world with no roadmap provided. Happy one minute sad the next, food had no taste. The day was meant for sleep and the darkest deepest night time found him wide awake with nothing on the screen, staring into a void. That spring, after a winter of watching her son struggle with himself and no answers forth-coming Daniel's mother made the call. It took three calls to make contact. When she finally got the return call, during the hour long conversation, she was told of a summer camp that provided a wholesome outdoor experience. 'It is out of the city, out of your state actually.' Daniel was not told of that call.

She signed Daniel up. This would be Daniel's first time out of the city. A summer in rural Maine.

Daniel continued to reflect even as he turned the pages. It was nearly dark, the words becoming a blur, squinting he put the book down. He rose, stiff and cold. As the sun shifted and lowered, inside the shack it became colder still. The tea kettle cold to his touch. The stove not fed since before first light. Dark enough now so that smoke would not be visible, Daniel wadded up pages from an old Sears and Roebuck catalog and tossed them into the ash. He methodically stacked shavings and small twigs onto the wadded pile and struck a match.

What had once been the shack for the maintenance man for Camp Deveraux housed a small stove, a rocker and a three by six foot bunk. As colors emerged from the catalog the sticks took charge and soon Daniel was strategically placing finger thick branches onto the pyre. He held his hands over the open stove and was rewarded with a bit of warmth. He added to the kettle from a jug of water, closed the lid and placed it on to heat. He turned to the window. The lake was deserted. No lights visible from the distant shore. Just as the trees had shed themselves of summer past, the lake was left with few year round residents. Seasonal camps had been drained of life sustaining water and buttoned up like a man of the cloth. The lake itself stood motionless. Boats and docks removed now dressed in colorful tarps dotting the shore. A layer of ice would soon make a lasting appearance—oozing up and thickening like a thanksgiving gravy. Once November chilled the water to temperature—December and January would add the ice to the drink allowing small shacks and growling machines to take up short term residence. Daniel warming slightly allowed his face to soften. The little stove spit and crackled, light from this dance sending flickers into the emerging shadows. Daniel opened and set a can of beans on the stove to heat. He smiled to himself, his first visitor of the season would be joining him for dinner. A special guest.

***

Four days off and snow on the Mountain—mixed in with a little man-made stuff—I planned to hit the slopes Friday morning. It was nearly dusk. A gunshot echoed across the lake, I smiled hoping maybe one of the boys bagged their deer.

My first hunting season in Maine. I didn't have a gun but I had taken dead aim at getting some dads' involved with the school. Following up on the two stories that had hunting as a theme, I had invited the local game warden—who just happened to have two kids in the school—to come in and offer a hunter safety course. Several other fathers came in as well and it was well received. *A whole world of learning takes place outside these books.* The next opportunity would be a snowmobile safety course and two of the boys had volunteered their dads for that. I sat in Ed's chair as he went about preparing the Thanksgiving meal. He was whistling and humming away. I was glad I had welcomed him into my life. Luke had called several times and loved what he was doing, so no ski lessons for him this year. I sighed. Outside it was now night time dark, temperature of thirty four degrees with a wind chill. Hunting season will be over soon. The kids had been antsy the last couple of days. None of the mighty hunters had bagged a deer yet, Thanksgiving break provided the last hope. "Pretty soon," offered Ed when I asked about the meal. I grabbed my lesson planner and snuggled further into Ed's chair taking stock of how the year was shaping out, giving thanks and all that. The first dance had been a success. Several parents volunteered to chaperone. The kids dressed up and it seemed to go off without a hitch.

Well almost without a hitch. The custodian Evan volunteered to chaperone and I couldn't come up with a reason why not, which was fine till about half way through the evening when he asked me to dance. I stammered and stuttered but not wanting to cause a scene I finally agreed to one dance. I held up one finger like a teacher about to scold, offering a visual to my words. "One dance." I guess the guy is nice enough but the kids viewed the dance as me being pinned to the guy. Twice since I have had to refuse a date, coffee maybe? a movie? Dinner? He never takes no as an absolute.

It's becoming a problem. Darlene even kidded me for god sakes. I mega sigh.

On a positive note, group learning is reaping rewards I hadn't even considered. The older students have adopted the role of mentors and are taking an interest in their charge's success. I have not observed a single instance of bullying in the classroom, at recess, or on the field. The only disciplinary action of note had involved a fourth grader—and a meeting with the boys involved and their parents had a happy ending.

Suddenly an adult bully enters my mind. I sigh. Leave it to the adult. I remember the morning. *The door opened and suddenly he entered armed with a note book and took a seat in the rear of the class. He did not speak. I suddenly found myself under official observation. Teams of kids were using candles to heat up beakers of water to explain evaporation and condensation. The morning frosts that covered everything outdoors as air temperature rose and fell overnight was the catalyst for the experiment. He sat busily jotting down notes for the full ten minutes he was in the room then rose and left without comment. Even the students felt uncomfortable. Several of the boys muttered under their breath. He had his secretary call the next morning and suggest we meet to go over his observation.* **That afternoon—the very day Thanksgiving vacation was starting—I found myself on the receiving end of a one sided conversation.**

I knocked and entered. He did not greet me he simply voiced, "Bunsen Burner. He let the two words sit there a moment. "Do you know what that is?"

I was still standing in front of his desk. "Yes. I do."

"I didn't see one being used during that experiment."

I was taken aback but managed, "There isn't one in the school sir, I just made do with what we had."

He remained quiet but poised for another verbal attack.

"Would you care to know how the experiment turned out?" I breathed in and sat down without invitation.

"Miss Standish I already know how this experiment is going to turn out." He looked at me oddly.

"What do you mean?"

"You don't think I haven't got people whispering of your radical approach to teaching?"

"No one has complained to me. Certainly not the students."

"Of course the students don't complain, they are having too much fun to complain."

"Is that it then, students can't be learning unless they are bored to tears and filled with angst with what they don't understand?"

"As I tried to explain to you earlier and perhaps I wasn't being as clear as I should have been—this is not a private school. You are teaching at the end of the pipeline here. Don't set these kids up for failure in the real world. Some of them won't finish High School for God's sake, they will join the work force where nose to the grindstone is what will keep them employed. They don't need this community learning you're offering. Just keep them busy. Those who can will and those who can't will go to work somewhere. I don't know if you are aware, but I taught in that little building for years. I was the Principal when it first opened and it has been run like a tight ship from the very beginning."

His cards were now on the table. This is still his school we are talking about.

"Is that what you truly believe sir? If so, I am glad you are no longer in the classroom." I stood, "Evaluate me as you will, I am offering what's working for all the students." I looked him dead in the eye and probably ended my stay here after this year when I said, "I won't go quietly."

"That's unfortunate. Here's your copy of my observation which you will note I have deemed unsatisfactory." He gave me a tight little smirk and wished me a happy Thanksgiving.

The memory of that meeting brought a sigh. A bully for sure. I closed the planner and drew in the smells of the upcoming meal. The phone rang. It was my Mother.

"Happy Thanksgiving dear, will you be having turkey?"

"Hi Mom. Ed just took out an apple pie and it smells heavenly in here. The turkey is resting. Biscuits are going into the oven right before my eyes so I'll be stuffing my face about twenty minutes from now. How about you?"

"I'm alone again." My mother sighs. That man I thought was so wonderful, well he found a different bunny on the bunny slope."

I thought back to the little bunny I had seen earlier in the week and imagined my mother with long ears trying to attract his attention. I chuckled.

"It's not funny. I'm all alone here. Can't you come for Christmas at least? That's only a month away."

Ed signaled me that he needed my help at the stove.

"Let me think about it, I'll get back to you. Treat yourself to a dinner in town, I have to help Ed."

I awoke in my room from a turkey induced coma with a little drool at the corner of my mouth. I wandered into the living room where Ed too was digesting his dinner in the good old fashioned way as well; his snores told me he had enjoyed the meal as much as I had. There came a rap on my door. I stretched and turned on the outside light. It was Henry. I didn't even know he knew where I lived. He didn't say a word just nodded. "Come in and sit, can I get you a turkey sandwich?"

Henry smiled, "That would be nice, I fear what will be offered on my next stop will test my resolve."

I looked at him oddly. *This man speaks in tongues.*

Seated at the kitchen table, with a plate of leftovers and coffee to wash it down Henry ate sparingly. When he had finished and was wiping his chin I followed up on the question I had raised and he had ignored a while back. "Tell me about those stones Henry. Recently someone else asked about them. What's the story?" What followed was another of our recently discussed literary terms—symbol.

"Do you dream Melody? You have a wonderful name. It speaks of peace and harmony, the wind gently moving leaves, water washing over rocks, melodic." He took my hand and studied it. He then removed a shell shaped object hanging from rawhide under his shirt, etched in it a hand with a swirl in the middle.

Ed continued to snore.

He let me hold what appeared to be polished bone. "My people consider the hand a key to what is inside a person's soul. Their accomplishments, their work, and personal history. The swirl in the middle represents the ability to see beyond earths boundaries. We all possess this ability if we allow ourselves."

Then Henry went from symbol to personal.

"Let me tell you what I see when I study your hands Melody." He continued to hold my hand as he examined my history and perhaps my future.

"You are in a new place yet observe and question. You have followed the rules yet seek a greater truth. You have a sense of what is needed yet lack support. Trust these hands Melody, they will lead you to the truth."

"Henry, can you give me a little direction at least."

From personal back to symbol.

"The stones that you speak of are merely reminders that we all share the same world. We are our brother's keepers. I will offer this much for now. They stand vigil over one who has no heart, no hands, a self-absorbed history. They have been here since the one with no heart or hands arrived. They will remain until the gloves are removed and the lack of heart exposed. You have that power. Your heart is strong, your eyes clear, your heart and hands capable."

I sighed. Not sure I had been helped but reassured never-the-less.

"I have a question for you." He put his necklace back on and again took my hand. "What will become of Waren? It seems his family has left for good. Will the authorities be involved? I have no place for him and he should not stay alone through this long winter."

I felt the power of this man charge through me and from his hands to mine, I knew he knew I held the answer.

CHAPTER SIXTEEN

Behold A Pale Horse

Thanksgiving night, well fed and turkey tired Henry knew he had two more doors to knock upon before finding his way to his cabin. The stars were out and clouds that would normally be pulling up the covers on the night seemed to be awaiting two more stories. The wind blew pages across the sky at a furious pace, a sliver of moon illuminating the action. Henry looked up. He had read this story before and the ending was always the same—snow soon to follow. Mother moon, a mere fingernail of her full self, offered no guidance for the first story he was about to hear. "Come along Snow dog, we need to walk off that meal." He rubbed the stiffness from his knees.

He knocked. Wood smoke reached his nose before the sound of a scraping chair reached his ears. The door squeaked open and Daniel, a silhouette, framed in the leaking light from the stove behind him stood in silence as if asking a password. In fact he was waiting for a password.

"Behold a pale horse," Henry offered. Daniel moved and gripped his hand.

As Henry's eyes adjusted to the dark with-in the dark he closed the door and moved toward the little bursts of blue light coming from the cracks in the stove—a dying fire. He smelled onions and meat of something long dead. A faint smell of an earlier brew of coffee hung in the air as well. "A little more light would be useful Daniel, I have not gazed on your troubled brow for at least twenty or more of these white man's celebrations." He shivered. "I can feel the wind through your walls." He smelled Daniel in that moving air, a sour smell of despair—fear even. "Let us add more heat, these old bones of mine retain no warmth." Henry continued to rub his hands one upon the other. Daniel had not yet spoken.

The flare of a match held over a candle brought to Henry's mind shadows of many councils held by firelight in his youth. "It is good to see you Daniel, even in such weak light. You left a sign on my porch. How can I help?"

Daniel set the candle in a used tin tuna can then proceeded to add small sticks to the fire in a very deliberate way. His mind seemed to be deliberating as well. Finally he spoke, "Why did you desert me Grandfather?"

Henry pondered the question. "Have I not always been with you in spirit?"

"What happened all those years ago? To me, to our family? Mother tells stories of my father but she has never told me the whole story?"

"Let us make a new pot of coffee. You are here for a reason. I will tell you all you wish to know. You have a right to know."

During the next hour Henry explained how he had fallen as a man and as a grandfather. "I doubted myself for a long time and attempted to drown that doubt every night in liquor. I thought of you often. But did not act. I followed the man who killed your father with the intent of ending his life." Henry turned twice in a circle as if conjuring up the event. "I went to his home one evening. Half-drunk and filled up with anger. I had convinced myself that would end my pain." Henry looked at Daniel as he had remembered him at age six. "A small boy about the age of you when you left, answered the door. "I nearly collapsed. In that moment I saw you, Daniel. In that little boy's eyes the questions you have had all these years were forming." *Henry was in that man's home right now. He could smell the cigarette smoke and the aroma of fried food wafting in the doorway.* "I had only to complete this mission and the boy would forever carry the same hurt and anger and self-doubt that has shaped your life. In that moment I turned away. Away from the anger, the drink, the need for revenge." Henry's eyes were clear.

"I tried to reconnect with you at that time. I was not successful. Until your Mother called in desperation I had no way of knowing where you were. Some things I did do. I stopped drinking. I became a watcher for this town, for its children. When your mother called I made arrangements for you to come here those three summers, Daniel. From a distance I watched you arrive on that train, brittle, unyielding. From a distance I saw you over time slowly soften, to accept warmth, to begin to understand yourself. I hoped those summers would heal you."

Daniel spoke, "Why didn't you make yourself known to me?"

"I did not feel worthy. There was self- loathing that I carry to this day. I had abandoned you. I had no right to reclaim you."

"Yet you watched over me those summers?"

"Come out-side I will tell you a story."

The two men walked down to the water. They found a spot where the lake met the night sky. The water was moving in the wind and weak light reflected off the undulation. "I never held the white man in high regard. For a long time I fought against many wrongs I perceived. I changed my view when I began working for this camp."

Daniel looked at him quizzically.

"It was here, at Camp Deveraux that I taught children the power of water. In every stroke of their paddles I introduced them to the power of team work. When we achieved harmony of stroke I gave them a brief history of our people. On this lake they found balance, reassurance. In these buildings they explored their inner spirits. On the river we stopped and examined carvings. I completed my own healing by watching the good that was done here."

Henry was nearly done. "I told you a story many years ago. It was before you could read. I was sitting in your home looking at a children's book, I don't recall the title. Anyway you didn't seem interested so I simply looked at the picture of the white horse on the cover and created the story that became our story. Our secret password. You must remember a bit of it because those were the words you left at my cabin, <u>behold a pale horse</u>."

Daniel nodded. "That story kept me from hurting myself, grandfather."

"So you see Daniel I have always been with you. I am so glad to see you after all this time. How can I help you?"

"I might have hurt someone."

"In what way did you hurt someone?"

"That's what I'm not sure of. I can't remember."

"What do you remember?"

"All I remember is what I was told by the police. They woke me from a cell and told me to come with them. I sat in a small room and they kept suggesting I tell them the whole story. I didn't remember any story—which made them mad. They kept at me for an entire day. Telling me I must remember attacking my landlord and running away from the scene." Daniel raised his eyes. "Grandfather I do remember seeing my landlord lying in a pool of blood but I didn't hurt him, I swear!"

Henry took Daniel's hand. He closed his eyes. The hand told of a tormented soul, but a gentle one. It did not hold the same positive history and strength and resolve he had felt in the hands of the young school teacher. In these hands he felt few achievements, a personal history of despair and a cloudy murky future. But he did not sense violence. Deep within this grasp he felt himself. "You did not harm this man Daniel, I can feel it." Henry stood back, "Why did you run away, Daniel?" They found a stump and sat down. As Henry waited for an answer he thought of his necklace passed down through the generations that spoke to him. A swirling in the life line part of a hand that connected him to the Great Spirit.

Daniel looked directly into Henry's eyes, "Because I thought they might be right. I honestly don't remember. I couldn't be locked up again." His eyes filled.

"Why were you in that cell, Daniel?"

"I was off my medication for a while and acting strangely I guess. The police found me and decided I was the one who had hurt the man." Daniel stood and paced. "I think I did hurt someone on my way here, Grandfather." He paused, deliberated again and continued, "I thumbed a ride and after a distance the man pulled over and demanded money. I didn't have any. He tried to check my pockets." Alarm then surfaced in his voice. "I hate to be touched, Grandfather. I-I struck him with my fist and he was bleeding when I left." Daniel began to cry—a low keening sound that reminded Henry of an animal in distress.

Henry the one person other than Daniel's mother who could lay hands on Daniel rose and brought him into an embrace. Henry could feel the raging river that was tearing through the canyons of Daniel's soul. He would comfort this man. He would heal his grandson.

Henry walked Daniel back to the cabin to the rocker and sat him down. By the light of the candle he re-set the water to boil. He found other things too. Food that was not store bought. Thinking back to the board meeting and the supervisor's report he nodded his confirmation.

Daniel, Daniel, Daniel.

And so after a restless night, (too much turkey and pie, maybe) I actually think the last question Henry laid at my feet was what had me twisting the blankets into a Gordian knot. I awoke with no answers. Ed was standing at the window watching the squirrels once again. I stood in the doorway listening to the little chuckles he was mostly keeping to himself. He was talking quietly to them as if they were his children.

More dialogue for my book perhaps. "Ed what's for breakfast?" he likes it when I put him in charge. I had to speak up though, get his attention, his hearing was horrible getting worse, even with the two appliances he had stuck in his ears. It was humorous if a bit sad to watch him take them out with the thought he would hear me better. Truth be told we mostly communicated with him hearing sounds and then turning so he could read my lips.

"I'm going skiing today Ed. So I need a hearty breakfast. How about eggs, left-over turkey and stuffing, and a piece of apple pie for dessert?"

"Coming right up ma'am," then he saluted. I had to laugh. He really was a good addition to my life. Which got me thinking as I sat in his chair while he cooked, whistling all the while. *How would Ed like having a kid around? How would Waren like having to keep repeating himself to be heard and understood? Oh well maybe a few trips down the slopes will show me the path.*

Karen pulled up outside and I walked my skis and boots to her Suv. She sat drinking from her travel mug while I attached the skis to the rack and deposited my boots in the way-back. When I finally closed the door, strapped my seatbelt and turned to say good morning, she had a bemused look on her face. "You look like a real skier. I'm dressed like a permanent resident of the bunny slope. Are you sure you want to ski with me?"

I looked at her outfit. She did look like she had just been fitted top to bottom by an interior designer—everything matched and coordinated. "We'll have fun, no worries." I chuckled to myself. *I find myself thinking how my own vocabulary is acquiring little pieces from my students. I had never used the phrase—no worries—until I met the always happy Troy and his little reassurances.*

Karen glanced over, "What are you smiling about?"

"Oh just thinking about the kids I teach. I'm really glad I came here. I'm learning as much about myself as I am anything else."

"So what have you figured out? About yourself I mean?"

"Well, that I genuinely like what I am doing. And how malleable kids are. These kids don't have a lot, but they have each other and they are givers not takers. Their parents too. Different kids' everyday are starting to step out of their comfort zone and taking a risk. A raised hand to offer an opinion or volunteer to read aloud. You know how huge that is for some kids?" Karen nodded her head.

"We have new basketball uniforms for the boys and girls and the cheerleaders too. I am beginning to think we need to create little community schools like this one instead of these huge warehouses we are building across the country." I was on my soap box now. "Let students be part of their own learning and tap into the world outside the glass. I know being here has forced me to look at learning and teaching differently. When I came here and realized I couldn't effectively teach thirty- two kids from three grades in a traditional way I either had to fake it or change things."

Then I sighed and added a punch line. "That being said, I'm in the dog house with my immediate boss. I think he would like to see me gone by the end of first semester." I looked to see if Karen was really listening. "Don't say anything, but I may be about to do something else very non-traditional."

Karen put her cup to her lips. She bade me continue. "Bare your soul girl. I won't say a word."

"It's right in this minute that I decided." I sighed. "I'm going to ask Waren to come live with me and Ed."

Karen's eyes widened. She didn't say a word.

I pleaded my case. "He's living all alone in a run-down twenty-foot trailer. His family is gone." I cleared my throat. "You know I've been tutoring him. Have you met Henry?" Karen hadn't said a word she kept both hands on the wheel. "I think it could work. So there now you know, what do you think?" I sighed, everything on my mind had escaped my lips. Defense rests.

"Girl you are a piece of work. Do you think you could stretch yourself any thinner? Let me review for this quiz. She spread her fingers, counting on the steering wheel. *I was reminded of Shelley counting the hows and whys we should hold the dance.* You are teaching three grades—you are the principal—you are about to coach your second sport of the year—you already have an old guy you are not related to living under your roof—your supervisor is looking for ways to get rid of you—and now you want to add a thirteen year old to your Christmas list!" She waved the full hand of fingers and thumb at me. "I think we need to turn right around. I don't think you have time to ski." Then she laughed right out loud. "Melody what are you thinking?" She sighed. (*Catching around me I guess.*)

"I know on the surface it might sound a little too much but I think Ed and Waren would actually be good with one another. Ed loves people and animals, he loves to read and he knows a lot of man stuff like repairs and tools. I think this could maybe work." Case closed.

"Well you've obviously convinced yourself so that's half the battle. Enough about work and home. Help me learn to parallel ski today. Starting on the bunny slope of course."

***

Henry awoke after a short night. On his walk back to his cabin he tried to come up with a plan for Daniel. He stopped at Waren's trailer but there were no lights, the boy obviously asleep. Now he had two others he was becoming responsible for. *Three if you counted the new school teacher. I am an old man, the smoke in my chimney doesn't soar like it used to.* Remembering a time when he had allowed too much creosote to build up and the roof nearly catching fire, the chimney roaring like a locomotive, he chuckled aloud. "Perhaps I have one more chimney fire left in me, we'll see."

CHAPTER SEVENTEEN

A Season of Holidays

From Thanksgiving to Christmas is always a challenge in the classroom. I remembered in the private school in New Hampshire, even the most motivated of students seemed to lose their focus as they mentally prepared for the holidays. It was no different here in Maine, though some of the holiday plans were a bit more modest. No Jetting off to a holiday in a different State or possibly a different Country. Here it was just a welcome vacation from school, maybe a snowmobile ride or a visit to a relative. The holiday in the air feeling all began that Monday morning after Thanksgiving with a report out on the hunting efforts. Two of the boys had been successful in bringing home winter food in the form of a deer. They were standing a little taller this morning. Another boy shot two rabbits and most of the others were with a Dad or Uncle who had bagged and tagged. Everyone seemed to know someone who had harvested a critter. I listened. Then I dragged out a poem I had read from a little known writer, R. Wesley Clement. To me it summed up what the boys were trying to convey. I handed out a copy and read it to them asking them to follow along.

LEGEND OF THE FALL

There is a legend beginning in the great far north
two brothers straight and true,
For most of the year they are family men
doing what good men do.
Come November though when skies turn gray
when dawn brings an icy chill,
clad in orange garb they seek the yard
of the deer they mean to kill.
These two brothers respect the hunt
the quiet of the wood
within this stillness pounds beating hearts
a love that's understood.
For three long weeks they have tracked their foe
thru Birch and Fir and Oak
heard gunshots in the distance
held their ground when rainstorms soaked.
In a tree stand high above the ground
to the east appears first light,
on this last hunting day doubt fades with the gray
the two nod as to say, today things will be set right.
Slowly the world curtain opens
like a spotlight the sun starts to glow
to a stage walks a deer
sniffs the air shows no fear
of a fate you'll soon come to know.

With reverence for this gift from God
a shot rings thru the trees
as the echoes still one quest is filled
a brother quietly pleased.
Wait now that's but half a tale
one brother's trail yet runs cold
then in a moment of inspiration
an old timer's story is re- told.
'Stay near the entrails warm and steamy
the smell of death will ride the wind
your patience will soon be rewarded.'
a shot rings out again!'
Later as the sun completes its trip to bed
and the moon takes to the sky
glasses are raised by two brothers
toasting two deer hanging high.
It's a story soon to be legend
for all that's been written is true
two brothers, family men, hunters,
doing what good men do.

I read the poem to the entire class then asked them to tell me what they thought the author was trying to say. The boys focused on the hunt and commented on how the second deer was bagged. 'Pretty cool,' was the term they used. The girls saw the closeness the brothers seemed to share and included family in their interpretation. One girl didn't like the fact that two deer had been killed. She didn't like guns either. Minority opinion in this room for sure. But nobody tried to change her mind. Her opinion. Left it at that.

Then they asked me what I thought the author was getting at. I told them that I had been given a little insight they hadn't been privy to. The author was simply creating a lasting memory for the two sons who had told their dad about their adventure that season. A true story put to paper.

The snow outside that had fallen on Sunday night had delayed school till ten am. The start of a season of school delays and cancellations upsets the regular, one day following another, education train. So mix snow, school closings and delays, with the strains of holiday music already ruling the airways and right then I knew we had to mix things up in the classroom. We brainstormed who we might invite into our class who could hold our interest and maybe teach us in the process. Ruth suggested an aunt that made rugs. She got support from six others—a real possibility. Mike said his dad repaired snowmobiles and could teach us all a trick or two—the boys liked the idea. I suggested that we invite at least one speaker who could tell us more about where we live. "We will be studying Maine History after the holidays so let's get a head start." Various names were dropped but in the end the name that everyone agreed on was Henry Strongbolt. "My dad says he knows how every road in this area got its name and the lakes and ponds too. Plus he knows about Indian legends."

So for three full weeks before Christmas we would learn to make rugs, repair snowmobile engines and explore our community's roots.

"Oh yeah we still have math, reading, Science, and grammar." The class groaned. But in shorter doses I remind them. And maybe in a different form. They nodded, however reluctantly.

The trick at recess was keeping snowballs from taking flight. Since it appeared to be a losing battle I arranged a competition of skill. It seemed to fit the bill and I didn't have to dole out any detention time. By the third day after the storm the sun had done due diligence and melted the plowed playground straight through to the tar. Basketballs began bouncing again, all was well with the world.

Speaking of basketball—we have no gym of our own so we have one day of practice in Solon, one in North Anson, and one in Anson. The boys and girls travel together for both practices and in two weeks our first game. The P.T.O. purchased new uniforms for the boys and girls and the cheerleaders as well. They held a raffle and also placed jars in the area businesses. Each jar had a photo of our teams trying on the old high school hand- me-down uniforms from ten years ago. The photo spoke volumes. Our boys and girls looked like they had all gone on a crash diet. In this case a picture was worth fifteen hundred dollars.

With so much happening in their lives in a short span of time, the classroom atmosphere was almost manic. Our first visitor turned out to be Ruth's Aunt Flora. She came in with boxes and boxes of old rags and a dozen pair of scissors. She first displayed several of her creations, very cleverly made, each one a theme. The students were put to the task of ripping or cutting strips from old sheets, shirts, pants, socks and coats. Aunt Flora showed them how to hand sew the strips together at one end then begin the braiding process. By the end of the presentation the kids all knew what Mom was getting for Christmas and it hadn't cost them a cent. Lots of smiles and thank you very much, as Ruth's Aunt left us. We learned a skill and had a good time doing it. Several math skills were employed as well.

With the weather iffy I gave permission to spend some valuable recess time completing Mom's present. Half the boys gave up playground time if you can believe it.

When school ended on Thursday afternoon I had made two decisions—well three really, but the first two would be taken care of this afternoon. The snow on the road was melted but the sides would keep their grey-white, slightly raised banks for months to come. During the next four months the shoulders of the roads would bear a heavy load of snow, ice, road salt, and slush. My first decision had to do with that knowledge. *What had I been thinking when I bought this little sports car.* Driving into town for groceries and meetings—some late at night—I realized I would probably get myself stuck, stranded, or worse. So this very afternoon I was going to Skowhegan and trade my car in for a larger vehicle. This first decision had to do with my second. I was nearly to Waren's road and I was still framing how I was going to ask him to come live with me and Ed.

Waren and Henry were just now putting the finishing touches on a two foot wide path. The sun hadn't found its way into this mess to lick away the cream. I parked on the roadway. Henry had a big smile on his face. That man can read my mind I swear. Waren on the other hand gave nothing away. Whether Henry had voiced the possibilities to Waren remained hidden inside a mouth that shared nothing at the moment. A nod of the head to acknowledge me then a shovel full of snow thrown over his shoulder.

While closing the door to my car for nearly the last time I suddenly had a brainstorm. Suddenly I was relaxed. I began to whistle. Pete recognizing the car and the driver barely raised his head from the steps. I nodded and announced, "Different lesson today, Waren, today it's a road trip."

Henry continued to lean on his shovel and smile. *Probably already knows, maybe already knew what I was going to propose.*

"So Waren," I announced when we were settled in my car, "how about you help me trade in this little rig for a big rig? I have no idea what I'm looking for but it has to be good in the snow. Would you help?"

Waren looked deep into my eyes and spent some time there trying to figure this all out. Then he nodded and the slightest of lip movement told me inside he was excited. I smiled and waved to Henry and off to town we flew.

As I shifted through the gears and hit the forty-five mile an hour speed limit, so too did Waren begin to become more verbal. "I know cars Miss Melody. I study them actually. I think you should get a Jeep. Something with four-wheel-drive for sure."

I looked over and for the first time I saw light behind those eyes. "Well Ed, he's the old guy who lives with me, he used to be a mechanic. He said no matter what I decide, stick with American made."

"Yup, Chevy, Ford, Chrysler, Jeep. They're all good. Stay away from that foreign stuff. Jeep is American. You thinking new or used?"

"I still owe on this one so I'll probably trade for a used one. I made a good down payment when I bought this so I should have at least $5,000 in equity."

"You know what they are going to say don't you?"

I looked at Waren. "What are they going to say?"

"That they won't be able to get rid of this little sports car till spring and so they don't really want it. They are going to do you a favor though. Cause you're a teacher and all, they'll take it off your hands." He smiled then.

"How do you know all this?"

"My mom, when she was around." He closed down for a moment turning to the window. Then turning back he continued, "Anyway she said It don't matter what it is you're buying, if it's a woman buying it, they will try to stick it to yuh." He threw up his hands. "That's a Fact. I'll help you find one you like but if the old guy was a mechanic, I'd take him with you when you trade. They won't mess with a guy who really knows cars."

I absorbed what this young man was telling me and realized he might not have the grades but he knew how the world worked. "Well then let's go window shopping and we won't let anyone know we are serious shoppers." I smiled, "And they will just leave us alone."

"I think that's best ma'am," he nodded.

When we had finished checking out all the brands I took Waren to McDonalds and watched him polish off two Big Macs, fries and a coke. I settled for a fish sandwich and a diet coke. It was dark, and the roads after the days warming and melting were just wet enough to be slippery. The temperature had fallen to just above freezing. Waren played with the tape deck. Choosing a tape, inserting, playing a song then switching tapes all the way back to Embden. Did you find a favorite?"

"I choose <u>The Little River Band,</u> that song <u>Cool Change </u>does it for me, I feel like they are talking about me."

I had to swallow, this kid goes deeper than those waters in the song. "Let's just pop in to my place for a minute. There is someone I want you to meet."

When the two shook hands, Ed immediately asked Waren about the different vehicles we had looked at.

Waren described make, model, mileage and his opinion on each.

Ed paid close attention, reading Waren's lips. He smiled. "You had a good co-pilot with you Melody. This young man knows automobiles."

Waren smiled shyly, quietly pleased with himself.

Then I took over. "Ok both of you sit down there is something we need to discuss and it's not cars."

For the next half hour we talked about what it might look like, us all living under the same roof. I thought Waren would be against it but he listened attentively. Ed liked people, he just had trouble hearing them. Waren could hear fine he just had trouble understanding the cruelty and abandonment he had experienced at the hands of people.

Ed had made a delicious Lasagna and home-made biscuits. Waren and I looked at one another. We didn't tell Ed we had already eaten. Waren winked and dug right in, polishing off two helpings. With his second glass of milk half gone he grabbed two cookies when they reached the table. The meal over, Waren helped me clear the table and do the dishes. He went over to where Ed was looking out the window. The outside light cast shadows just yards beyond the camp, but within a small circle of light Miko and his family were taking center stage. Ed had set up a little feeding station out there and visually tracked their movements all day long. The two talked quietly but I could see that Waren had placed himself directly in Ed's visual range. Ed could read lips and Waren had quickly picked up on that. I had homework to do so

I went about my work, leaving them to fill in the blanks. When I had given them a half hour or so I motioned the two to the couch. "So, can this work?"

Ed spoke up, "I'm going to teach him how to tear down an engine and put it back together. Maybe a snowmobile engine. Waren's going to help me set up a little tarp covered work area. We can plug into your outside electric and work into the evening. I know where I can get a gas heater and some drop lights."

I had never heard Ed say this much.

"So as long as it's not too cold we can work through the winter." It was settled in Ed's mind.

"I take that as a yes from you too Waren, correct?" Waren nodded shyly.

"Ok, let me get you back home. We'll get you moved in Saturday morning. Right after you Ed and I go get one of the vehicles you recommended. I'll get Miss Nichols to follow us to town. Waren, you won't mind riding to town with Miss Nichols will you?"

The look on Waren's face told me he didn't mind at all. "Oh and one more thing Waren, you have to return to school."

Waren paused, thought before he spoke. "That's not a deal breaker ma'am."

CHAPTER EIGHTEEN

Pests Surface Out of Season

The three DeBloise brothers puttered in the yard on this December morning. One sat in a plastic lawn chair sharpening a chainsaw while the other two fiddled with an old diesel tractor. Their mindless sputtering—not dissimilar to a balky chainsaw—left their mouths and was captured and disbursed in vapor trails similar to the little balloons of narrative in a comic strip. The three brothers lived as one family in a makeshift dwelling supported in the middle by a trailer. One that seemed to be grimacing like Atlas trying to hold up the world.

Three mongrel dogs, all tied to a separate pile of debris, endured a six foot radius of movement. Yapping the day through once the brothers left for the day—meek, heads down, quiet in their presence. The structure, a series of appendages shaped like a tepee covered with tar paper, one little window in each. The overall effect was of a winged moose fly trying to decide who to bother. This eye-sore stood out as a blighted shadow in a vast mountain range in the western part of the state of Maine. The building and all it could not digest - cast out in all manner—could from a short distance be mistaken for a garbage disposal site. Wrecked equipment, pieces of salvaged snowmobiles, used up tires—all lay where they had expired. Green tarps half buried in snow, covered broken furniture, chairs and a discarded mattress. Black five gallon pails salvaged from their woods operation stood as a wall at the edge of the woods. A swing hung from one rope, boards leaned against trees. Oil barrels of food trash spilled over their tops. A row of silver gas canisters lined up against the building gleamed in the morning sun. The supporting trailer had been placed in such a manner as to allow movement from one appendage to another without the need to see the light of day.

Two of the brothers had stay at home women—not married—who attempted to tame three kids aged two to seven. Spawned by fathers who apparently had never been properly civilized themselves, the women had their work cut out for them. Feral would properly best describe a first impression.

Bruce—the first if you care to view him in chronological order—showed no respect for women or kids and barely tolerated his two younger siblings. The oldest—the most capable, and the meanest. Bruce ruled the roost.

The three brothers worked the land in a disjointed, no rhyme or reason—sporadic—haphazard—half-hearted effort—with no commonality of purpose. The fall and winter found them harvesting woodlots for local landowners. Spring, summer, and early fall they tended their pot plants. Hired to cut woodlots by their neighbors often as not out of fear of what might happen if they didn't give the brothers a little something to do with their time.

When approaching a prospective landowner, the terms of a contract were made clear from the outset. Bruce did the talking, "We do what we do, your trees will get cut, you'll get paid—end of story." The few times a landowner had balked at the terms being offered he had lived to regret his decision. Bruce the persuader, in one instance parked his old beat up 4X4 pickup at the end of the man's driveway for a solid week. Just off the property. He scared the be-jesus out of the man's family every time they left the house. He nodded and smiled, revving his engine. Through missing and rotten teeth, mouth open, nose to the sky he sniffed the air, then shouted out, "Can you smell it? The smoke. You can smell it! Somethings burning—or about to." Then he smiled and showed those few teeth that looked like they had suffered the very fire he spoke of—black stumps remaining. "Good thing I'm around to watch over your place don't'cha think?"

And of course there was the lineage and history with the DeBloise clan to consider. The men's father had been a boil on the backside of this little numbered township for as long as anyone could remember. Their father, Francis, who had fled Canada, entering Maine by sneaking through the woods above Rangeley had violated people and property for as long as he lived. Once safely in a lumber camp somewhere near Stratton, he set about to become a property owner. Not with fondness he was named *Pig man.* A term that would eventually cover his vocation as well as his habits—the name was not uttered in his presence. Francis was not a large man in stature but when you added in his temper and the smell that emanated from his person he seemed larger. Francis did not bathe, shave, or change his clothing. When a yellowed undergarment gave way he simply covered the remnant with another garment. He wiped his hands on his clothing during and after eating. The boys' mother, Francis's wife—Mother—the only name the boys had ever heard her called—existed solely as a conduit for the old man's desires. She tolerated the boys the same way she handled the litter of pigs she was given charge of. When Pig Man was out and about, she fed the pigs and she fed the boys. Mother was for all practical purposes a prisoner in her own house.

The two younger brothers with women inhabiting separate appendages in this dwelling were following the same model.

Mother DeBloise died of life-failure at the age of forty- two. The boys by then old enough to fend for themselves got their remaining training in slovenly habits the good old fashioned way—they learned them at the trough. Filth was a constant. Pig Man's belt set the rules which changed sometimes hourly to suit the old man. Out and about, chickens disappeared, gardens got raided, people got threatened and occasionally beaten and it was wise to order your pork from the pig man every fall.

Good old Daddy taught them the family's other business as well, raising a late fall harvest grown in the shadows of tall trees beneath a canopy of foliage that defied detection from above. Their little squalor was off the grid. In the end the boys were eager, ready and willing to carry on the family traditions.

When Pig Man died they burned the shack in which they had been raised—everything in it—no family treasures, pictures— nothing. How he died would always be a mystery. The pig sty that backed up to it was burned as well. The boys, barely teenagers at the time let their father lay in among the pigs for two days before calling it in. "He must have fallen in there and had a heart attack," they told the one deputy who found his way to the place and looked at the small part the pigs had ignored. "We were working away at the time," they offered.

In actuality the old man passed in his own filthy bed and found his way to the pig sty with an escort. Whether he died of natural causes or had some help getting to the sty in the sky never seemed all that important to the authorities. The trailer and add-ons now sat where the shack and sty had been. (*When the wind is right, you can still smell pig—perhaps a little getting in the last word from dear old dad after all.*)

The brothers poached year round for their meat and made a trip into neighboring North Anson once a week for milk and bread, mustard and catsup. Liquor and diesel fuel was about the only time they made it as far as Madison.

The two women, their freedom modeled after the boy's mother, were treated better than the boys' mother but still not normal. The brothers took the women's request list scratched out what they didn't deem essential and took turns making the purchases. The two women, emptying bags finding many of their needs ignored, exchanged a lot of silent headshakes.

Things were changing though. This year <u>Scab,</u> now seven years old was attending school for the first time. (Her given name was Eliza, though Uncle Bruce insisted his name for her was more accurate.) He gave her the name soon after birth when she seemed always at her mother's breast, wailing when she had to be forcibly removed. The name continued to dog the little girl as she soon latched onto her mother's arm and following that became an appendage to her mother's leg. The soon to be seven year old had started school at the little elementary school in Embden in September. It was a mile and a half through the woods to get her to the main road where she could be bussed in. The job of getting the little girl ready and out to the main road every day fell to her mother Rhone, virtual prisoner of Bodine. Rhone was allowed the trip only because the brothers were too lazy to do it. They had talked of home schooling, but it ended there—talk. Enrolling the little girl into school even if it was a year late was the one battle Rhone had won. She was determined to give her daughter at least a smidgen of a chance for normalcy. She had a two year old son but she knew he didn't stand a snowball's chance in hell of ever being civilized. Father Bodine already had him nipping at his beer cans. "You raise the girl I'll take care of Blister here, he loves his pappy don't you boy?"

Bruce the oldest directed all family activities. His two younger brothers were scared shitless of him and never questioned his direction. They had a fifty acre woodlot to cut and they had been kinda at it since the black flies disappeared. Bruce looked up from beneath the skidder, his youngest brother Byron was just sitting there in that plastic chair apparently lost in thought. "Hey Numbnuts how about bringing me a 7/8th socket wrench, you've about filed the teeth on that saw down to the gums." He smiled then.

Byron looked at his brother, followed the vapor trail and felt another bug bite of animosity itch his skin. He nodded, rose and straightened his five foot seven inch frame and bounced a silent *screw you* right into his brother's face then turned to retrieve the wrench. He smiled to himself. *Speaking of gums you're about down to that yourself ain't yuh brother?* These little silent responses to his brothers' attacks kept him in the fight—at least in his own mind.

Brother Bodine was chuckling at the name his younger brother had just been called, *better you than me,* he thought to himself. Wood smoke was curling up into a clear sky with the sun marking the time at near 8am.

Bodine's woman, Rhone, (a not so very happy woman if we are keeping things real) watched three lazy good for nothings who would be wasting half a morning just getting ready—to get ready—to get to the job a dozen miles away. They might—if they get a move on—get in three hours of fighting one another before dark. She shook her head. Her husband Bodine was the best of the lot but under his brother's iron fist he had become as useless as gray water. She turned her head as Bruce opened that dark gaping hole. Lately he was throwing looks at her that raised a pulse in her back teeth. She cringed, thinking of the winks that accompanied those rotted stumps. His open mouth leer, tongue moving across a razor blade of lips like a windshield wiper. She shuddered trying to shake loose the image.

Her best and only friend, her not really a sister-in-law Paula, was pregnant again. *No end to this sad fairy tale, no Prince Charming on the horizon. Shit even a Prince couldn't find their way to this hell hole - though if the wind was right,* she chuckled to herself. The vast forest of evergreens peeked into a scarcity of windows. She moved through the maze of walls always in shadow realizing there was a reason the fairy tales she remembered as a kid always warned about the dangers of the forest.

One of the three kids started yelling about then and she turned to face one of the wild animals that had been spawned there. "Yours Paula, go find your mother, she'll settle it." Then Rhone hollered to her own daughter, "Eliza, get a move-on that damn driver won't wait a second if you're not out there by the road." The little girl grabbed her back pack and dragged a wrapped sandwich from the table and a brownie as well. She snuck the brownie into her nap sack. This is a grown-up dessert', she had been told last night with her hand getting slapped by Uncle Bruce. *Well she was old enough to go to school, so there!*

Bruce hollered, "So Scab, remember, any of those kids give you any crap you kick em' right where I told you—you hear?" He then grabbed his crotch as part of his own show and tell, laughing like an idiot.

Rhone gave him the darkest thunder-cloud look she could muster and grabbed her daughters' hand.

The bus was shifting gears—the son of a bitch hadn't even stopped. Just slowed down—ready to leave her daughter stranded four miles from school. Rhone reached the roadway and hollered loud and with enough emotion to bring the bus to a sudden halt. Her snowmobile smoking like a wood fed fire, she pulled directly in front of the bus and looked the driver dead in the eye holding his attention with her middle finger. When she had his full attention she motioned for him to either open his window or get out of the bus. She had something to say.

So on this morning of December mornings lots of forces were coming together that would test the new Principal of Embden Elementary in ways no one could have imagined. Well, maybe Henry.

***

One more week to go before Christmas vacation. This week the boys all declared they wanted to become mechanics. Mike's father brought in two old snowmobiles for the kids to learn on. He explained the similarities all combustion engines share. "It's pretty simple really," He began the discussion in the classroom. I was impressed with how he tied math and science skills, reading ability, and good common sense together for the class. "A good mechanic can find work anywhere he goes. And he can save a ton of money buying what needs fixing, if he can fix it himself."

He began at his beginning. "My dad got me interested when I was a kid asking for a scooter. You probably know them as dirt bikes now." The boys recognized that term and perked right up. "He told me," 'if you can get one of these junk cars in the yard started, I'll get you your bike.' "Then he showed me what I'm showing you this morning and answered any questions I had. I had plenty at first but just like a puzzle it came together; this part makes that part move and so on. It wasn't long before an old fifty-one ford we had sitting in the back had a plume of blue smoke announcing its rebirth." Like he was reading a book to the kids he announced, "Chapter two. I took some classes in high school, then went to a two year mechanics school and I've been employed ever since," he smiled. "Always had working transportation too." He shifted gears, "If you want to work for yourself, this here's one of the best ways I know to do that." He moved to the window. "Final chapter. Pay attention and we'll breathe some life into these two old castoffs on my trailer and one lucky kid is going to be driving it home come Friday." Another shift, and a look in the direction of the old guy who had been waiting patiently, "Now let me introduce a man who could probably still teach me a thing or two about engines—Ed Crone."

The time we normally devoted to math and science classes this week included various wrench and socket sizes. We learned tolerances, carburation, gaskets, transmissions, spark, pistons, lubrication and another dozen terms that were explained as the need arose. Between Ed and Mike's dad we were just getting ready to take the class out to his trailer and get hands on when Mrs. White motioned me to the door.

Mrs. White looked pale white.

"Whenever you have to show up at my door unannounced it means trouble. What's happened that's bad so close to the holidays?"

"Sorry Melody but this is bad. Worse for who's involved." Mrs. White's eyes revealed the level of bad she was privy to. "Mrs. Poulin needs you. You aren't going to believe this."

I sighed, gave the class a stern warning and followed. One quick look at the sky revealed the story was already out—dark clouds were replacing what had been a sunny morning. Mrs. White covered Marie's class and we went into the little office-infirmary. Only place for privacy space in the building. "In all my years I have never run into this before. I'm not sure of what this even is."

"Start at the beginning Marie, we'll figure it out together."

Marie took a deep breath, calming herself. "The little DeBloise girl, a kindergartner, shared a brownie with two other children at recess. All three of the girls have become sick and dizzy. I went through Eliza's back pack and found the wrapper, it smelled like marijuana, big time. Soooo Principal Standish it seems we have a drug case on our hands." She let out that deep breath. A sigh really.

CHAPTER NINETEEN

Mountains, Monkey Wrenches, and Monkey Business

After my talk with Marie, I called two of the parents then waited with the three girls in the infirmary. I sent Eliza into the kitchen to stay with Darlene while I met briefly with the mothers of the two sick little girls. They were mad at their daughters. Mad at the school. And just in general pissed for having to leave their jobs to come pick up their kid. I assured them I would handle this in the best possible way. They did not want their kids labeled drug addicts at age five and six and they did not want to be an agenda item at a school board meeting. I told them I did have to involve my bosses but I was hopeful we could keep this as a discipline incident here at the school. We shook hands and they half dragged the girls to their vehicles. A parting shot thrown in my direction, "Somebody needs to get that DeBloise tribe out of our county—our school at least. We'll leave that to you Miss Standish. They are animals."

I sighed. Darlene who was still in the building sat with Eliza. Returning to my classes I found them all handling various engine parts one after another. They had to name the part and its function before passing it along. It was like playing the game Gossip—with a twist. Ed announced the part and its use aloud then handed it off. Listening skills were required. Both these guys were born teachers. I spotted Waren with his head under the cowling of the snowmobile with Mike's dad pointing out things to him, Troy, Sam, Tracy, and Fred. Everyone was having fun but taking it serious at the same time. The girls while not ready to get grease under their nails were attentive and respectful. I found Mrs. White and asked her to watch over the activity for a little longer and I went in to make the call. I maybe over-stepped the chain of command but felt I needed to let the Supt. know what had happened before talking to the Elementary Supervisor—*I just don't trust the judgement of that man.*

"You know I haven't been out your way to visit since the board meeting so let me get my things together and I should be there in about half an hour. Do you have someone who can cover your classes?"

I was about to tell him about my guest speakers but at the last minute decided to let him see for himself what was going on in the name of education at the Embden school—before he heard it through the grape vine.

While I waited I reviewed the little bit of a record we had on the DeBloise girl. There wasn't much. She was seven years old, and the name of her parents was listed. There was no contact number, just a note that announced that if the little girl was ever sick she could just tough it out till school dismissed. I raised my brow, I would have to run this by the Supt. as well. I had no experience with something like this. What laws were we flouting if we let all this pass? Should I have called the Sheriff? I went to the kitchen where Darlene was giving the little girl who seemed fine now, a bowl of Jell-O. I decided to sound her out.

We went in to the food pantry and whispered, "I have no idea what you should do Melody but you can bet the entire town will know what happened by sundown no matter what."

"Have you ever met any of this family? They sound a little rough around the edges?"

"I haven't but my husband has seen their handiwork. He works in the wood mill and a lot of the hardwood that's cut comes there. The truckers who haul independently bitch about the wood piles these DeBloise men create. She tried to find the exact words. 'Piled up like a kinda bad hair day their wives throw at them—and the headache that goes with it when a little loving is requested.' She chuckled at that. "Leonard doesn't swear but he will quote nearly verbatim when necessary. His quotes concerning these brothers are filled with raw language, but he always finishes by saying—'remember I didn't say that.' "From what I gather from my husband the older brother is the mouth piece who menaces everything and everyone he crosses paths with."

I went back to the office to wait for my boss to show up. Darlene agreed to stay and watch Eliza until school ended. I had to focus my thoughts on how best to approach this. There didn't seem to be any good way out of this without a confrontation with the parents. There was a knock on the door. I thought it was the superintendent—it wasn't - it was the custodian-bus driver, Evan.

"Miss Standish, I just came from meeting with my boss, the transportation supervisor. He said I should talk with you," he stammered—a little embarrassed—"I-I was threatened this morning."

I waited, not having any idea where this was coming from.

"It was the Debloise woman, we've got her kid—kindergarten I think. She said if I leave her daughter by the side of the road one more time she's going to turn me into road kill—she gave me the finger too." He sounded like a little kid whining.

I was shocked to hear that name twice in the same day. "Well Evan I can't offer you anything immediately. Your complaint is going to have to stand in line. I will deal with it though. By the way have you left her there before?"

"I have a schedule to keep. They know the time I'm coming through, it's up to them to be there."

"So you have left her?"

"Coupla times yeah, she needs to be there."

"And you didn't see the need to tell someone—like myself or Mrs. Poulin?"

Evan hung his head, "Never really thought about it, probably should have huh?"

"Since it's me the parent is going to ultimately have to deal with, yes Evan, you should keep me apprised of anything that affects this school or the kids in it."

"Yes ma'am—say would you let me buy you a cup of coffee some afternoon?"

It was time. "Evan, honestly, we've had this conversation. I drink my coffee in the morning mostly and it's generally with Darlene. You're more than welcome to join us but without trying to hurt your feelings that's probably going to be the best I can offer."

Another knock on the door sent Evan on his way - head down. My big boss entered. We shook hands.

I decided before we got down to the business at hand I would let him see the hands-on-teaching taking place. "Walk with me." We got outside just as a plume of blue smoke rose along with applause from thirty-two students. Most had grease on their hands and more than a few, grease on their faces. Ed and Mike's dad were beaming. When they saw us there they cut the engine. The Supt. held up his hands as if inviting explanation. Dwayne, never bashful but this time filled with knowledge, must have seen this as one of the teachable moments I was always espousing. He explained it all in a very understandable way. He even included a little of the math and science part of it - which I very much appreciated. Not to be out done, Ruth had disappeared into the classroom and brought out one of the rag rugs we had created a week ago.

Honestly I didn't have to say anything at all. I thanked Ed and Mike's dad and Dwayne and Ruth. We went back to the office with my boss trudging behind. He was a clever fellow and rather than complimenting me outright, was cautious in his support. (Doesn't that sound like every Supt. you have ever met?)

"It's always good to involve the community when you can. Just one of them speaking in support of you at a board meeting silences the fence sitters." He smiled. "Who was that Ed fella, I don't think I've seen him before?"

I had too much ground to cover to fill him in on what my private life looked like these days so I told him he was a friend just offering his knowledge.

I brought the conversation around to what had happened in Marie's class and the short conversation with the two parents. I informed him of what Darlene knew of the family and just for the drama of it included Evan's morning and the note in the little girl's file.

"There is no way of contacting this family short of a snowmobile ride, is that what you are telling me?"

"Seems that way."

"Well Melody, I'm fifty seven years old and I am not a cowboy so I think we need to let the Sheriff handle the legality of this. For our part I say we invite the parents in and explain that we aren't going to punish this little girl for their poor behavior. How does that sound to you? Your driver can hand the mother our request in the form of a letter I will draft this very afternoon. There will be no misunderstanding in the letter. I will give her a week to respond or the little girl and her parents will have to come in front of the full board to get back in school."

I nodded, this man has good common sense.

"I'm glad you called me. Now Wayne—your supervisor—he wouldn't see it this way at all." The Supt. seemed to struggle for how best to explain. "I inherited him. His ties are too close to the community for me to dump him without cause. He has already come to me regarding what he calls your outlandish teaching style. He showed me your first evaluation." He looked at me over his glasses. "As I said he's here for the long haul but he's smart enough not to challenge me. He figures if he documents, documents, documents, he's covered his behind. I'm sure he figures he'll outlast me, you too probably. But for the time I'm here you and your approach is safe. I wish more of my teachers dared to challenge the system a bit more." His eyes widened, "You know the more I think of it—maybe I am a bit of a cowboy." He hitched up his britches, winked at me and left me standing with my mouth open. I didn't even sigh. "Now let me get to that letter."

I walked back to my classroom to tidy up the afternoon and present both men with a certificate thanking them for their contribution to the education of Grades 6-7-8 December 1980.

Next week is a four day week. Henry will be our guest speaker and I have no idea what he's going to say. Then its Christmas vacation, WOO-HOO!

All I Want for Christmas Is...

We got the snow all the kids at school were clamoring for. Secretly I wanted snow too, so I could try out the four wheel drive-ability of my—new to me—Jeep Cherokee sitting just out-side my door. After Waren and I visited the three dealers and compared the corresponding brands they offered and the prices, Waren chose the 1976 solid red, Jeep from Peoples Garage. I returned with Ed and let him do the dickering. Having a hearing loss can pay dividends it seems when listening to a salesman. Ed only heard and responded to the words that got my name on a contract and the price he suggested in the first place—love that man. Then over the weekend the two new men in my life, cut, setup, and decorated a small tree. The tree sported things they had found outside. Leaves that had been blown into small spaces where they retained their color. Acorns they managed to find before they were claimed by Mikos' family, birch bark white as snow, and sprigs of hard red berries found somewhere in their wandering. Waren drilled little holes in the acorns and strung wire through them. Very clever. "He loves that drill," Ed told me. Ed had sewed the berries together in a string that made a loop around the tree. We had all shared several bowls of popcorn and managed to keep our mouths shut long enough to make a garland of white. Already one present wrapped in red tissue—long and thin standing against the wall behind the tree—no name on it—raised my curiosity.

With the tree a silhouette in the window, I hunched at the kitchen table with my books and planner. It was Sunday December, 14, 1980. Hearing the words of support my Supt. had offered in our brief meeting I continued looking for new ways to get the students to engage. This week Henry would most certainly offer a solid history of the area and I had no idea what else.

Darlene had also sparked an idea in my head and after Christmas break, groups of three will be helping her plan month long menus and learn the math and science that goes along with cooking for a hundred or so people on a daily basis. She has agreed to intern some future cooks as well.

Our Social studies classes have followed the John Jakes creation, **The Kent Family Chronicles** from prerevolution to the opening of the west. All areas of the 6th-7th and 8th grade social studies curriculum are now being addressed—just not in the normal fashion. The immigrants arriving from many continents have provided the <u>World Cultures</u> learning expected for the sixth graders. The harsh terrain and vast mountain ranges testing the mettle of those moving west adds to the students <u>Geography</u> knowledge. All the while those Kent descendants provide a rich tapestry of <u>United States History.</u>

One of the picture posters I had placed on the wall as I had prepared for students back in September will be taking center stage when we come off the Christmas break. We will be reading **Anne**

Frank: The Diary of A Young Girl. Beyond the obvious story line, I want the kids to think about the freedoms they enjoy in this country. *What if you had to spend your days hidden away with no hope of escape, how would you handle it?*

I will offer a list of questions we will explore within ourselves as we read the book. *Are we all capable of greatness? What is courage? Is your glass half full or half empty?* This fourteen year old girl, forced into hiding—not knowing if she had any future—recorded for all time in her diary, insights with a universal message. From that little hidey hole of an attic—for the two years left to her—Anne Frank offered a message of hope, honesty, and belief in a higher power. All the while seeing beauty in the world, even as her own world was slowly disappearing.

<u>Perspective, Insight, Honesty, Legacy, and Forgiveness</u>: Through the eyes and words of a teenager, Embden students will view a world that existed not that many years ago. Hopefully with the power of this story they too will never forget that freedom can come at a terrible cost.

Taking a break from my planning, I find the two boys (I call them my two boys—they like that) playing Cribbage. They tell me they will teach me the game over the Christmas break. A smell of fresh baked cookies is in the air. Ed has been teaching Waren the game of Cribbage, a game he played with his late wife. Waren is a quick study and just pegged a twelve hand about to win the game for the third time in a row. Ed throws up his hands and heads for the coffee pot.

"Say, Waren maybe you could offer me some strategy for my girls basketball team we haven't won a game yet. By the way bring me a cookie will yuh?"

Waren deposits the cookie looking at me with those serious eyes of his and as they say—from the mouth of babes. Not realizing it he offers up that <u>perspective </u>word he'll be given in his reading. "You need to have the cards to win, Miss Standish." With that he rejoins Ed who is not giving up just yet.

I had to laugh, he was right. The two tallest girls in the class had chosen to cheer and as gritty as the girls on my team are, we simply couldn't stop the pass into the middle to the tall girl that every other team seems to have. I thought back to the old line, *We may be little but we're slow of foot.* That about summed up my girls and our season up to now. The boys were winning half their games so at least they had hope. The girls on the other hand seemed to have come to terms with their basketball futures and the conversation pre-game seemed to be focusing on hair styles and what good looking boy might be in the stands. My pre-game routine lately was simply to offer encouragement and the old bromide; "Just have fun ladies."

"Road trip," I announce late Sunday afternoon. Ed, Waren, and I hop into the Jeep, put it into four wheel drive and go to Madison for pizza. The vehicle performed just as advertised and the pizza did its job as well.

I close my eyes Sunday night knowing there are just four days of school till vacation and no games scheduled this week. Only three agenda items I have facing me. First a meeting with the parents of the little girl who brought weed to school. I won't be going alone at least, the bus supervisor will be with me. I hope they understand that while the school is not going to push the issue, we did have to call the Sheriff's office and report it. I have no idea how the law will pursue this or even if they will but the school will be done with it. I sigh. On the bright side I need to do a little shopping of my own for the men in my life. Finally, I have to call Mom as well. I won't be going home for the holidays. *Let's see two negatives and a positive—that's still a negative in math terms—maybe I can dream up one more positive*—with that thought in mind I closed my eyes.

***

Chatter—that's the word that might best describe the classroom atmosphere for the first half of Monday morning. I finally had to raise my voice. The boys looked at me like, 'WOW! Where did that come from?' It was just prior to lunch and I decided to cut my losses and have a brief recess before heading in to eat. The snow had stopped, and thankfully it was not the snowball making kind. There was probably six inches of new snow atop the hardened inch on the soccer field so I suggested a game of snow soccer. We set up orange cones as our goals and chose teams. We had teams of thirteen on each side, girls and boys. The boys stripped down to tee shirts leaving their coats lying about like melted snowmen. We slipped and slided and beat on each other for the half hour and all that energy expended promised a relatively quiet afternoon to spend with Henry.

Henry came to join us for lunch in the classroom. Mashed potatoes, corn, fried bologna and a yeast roll shared room with what seemed a never ending supply of canned applesauce for dessert. Henry sat, seemingly amused by the students and the sounds of the classroom. He was going to spend the first hour of the afternoon in Mrs. Poulin's class helping the little ones fashion birch bark canoes—using construction paper. Regaling them with stories they would surely re-tell their parents.

Sitting there at lunch among my students he did not seem out of place. He told the students the Indian name for corn; Maize. He remarked on the bologna and had no idea what to call it, he joked with the kids about it—but left it on his plate. He rose, a pained expression even he could not hide crossed his features as his first few steps were halting. He was standing straight when he closed the classroom door. He left to work with Mrs. Poulin's class and forty minutes later he entered our classroom without being noticed. I was just telling the students about **The Diary of Anne Frank** we would be reading when we return from holiday. Suddenly he was just there. Henry could not contain himself, he raised his hand and asked to speak.

"I don't mean to interrupt but I have read this story. I served this country. I know of war. He was serious and he had their attention. "When you read a real diary, of a real girl, one about your age, remember. She is telling a true story that is nearly as old as mankind." Henry seemed to be looking beyond the classroom walls. He was dressed to speak to us, wearing leather leggings, a fringed vest and sporting a feather in his hat. "Throughout mans recorded history bad things have happened and have been recorded in many forms. The beauty and wonder of this story is that one so young could see beyond those terrible months, and give us all hope for the future." With that said he sat back down. I had nothing to add. I introduced Henry Strongbolt who will add to our knowledge of our area.

His long white hair hugged a lined face, his eyes twinkled with delight. He loved children. Several props; a lance, a net, a bow and arrow all lay across my desk. He also had brought a picture book of Abenaki artifacts.

He stood, "Many of you have seen me, and today you will begin to know me. I am Henry Strongbolt of the Abenaki. I have come to tell you of your land, your lakes, your rivers, your mountains. But before I do I need to tell you of my people. From the beginning. The white man speaks of God, to the Indian he was known as the Great Spirit. In the beginning the Great Spirit looked out over a vastness of black space. There were no colors, no sounds, and no light. Much was missing. The Great Spirit began changing all that. He introduced the sun. He brought color to the sky. With light to guide him he created water. He introduced sound and spectacle, through thunder and lightning. Still he was not satisfied. He fell asleep then and dreamed of two and four legged creatures of many sizes and descriptions. He created grass and trees for them to play in. He dreamed of things that could fly. All these things came to pass. Then he created man—to remark on his handiwork—to remember and record—to document and discuss. He created a circle of life, with all beings taking their fair share and no more. He created the stars to guide us." Then Henry smiled, "But you knew all this," he kidded and winked.

"What I wish to share with you today is not dis-similar to what the girl in your story will reveal." His eyes closed briefly, then he told a story of his peoples sorrow. "Mankind spread to different parts of the world. He explored and found others already there. He became envious of his neighbors. He began to take more than his share. He used force when challenged. He used the unknown to intimidate, to convince and to destroy. The mountains wept. The rivers flooded with those tears. Still it did not stop the greed. Disease and illness were created to discourage this ravaging, yet mankind multiplied and charted new waters. This very land, North America was one of the last holdouts. Hidden by what seemed endless water, my people flourished.

There were a million of us from sea to sea. Most of my people are men of peace. We believed the white man when he used that word—peace—to begin his bartering. Men of two languages, English and French pitted my people against one another. There was one fatal difference between the white man and the red man. We wanted only to use the land, they needed to own it. Disease and death were introduced in a hundred ways. In the end the white man won but we all lost. There are very few of my people left now and those who still roam this earth do it from land stolen from us then returned in parcels called reservations." He looked at a book lying on a desk, "Your very own history books will tell you a little of what took place. You will have to dig very deep to find the truth. My family, formed by the power of lightning, have never given up. We have adapted but not forgotten who we are. We are the Strongbolt family." He sighed then, "I am the last of my family who lives on the land, when I go it will be another forest disappearing, never to be replaced. I act as protector for one little piece of the past. Remember me when your trees disappear, when your families move away, when your way of life is changed forever." He handed around the book of artifacts and continued to answer questions, and there were plenty. "Tomorrow I will return and talk about how The Great Spirit used his imagination to actually create the lakes and rivers, the mountains and the forests."

When Henry ended, the kids all clapped. I was proud of them. I walked Henry to the door. Waren walked over as well. He shook Henry's hand and neither spoke, all was understood.

CHAPTER TWENTY-ONE

Snowmen, Snowballs, and Snowmobiles

Shouts of glee filled the hallway when the final bell rang on the last day of class signaling a two week break. Fred probably summed it up best when he said 'Miss Standish, you're nice an all but I think we all need a break—see you next year.'

The day had been controlled chaos. We watched two kid choice movies and had a class party where the drawn names from a week earlier found everyone receiving a gift from their secret Santa. I didn't usually allow eating in class but popcorn, punch and cookies were a center piece on this day. Let them Breathe. My desk was awash in gifts from the kids which included three new coffee cups, a Cross pen that I would cherish, two tins of homemade cookies that Ed and Waren will devour, a knotted rug and a dozen cards with Seasons Greetings. One gift had me laughing right out loud. No name on it but I had a suspect—maybe Ed would like a Corn Cob pipe.

Henry had returned on Wednesday just as promised. The students heard words and names for plants and animals that somehow seemed more appropriate—catchier anyway. Miko the squirrel, Tolba the Turtle, Azeban the rascally Raccoon, Mateguas the rabbit and Emden Lakes own loon—in Indian lore known as Medawisla pronounced muh-dah-wee la—the faithful companion. Messenger and teller of tales across the water.

These names all sprung from the lips of Gluscabe who was the first teacher. "So you are in good company Miss Standish."

Henry didn't dwell on the creation of the world, though it was clear he had an opinion. He just had fun with the kids and got them to look beyond what we see with our eyes. "Let us plan a night in mid-winter when we all come to this school and study the night skies," he suggested in parting. "The stars are spirit guides, they will take you wherever you wish to go."

When he had finished I thought to myself Gluscabe would be proud of his pupil, for Henry was an amazing teacher in his own right.

We had received snow over night that could be shaped, so three Snowmen stood sentinel waving good bye with their stick arms wearing various pieces of clothing scavenged from the lost and found.

(An aside—every month we laid out all unclaimed clothing along the corridor, each class walked the length claiming any article they had forgotten in the past month. After over a hundred children had viewed what was very clearly their clothing, the pile had barely been disturbed—hence—Embden sported the best dressed snowmen in town.)

Several snowmen showed visible wounds since the same sticky snow made for lethal missiles. With the kids gone, a silence settled over the building, I took one last look around and closed the door. *Fred you are so right, I need a break.* The janitor gave me a wink that indicated he wasn't giving up on that cup of coffee just yet. I just shook my head and sighed.

***

I wish I could tell you that I got that needed break and I suppose it was a little less hectic but an event took place on the twenty-third of December that shook me up. The Bus supervisor, Steve Caron called me that morning and told me we had to go see the DeBloise family and get some assurances his driver would not be threatened again. My Elementary Supervisor volunteered me. Since I hadn't involved him before, going over his head, he wanted nothing to do with the situation. *Thanks old WTF* I silently mouthed into the receiver as I spoke with Steve. "Today?!"

"I want this resolved before school starts up again or that little girl is not getting on the bus. I understand you might have reason to talk with the family as well."

"We sent a letter, I don't know if your driver delivered it to the mother or not?"

"She wouldn't take it from him. She ripped it up in the road. This is serious or I wouldn't be taking a snowmobile ride to that place two days before Christmas. I'll meet you at the school in one hour, wear something warm."

So another incident my janitor/bus driver/wanna be boyfriend/ hadn't reported to me. And he wants to buy me a coffee?

Steve Caron is a soft-spoken man but a big man who has worn well. He might be fifty years old but he looks capable. He drove up in a school maintenance truck hauling a trailer carrying two snowmobiles. He looked like the abominable snowman dressed as he was in a padded brown mechanics jumpsuit and a black stocking hat. I wore my ski parka and insulated overalls and had my goggles with me as well. We both had pack boots and gloves on. This is crazy.

Steve unloaded the machines and headed them in the right direction before we spoke.

"I am not looking forward to this conversation Steve."

"Confrontation is never any fun and from what I hear these people are hard core, but we can't have our people being threatened, Melody."

"I know, I know. Let's get this over with I have some shopping to do—and I have a hair appointment."

Steve smiled and removed his hat, sparse would describe his hair style. We both laughed.

The road had enough snow pushed into the ditches to give us a track and we traveled, one following the other to the turn off that enters the woods. A path slightly lower than the snow around it gave us the visual we needed to follow. The morning sun chased us, warming our backs. Shadows and filtered light took turns on stage as we moved through naked hardwood stands then ducked into the solid gloom of mature softwood. Our machines provided the only noise, with an occasional winter bird rising from a branch, going home to tell of these aliens in their midst. It's peaceful out here and I find myself sighing, my mind wandering. I'm on break and I hope to enjoy the outdoors during the next two weeks. A view of a mountain range well to the west peeks through the trees. I think of skiing. Within fifteen minutes or so we see a break in the trees. A hand drawn DO NOT ENTER sign appears, tied beneath a limb. One final warning appears, BEWEAR OF DOGS. I chuckle. The crudely drawn misspelling is located on a pole just to the right of what I suppose you could call a drive way. We have reached the DeBloise compound. Just beyond the sign, what had been scenic, turns into a junkyard dogs' fantasy. All manner of stuff is piled against trees or leaning on its own sporting white hats. A mattress, an open mouthed truck, skidder tires, sawed lumber, a rope swing, green tarp peeking out of its snow cover smothering piles of God only knows what. Upon our arrival large mixed breed howling dogs strain their voices and their ropes which are tied to three of those piles. Smoke is coming out of three different metal chimneys, hovering. Not willing to become part of the waste below.

All three brothers stand Weeble-like in front of a homemade skidder—from tallest to smallest—identically clad in denim coveralls, flannel shirts, quilted vests and ball caps. All offering a squinted vacant look, as if they are peering into a starless, moonless midnight. Dropped jaws reveals the largest Weeble displaying an absence of healthy teeth. The brothers in total add to an outsider's first impression. Summed up—it's just an awful mess out there.

Wouldn't you know it, the Weeble with the worst visible lack of oral hygiene opened up. His voice rising above the yapping. "Dogs heard you a ways off. Thought maybe you'd keep going and they would keep their yaps shut." He turned to face the dogs. "Shut up!" he screamed and the dogs melted. He scratched his head through his cap. He turned again and smiled.

Please don't do that, entered my brain.

"Then I realized there ain't no keep going, so you're here." He threw open his hands. "We was about to set to a day's work, so what do you want?"

The other two brothers had not moved. Had not changed expression.

Steve and I both got off our machines, exchanged glances and he began; one problem at a time.

"My driver was threatened the other day and we need to resolve any problems you feel you have with how the little girl is being transported."

Bruce spoke, but not to Steve. He turned to me, his whiskered face revealing sprouts of gray—the elder statesman—spokesman for the family. He spit black to the side. "I bet you're the new teacher I've heard tell of." He squinted, the sun still in his eyes. "Take off your hat let me get a look at yuh." He spit again then smiled. His open sore of a mouth had me swallowing my own spit.

Steve spoke up, "Is the mother of the little girl here, I need to talk with her if I could?"

"You mean Scab's mother?" Bruce was putting on a show now, "I spect' she's around somewhere." Then with a flourish, "this here's Scab's father, Bodine. You can talk to the lot of us, it's all group decisions here. Ain't that right boys?" The brothers, invited to the party came alive, stood up straight and awaited orders.

"Apparently it's the little girl's mother who brings her roadside so if you don't mind I would like to speak with her," suggested Steve.

Bruce planted a different kind of smile on his face. *And I know how this is going to end smile.* He spit out the remainder of the wad of tobacco he'd stored somewhere in among the stumps. Blackened drool painted a smile that appeared to have been squeezed through a knot hole. He spewed his words in a singsongy way, moving his body side to side. "Mind if you do, mind if you don't, mind if you will, mind if you won't." He seemed proud of himself puffing up while fingering imaginary suspenders. He continued, "Learned that little ditty at the old man's knee—over it as well," he winked. "So mister I don't mind anything you offer up as long as you don't mind if I don't."

The two brothers joined hands and did a little dance right there in the yard, mimicking the movements and quietly repeating the little nonsense rhyme brother Bruce had just spit out. The dogs joined back in. Bruce hollered quiet, not turning his head, and it was silent once again.

We glanced at one another, eyes widened. I looked around, even snow covered, squalor was the term you would use to describe this place. *Amazing what the mind conjures up. I ought to take a picture and introduce the word Squalor to the kids with a picture of this place as its definition. Waren's little trailer would seem tranquil next to this crossword puzzle.* I shook my head back to the present and squared my shoulders—my turn.

"Eliza won't be allowed to return to school if we can't talk this out."

Bruce opened that damn tragedy he called a mouth but the voice that reached my ears was softer.

Rhone had listened to Bruce long enough—this was her daughter we were talking about. Obviously Eliza's father wasn't man enough to intervene. "Just shut the hell up Bruce, none of this is your business." She stepped out into the light. "My name is Rhone, Eliza's my daughter. So you want to talk, let's talk."

Bruce swallowed his tongue as his face went crimson but he did keep his mouth shut. You could read his mind though, *He would take care of Rhone in his own way.* "Come on boys we've got wood to cut anyway. Nice meetin' you folks, come by anytime," he tipped his hat. Hair greasy enough to lubricate a chain saw. "I'll be seeing you little lady. Maybe my education ain't done and over with yet." He chuckled, "Shoot, did I just say, ain't. See I could use your help. I'll see you around." He winked. Then he turned to Rhone. "I'll see you too Miss Rhone, along about night fall." His meaning was clear. The men found their way to several snowmobiles hauling sleds loaded with gas and various pieces of logging equipment. They left in a roar, a cloud of blue smoke trailing them. The littlest Weeble Byron followed with the skidder eating that blue smoke.

Rhone asked if we wanted coffee. Coffee-ed out we assured her. There was no inside invite. She stood just outside the screen door. "Ok fire away, I'll do whatever you ask. I know I screwed up and I don't want Eliza paying for any of—this." She opened her arms to visual hopelessness, an explanation of what—this—meant.

I nodded, made eye contact and began, "Eliza brought an illegal substance to school, but we're willing to table that if it doesn't repeat itself.

Rhone nodded seeming to relax a little, like a little snow just melted.

However, we do need a contact number in case she gets sick or for any other reason we need to make contact, agreed?"

Rhone nodded her head thinking, "I can arrange that."

I looked at the abominable snowman to my right. "I'm done Steve."

"Ok, Mrs… "

"Just call me Rhone. There ain't no Mrs. here."

"Well Rhone can you tell me in your view what's happening with the pickup of your daughter in the mornings?"

"That damn driver!" she exploded. Then she paused and started again. "Excuse me, that driver, he doesn't hardly slow down. There is no way he can see if we're there or nearly there unless he stops. That's all I'm asking. Stop for Jesus sake. Look up the trail. You don't see us then move on, end of story." She shook her head, she was trembling with emotion. "Lots of mornings he's five to ten minutes late, do we leave? No we don't leave. Have a heart dammit." She shook her head again. "That's all I'm asking, she's just a little girl." You could just make out a little head inside the screen.

Steve cleared his throat, "I'll talk with the driver but if there are further problems you need to contact me. You can't threaten my driver, especially in front of the other kids, Agreed?" He handed her his card.

Rhone wrung her hands savoring the outcome, then studied the card. "Yes sir Steve Caron, and thank you two for coming out here. There aren't many who dare to brave it. The Sheriff sent a little weasel deputy out here about the brownie and alls he did was share a bottle with the village idiots before he left."

I studied this woman as she spoke. I saw the look Bruce had given her. "Are you going to be okay? If you get my drift?"

"You know, a year ago I might have said no. But I have a daughter in school now and I realize me and that school is her only ticket out of here. I'll do what I have to do to protect that."

We left then, our snowmobiles sharing the only conversation on the return trip. I got off my machine helped Steve load them. All without comment. Steve broke the ice, "I hope that's the end of it. He fixed me with a look that didn't seem promising, "Oh, and Merry Christmas, Melody."

Finally, maybe, we could return to a holiday spirit. I couldn't help but think what kind of Christmas was awaiting the kids in that hell hole though.

Pig Man Comes to Christmas

Just as Darlene had predicted the rumor mill was delivering grist from the community at a production rate that would be envied by any Paper Mill in the state. In the short time since the little girls in Mrs. Poulin's class got sick, the scar tissue that covered old wounds concerning the DeBloise clan got a fresh look. Apparently the whole town was chewing the gristle. I got my first taste of pork on Christmas Eve morning.

I had cancelled my hair appointment the day before when the meeting with that family got Steve the bus supervisor and I rattled. We drove back on the same trail but nature provided no softening of what we had just witnessed. We spent an hour in the parking lot of the Embden School trying to find normal again. Steve had left with a wave of his hand and a final comment. "We are going to know the trail in there by heart before this is over."

I stopped in at the corner store in North Anson the next morning, my hair appointment re-scheduled for 10:00 am. I needed gas and while pumping, I was cornered by an older local with time on his hands. He came out of the store and found his way to my side of the pump.

"Let me do that." He craned his head around while squeezing the trigger. "I hear you are the teacher at Embden School, is that right?"

"I am. My name is Melody Standish and you are?"

Gallons were entering my tank and I had miles to go before I sleep. *Let's make this quick shall we.*

"Names, Grayson Haney and I think someone needs to tell you just who you are dealing with. Before you step into a hornets nest out there." He put out his free hand, "Let me buy you a coffee."

I would hazard a guess the man was in his Sixties. Younger than Ed. "I don't have a lot of time right now I have an appointment in Skowhegan at ten and I have already changed it once."

"I'll just finish up your pumping here. You go get the coffee ordered, it will be worth your time." He urged me on, "I'll give you the Readers Digest version, won't take but five minutes. But might save you a lifetime of regret."

"Who are we talking about, Mr. Haney? I really am on my way to an appointment?"

"Why the DeBloise clan of course."

I was jolted to attention. "Mr. Haney I just met them out there yesterday." I checked my watch.

"Yeah… well did you meet the Pig Man?" He saw me startle.

"Thought not… all you met was the pig slop, the residue. The fouled leavings."

"You need to be a little clearer Mr. Haney I have no idea what you are speaking of."

"Let's get you that coffee, I'll give you the end of the meal version of that family." He hung up the hose and handed me my receipt.

The morning crowd had moved on. Mr. Haney had me all to himself in the little eating area. He didn't even raise his cup to his lips before he began.

"My daughter's up there. Living with the idiot named Byron. Did you meet the little Squirrel eyed runt?"

In my mind I could see the shortest brother, first dancing around like a fool then leaving on that skidder.

Mr. Haney's mouth set like drying concrete. "Rumor has it I have a grandchild… but I've never seen em." He folded his hands around the Styrofoam cup, staring into the blackness. "The whole pack of em' is tainted, spoiled, like meat gone bad. The old man— the father—Pig Man, he terrorized this whole county for a dozen years or more. His sons are carrying on the family hatefulness—a meanness really." He shifted in his chair, "You've met them you say. Well let me tell you a little about the father. The slop don't spatter too far from the pail." He paused, moved his eyes closer to the cup of steaming liquid as if looking back in time. "I worked along-side of him when he first came to this country. His name was Francis DeBloise, he couldn't speak a lick of English when he first got here from Canada. He was like a wild animal that just wandered into our camp. He was running from something, you could tell." The man's eyes became as set as his mouth. "Francis he was strong though and caught on with our woods crew up in Stratton. That's where I met him. Had to point at everything to make him understand what needed to be done. We named him Canadian bacon at first—he loved his bacon at breakfast. Walked right back to where the cook worked and sopped up the grease left in the pan with biscuits. Then wiped his hands on his britches— what stayed in his whiskers stayed there. He worked hard, ate hard, played hard, and fought hard. Teasing him didn't last long. It wasn't but a week before everyone knew him and all his extremes. I saw him fight just two times. He used every appendage he'd been given, including his teeth. He bit the ear off a fella and spit it in his face. Then he laughed and put his arm around the poor guy.

All his extremes seemed to scare the shit out of the bosses and they made him a crew leader. They give him a wood-lot to cut and gave him three of the laziest workers. They didn't stay lazy long. He produced I'll say that for him. It wasn't long before he acquired a woodlot of his own—through threats made I believe—anyway he left our crew. But not before he was baptized with a name that stuck and followed him just like the grease in his whiskers. It was his habits—or lack of habits really—that got him his new name. That name followed him as close as his stink. Seems like we were seeing the future when we named him and he became that."

I looked at him quizzically, seems there was a little **foreshadowing** going on outside the pages of the stories we were reading in class.

"Like I said he did everything in the extreme. The extreme that got his nickname changed was his lack of attention to his personal self. Francis he didn't wash up for meals, he didn't bathe when opportunity presented itself. He didn't shave or get his hair cut. He didn't even change his clothes. He simply added a tee-shit to the yellow one that was rotting off his body. His pants were stiff as a board with his own filth. Got so bad men were double bunking so's they didn't have to be in the same cabin. He smelled bad. Fresh air didn't touch it. By the time he left the crew to cut his own wood he looked like an even wilder animal than when he first got here. And he smelled like one too." A little smile appeared as a memory emerged, "We all got to calling him **Pig Man**—behind his back of course, we all wanted to keep our ears."

I realized, I hadn't touched my coffee, I felt like I had spent this whole conversation underwater, just now surfacing. I sighed.

Mr. Haney was strangling his cup now and I surmised he was envisioning a neck with his hands wrapped around it.

"He moved away and settled into where you went yesterday. I asked you if you met him. Well he's still there right under the snow. When the wind is right that pig sty he built still stinks." A little light entered his eyes. "He laid in that pigpen for days when he died, rumor has it the boys put him in there."

The one sided conversation continued. It seemed Mr. Haney had been waiting a long time to unload and I allowed myself to miss my hair appointment once again.

I returned to my camp and called to re-schedule my appointment. The girl wasn't too pleased. She refused to re-schedule. Merry Christmas. I went to the yellow pages and the letter A provided me with a new place to try. I called <u>A Cut Above</u> and the owner answered. He would fit me in he promised but I might have to wait a bit.

Later that afternoon I sat waiting to get my hair cut. I held a magazine filled with new looks on my lap but couldn't get the conversation of several hours ago out of my mind. Mr. Haney said he left the woods business and began driving school bus for the towns in the western part of Somerset County. It was there he ran into Pig Man again a few years later.

He was early for his afternoon student pick-up when he observed a man dumping thrown out lunch food from a five gallon bucket into a larger barrel he had attached to the bed of an old four wheel drive pickup. When the man turned to return the pail he recognized the man as Pig Man—there could be no doubt. Pig Man recognized Mr. Haney as well. He wiped his filthy hands on his filthy overalls and approached him.

In his tortured English he informed Mr. Haney that he now raised pork and the schools allowed him to collect their leftover food. 'I still cut me some wood me but everyone like my pig meat so I raise maybe fitty, fitty- five. Would you want some my friend? Is best around.' He had looked around then and spotted the bus. "I see you drive bus for school now. Good for you, you not like woods business I could tell.' He laughed then, put the lid back on the school swill bucket and began his walk back to his truck. Then he turned once again. 'Got me own crew now, tree boys, name dem after men I work wit when first here from Canada. Bruce oldest, name him after man I chew ear off.' Pig Man laughed. 'Byron boy tree, member old cook who give extra bacon grease?' He winked and laughed again, pleased with himself. 'Bodine second son after boss leader. I get first wood lot from him. I try dosz names out with first litter of pigs. I get to know dosz names before boys even get here. Den Boys come boom, boom, boom, after dat.'

I was brought out of the pig pen by the owner of the shop. In his English accent he alerted me that I was next.

I quickly thumbed through the magazine with a hundred hairstyles but all I could see was the little girl Eliza with her hair obviously shaped with a soup bowl as a guide. Then I remembered my own father cutting my hair. Steve's parting comment and this morning's conversation reached my ears, *you're right Steve, we're going to know that trail by heart before this is all over.*

The owner, Alan, introduced himself and I sat down. "Did you find a style you'd like to try from that magazine? You look a little dazed.

I looked in the mirror and met his eyes, "Do what you think is best, just don't use a soup bowl, been there and done that and lately seen that," I kidded.

He looked at me oddly, then got it and grinned.

I got my hair done and treated myself to a manicure—Santa Claus Red on each digit should keep me in the spirit. I bought some ice fishing traps for Ed and Waren. I even sprung for a hand auger that would go through a foot of ice in a heartbeat the salesman guaranteed. I also bought new jeans, a denim jacket and three different colored tee-shirts for Waren. I didn't know how he'd take it but I bought a six pack of new underwear and sports socks as well. One personal gift, a new Sony Walkman tape player which will be the last present he gets to open.

The one gift I got for Ed was a Harmonica. Strange, right? He told me it's what he always wanted to learn to play.

It started snowing again and by dusk six inches had accumulated. Ed had made a fish chowder. Fish chowder and oyster crackers was a tradition in his family. Tonight we're trying it out. Later we sat around listening to Christmas Carols. The men challenged one another in Cribbage while I pawed through tins of cookies, munching on one while grabbing another; all the while abstractly looking for the hairstyle I had seen in that magazine. I found it and went to the bathroom mirror to check out how it differed from the cut I was wearing. Both men in my life had told me they liked my new hairstyle. Lights were out by eleven and I slept like a baby, it seemed the two men in my life I could rely on were at peace themselves.

Christmas morning dawned cold and crisp. Ed was already up building a comfort fire to augment the furnace. He had the coffee pot on and this morning we would be sweetening it with egg-nog, another Ed family tradition. I sat across from him, tasting this sweetened potion. Dipping in a cookie, I was reminded of the lack of traditions in my own family. I smiled at the old guy and toasted him. *(I guess I'm starting one this morning.)*

Waren slept in, which seemed odd to me until another Christmas morning revelation struck. He probably had no reason to savor Christmas morning either. No household jubilant and antsy to open presents. Waren was the way he was for a reason. Well this morning maybe we can begin to change all that.

I never did get to ski during the two weeks off but I learned how to play cribbage, how to split wood, how to ice fish and how to listen to music on Waren's Sony Walk Man while walking on the new snow shoes my two boys had given me for Christmas. Ed practiced his harmonica for hours in his bedroom. When satisfied with a sound he walked to the window and tried to find an audience. Neither Miko nor his family appeared beyond the glass. I don't know if Ed really hears it or not, but we do. "Could have been worse," Waren deadpanned, "He could have wanted to learn the drums."

So as I said, I spent as much time outdoors as I could. I walked to Henry's cabin to say hey, but Henry and snow dog were gone. Waren's dog Pete was there. He recognized me and hardly raised his head from the step. I waved and continued my trek. I walked miles those two weeks all by myself and gained a different perspective of the natural world. I also got an idea I was going to take to the Parent Teacher Organization. *Always the teacher I guess. Always with a new Idea.*

I had called my Mother and Father on Christmas day and got answering machines in two different places. Somehow in the warm environment I found myself, I wasn't even disappointed.

CHAPTER TWENTY-THREE

The War Reaches The Home Front

When school started back up I had thirty-two students in my room once again. Waren was his usual quiet self and the other students didn't seemed surprised he was there. I think when he showed up for the snowmobile repair demonstration, and again when Henry spoke, they knew he would be joining them after the holidays. Cindy a seventh grader, told me at recess they had all foreshadowed Waren's return. I laughed right out loud. At recess he had on his headphones and walked in rhythm to whatever song was moving him at the moment just outside the action.

In class we began the **Diary of A Young Girl**.

I started by asking if anyone had knowledge of the girl or the story. It seemed the boys had figured out she was the picture on the poster. Sam piped up, "I figured we'd get around to her."

"Good observation skills guys," I offered. "Okay let's see what secrets this diary reveals shall we."

I asked Angela to begin. With the students taking turns reading passages, I stopped them when a teachable moment emerged and drew comparisons with their own lives. Some areas of discussion I want to come directly from the students. Not to get ahead of myself but in the end they did not disappoint me. **Prejudice**—a powerful word, a hurtful word, an excuse word will take center stage.

But at first, the story unfolds in a most normal way, with a birthday gift. School, friends, gossip, Anne seems to be a perceptive girl who has been given a new best friend she can confide in, be honest with, and share her hopes with. At this point I asked if anyone in the class keeps a diary. Two girls do. We talk about having people in our lives we can confide in. It becomes clear that the majority believe Anne had it right, the safest place to bare your soul is to a non- speaking friend.

"Why is this book so important? I mean come on, who cares about reading girly gossip stuff." This comes out unsolicited from Dwayne.

"Well Dwayne you are absolutely right and if this diary continued in this fashion it would almost seem an invasion of privacy. It would never have been published. But what changes this from girly gossip as you call it, is the world Anne is living in. She didn't begin this diary with the knowledge that her writing would ever be read by anyone but herself. In the beginning Anne's thoughts and observations seem innocent and trivial to anyone but herself." I point a finger skyward, "Remember though, its 1942 a war has been going on since 1938. Rumors of Jewish people being swept up and disappearing have been running rampant. Anne and her family have seen changes forced upon them by the Germans but still believe they are safe. It's this innocence and belief that her people, the Jewish people, will somehow avoid the fate of being rounded up and sent away is conveyed in the simple girly gossipy things Anne writes about in her dairy. Remember the word **Foreshadow**? Remember how it was used in some of our other reading. In this case the author, Anne, doesn't consciously realize she is even using the term. Let's continue letting Anne tell her story. Give this a little time and you will see why this book is considered such a treasure."

Dwayne grunted, giving me the benefit of the doubt. He had seen me kick his butt in a game of Pig. I missed the foreshadowing the name of that game—Pig—was sending my way but I would see it soon enough. Irony as well.

By page 8 the students begin to see how being Jewish puts Anne and her family under scrutiny. Forced to wear a yellow star they begin to experience all the prejudices and restrictions the invaders—the German army—can muster. This is just the beginning.

***

The New Year meant a change of address for Daniel. Henry had spent the two weeks the students were away from school trying to find a place for Daniel to stay. On the last vacation day he knocked on my door. I was his last hope he said. "I don't have any room here Henry," I said. He smiled and took my hand and our eyes met. Then he asked to speak to Waren.

***

At lunch time Mrs. White delivered a message from Mrs. Poulin. Eliza, the little girl who had recently brought an illegal substance to school, was not in attendance. I closed my eyes and sighed. I checked to see if the school had received any mail from the girl's mother Rhone. We had not. I checked the phone log to see if any messages had been recorded in the past two weeks. We had not received a call from Rhone. I decided to call the Superintendent.

***

It was in the afternoon a day later—the little girl was still not in school—when the superintendent followed up on the conversation of a day ago. "No sir she wasn't here again today and no call."

"Well we need to go out there. If she doesn't show up tomorrow morning call me. I will arrange to cover your classes. I will accompany you. The Sheriff and several deputies will go out there with us. From what you've told me the mother and daughter may be in danger from that older brother.

***

Henry moved Daniel into the little trailer Waren had lived in. Henry counseled Daniel every morning. Waren had cut and split several cord of firewood before moving in with me. There was no running water but a stream nearby provided water that could be boiled for drinking water, dishes and hygiene. Daniel now used his little ax to keep a small hole in the ice just off shore to supply water. This morning Henry showed Daniel how to set a snare for rabbit. Daniel drew the rabbit and the snare on his pad. Henry commented on how well he drew. "How are you feeling Daniel? Your pills are gone yet you stand and eat and drink and sleep."

"Grandfather, the quiet here, the beauty of the woods. There is a drawing in nearly everything I see. I have held my breath since I started on this journey. Today I am gulping huge lung-fulls of un-touched air. The weight is gone from my heart. Thank you." He took his grandfather's hand.

Henry looked at him. He drew his brows together, took Daniel's hand then smiled. "You are better Daniel, I am beginning to sense a change in your purpose."

***

With the added knowledge about the roots of this clan Grayson Haney had provided running through my mind, I sat behind Steve as he led the Sheriff and two deputies on snowmobiles along the little track. I wasn't hopeful. My Supt. was traveling just behind us with an odd look on his face. A happy look, like he was glad to be out of the office. Boughs sagged, heavy snow brushing our hats and shoulders warned us to turn around. It was 11:00 am. The sun providing no warmth or encouragement just light. When we reached the DeBloise place it seemed nearly deserted. The snow that had fallen over the past week lay like a layer of cotton candy, uneaten. Three mongrel dogs announced our arrival. They were tied with rope and the short length of their imprisonment had worn away three circles of brown. There was no quieting them, they looked emaciated. I focused on the house. Looks can be deceiving, irony was afoot. The roof with snow covering the black tar paper like vanilla frosting feigned innocence. Frost covered windows signaling a ginger bread house with warm smells and sugar plums within I knew was a fairy tale. My last trip here suddenly flooded my mind. *Get a grip Melody.* The Sheriff knocked. We all looked at one another. Each carrying an imagined ending in our minds.

The Sheriff knocked once more shouting out his authority. Silence screamed from within. He opened the door. The hodge-podge structure provided a maze to navigate. With frost covering the windows the rooms were in deep shadow. A flashlight was turned on. A sour smell rode the stagnant air that seemed colder than the outside temperature. There was blood on the kitchen floor and broken glass. We all looked to one another, no one spoke. We educators were sent outside. It was in a back bedroom that blood was found on the bed clothes. No one was home.

CHAPTER TWENTY-FOUR

Petroglyph Man Wears Plaid

The Sheriff had sent the Superintendent, Steve, and myself out of the trailer immediately. He called ahead to Skowhegan State Police barracks for a forensic team "And bring the dogs. Get some heat in those stoves, all of em' and light those lamps. Don't touch nothing without gloves, this is a crime scene. Call the animal shelter too. Those dogs are starving to death."

Steve looked to the sky. There was nothing left to say so let's talk about the weather shall we. "Gonna snow by nightfall, it's clouding up fast. Let's get you back to school. You alright to do that?" I look back toward the house. "I'll make sure they keep us in the loop." The supt. gave me a quick hug and whispered, "You shouldn't have to see this stuff, Melody."

I sighed. I did have people covering my back and there were thirty-two kids waiting on me. Anne Frank had a lot more to deal with this morning than me so I answered, "Yes I'm ready."

The hum of the machine under me lulled me briefly into thinking about my to-do list. It was time to add that curriculum staple, Grammar. I had avoided the issue for as long as I could because in general, kids hate the mechanics of their written language. On the ride back I realized with what I had just witnessed I couldn't bring myself to deal with any more trauma today, so Anne's fate would be postponed.

Subjects and Predicates would headline our afternoon. I had been giving this topic some thought and had actually thought of a new way to diagram that might be kind of fun—kind of—the operative words. This would also be an opportunity to get a little ahead of ourselves and ease into the history that would be taught in the second half year, Maine History. <u>(An aside: I had reached out to a husband and wife who each teach History and Social Studies classes at Carrabec high School. Their knowledge and passion for the area had me sitting in the middle of a canoe in the Kennebec River on a glorious Sunday morning in late September. Eric and Sue Lahti met me at the Evergreens Campground for breakfast. During the meal Sue told me about the significance of where we were. It seemed Benedict Arnold and his men on their march to Quebec had stopped here—a well-known Indian resting place. With a second cup of coffee sloshing around in my stomach, the ripples and currant and occasional dip of the paddle moved us to the Embden side of the river. We pulled in and Eric managed to tie off the canoe and help Sue and I up onto a large out-cropping of rock. Eric teaches a class in Archeology and is one of the most knowledgeable Historians in the area. He pointed out various etchings that have adorned the huge rock for hundreds of years. I took pictures.)</u>

It was from one of these pictures, recalling a grammar game my mother used, that I created my model for teaching Grammar. This afternoon three different colored gramma books sat unopened on the kids' desks. I told the kids to blow the dust off them and open to the section, Eight Parts of Speech. This should just be a review and reminder for most of the students. We needed to put some clothes (Grammatically speaking that is) on the handout in front of them. Today we would simply go skinny dipping. I told them of my day on the Kennebec and explained briefly the reason for my voyage. "We will spend some time in the coming weeks doing our own exploration of Maine and if things work out I may have an incredible surprise for you in the spring. For now we will just get to know that man in front of you. I have named him Petroglyph man. He will bend to your will as you cover him in clothing, movement, emotion words and actions.

I let the students study the drawings. For today we will draw him as he stands on that rock. Let's begin with a subject and a predicate."

"Remember the <u>Hang-Man</u> game you have all played.

That's how we will start with **Petroglyph Man** on the board. The difference will be he will already have taken form. I looked around the room, made a decision;

"Waren would you do us the honor?"

Waren looked at me oddly, head slightly canted then he slid out of his seat, straightened and moved to the board. He did not say a word. He studied the picture and drew a long vertical line, attached two stick legs, two stick arms and a circle for its head. He returned to his seat.

"If you pay attention you will see in the next week how we can make this stick man do whatever we want. We can dress him in any fashion we choose. Make him run, dance, laugh, or cry. The eight parts of speech that you have studied before are like different wardrobe choices. The nouns and verbs that make up a sentence are not necessarily that exciting. It's when we add layers of adjectives and adverbs and other parts of speech that **Petroglyph Man** will really come to life." The kids were listening, paying attention—to grammar no less. "Does it matter what we dress him with? Why is grammar important?"

Rachel raised her hand. "For me Miss Standish it will let me see who he is, where he lives and why he's happy or sad. I can even meet his family and friends." No one snickered, or made comment. They were listening.

I had to smile, "Thank you Rachel. So who wants to dress **Petroglyph Man?**" A fistful of hands rose. The mystery of **Petroglyph Man** was about to be solved. It would take us a week but in the end we would all know who he is, where he lives, what he eats for breakfast, and the color of his favorite shirt. I handed out a worksheet with the eight parts of speech and a brief explanation of how they are used in a sentence. This worksheet is a review of things they have been taught in earlier grades. Hopefully most of it stuck. If not maybe it will after we finish. I want this to be fun not tedious.

As the students begin creating their own sentences identifying each part of speech, my mind returned to this mornings' events. **Petroglyph Man** was forming in my head, I knew who he was, where he lived, and the color of his shirt. *Bruce DeBloise stood at the board in his wrinkled, faded, plaid shirt his open sewer of a mouth twisted into more of a putrid pout than a smile, 'You going to make the stickman dance pretty, teacher? Mind if I do, mind if I don't.' Holding petroglyph man up like a stringed puppet, making him dance he winked and spit a black stream of bile right at my feet.* I shivered.

PJ noticed. "I can get your sweater for you Miss Standish, if you're cold."

I met his eyes, "Thank you PJ, I'm fine." But I wasn't fine and the sigh that left my body involuntarily was like a punctured tire. The entire class seemed to hear it and collectively their body language told me they were concerned for their teacher.

The girls lost their game this afternoon—the boys won— and the cheerleaders cheered in both defeat and victory. I have to confess I went through the motions. I don't remember the scores or anything about the three hours on and off the court or the bus. When I pulled up outside the little camp I was sharing with Ed and Waren I felt exactly like a naked **Petroglyph Man**. Physically, emotionally, and mentally drained. My limbs ached. I stiffly marched directly to my room. To bed with no supper, barely greeting the men in my life. Two descriptive words best describe my emotional state, bewitched and bewildered.

***

I begin smelling my own unique self, first the subtle perfume that is losing the battle to a smell of fear, a smell that's like wet wool, a disturbing smell. My pores begin emitting a vapor that clings to my shirtsleeves then begins a run down my chest inside my shirt in liquid form. All the warning signs imaginable flash in my head. Every alarm bell rings out—this can't be good. My mouth goes dry, trying to swallow my fear is useless. For good measure—the dark—so thick I can taste it. That great quantifier—darkness—the back drop of a hundred childhood nightmares. I can feel I'm in difficult terrain not easily traveled even in full light. My chest tightens and flattens as if a terrific weight has been attached. Enters my screaming mind a phrase I have used dozens of times—half kiddingly in most situations—but not now. **Scared as Hell.** *My back against a tree trunk shrinking into the bark trying to make sense of it all there is an absence of sound. I sniff the air, strain my ears, my heart thumps and its pounding in these same ears—deafening. I manage a deep breath. In this absence of sound I peer into the blackness conjuring up the worst outcome imaginable. I touch my legs, scratched and bleeding, comfort my arms sore from squeezing through the undergrowth. I strain to capture meaning from this nothingness, reaching into the darkness for anything that might bring recognition and balance to my senses. My eyes ache from the strain. Another forced breath is released, labored, painful, a breath that has nothing to do with staying alive—but rather the one thing I need to bring under control before I can even marginally move forward. It* *is the only sound, and it is coming in ragged desperate gasps that surely can be heard by anyone or anything nearby. A long shuddering sigh leaves my lips sending a quiver the length of my body. I look up, all my spirit guides remain back stage behind an ebony curtain.*

In the distance a branch snaps, then a possible footfall, rustling leaves—almost a relief. Did I hear a giggle, a cackling sound? **No** *I am not crazy—not imagining this. It's really happening—I'm not alone. A ragged sigh starts at my toes then finally leaves my body, I weep. I hear the words,* **'mind if I do, mind if I don't.'** *I start.*

But in that moment of despair a different voice reaches into my head. A voice I have come to trust, it speaks to me. Follow my voice Melody. **'Take my Hand Melody.'** *That single voice is joined by thirty-two others. Together we set the rules, Stop, Look, Listen. We read stories of facing and overcoming hardship. I need to focus on these two separate voices. One has assured me of the strength of my character while collectively the voices of my students have come to trust me and depend on me. I have to find a way out of this. What would Rainsford do I ask myself? The word* <u>palpable</u> *enters my head and is soon joined by the word* <u>anxiety</u> *in all its forms. I take a leap of faith. I'm running.*

I wake with a start, lurching upwards, breathless. Frost covers my window yet I am soaking wet with sweat, blankets wrapped around my neck like a coiled snake. I sit up struggling for breath my heart pounding. My feet hit the floor and I make it to the bathroom before what remains of yesterday's lunch empties into the bowl. I dry heave the emptiness. A long shower and a phone call later I find Ed and Waren sitting across from one another in quiet conversation. Coffee and the cribbage board making an early morning appearance.

Waren looks up, "We going to put some winter clothes on that **Petroglyph guy** today Miss Melody. It's cold around here this morning."

Can this kid read my mind?

Ed picks up when Waren finishes, "Thinking of a pea soup to finish up that ham bone Melody, how does that sound?"

I look at my two men, I feel grounded again. Neither mentions me missing last evening's meal. "You two guys are up early. Can you make some biscuits to go with that soup, Ed?" I smile.

Ed smiles back. "You got it."

"Waren, if you want to ride in with me this morning I could use a little company? I'll wait."

"Sure beats that damn bus… " catches himself, "sorry ma'am, that sorry bus."

I had called Steve first thing this morning after my shower. I left a message on his machine. I was going to face all this head on. I had run from that son of a bitch Bruce all night long. He left me only when I joined Rainsford in the water, searching for an island of hope. It may have been a dream but upon waking I was indeed soaking wet and my blankets resembled a rough and rocky shore line.

Ed looked at me quizzically, but hid his questions in his cup of coffee. He had seen me like this before—preoccupied—but not in this extreme.

Waren the observer, fed his curiosity a bowl of cheerios and moved to the window to watch the family of squirrels navigate the snow. His remark whether directed at the squirrels or me I couldn't say. "Looks like a long winter Miss Standish," our eyes met. "Me and Ed are pretty good with a shovel, you need to get dug out, just let us know." He nodded and slurped down the milk in his bowl then went in to shower.

Steve called me back. He had just gotten into his office. I nodded my head as he spoke. Things were better than we had imagined but just barely. 'We'll meet and talk at school.'

Old Comfort Clothes and New Digs

After moving in to Waren's trailer Daniel had returned to the caretaker's shack deciding to take one last look around. In lifting the cheap little mattress to make sure he had left no trace of himself he discovered a ring of keys attached to a steel support brace. Whether the last inhabitant hid them on purpose or simply forgot them he couldn't say. Before he left this place exactly as he had found it, a walk through the positive memories from his camp experience now seemed in order. There might even be a few dusty books or magazines left behind he could claim. The main part of the camp was undergoing a transformation. In the spring workers would return to continue updating the buildings.

Henry, sitting with Daniel on a quiet night back in January nursing a cup of tea told how Camp Devereux had continued the summer experience for hundreds of children until a handful of years ago. 'I met the lady who started these camps. She is the reason you were able to make the journey by train those three summers. I know her story.' Henry got up to claim the last of the hot water for a warmup of his herbal tea. 'She was a woman who single handedly changed how children like yourself and others with different challenges were treated and taught. Scraping together the funds to start this and other summer camps around the nation she put her own property in jeopardy.' Henry shook his head and sipped his tea. 'Her formula was simple, concocted of all that surrounds us. To the air and water she mixed laughter and companionship and teamwork. She created an outdoor experience which was unheard of in her field. She was a gifted teacher.' Henry paused, his features darkened. 'In my time,' he continued, 'I have found when good is the purpose, a rock will expose itself to the peril of the canoe. Our benevolent Uncle Sam is easily influenced by spitting words and forked tongues.

The echoes of laughter you hear in these buildings—of happy children—were silenced by bureaucracy.'

Daniel had listened but his mind was on the summers he had spent here all those years ago. He had arrived for the first time on that train filled with others of his age as well as younger and older voices. Some of those voices, counselors. The voices in his head slowly began to quiet that summer. Learning to paddle a canoe for the first time, his first swimming lessons. It was a summer of firsts. First time on a train, a horse, first time sleeping in a tent. First time singing around a campfire. First art lesson. First group of boys sleeping in the same cabin. First time jokes played on the counselors and boys in other cabins.

It had taken a full month for Daniel to even begin to adjust. Everyone had left him alone though, 'let him wallow in his misery, he'll come around,' he had heard one counselor exclaim. The counselors did not force things. Each camper was allowed to assimilate according to their particular distress. Looking back— for Daniel—it was the art teacher Mr. Semple, who found the real

Daniel first. 'Your drawings of animals are very unique, Daniel, I believe you capture their spirit.'

Daniel wasn't sure what that meant, but Mr. Semple certainly did. 'When most artists draw it's merely an outer shell—a flower, a tree, a bird, a sunset, a deer or a moose—you can't see what is within.' He held up Daniels sketch. 'Your drawings seem to draw a breath of life to explain themselves.' He pointed then to the squirrel Daniel had captured scampering up a tree, looking back as if posing for a camera. 'That squirrel speaks to the viewer Daniel, and he's not a happy squirrel. I can tell from the disgusted look on his face. He is telling us to leave him the damn alone. He obviously has things to do.'

From that conversation, little by little, sketch by sketch Daniel quieted the voices. Mr. Semple sought him out. He found him in the lunch room and they shared peanut butter and jelly sandwiches. Not telling Daniel, he made sure the other counselors were aware of how gifted he thought Daniel was. Mr. Semple was a well-respected artist. The counselors responded by trying to eke out other talents Daniel might possess. Slowly Daniel's frozen exterior melted. A sense of humor emerged and was even vocalized on occasion. Daniel began showing an interest in the natural world and his sketches reflected it with background flowers and trees and water and rocks propping up the animals he drew. Daniel's growth and the valuable work being done at Camp Devereux was on full display when on the last camp day Mr. Semple, at the awards ceremony, honored Daniel as the most outstanding art student of the summer. Students were the focus, with dozens of awards presented for their successes. The entire camp walked by the pinned up display of how Daniel had viewed the last eight weeks. He received a standing ovation. From the beginning sketches that followed his arrival on the train, to the last sketch finished just yesterday, Daniel's journey was mapped.

The demons did not leave after returning home but Daniel now had an antidote in the form of pen and paper that kept him from reaching the ultimate despair. His art work and that vague ache of someone lost sustained him. Over the years, at times regressing and being medicated, he found that he truly did see the world through a different lens and that was ok—most of the time. Though the three summers in Maine changed him, life had not been easy for Daniel. Back in the city he barely made it through high school, a marginal student loved only by the Art department. After that he became a struggling artist who lived on the margins. He trusted too easily and was often taken advantage of. The incident with his landlord, whether real or concocted forced him to get out of the city. He was determined the second half of his life was going to be better. It had been with this in mind that he had begun his trek back to Maine. He was running, but now after reconnecting with his Grandfather perhaps he could begin running towards a future rather than away from the past. He took the keys and began to look around. Most everything had been removed. A closet that had not been ripped out contained a dust covered yearbook from 1969. Daniel thumbed through it. The pictures and activities shown mirrored his own experience from years earlier. Noises and smells emerged from the pictures, taking him back. He found a form letter that campers were encouraged to mail home. He remembered the form letter he had mailed in the first two weeks where each block he had checked reinforced his unhappiness. Each pre-written letter came with little pre-printed squares of generic joy that emphasized the positive. A single line allowed room for a dissenting opinion if one could muster the energy to write it down. Daniel remembered, like it was yesterday. His first form letter home. No blocks of contentment checked off but rather a scrawl and scream of despair—cleverly written to pass the censors—his counselor kiddingly had informed him. He took the counselor at his word. His letter home vague, but his meaning clear. He noted his days were not blocks checked with headings of, (best day yet, sunny skies, exciting, full of friends) but rather the scrawled cryptic words (too long.)

In response to the blocks that spoke of what he had learned so far, he wrote: rain coats are not water proof.

On another line he noted: Camp leaders never pause to breathe.

His favorite activity was sleeping he'd written.

On the subject of food, he noted: peanut butter covers all mistakes.

And on the last line provided he had managed a full sentence: If you don't get lots of letters it's because my hands are numb from the cold water.

Daniel didn't sign his name, he had drawn what might have been the world's first smiley face. One that could have easily been mistaken for a grimace. He sealed the letter.

He shook away the memories. He sneezed in the dust and closed the door on Camp Devereux for the last time.

CHAPTER TWENTY-SIX

Population Explosion

Daniel had moved into Waren's little trailer with only Henry bearing witness. Plenty of wood cut to last the winter and unlike the outside, Waren had kept the inside tidy. Henry checked the corners for signs of rodent activity finding three dead mice in traps Waren had set before he left. Any mouse relatives visiting must have gotten the hint for there were no recent droppings or chewed bags to be found. Daniel lit the fire and the kerosene lamp. A single picture on the wall of a pretty woman holding a small boy could only have been Waren and his mother in a happier time. Daniel thought briefly of his own mother but knew he was not quite ready to go back to that world, if in fact he returned at all. Henry struggled in, carrying a canvas tote of wood. He took a breath. "You will be safe here Daniel."

Daniel nodded. "Thank the boy for me Grandfather." "You will be able to thank him yourself in time." Daniel nodded and closed the door as Henry shuffled down the two steps. He looked around. The little kitchen with a sink had no plumbing, water emptied onto the ground beneath the trailer. He glanced out a window, a plastic outdoor toilet scavenged or stolen from a construction site stood just within his vision at the edge of the woods. He went back to checking his new digs. There was no refrigerator obviously. A 20 gallon red plastic cooler could be packed with ice but stood open and empty. Daniel supposed a snowbank would work for now. The stove was wood fueled with a flat surface large enough for boiling water or hold a frying pan. A plastic gallon jug of water sat on the edge of the sink. It was frozen. The shelf over the sink was filled with paper plates and cups. The small table which could seat three if its tiny leaf was opened completed the kitchen area. The utensils to work with included a can opener and a single kitchen knife. Plastic forks, spoons and paper plates shared the space beside the sink. Daniel didn't have to get up to check out the remainder of the place, he simply turned his head.

The bedroom with a single bed and mattress had no room for a bureau. What was originally a bathroom was stripped of its function, now containing a little cot. Three small windows. One a circular port hole that didn't open allowed leaky light to accent the dark and cramped accommodations.

Daniel sat in one of the two kitchen chairs with his pen and drawing pad, sketching. The tea kettle began to sing. He poured boiling water over a tea bag mindlessly steeping his brew—the water slowly muddying. Staring into his future much as a reader of tea leaves—he felt hopeful. Out of his prescription yet the anxiousness had not returned. Henry had calmed his fears and would come every other day or so to check on him. Henry had also offered a possible source of income for Daniel. As he brought the paper cup to his lips, he accepted the bitter brew with not a grimace but with a sigh of satisfaction. He began adding background to a drawing that seemed hopeful.

***

Bus supervisor Steve and Melody fortified themselves with an early cup of coffee. Melody did not share her nightmare but listened to a real live horror story involving the same man who had chased her through the night. The little girl Eliza was not hurt but had been traumatized. Rhone and the little girl had been left at the door of the hospital in Farmington. Rhone's jaw was broken her eyes blackened and her nose swollen—pushed to one side. She had not spoken and would not write down what had happened. Eliza the little girl, obviously a witness, turned inward and did not speak at all. The sheriff was going to Farmington to interview Rhone today. The little girl was with child services for the moment. "So I guess our issues are on the back burner for now and possibly over and done with. So thank the lord and pass the peas."

"Steve how can you say that? Where's that woman going to go? And little Eliza she's one of ours." My eyes were wet.

Steve looked at me, "You can't save the whole world Melody, much as you might want to."

"I know, but the little corner of it I'm responsible for, I can try to save that, can't I?" I could feel myself steel.

Steve got up walked to the counter and returned with the coffee pot. "You might need a second cup young lady, but I have to say I wouldn't bet against you." He rose. "Well that's the news bulletin for today, if I hear anything else I'll keep you informed."

At school and on my way down the hall I looked through the glass into Mrs. Poulin's classroom at a room full of rug rats all engaged in various activities. *I will save that little girl,* I said to my reflection.

In class we left the Kent Family as the civil war stormed through the south. U.S. History taught through the historian author John Jakes had been successful, with the kids actually taking an interest in what the family would experience next. But I wanted to include one of my all-time favorite stories to our reading. Across Five Aprils will offer a different view of the tragedy that was the civil war.

We spent more time with grammar and **Petroglyph Man** is wearing the latest fashions as students begin sprinkling their writing with more detail. We had talked about including all their senses in their observations in science and it seems to be paying dividends in their writing. Emotions too were making an appearance. We left Petroglyph Man hanging and numbers replaced letters as a math assignment was started. Students were busy with their math work so I picked up a students' written assignment summarizing what she had learned from the past four months of US. History. She had written the assignment in verse:

The history in our textbook
reminds me of Petroglyph Man
naked facts, nouns, and verbs,
our history like the stick man.
The Kent family brought texture
a fabric of feeling appeared
anger, loss, love and toil,
while blood ran through the soil.
From breaking away from our Mother
to adopting a nation's grand plan
to a time we kill our own brothers
to the wild, to find our own land.
We're taught nothing worth doing comes easy
In one family's struggles we've seen it's all true.
Each morning, with hand over heart
I understand Miss Standish, I do.

Tears enter my eyes as I look at the student, their head down plugging away at fractions. "Thank you, Julie," I whisper.

I continue to be amazed with my students and the way they learn best. Just after Christmas break on a half day Wednesday I went to the High School for an afternoon workshop on learning styles. Perhaps I'll learn even more.

The idea behind finding the best way students learn has been around for a decade and it has finally found its way to Maine. What I took away from the workshop were mental pictures of my students who on the surface anyway, seem to exhibit certain of these styles; in the way they communicate orally and in writing. As the presenter explained the nuances of these styles, I was mentally watching the body language of my students when they are on task and even when we are at recess. I am not a trained research scientist but at least part of this model makes sense to me. WOO, WOO, I am a researcher, who knew?

I have not heard a word from Steve regarding the little girl or her mother. We have one week left of basketball and I can't wait till it's over with. The boys will be in the playoffs while the girls will be able to devote more time to hairstyles, current movies and music. And dare I mention—boys.

We need a weekend. Students have been sneezing and coughing and blowing their noses all week long. No flu yet but I fear it's just a matter of time. The boys still remove their coats and sweat shirts five minutes into recess.

Waren waited for me after school this last Friday in January. The sun held no warmth, the roadway showed no melt, the snowbanks dirty with sand. Just half way through winter. When we got onto the dirt part of the road—on a whim—I pulled over to the side. Waren looked at me curiously. "Would you like to get us home Waren?"

He was out of the Jeep and around to my door before I could exit myself. He got in, adjusted the mirrors and buckled up. I looked at him and sighed.

He winked and said, "No worries Miss Melody," then finished, "I picked that line up from Troy."

I nodded and smiled. *I love this kid.*

"So what do you think your learning style is, Waren?"

He hemmed. "Honestly, I think I'm auditory. My imagination works better when I picture something from a sound or something I have heard." Then he turned slightly in his seat, "Like, I can see the entire Kent family from the description in those books. It's like you said Miss Melody, put some clothes on that man." He smiled.

I laughed, "Glad you've been listening."

Stewed beans and biscuits were on the menu. Ed seemed quieter than usual and didn't suggest a cribbage game. He went right to his room. I looked at Waren, he shrugged. I'll probe a little in the morning.

"I have an idea Waren. Friday night the high school is hosting a good Madison team. Want to go cheer for the Cobra's?"

CHAPTER TWENTY-SEVEN

Everybody's Talking at Me.

Saturday morning dawned with a red sky and a warning from Ed. I didn't witness the horizon as I slept in till well after nine. When I got up Ed gave me the weather report in the form of an old sea captains weather verse; *"Red sky at morning, Sailor take warning."* Then he gave me the details, "Heavy snow before nightfall, high winds, and stay off the roads."

I gave Ed the look. He grinned and confessed, "I added the stay off the roads part. Those weather people aren't smart enough to tell people that."

I wandered to the window. True enough, clouds were covering up just a nightgowns worth of blue, racing and piling up against one another like the clippings at a sheep shearing contest—same colors of off gray and wooly texture as well. The lake was deserted. A single ice shack visible, no color or movement of life anywhere in sight. **Bleak** would be my word for the day. I nursed my first cup of coffee at the table. Sitting there I was thinking about how best to end **Anne Frank: The Diary of a Young Girl**, when the phone rang. It was my Mother. Her first words reaffirmed what she mistook as wisdom.

"I told you your father was losing his mind, here's the proof. He's seriously dating a thirty-seven year old. I told you, you wouldn't listen." She continued rambling on. I held the receiver away from my ear and counted to ten.

"Well dear what do you think of all this?" she was just warming up.

"Good morning mother. I am doing well, teaching is going well thanks for asking. We're going to get a big snow storm before night fall, Ed tells me. And rumor has it in two days the ground hog is going to stiff us with six more weeks of winter, that's what's happening in this neck of the woods." I sighed long and loud. Like I said, Bleak is the word for the day.

"I have no idea what you are going on about but it's clear you have no sympathy for my plight. When did you become so hard core, Melody? I remember you as the little girl who wouldn't swat a mosquito if you were being bitten."

"You're right Mother I have developed a thicker skin. And compared to what has been thrown at you, it doesn't begin to compare with my students' lives."

Mother sputtered, "Well, then don't expect weekly updates from me, you obviously side with your father in this."

"I have no idea what <u>this</u> is, but you and dad have been done with each other for months now. So pardon me if I can't get all worked up." I stood up as if she could see me and ended, "Good bye Mother." My hand was nearly cramped from squeezing the receiver. I was shaking.

I made it to my tote and brought Anne Frank to the table, ready for that second cup, when the phone rang again. Ed was studying something outside the glass, while Waren was reaching in the cupboard for a cereal bowl. I managed a, "Good morning sleepy head, did you enjoy the game?" He nodded.

"Hello."

"Hey Melody it's me Luke, you do remember me?" A nervous chuckle followed.

I absently smoothed my hair and sat up straighter. I cleared my throat, I feigned cheerfulness, "Hey Luke, how have you been?"

"Actually that's why I called, I have been really good. I love the job and the area."

"Well good, I'm glad you aren't stuck in the desert with no water and slowly dying of thirst." I could sense my own well of happiness about to dry up a little more though. *Can you read someone's mind over the phone?* I decided to drop the shoe before it was dropped on me, "So what's her name, Luke?"

Silence, then a very weak, "How do you do that?"

"Past practice Luke. And a belief that no good comes from calls out of the blue on a Saturday morning."

Luke stammered, "I-I didn't mean for it to happen, Melody."

"I hope you didn't use that line with the lady, Luke."

Luke was baffled. He stuttered once again, "I-I-I'm sorry, Melody, you are a wonderful girl."

"There's nothing to be sorry about, I liked you, you liked me. Things happen. I wish you the best Luke." I hung up before Luke could begin to feel the tears in my voice. **Bleak.**

Snow billowed from the sky with no pretext of offering up a winter wonderland. It began to strike the windows in its second hour and we lost three hours of day light. Dark at three pm. Luke had retired to his bedroom and when I took him in a plate of cheese covered nacho chips he had his feet against the wall, headphones in place and a pillow beneath his head. Hunkered down was the boy.

Ed was asleep in his chair by the window counting the shorn sheep who had given their fleeces to this storm.

Once more I brought Anne to the table. I read student papers whose combined efforts offered a clear picture of what **bleak** really means.

Not to give our stickman credit but the cold hard facts revealed are difficult to ignore. As I read what Anne had endured an ever more telling chronology appears:

Her bike is stolen. She cannot ride public transportation. She has to wear a yellow star. There's already talk of having to leave her home and go into hiding, When forced into hiding the family get on one another's nerves. There is a constant fear of discovery.

Another word, <u>Anxiety,</u> appears in nearly every student paper in one use of the word or another. The dictionary definition offers every feeling Anne experienced before and during her confinement: (A painful or apprehensive uneasiness of mind. A fearful concern. Marked physiological signs such as raised pulse, sweating.)

Anne had actually begun experiencing anxiety in subtle ways in the opening pages of the diary.

At the opposite end of emotion the word <u>Mundane</u> emerges, as day after day of being closed in marks the calendar. The walls, the whispers, the sameness day after day is a form of anxiety in itself.

Anne grows up right before our eyes during her two years of confinement and her diary allows us to witness her introspection. Her hopes for freedom continually dashed through the voice on the radio. Her feelings of a different kind of love emerge as time passes, subtle yet undeniable.

Near the end of one student's paper they write—it's as if Anne knows and prepares for how her diary might be viewed in the aftermath of the war. Anne had written, 'I <u>want to go on living even after my death.</u>'

In time Anne discovers love but has difficulty voicing it even as she senses Peter has discovered it too. Love amid all the rubble just beyond the window.

I gather the papers and holding them all in my hands come to a decision. I will not grade these papers individually, but collectively just as I have read them. Together, collectively, the class has truly embraced the lessons of the story. I will hand the papers back on Monday then announce the A they will all receive. I will also let the students know the final fate of Anne that the diary does not reveal.

***

Through writings that took place later as facts were gathered and the diary lay unpublished, Anne has perished but her story does in fact come to life. Anne achieves her wish to live forever.

One more call comes in, it's Steve. It is as we thought all along, that bastard Bruce beat her up and terrorized her daughter. "Rhone wants to see you Melody. She wants you to help her daughter."

CHAPTER TWENTY-EIGHT

Splish-Splash I Was Taking A Bath

Bruce gnawed on what he saw as a betrayal of the family hierarchy. *Rhone had to pay and a lesson taught, just like that little old teacher would repeat, repeat, repeat, to make it stick in those kids heads. Just like Daddy repeated his own self every time he laid on a lick.* As his saw cut into a big pine, the chips hitting Bruce in the face, he visualized, then verbalized to himself how this would end. He hummed repeated verses of, *mind if you do mind if you don't,* adding little twists that sparked a chuckle. Within an hour he had it mentally laid out. He would let Christmas pass. Let her think I've forgiven her. But when he was ready. His two brothers would be ordered to gather all the kids but Scab. Byron's woman Paula didn't need to be witness to this either. A nice little after holiday vacation for the family down in Augusta, indoor pool and a week away. He had money stashed from short changing his brothers over the last few years. The saw chewing through wood covering his humming; a sudden thought, *he could come across like the hero in all this yet.* Bruce's thoughts ended as the tree, breaking branches as it toppled, caught up in the branches of the tree next to it. "Well shit." His eyes followed the trunk to where it disappeared into the branches of the standing tree. "Well there then," he said aloud, "let the boys clean up this mess I'll just go make plans to clean up the other one." He left the woods returning two hours later. The plan as solid as a twitch of wood.

A full week had passed and if Rhone had worried, Christmas had her dropping her guard. Bruce gave his brother's an extra little bonus and told them to spend it on their families. The Friday after Christmas Bruce sprung the trap.

Bodine seemed confused when presented with the plan at about four pm. that afternoon. "Why ain't Rhone and Eliza invited, Bruce?"

"Your woman and daughter are the cause for those people being in our business. That deputy showing up and then the two education idgits following him." He smiled then, the benevolent brother, "This little vacation is my after Christmas present to my two favorite brothers and their kids." He put an arm around his brother, "Course, Rhone and Scab, all they're getting is a lump of coal for their actions," he kidded. "Any more questions?" Bruce raised his brow, loomed over his brother and continued. "Now I got a little business in town but I'll join you tomorrow. This here hotel has got an indoor pool so have Paula pick up some suits for all of us and the kids at K-Mart." He peeled off a roll of bills. "You should be able to find the place all easy. Here are the directions, all spelled out for you. Take the Bronco. I'll use the pickup."

The first Rhone heard about all this was when she followed a scurrying Bodine rummaging through a laundry basket trying to find his cleanest dirty shirt. "You are going where?"

"Brother Bruce is taking the family on an after Christmas vacation. Sounds like fun don't it? I ain't never been on one of those. He's paying for everything too."

"So am I invited on this little trip? And why so sudden?" What's your brother up to now?"

"He ain't up to nothing Rhone it's a little present he's been planning for us that's all. Well most of us."

"What does most of us mean, Bodine?"

Bodine's eyes lowered and he mumbled, "He's pissed at you and Eliza for getting the law down on us, so all you're getting is a lump of coal Rhone, Eliza too." Bodine looked sheepish but shrugged a what-you-gonna-do. "Hey we had a good Christmas didn't we? Hell Bruce paid for part of that too. He whistled a little and finished getting clothes together for himself and their little boy Shamus. *The word foreshadow was not part of Bodine's lexicon.*

Rhone looked at her husband, she shook her head. *He is oblivious and hopeless. He don't even see the shit storm forming.* She grabbed her boy Shamus and gave him a big hug. Her eyes wet she whispered over and over the name she had found in a book and fell in love with. Like everything else in this damn place Bruce had to put a sour spin on everything including her children's names. "You go tell Eliza she ain't going, that ought to go over big."

Bruce had re-named Rhone's little boy Shamus, (Sinus.) In truth the little boy did seem to have a river of green snot running down to his lip and consequently into his mouth pretty regularly. When told that Bruce was going to join the family tomorrow, Rhone knew Bruce had been planning pay back all along.

When the screen door slammed, Paula looked back helpless to what she too knew Rhone was going to be facing. The quiet set in. Rhone didn't wait for the Bronco to leave the yard before she acted. She knew what she had to do. If only she had time. She breathed deeply and hollered to Eliza who was crying her eyes out in her bedroom after hearing she wouldn't be swimming in Augusta. Rhone threw a few pieces of clothing in a garbage bag and pried Eliza from the bed and fed Eliza's struggling reluctant arms through the sleeves of her winter coat. The little girl broke loose and threw herself across her bed spreading out like a toppled scare-crow. Rhone went to the drawer looking for the keys to the only remaining transportation. She grabbed a snowmobile key and ran outside. She started it up, revved it then backed off bringing it to idle. She was breathing heavily, her chest stepped on. Fear beginning to set in. The stark woods seemed to be closing in as well. Dusk was settling. She returned to her daughter. Kneeling, capturing each leg in turn she forced the little girl's boots on. She heard a single vehicle. A loud one. The pick-up. Bruce. She sucked in some air. She was too late. She shooed Eliza into her bedroom and closed the door. She returned to the kitchen turned off the gas light over the table and sat quietly. Waiting. Waiting. She could hear her heart beat keeping time with the echoed rattle leaving the throat of the idling snowmobile between yelps of the dogs.

Bruce noticed the snow machine idling and smiled to himself. He sat in his pickup fiddling with the radio trying to find a country song. In no hurry now with the remaining transportation sitting there all dressed up with no place to go. He opened his door and shut the damn dogs up with one bellow. He turned off the truck then the snow machine. He looked around at the quiet. *Well happy holidays.* He was actually feeling a little festive. Maybe he wouldn't go so hard on her. *If she treats me right* his mind added. His steps spoke aloud as the crunching sound of dropping temperature was hardening the days melt. He mouthed a silent little, *mind if you do* to a made up tune. He chuckled aloud. He opened the door. Peering into a darkened kitchen he could just make out Rhone's shadow at the table. He walked over and calmly placed a bag of candy and a fifth of liquor on the table. Still humming, he turned and locked the door. Rhone scraped her chair back, rose and stood with her back to the sink, facing whatever would come next.

Bruce broke the silence, "We're gonna have us a sweet old holiday time, Rhone. He lifted the bag. "This here candy's for the Scab. Get her out here." He struck a match, holding it for the longest time just below his eyes then reached and lit the gas lantern. Rhone watched his face twitch as even now he seemed to be formulating his next move.

Rhone trying to think on her feet, hollered to Eliza, her heart racing. The little girl still sniveling, still in her winter coat, resembled her baby brother as she entered the kitchen, snot glistening. Her tear streaked face red and puffy from what had been a half hour wail.

When Bruce handed her the bag of candy, the little girl thinking her Uncle had a change of heart, brightened. "Merry Christmas once again E-lize-ah," he dragged out. "Could-a-been, should-a-been, a lump of coal you know." He pointed a finger at her. "Now go suck on those and leave your mother to me. We have things to discuss. Don't we Rhone?" He worked his wrecked mouth into a grin. "We're gonna share a holiday drink, maybe toast a better year, try to work things out. It's all good. Ain't that right Rhone?" He looked Rhone in the eyes, winked and opened that god awful mouth in a smile.

"Go on Eliza, and close your door," whispered Rhone. She felt caged and trapped and helpless.

"I'm sure your beloved told you of our vacation celebration Rhone. Why don't you open this bottle and we'll toast the good times, the bad times, the present times and the future. Hell you might get to swim in an indoor pool when this is all over."

"What do you want from me Bruce? All I did was fight for my little girl's future. She's the only light in this god forsaken place."

Bruce studied on that for just the barest of time. "Just open the damn bottle and bring a couple jelly glasses with you. I like your feistiness. You might get to Augusta yet—Scab would like that."

Rhone with her hands shaking managed to open the bottle and approach cautiously. The fingers in her left hand squeezing the rims of the jelly glasses, the bottle neck in a choke hold in her right.

Bruce waited till she began pouring. Her eyes looked down. At that moment he put an arm around her waist pulling her down onto his lap. His other hand closed on her breast. Rhone exploded. Straightening, turning and swinging the bottle at Bruce's head she struck a glancing blow, knocking him to the floor. The glasses crashed and broke, a chair tumbled. Time seemed to stop—but not really. Bruce found himself looking up at the lantern above the table shaking his head trying to focus. He touched his head and found blood. He groaned. He shook his head once more and ever so slowly rose to his knees, breathing hard. Standing above him with the bottle raised, whiskey running down her arm, Rhone was ghost white but appeared ready to strike again. They eyed one another.

In a burst of outrage Bruce rammed into Rhone's knees tipping a chair into the table. Rhone screamed, hitting him across the back on her way down. She landed hard. Broken glass cutting her right hand. Bruce growling like an animal was on her before she could begin rising, hitting her twice. The first blow breaking her jaw and the other closing an eye and flattening her nose. She lay still. All was still. Bruce rose, still woozy from the blow he had taken, his breath ragged. He picked up Jack, studying the little bit of liquid fire left and swallowed straight from the bottle. He righted a chair and sat down for a minute still clearing his head. He rose, stood over Rhone breathing hard, mumbling, "Mind if I do, mind if I don't." No festive spirit in these lyrics now. "I don't mind if I do, Miss Rhone." Holding the bottle to the light once more, disappointed with the liquid lost, he downed the remaining little bit of whiskey. He grabbed Rhone by her sweater and hauled her to his room.

Eliza hearing the noise, had snuck back into view. Sucking madly on her favorite orange colored tootsie pop, eyes wide. Bruce noticed her and gave a mighty roar sending the little girl screaming back into her own room.

It was dark in his room. He lit the lamp. Rhone lay in shadow across his unmade bed blending in with the bedcovers. Bruce sat down on the edge, he was tuckered out. Breathing hard. The foul smell of his breath reached him. He watched what he did next as an observer from a different dimension. When Rhone didn't wake up and try to fight him off, Bruce got a little scared. He slapped her lightly. "Oh Rhone, anybody home? It's morning time." She was still breathing. He watched her chest rise and fall. Suddenly his mind filled with dear old Daddy applying the forfeit to his mother. *You have to pay a forfeit Rhone.* He began stripping Rhone's clothing. Mumbling to himself one of his Daddy's little homilies. "A woman's work is never done all the day you'll have no fun, now you have to pay a forfeit." He started and finished his business, then lay there wiping the blood from his head with a pillow. Rhone was still out. Feeling a little uneasy now that he'd done the deed, he looked at her lying motionless. *Shit, why couldn't you just be nice for once?* He sighed long and loud. *I'd better get her to a hospital.* He could dismiss this little fracas as consensual if she even figured it out, but if she up and died he'd have some explaining to do. The observer was left just shaking his head.

Rhone was left on a bench outside Farmington Hospital. Eliza directed to count to a hundred with her eyes closed then go get some help for her mother. "Keep those damn eyes closed Scab and suck on that pop till you hit a hundred or I'll know. You don't want me to know, now do yuh?" The little girl did just as she'd been told and Bruce was long gone when the hospital door opened.

CHAPTER TWENTY-NINE

Lost and Found

It wasn't until Sunday—January already old news—that the shortest month of the year poked its head up through a foot of snow fallen over night. February 1, 1981 will forever live in my memory as the day I learned I could not save the whole world. It was the day I grew up.

Ed had been quiet all of Saturday since issuing his weather report and appearing to have regained his sense of humor that morning. He rocked quietly in his chair throughout the afternoon watching the snow hit the window. He barely touched the beans and hotdogs on Saturday night though he did tell me my biscuits were getting better and better. He turned in with a little wave of his hand. I busied myself with lesson plans and those damn phone calls so the day passed. Saturday evening Waren played solitaire with his head phones on. We took turns looking out the window watching what looked like a real blizzard giving us front row seats though the screen remained a solid white. I re-read, skimmed really, Across Five Aprils, it was as good as I remembered. With snowflakes like guided missiles hitting the window from all angles then melting down the glass we both turned in. The sound of a howling wind had me shivering under my covers. We all slept in. The coffee was not on when I entered the kitchen at ten am. Waren rose shortly after I had the smell of coffee wafting through the camp. He went to the window and exclaimed, "Yup that's at least a foot of snow right there." He inhaled a quick bowl of cereal and went out to start shoveling. The snow had stopped but the wind was still howling. No sun to warm our spirits. After a long shower and while my hair dried, I took a look at my long neglected personal writing. I really wasn't getting it done. I sighed. On the other hand when I thumbed through the last months' lesson plans, I was amazed at what the students had accomplished. I smiled. Checking the clock it was noon time Sunday. Hmm, still no appearance from Ed calling out for lunch—still no Ed in his favorite chair. Waren had cleared half the driveway, some blowing back in. He gave me a little thumbs up when he caught me checking his progress. Ed wouldn't want to miss this. I knocked on the door to his room. There was no answer. I opened the door and again quietly called his name. The shade was down so I turned on the light. The blankets remained still. I walked to Ed's bed and looked down. Ed had passed in the night, his blankets tucked tightly up around his non-hearing ears. I sat down beside him laid my head on his shoulder and cried my eyes out. I didn't shriek or holler for Waren I just sat there and cried. During that cry I reflected on what the man had done for me. What had started out as a call for help from Ed had turned into a grandfather figure who added a new dimension of understanding. So much you can learn from the elderly. I will miss him terribly.

Waren and I cried together and though we didn't hug or hang on I think it further bonded the two of us. Ed had made both of us better people.

I called Steve. We had become friends as our paths crossed over one matter or another. He expressed his condolences then told me to let him make some calls and get someone out here to remove Ed. "I'd say based on what you've told me about his wife's funeral he would want this kept simple. You can't bury anyone this time of year anyway."

Three-thirty on that Sunday afternoon an ambulance connected to a funeral home in North Anson showed up and took Ed away. Waren and I sat there wordless. An hour of silence later, Waren invited me to the table. "Ed would want me to make you a better Cribbage player, so get ready to learn the hard way." He smiled through his tears and shuffled the cards.

My mind raced all night in a hundred directions. When I woke I felt as mentally exhausted as having spent a day in front of the class.

CHAPTER THIRTY

School Daze

Monday morning comes around no matter how your weekend goes. Waren and I drove in together. The storm had transformed the lakes and camps. The trees and their appendages, like our stick man, now stretched out fully clothed. The snow banks were car window high and the road itself a muffled white carpet. The school parking lot was cleared but mountains of snow stood on each end. The smell of fresh rolls assured me the entire world had not transformed over the weekend and Darlene was her old common sense self. I opened the door to the classroom for Waren and returned to the kitchen.

"I heard about your house guest. I'm sorry Melody." She handed me a cup of coffee.

I nodded my thanks, and sighed. "You probably heard about the DeBloise woman and daughter as well, I assume."

"Nothing escapes the eyes and ears that surround Embden Pond. You know the old saying, (Sound travels around water.)"

"The mother is asking to meet with me. She's still in the hospital but I'm assuming it's about her daughter." I took a sip of coffee. "Has that brother been caught yet?"

"From the scuttlebutt out there the mother is still not saying who did this to her. So no, I think he's still on the loose."

I sighed again and went to my classroom. This week we will spend time reviewing what we have studied for the first half year. At the end of the week the dreaded MidYear Exam. I have to justify my existence after-all. The students arrive a little subdued as well. The Blizzard, too much shoveling, being snowed in, I wouldn't offer a guess. I knew my reason for a quiet beginning so I shared. "I'm sure some of you have heard that Ed, a man you talked with and learned from, has died. We will have a class discussion on what the man meant to us. We have to talk about these things. Then we will move on."

The whole day including lunch seemed to take place with a foot of snow insulating our sounds, our footsteps, even our thoughts. Quietest day since I've been here.

I drove Waren home and then went to meet with Steve. My Supt. was sitting in one of the two chairs when I entered without knocking. "I'm sorry Steve I didn't know you had a meeting, I should have knocked." I stammered, "Dr. Hatch how are you sir, sorry about that."

He put up his hand, "Come sit down Melody, we were actually discussing the mother and little girl, Steve tells me she would like to meet with you."

I nodded.

"You have no idea why?"

"If I had to guess I think it is probably about her little girl and her education."

"That's what I'm guessing as well. Do you have an idea what we can offer?"

"Not really sir. I just planned to listen, then explore possibilities. I'll probably be picking your brain for ideas."

The Supt. nodded. "By the way, I'm sorry for your loss. Steve told me you were close to the man who passed this weekend." "Thank you sir. He had become kind of a surrogate grandfather I guess, so I am going to miss him."

He cleared his throat, "Would you like someone to go with you to meet with this lady? It might not be a bad idea."

"I think she might open up to me if I am by myself. I understand she hasn't even named that evil man yet."

"I am not telling you what to do but consider your own safety in all this. Steve told me he made some vague threats to you on that first visit."

"I will be mindful of that sir. And I will keep you informed of whatever is discussed."

"So Steve, anything to add," Dr. Hatch gestured.

"Just be careful. You are a woman on a mission and I won't warn you away. I'll simply repeat what I said the other day. You can't save them all." He picked up a post- it-sticker and handed it to me. "That's the phone number and room number for Rhone."

When I got back to the camp Waren was just finishing up cutting out a little tin of biscuits. "I know it's not Saturday night but, I'm hankering some beans and hotdogs and biscuits. That work for you?"

It seems a little of Ed has rubbed off on Waren and he is going to medicate me with comfort food. I nod and sigh. "Let me check that biscuit batter, you're a newbie. Ed told me mine were near perfect."

Waren smiled at that.

After supper I called the hospital and asked them to deliver a message to Mrs. DeBloise.

***

Henry stood at the edge of the woods and looked into the yard of the DeBloise brothers. Snow covered every possible edge and corner of the natural world. Trees cloaked in the color we deem innocence shared the moonlight with waste created by man. Tires, broken machinery, shrouded coverings turned white as a bed sheet. A portable toilet, the door wide open half full of new snow. Henry knew this place. He had known the father. Henry did not share the view that all can be saved. He focused on the true innocents—the children. He fingered the pebble in his pocket it was safe and warm. He rubbed it once more and spoke silently to the one it was meant for. *I will find a way.*

It was nearly nine pm. when a knock on the door startled me out of the end of the civil war. I was just finishing a review of Across Five Aprils, by Irene Hunt. Waren was already holed up in his room either reading or listening to music.

Standing at my door like an army officer from our recent readings, bearing bad news, is Henry Strongbolt.

After taking my hand, Henry asks for a glass of water. I tell him to sit and we move to the kitchen table. As a kid, and in my own experience of writing lesson plans and deciding where to live and who to live with, the kitchen table serves as the courtroom. Decisions, good or bad, are constructed here. Henry asked for water but he knows I will suggest coffee which will signal a real conversation is going to take place.

While the coffee percolates, Henry found his voice. He takes a pebble from his pocket places it on the table and begins. "When this school opened in 1962 my family had already lived in Embden for two-hundred and more years. I turned fifty years old in that year and it was in that year I lost my only son. I was married once." His eyes closed briefly. He looked to the window, the darkness a screen that was about to reveal some of his past. "The incident that claimed my son took place in a town not so very far away. My son, Ibsen, was twenty- six. He had a son as well." the only sound in the room the coffee beginning to perk and the soothing voice of Henry. "My grandchild was born of an Indian father and a white mother." He smiled then. "He carried enough of my sons color and features to be recognized as Abenaki. My grandson attended one of the smaller schools in Embden." He turned slightly in his chair, an aside coming. "Did you know that at one time there were thirteen schools in the town of Embden? Imagine it." He breathed in the smell of brewing coffee. "Anyway in 1962 Embden Elementary opened combining the remaining schools. In the smaller schools everyone knew everyone, they lived within a mile or two of one another. There was peace, understanding and acceptance. My grandson spent his first year in one of those little schools. In the year that Embden opened, not only did I lose my son but I also lost my grandchild." A pained look crossed his face. "When school began I had high hopes. I had begun teaching my grandson his native history. My son had taken a new job working in the woods and was promoted to crew leader within a short time." The coffee signaled its readiness and I poured us each a cup. We sipped in silence. Waren left his room to use the bathroom and joined us briefly to give Henry a hug. Waren was growing as a person right before my eyes. After Waren left us I warmed our coffee and Henry continued. "The white man has a word that signals everything—and nothing as well. The word is if. If my son had not been killed in a bar by the man who was passed over for the promotion. If we had continued to send our children to the smaller schools. If the present Elementary supervisor had not been chosen to lead this new school. Ahh, a lot of ifs." He sipped. "While I grieved the loss of my son, as the white people say, I went off the deep end for a time. I neglected to care for my grandson properly. I let my grief cloud my vision. I consoled the past and did not properly address the future. By the time I found an inner calmness, my grandson and his mother were in a different state. In those months after he lost his father my grandson was grieving the loss of his father and me as well. Did he lash out? Yes he did. Was he outrageous in school? Most certainly. Was there an adult on site who should have been able to connect the dots? Oh yes there was." Henry drained his cup. He waved away a refill. "Your boss carries a stone in his heart. His response to all issues is contained in a manual. His brain has no need to engage. With my grandchild he meted out stimulus and response punishments that did nothing to help resolve the underlying grief the boy held in his heart. My grandson was made to stand in the little office in a corner in the dark. There was no discussion. My daughter-in-law reached out to me and I failed her. In the end she moved far away to join a sister in another state. I was forbidden to make contact. Years later it was a mother's despair that allowed me to see my grandson again. Even then it was at a distance. He is here with me now but that is a story for another time."

He picked up the pebble and slid it over to me. You asked about the stones. "This pebble represents one of the children in your school. Yes, Melody it is me who tends that little basket beneath the fence." He smiled, but in a sad way. "When I finally made peace with myself I resolved to watch over the children of this school. I resolved to attend every meeting that is associated with this school, to know numbers and where they live. So since losing a son and grandson I have been a watcher, and at times an active participant in the lives of the children of Embden." He sat up straight. "Now let's get to why I knocked on your door."

CHAPTER THIRTY-ONE

Rhone

A hazy history

Weeks after the attack Rhone had still not named Bruce as her assailant. For the first two weeks she was heavily sedated with a broken jaw, and a slight concussion. This morning she asked for a mirror and the nurse took that as a good sign. She looked at herself. Her blackened eye was now a shade of yellow green and her nose while not broken had a little bend that brought a chuckle to her lips. "Well now don't you just look like the capable mother," she managed through a wired jaw. Her reflection offered no retort. *You are a long way from that stupid little high school girl, maybe should have listened to Mom.* She sipped on some iced water through a straw and lay back down but kept the mirror in front of her. A different reflection entered the glass and Rhone was studying in her room. That seventeen year old girl about to graduate from high school. She was pretty, popular, and spirited; life of the party which kept her on everyone's guest list. It was at one of these parties she met the future father of Eliza and Shamus. Bodine was a little older and had some disposable income that he enjoyed spending on this beautiful young thing. Rhone liked that nothing seemed to bother him. Mellow is the word he used to describe himself. He told Rhone he had experienced enough drama as a kid to last a life time. He told her he had two brothers, one mean and one a little slow and that he worked in the woods with them. He introduced Rhone to one of his woods products. After her first time with Marijuana, Rhone understood mellow. Her first summer out of high school was just the best time. No curfew, no school to even have to think about and certainly no need to think about the future.

Bodine was twenty and Rhone just turned eighteen when Eliza was conceived. Through a haze of marijuana smoke they actually kinda liked the idea of having a kid. When Rhone broke the news to her mother, her mom tried to have a heart to heart, an honest one. Rhone didn't have any religious convictions but just felt she was ready to take on parenthood. Rhone's parents agreed to let the young couple live in a back bedroom, Rhone's old room. The first five months of the pregnancy they came and went as they pleased. Two kids. When Bodine got busted for having marijuana on him and spent a weekend in jail, Rhone's parents kicked him out.

Stubborn Rhone sticking up for Bodine left as well. She had not met the brothers.

She and Bodine left the tar and the bronco landed with a thud onto an old skidder road. If Rhone had observed the foreshadowing being offered up she would have realized she was in for a rougher ride from here on out. When they pulled off the road and finished the trip on a four-wheeler into a yard where a single trailer and a porta potty sat she was offered a visual clue as well. Rhone thought they had taken a wrong turn and found a junk yard. Three dogs howled until Bodine hollered them shut. Even then they continued to strain against their chains, whining. As they made their way to the rusted door, Bodine set the stage for how things worked in this place. "Now Bruce, he's kinda the boss and he's quick to temper but you leave him to me. Besides he loves a pretty girl." Bodine was actually a decent looking guy and when he smiled his eyes smiled as well. "You see that stack of lumber, we been talking about expanding this little place so it's all good. We'll be able to party some right here, so it's all good," he repeated. Leave it to a girl in trouble to be dazzled by a smile, a thirty foot trailer, and the knowledge that her pride won't allow her to go back home. Bodine seemed to be on board with the baby and that's what matters isn't it?

Bruce was all nice and understanding when he first met Rhone. Maybe things would have worked out differently if Rhone was a weaker person. There's that foreshadowing thingy again.

The addition became the focal point of the late summer early fall. Architecturally the plan resembled a three sided building with the existing trailer the support for the inside walls. There was no foundation just concrete blocks strategically laid where a woods skidder had mostly leveled the ground. A floor built on top of that. All sides came together in a peak that joined together two feet above the trailer roof. There never had been any electricity so bottled gas would continue to supply light. Three metal chimneys popped their head through a tarred paper roof and we're done here.

In October with Rhone sporting one of Bodine's shirts to help hide her expanding girth and imminent birth the brothers celebrated the birth of their new house. Rhone wasn't drinking, but she was the only one. Byron the simple brother had found a girl that found his odd ways adorable and they had retired to his new room. Bodine was hammered and passed out. Bruce who always seemed to be watching Rhone from a distance decided this might be the time to get to know his future sister-inlaw a little better. He started off nice enough. He smiled, his mouth with teeth already on their way south looked like a storm cloud gathering.

Rhone laughed out loud. "I'm not laughing at you Bruce, it's just I can't even believe you'd want to see this body right now." Rhone pointed to Bodine's shirt stretched to its limit. "I'm with the man who owns this shirt. There's a million of us out there just waiting to be swept off our feet and taken to a castle in the clouds, just like this one." Bruce backed off but he never quit the fight completely. The battle had lasted seven years. She spoke aloud to the mirror, "I guess he won the war."

Her own voice brought Rhone out of her daze. She took a deep breath, studying her eyes. "Or not." Oh yeah that son of a bitch is going to pay big time. She got out of bed and went into the bathroom. Sitting there on the toilet combing her hair, her hands moved her mind. She needed to frame what and how she was going to address her situation with the school teacher. First things first.

Are You Kidding Me?

Bruce, after several days at the motel, called the hospital in Farmington to make sure Rhone had survived. They wouldn't give him any information but did confirm she was still a patient. He had a decision to make. There was sure to be an investigation. Who knows what that stubborn Rhone is going to say? And Scab, she could certainly place him there. Best to stay away for now. The noise and smell from the pool was making him ill. And when he wasn't bossing his brothers, he was finding he didn't much care for them. He sipped Whiskey and a splash of Ginger-ale from a paper cup studying them from the balcony looking out on to the pool. *Maybe I'll just leave one more clean-up to them and spend the winter in Florida.* He rose, walked back into his room and placed a call. When the week ended and his brothers were ready to leave, Bruce was nowhere to be found.

***

The crew landed back in Embden, on a Saturday. Brother Bruce had extended their vacation a week and Both Bodine and Byron had stayed in a stupor the whole time. This morning they were still drinking. Paula, eight months along, drove the Bronco along the old skidder road, sliding back and forth and through the snow that had landed since their departure. Already missing the weeks of relaxation she had just experienced; someone else picking up towels and bed sheets and straightening the room. Well that was over. They had widened the track into the place when they added on and in four wheel drive you could get there from here... . Barely. Paula noticed there was no smoke coming out of any of the metal stacks. The windows all frosted up. *Oh great I get to freeze my ass off, build a fire, feed these two baby brats and their big brat fathers*, she shook her head. "You two lazy good for nothings, how about you go build us a fire? I'll stay here with the kids till it's warm in there."

Bodine and Byron nursing their third beer since Augusta thought that was a terrible idea. Stealing a page from their brother they chanted "Mind if we do, mind if we don't, don't mind if we don't," then they clinked bottles laughing like hyenas. Paula studied the mirror, four blurry eyes challenged her from the back seat. Paula shook her head muttering. "Well you keep these two with you at least. She slammed the driver's door. It was then she heard the silence. The dogs were gone.

Curious, she waddled to one of the hanging ropes. It was whole. Someone had turned the dogs loose. Through foot deep snow, still muttering, then thinking, *Funny, Rhone always keeps the steps shoveled at least. At the door her mind registered the yellow tape.* Her eyes widened. She pulled away the tape and entered the trailer. It was dark and freezing. She peered into the twilight and smelled alcohol. She edged forward and stepped on something that crunched beneath her feet. She sensed something was wrong. She struck a match to the gas lantern and a crime scene immediately filled her head. She caught her breath and found her way back outside hollering for the two brothers to get their asses in here. Bodine watched her mouth move from behind the rear window. "What the hell is she saying?"

Even in his drunken stupor Bodine surmised upon entering what had happened. He followed the blood trail from the kitchen to his brother Bruce's room. He saw the blood on the pillow and sheets. He made it to the yard before throwing up his anger. With leaky eyes he straightened. Hollering, "You kids stay in the car. Byron. We all need to get out of here." He re-entered, walking around the mess and looked in the little secret hidey hole where they kept their cash stash. Company money they called it. It was gone. He pulled on his hair and screamed. He ran back outside and dry heaved in the snow. "Paula you get in the back seat. Byron you're riding shot gun. I need to find my wife and kid. AND I need to find Bruce."

CHAPTER THIRTY-THREE

All I Was Going To Do Was Listen

I entered room 222 the lights were off, a grunt reached my ears. I snapped on a light. Sitting in a cushioned chair dressed in new jeans and a pink collar shirt, Rhone was holding a writing tablet. Just sitting there in what had been the dark. A folding chair sat alongside. I couldn't help but think of the board meetings with chairs placed for the audience. *Who's going to run this meeting?* I took her hand, sighed and sat down. She immediately handed me the tablet. I could sense the emotion bleeding onto the page. She had tried to disguise it by creating a grocery list approach but it was clear, this lady was desperate. I focused on the words: I have one daughter I will not lose her.

Going back to my parents is not an option. At least not at the moment.

Going back to Bodine is not going to happen. Ever.

I have a son who I love but might have lost already. I hope not.

I looked up then. Rhone was silently crying. I took her hand again and returned my attention to what followed the one purchase I was being asked to make.

Can you find a safe place for me and my daughter?

CHAPTER THIRTY-FOUR

Brother Where Art Thou?

odine went to see Rhone one time at the hospital. Rhone wasn't speaking yet but she moved her hands feverishly as she filled in the blanks for him in writing. <u>I'm filing charges Bodine just as soon as these wires come off. I want to say it out loud.</u> She looked at him with fire in her eyes. <u>Your brother Bruce beat and raped me and traumatized my daughter.</u>

Bodine lowered his head, "I'm sorry Rhone, I never meant for any of this to happen."

Rhone scribbled, <u>Bodine you and your brother are like puppets and Bruce pulls your strings. We're done you and me. Eliza and I are making other plans, I want Shamus too just as soon as I settle.</u>

Bodine threw up his hands, wild eyed. "Bruce is in the wind. He stole our money stash. Now Byron and I are going to have to start over." Then he softened, a plea in his eyes, "Can't we start over too?"

There was steel in Rhone's eyes. She scribbled with emotion. <u>Not going to happen! I let too much go on for too long. Eliza and Shamus deserve a life. I'm going to try to give them one.</u> She put down her tablet turned her head away laid back down and closed her eyes.

***

Fifteen hundred miles away, in Daytona Florida, in a little trailer park Bruce DeBloise raised his head. He winced and immediately eased his greasy head back onto the pillow. *Whoa, that hurts.* He turned to his left, his new teeth stared back at him. Clackers, he had named them. Hated them. But he had to admit he was having more success with the ladies. A recent success story lay snoring beside him. His first trip to a dentist was prompted by the ever increasing migraine inducing tooth-aches he'd been having since getting down here. The man pulled em' all. Black stumps and bad breath had the Dentist muttering to himself. Bruce muttered as well when he found out the cost.

His mouth remained sore from the new teeth, and he gargled with whiskey. "Prescription medicine," he kidded.

The woman lying beside him the only benefit of these pieces of plastic near as he could tell. Other than the lack of that terrible headache of course. The ache in his head this morning wasn't from his mouth but rather too much tequila last night. He hadn't gargled it either. He tapped the woman on the ass and woke her. "I need some aspirin, breakfast and about three glasses of water to drown that Mexican son of a bitch. He rocked her shoulders. So get up and bring me a glass of water and some aspirin will yuh?"

The woman moaned and simply stuffed her head under the pillow.

Bruce in no mood to repeat himself simply put his hands over her pillow and pushed hard and long. The woman began to thrash. Bruce finally let up, pulled off the pillow and asked, "Message received?" The woman breathless and gagging stumbled to the bathroom.

Bruce laid his head back putting his hands behind his head, smiling. He thought briefly of a new found dilemma, he needed some money. Damn Dentist. Only one person knew where Bruce was hiding out, him a trusted dealer in Maine. He reached down for his wallet in his pants on the floor. He became woozy, nearly blacking out. Whoa! He got his breath back and found the number for his lifeline. Bruce would be calling for a little store credit. He dialed the number. "Hello," that was all, then he listened. It was like he had dialed in a news show.

"So she told the cops."

"My brother is looking for me too?"

"So can you front me some cash?"

"Nah, that don't change our business plan, I'll take care of her and my brother too comes to that."

Oddly he checked his watch. "All right, the snow will be leaving fore you know it. You wire me a thousand dollars and I'll see you in six weeks."

He rolled out of bed. Sliding into his jeans, as he threw on a tee shirt, he lost his balance and landed back on the bed. He lay there a moment, having to laugh at the idiocy of his predicament. He went to the bathroom guzzled another glass of water and peed on the toilet seat. The woman stood near the door, dressed now, still shaken. Eyeing him, shaking her head. He winked at her as he zipped up, "Thanks for the water and the drugs honey," He smiled. "I'll drop you off, I need some breakfast." He sang his little mind if I do, mind if I don't ditty just under his breath over and over, chuckling to himself.

When he pulled over to the curb, the woman, still scared to death by what Bruce had done to her, exited as fast as possible.

She threw out one deadly dart before slamming the truck door shut. Looking Bruce right in his puckered mouth, she fired, "You forgot your fake smile on the nightstand back there handsome."

***

Back in the frozen north, winter vacation was underway. Waren got his first ski lesson. His learning style was apparent when after listening to me explain the basics he took to the slopes like he had done this many times before. He had begged me to allow a snowmobile engine in his room. Remembering how he and Ed had planned the winter I couldn't refuse. "Don't get that thing to working and try to start it up in here," I admonished. Mike, the son of our visiting mechanic was in there with him now. First visit from a friend. Lots of firsts.

Rhone and her daughter spent the week at her parent's house helping them with the renovations that would create space for her and her children when the school year ended.

I caught up with what was happening with my parents which is a Mexican standoff at this point. My father is indeed living in a little beach town in Florida, and he is seeing a younger woman. My mother has reluctantly retained a lawyer. In conversations with both I have refused to take sides which seems to bother my mother. Talking with her is like hearing one of my students arguing about who started it. It doesn't matter. You're both going to have to face the consequences.

I thought a toasted peanut butter and jelly sandwich would taste good about now and hollered to Waren and Mike, did they want one? I delivered their sandwiches along with glasses of milk, then moved to Ed's chair. He came to mind, I sighed. I realize I still missed the old guy. Miko seemed to be offering the only movement on the lake at the moment. Ice shacks dotted my view but there was no smoke visible and no colorful out- fits either.

I opened the next story the kids are going to be assigned and began reading. **Donn Fendler, Lost On A Mountain In Maine** had been introduced to me by a history teacher at Carrabec High school. Early in the year Andy Carbone addressed the five eighth grade teachers who would be teaching U.S. History and in the second semester, Maine History. He told us any success he would have later on with these students depended on how we treated History. 'Let them have fun with it. Do hands on projects.' He then gave us a handout of possible resources that could help us do just that. Miko climbed up onto the window ledge and looked in. I think he misses Ed as much as Waren and I.

CHAPTER THIRTY-FIVE

Starry Starry Night

When school started up, Waren was riding shot gun and little Eliza was meeting my eyes in the rear view mirror. I walked her into Mrs. Poulin's room and gave her the scoop. Eliza would be finishing the year at Embden. Marie looked at me, didn't say a word thankfully, and then smiled.

The kids took a while to settle down. Maybe I had a lot on my mind but I felt out of sorts. I raised my voice. Waren caught my eye. He gave me a little nod indicating things would all work out. I sighed and apologized to the students. Troy spoke up, "No worries Miss Melody, none of us wanted the week to end either."

I had to laugh, "I guess you nailed it Troy, the week was too short." I rose from my desk, "Let's take a break before lunch and this afternoon we will plan the night time star gazing event. Remember, Henry promised us a night to remember and it's coming right up."

During lunch I was still pre-occupied. I didn't see what the kids were passing around. When the clock struck one, we were discussing a proper name for our night under the stars. There was a knock on the classroom door. I hollered come in. It was Darlene ushering in Eliza's mother Rhone, holding a big old cake complete with candles. I looked at Waren. He shrugged a what are you gonna do and all the kids sang happy birthday to me. While we ate cake and ice cream and I read all the little nuggets of affection the kids had added to the card, Rachel asked to play a record that might offer a theme for next week's night time event. "I think it would be a good song for the spring concert too," she offered.

Don Mclean had made history with his record, **Bye Bye Miss American Pie**, but it was the other side of that record we heard that afternoon. **Starry Starry Night**, held a mixed message and we ended up talking briefly about suicide. But we focused more on the music and how the descriptive words used nature to describe someone's personal pain. When we study the night skies we'll all view them through our own experience. For this afternoon we focused on the reference to a starry starry night and made our fliers that would go home inviting parents to join us. The afternoon flew. Embden Elementary was back from vacation and running on all cylinders.

CHAPTER THIRTY-SIX

Star Light Star Bright

One of the parents called me, all excited. An amateur stargazer, he offered to set up his two Hi- Power telescopes for the evening. He also had a video of the heavens with overlays connecting the various constellations, he would be willing to do a presentation before we go out into the night. Icing on the cake—he was a school board member. *This is getting better and better, this is community learning,* I smiled.

Henry knocked on my door Wednesday evening, as usual he just appeared. Tonight though he had someone with him. "This is Daniel." Announced in such a natural way, *why of course this is Daniel*, I thought, *enough said*. Henry then noticed the little girl and her mother seated on the couch. He nodded and smiled. Introductions all around then Rhone took her daughter into their room. Waren, Daniel, Henry and I sat around the table. We all silently eyed one another. "Would anyone like coffee?" Three hands rose as if testifying.

"Daniel is my grandson. He is living at Waren's trailer. He is an artist."

Henry continued to amaze me. Not sure this announcement begged a response I continued to prepare the brew.

"Daniel tell them what you do."

Daniel began in a halting voice, already dismissing the idea he was about to present. "I'm not sure the kids will like my sketches. They aren't like photographs. They will probably think they are weird." He laid down an envelope.

"Well I'm a kid," said Waren. "Let me see them, I'll give you my opinion."

Henry smiled. I filled our cups while Daniel laid out a series of sketches. The ones he had chosen to share included animals looking into the heavens. Stars peeking from their height onto mountain peaks. Several Constellations wearing animal skins that echoed their names. Waren was blown away.

I studied the sketches my mind racing ahead of myself. There was a sketch of Miko the squirrel wearing an expression I would have difficulty putting into words. I looked at Daniel in amazement. He would be the perfect illustrator for the book I continue to imagine. I saw the constellations Ursa Major and Ursa Minor, (my Little Bear and my father's Great Bear) sketched in a way that gave them life. I cleared my throat, "Daniel it would be an honor to share your work with the community tomorrow night. Your sketches are beyond words."

We invited Rhone and daughter Eliza to join us. I was interested to see Eliza's reaction to the sketches. She wasn't frightened. She picked up each one, studied it, then gently placed it back exactly as she had found it. "Well, her mother finally asked, "What do you think?" Eliza looked directly into Daniel's eyes and said, "How did you know?"

Daniel simply smiled. He had found a kindred spirit. Eliza reached out and took his hand.

I invited Rhone and Eliza to join us tomorrow night.

***

Thursday night the kids arrived hungry and excited. This was something they had never done. After a delicious meal and dessert the lights were dimmed for the video. "Before I show this," the parent explained, "I want to play your theme song, **Starry Starry Night**. Kids, in my view you couldn't have made a better choice. I work for a social service agency where many of my clients see a very different starry starry night when they look up. We have to learn to listen to one another and not judge." My eyes were wet. His eyes misted slightly, "I'm going to hand out the lyrics. Follow along. Listen to the words then I'll start the video."

Daniel followed up with his interpretation of the heavens by showing several of his animal sketches. When Miko showed up in one of the sketches, Fawn piped up, "So that's where our little squirrel ended up," all the students laughed. Gary followed that with, "I told you he would show up in a different chapter," more laughter from the students. The adults looked confused. "Inside joke," I offered. Waren didn't say a word.

Outside with telescopes focused on various parts of the night sky, our parent astronomer shifted them to follow Henry's legend of the creation of the heavens. Students and parents were treated to an evening of art and science mixed with mythology. I have to say it was the best group lesson I have ever witnessed. Lots of handshakes and hugs accompanied the students and parents to their cars that night. Daniel walked me to my car. "I have never heard that song before, Miss Melody" He was about to confide in another person. "When I read those words my past life passed before my eyes. So many times I thought of ending it all. The one thing that kept me going was my drawings and the memory of my grandfather. You are doing good work here. Creating good memories. I just wanted you to know." With that he joined Henry and walked towards the West Shore Road.

I sighed. Waren, Rhone and Eliza piled into my Jeep. And off we flew. We passed Henry and Daniel and I tooted. They waved.

***

While my students greeted the first day of spring and the impending end of the third quarter of the year with a collective sigh, Rhone too was making plans for the end of the year. She had shared the news one night in February that her parents were going to take her and her daughter into their home at the end of the school year. They were in the middle now of renovating attic space into a room for their granddaughter. Their grandson if he joined them would have his own room next to his mother. Rhone had spent the week of February vacation helping with the renovation.

Rhone had some other changes she wanted in her life. She wanted assurance that Bruce would not be back in the picture. She called the Sheriff's office. No they had not found him. They were sure he was still out of state, there was a warrant out for him no matter where he surfaced.

"Have you spoken with Bodine?"

"We sent a deputy out, he's living back out there in the williwacks. He's been advised to call us if his brother appears. That's about all I can tell you ma'am."

I was glad Rhone had an end game. I had Waren's future to plan for. That was enough. If my private life could mirror how well school was going it would be a breeze. Maine History is going to provide the meshing of three grades and disciplines covering five subjects: History, Geography and World cultures, as well as Literature and Science. Ten pm. and I'm just finishing up reading Donn Fendler's story, Lost on a Mountain in Maine. This story will help my students realize the power of persistent ceven as it highlights Maine's rugged geography. One final time Henry will speak. Not of legends but rather historical fact that places his people on the shoreline when our European ancestors first stopped by.

Man on the Run

Bodine and Byron found themselves working the wood lot by themselves and frankly it seemed quieter. Fewer trees snarled up against one another. The two brothers actually talked problems through before reacting. It was the last week of March, the woods still wearing ten inches of snow, softening under foot though, suggesting an early mud-time. They had just yarded out a twitch and added it to what would amount to two wheeler loads. "This might be their last trip in here, I don't think the road will hold up after this week."

Byron nodded his agreement. Suddenly he heard a noise. He looked to the sound and his eyes widened. Brother Bruce was peeking around a tree like a little kid. Byron excited, nudged his brother, tugging on Bodine's shirt like a little kid himself. Bodine turned his head. Bruce took off his hat and gave his brother his new Ipana smile. Bodine studied this new look. "You crazy son of a bitch what did you do?"

"I got me some new munchers, like em?"

Bodine hardened his look. Neither man had moved. "I'm not talking about new teeth, Bruce I'm talking about what you did to Rhone and my daughter. She won't have nothing to do with me."

"Y-e-a-h," Bruce dragged out, "sorry about that." He looked sheepish for a second or two but then the old Bruce emerged. "Did you know she struck me with a bottle? Pissed me off. Kinda the last straw." Then he brightened. "Brother, I was even in a festive forgiving mood when I got there. I was gonna bring her and Scab to Augusta, surprise you."

Bodine looked skeptical. "Well she's pressed charges on you which just might end up being the real last straw." He moved a little closer to his brother who was keeping the tree between them. "A deputy keeps popping in. Quite a list of charges he's laid out. You might want to stay gone." He took off his own hat. "Byron and I are done with you that's for sure. You stole our money too."

Byron nodded, he spoke up all animated, flubbing his brothers' lines, "Mind you do, mind you don't, mind we won't," followed by a self-conscious glance to the ground.

Bodine had to smile. "Byron might not have your words right but his meanings clear. We're done with you." He stared his brother down. "Since we was kids Byron and me followed your every word. Took the blame when we could to keep you from getting the belt. Those days are over." He turned to walk away but then turned back, "I might add, the next time that Deputy shows up, I'm going to put a little bug in his ear. It's near mud-time Bruce." He raised his eyebrows, "Easy to track a man during mud-time."

Bruce put his hat back on, shook his shoulders. "Her word against mine. You might ask her to reconsider. It might be in all our best interest."

Bodine took a step forward, "You come near her or my daughter." Bodine widened his eyes, stretched to his full height, "Brother or not, I'll flat out kill you."

Byron nodded and stammered, "And I'll help."

Bruce didn't say a word. He studied these two men who in his own mind he had taken beatings for. *The world sure does change. And its women who's changing it. Well, we'll see about that.*

CHAPTER THIRTY-EIGHT

The Ides of March and April Cried

The sun was staying in the sky a little longer everyday it seemed. This afternoon I strapped on my snow shoes and headed out on a snowmobile trail just across the west shore road. The snow was becoming more granular with each days melting. Waren had walked to his old place to hang out with Daniel, his new friend. Rhone and Eliza were preparing what promised to be a delicious supper. I faced the late afternoon sun and found a rhythm to match the song in my head, breathing in the new spring air. My mind opened and I took stock of how the day had unfolded. Learning styles seemed to be churning through the minds of my students. I had encouraged the students to explore their strengths. Today showed me it was having an effect. Laura, a quiet girl asked if she could show what she had learned from the book **Donn Fendler, Lost On A Mountain In Maine**. She lifted the cloth and a model of the mountain and some of the terrain he faced emerged. Two months ago Laura would not have considered how using the sense of touch aided her understanding. I can't wait to see the finished product. Waren had finished the story in one reading in his room with his headphones attached. He turned in his report over breakfast this morning. He had his curious little smile attached peeking up over his cereal bowl as I read. Poem, or lyrics to a song—I couldn't decide. I looked at that head of hair hiding a beautiful brain and my eyes watered. I was about to comment then thought, I don't have words yet. I need to read this again. He looked up hopefully.

"We'll talk about this tonight."

Mind wandering allowed foot wandering as well. Suddenly I was staring at Henry's cabin. Silence and shadow. Then I saw movement. Pete, Waren's dog was lying in those shadows and he rose to check out his intruder. When he saw it was that lady with the toy car he laid back down. Waren had expressed regret in leaving Pete but Henry assured the boy he and Snow dog would take good care of man's best friend. I waved. He ignored me. On I go.

My mind continued to wander. Suddenly my body landed on the trail as I hit a patch of ice and went down. *Now there's some learning using the sense of touch Melody, ow that hurt.* A bird on a limb I was staring up at witnessed my fall and seemed to enjoy the spectacle. One of Daniel's sketches came to mind as I lay there. *He is pure genius. And he's going to work with me,* I smiled through the pain. I managed to get back but I was a hurting unit.

When Waren returned, Rhone was putting a plastic bag of ice on my hip, Eliza watching. "What happened Miss Melody?"

"I let my mind wander Waren. Obviously visual learning is not one of my strengths," I chuckled then and groaned.

I went to bed early, my hip really ached. I got up and took some Tylenol and watched the hours pass. Finally I slept. My alarm still went off at five. I rolled over and sat up. When I tried to get to the bathroom, my right leg wouldn't cooperate, stiffness and a dull ache had sat in. I waited until six then dialed the number that would arrange a substitute for me. Twenty minutes went by and the phone rang. 'It seems there are no subs available Melody, sorry.' I was just going to have to tough this day out.

Waren drove me to school and when we got there he assisted getting me into the classroom. Within ten minutes he returned carrying one end of the fold-up cot we used in the clinic. Miss Nichols was handling the other. Darlene delivered coffee and a roll. When the kids arrived on the busses, Waren was standing at the entrance to the mobile classroom quietly directing traffic. I had armed him with the day's lesson plans. I stretched out in the front of the room with a load of Tylenol under my belt and was soon sleeping like a baby. I did not hear a peep all day as students tiptoed through their tasks. Mrs. White handled recess and lunch and popped in from time to time. There would have been no need. I did miss one visitor. Wouldn't you know my boss old W.T.F. would pick today to pop in for a visitation, i.e. evaluation? Several students put a finger to their lips. W.T.F. was clearly out of his depth. Waren told me the man stood there shaking his head, spun like a top and left without comment. Oh well, I'll just have to deal with that when the time comes. I choose to focus on the love and respect the students showed me by their actions that day. It will forever be one of the fondest memories of my time in Embden. My hip was feeling better by dismissal and I was able to thank the students before they left for the day.

Students had a week to get in their report on the book **Donn Fendler, Lost On A Mountain In Maine**. Many had finished early. I carried a folder of those home with me. Very different learning styles were represented in the reports sitting on my kitchen table, freshly cleared after a Macaroni and Cheese dinner. Eliza sat beside me. I stretched and yawned. *How can I be tired after sleeping most of the day?* The first report was what I would term traditional. A cover page with the students name at the bottom followed by three pages chronicling Donn Fendler's nine harrowing days. Certainly the student had read the book but it was like reading a police incident report; this happened followed by this, then this. The good take-away was that he had clearly read the book.

Waren's report surfaced. I had promised Waren I would react to this before my mishap. I re-read it.

WHEN WILL I SEE YOU AGAIN.

Night time claims middle of day
any wonder I lost my way?
Shivering cold through rough terrain
a scrabble through briars
that caused me pain.
When will I see you again?

Rounded corners, nature's doors
a world of fog covered windows,
there are no floors.
I'm right here, please don't ignore me.

I shout to granite walls
silence calls back
memories of a scouting tip
I'll try a different tack.
Downhill to where water flows
I doze a moment then on I go
to where you can hear me
Why can't you hear me?

I'm hungry, tired, and soaking wet
was that a bear?
My pulse races, a full body quiver
a cabin in the distance
I'm almost there.
I really want to see you again.

Look around each corner, open every door
There is no sky hear the mountain roar
You must be near me
I hope to God I see you again.

Little kids fairy tales, lost in the woods
Indian legends where you're lost for good
Nothing emptier than the great outdoors
Unless I can see you again.
Is that water?
Praying now I see you again.

I am simply blown away by this boy. I may need to frame this.

***

Reaching out to the high school staff is paying dividends I could not have imagined. The high school has written a Drug and Alcohol Grant that is putting the community into their curriculum for the last nine weeks of the year. Since all the towns in the district are surrounded by water it seems like a natural way to celebrate what those waterways have provided, past, present and future.

The science curriculum is studying water quality, vegetation, fish and wildlife, erosion, and rocks and minerals in our area.

Social Studies is touching on the people along the river past and present. The Indians, the early settlers, the soldiers, the use of the river for navigation, agriculture and industry.

The English curriculum will include student initiated interviews with older citizens to capture their personal stories of the river drives, the old mills, the early schools.

The Art Department will send its students into the field to capture photos or create original drawings, paintings, and collages. Some will try to create an archive of early drawings, maps and old photos.

School wide field trips will deliver bus-loads of students to community locations, including Wyman Dam and Scott Paper woodlands where thousands of trees are planted and managed. At the Piper Farm in Embden students will experience all phases of farming along a river. Also on the river a fish farming enterprise called Aquaculture is underway. Near the Embden School the Fish Hatchery will receive students from all five towns. This community event will end with a special surprise. It can now be revealed.

The entire High school and my class of thirty-two will meet at the Evergreens Campground in Solon and ride the river for four miles in white water rafts. Along the way all students will visit the Petroglyphs, home of our own Petroglyph man. We will lunch on an island in the Kennebec and finally come ashore a mile from the High School. To add one more superlative to the mix, NBC national news is coming along to prepare a report for their <u>Sunday Morning</u> news show.

I carry all this excitement to bed with me. This small school district is blessed with committed talented teachers and students. I sigh with contentment and I sleep soundly.

CHAPTER THIRTY-NINE

A Quote for the Ages

I decided it was time for a show down with my supervisor. I had in hand his latest evaluation. I also knew the last quarter of the year was going to involve even more untraditional teaching methods. I decided to go on the offensive. I called his office and made an appointment. This was my first year in this position and lately with the relationship I was forming with teachers and students and even community members I did not want it to be my last.

I knocked on his door. Wayne T. Folsom invited me in. He had a big smile on his face. "So you're awake are you? When I visited last it seems a student was in charge. Care to explain?"

I looked him straight in the eye. "The short answer is I couldn't find a substitute. The long answer is the reason I made this appointment." I opened the tote I had with me. "I'm going to explain what the last nine weeks of school are going to look like for the students I'm responsible for. Then I'm going to make you an offer you can't refuse. The offer is going to be in the form of those test results that seem to govern your life." He looked curious but said nothing. "I'd like to quote the scientific philosopher, <u>Karl Popper,</u> being a former science teacher I'm sure you know his work."

Grudgingly W.T.F. nodded.

"He said and I quote, **No rational argument will have a rational effect on a man who does not want to adopt a rational attitude**. So before I continue can I expect you to be rational if I can prove using measures you deem acceptable, that my students are learning?

Wayne studied me for a moment. "What measure are you proposing?"

I sat down.

"The standard tests that measure reading progress, a writing sample, math proficiency, science and social studies norms. The students take them in April every year isn't that so?"

"That's true. And what if they don't reach the bench marks you're suggesting?"

"Some of them most likely won't reach grade level, they never have. I have looked at their records. But I'm betting even those students will show improvement over what they have achieved in the past." I stood up. "The kicker here sir is a number of these students are going to score off the charts. I firmly believe they are going to have tremendous growth in their understanding and application of concepts in many disciplines."

I stood up. I cleared my throat. "I feel so strongly that when these results come back in August, if the tests don't show that measurable growth, I will resign my position, no fight no fuss. You have the summer to be lining up candidates to take my place if I fail." I sighed. I opened my planner and handed him the outline of the non-traditional learning planned for the last month of school. He didn't say a word.

"So just stay away and let me do what I do best—that's teach." He looked at me but there was nothing to say. I gathered my things.

When the door closed behind me, I silently thanked Henry.

CHAPTER FORTY

When the Mud Dries

My little camp was beginning to resemble a classroom. Eliza and her Mom were at one end working on Eliza's assignment while Warren was reading, slurping a bowl of soup. Daniel and I were studying some of his art work that would be used to illustrate a story I fully intended to write, soon. "Melody maybe you can write your story around the drawings instead of the other way around."

I looked at Daniel, "I hadn't thought that way but maybe it could work. Leave me your drawings and in the quiet of the night I'll give it a try."

"That sounds good." he rose. "I need to go meet Henry anyway. We're going to do some night fishing, the ice has gone out of the pond."

"Can I go?" asked Waren.

"Not on a school night Waren. Daniel, ask Henry if he could take Waren fishing over the weekend."

Waren looked disappointed.

"Waren, you are about to have a whole week of nights. I'm sure you and the boys," I winked at Daniel, "will find some mischief to get into."

Waren sighed.

Ohoh, it's a disease. I chuckle to myself. Waren just looks at me and shakes his head.

With Daniel gone I sit trying to fashion a story using his drawings of a squirrel whose expressions seem to beg a story. Rhone and her daughter finish the assignment, rinses out Waren's bowl and the two go to their room. Waren has something on his mind. He fidgets and pretends to be reading but I can read his body language.

"Ok out with it Waren, what's up?"

"I guess it was that last story we read, its got me thinking about my mother and sister. How I have been kind of lost—not like Donn—but still." He rubs his face, "I really don't want to live with them but I'd like to know they are alright." He studies me with those brooding eyes before continuing, "Miss Melody, you and Ed and Henry have changed my life. I feel safe in my own skin for the first time. I even have an idea of what I want to do with it." He holds up his fingers like a peace sign. "So two things. One, can you help me find my mother and sister?" He bends one finger. One request left. "Two, can I continue to live with you through high school? I will work and pay my share of everything." His eyes mist.

My story of Miko the squirrel would have to wait another night, I fold Waren into my arms and we cry together. This is the first time Waren has truly let me in. I have a lot of thinking to do.

***

After leaving Melody's camp and the light and life within, Daniel struggles to find his night vision. As his eyes adjust he catches just a glimpse of movement to the left of the camp. He peers deep into the darkness but nothing emerges. He stood stock still. Squinting. Opening and closing his eyes as if adding lenses to a camera. Still nothing. He shrugs and walks to Henry's cabin. Pete and Snow dog are straddling the little step in front of the door. He steps over them and knocks. The smell of wood smoke and pine trees surround him. Henry answers the knock and soon they are in a canoe sitting fifty yards off shore. Each quiet in their endeavor. The water is quiet. Henry suddenly points and speaks in a hushed tone. "Daniel, look to your left there is a Moose in the shallows." Daniel peers into the darkness, no moon light or stars tonight. He hears water splashing. Eventually he catches a shadow. He is reminded in that moment of what he had seen or not seen outside Melody's camp. He tells Henry. Henry takes it in without comment.

***

April vacation starts at the end of school today, April 17, 1981. Baseball and softball will officially begin on the Monday we return. The frost is gone and the fields are drying quickly. The talk in class is of going fishing, a dance tonight at Mark Emery then Easter on Sunday. Community learning will be what we will come back to. The kids seem excited about doing some stuff with the high school. Eighth graders already beginning to act like they have out grown the rest of us. They are ready to be freshman right now it seems by their attitude. I find myself having to bite my tongue. Hopefully it's the needed vacation that is sparking this and when we return we'll be so busy they won't have time to complain about every little thing.

Darlene had some news this morning over coffee. "It seems Eliza's uncle has been caught, charged, jailed and bonded out in the past couple of days."

"What will happen next?"

"I assume Eliza's mother will have to testify. I haven't heard when that will be." Darlene peers at me over her cup. "You might want to let the lady know he's out and around. If you haven't heard any of this she probably hasn't either."

***

Daniel came to supper tonight, armed with a fist-full of drawings he seemed to be mass producing. Using a squirrel as his subject he is finding different expressions and places for the little guy to explore. A limb, a mail box, the end of a canoe, a roof top, a window sill. Each picture is a story in itself. I think Daniel's idea from the other night is just the spark I need. Rhone is packing for a week- long stay at her parent's home. The little girl is doing well for what she has been through and right now is studying one of Daniel's drawings. She then puts a pencil to paper herself. Daniel and she are discussing the finer points of art so it seems like a good time to fill Rhone in on what I have heard. She opens her eyes wide then shakes her head.

"You will have to testify, right?"

"Oh yeah, Eliza too, according to the county attorney."

"Should you be taking some precautions? If you two don't testify he walks, correct?"

"I'm just now hearing that he's been caught and released." She shakes her head once more. "Now doesn't that just sound about right?" She has to chuckle, shaking her head. "Melody it's a mans' world. Even the people supposedly on my side don't take what's happened serious enough to give me a heads up."

"What are you going to do?"

"What can I do? Pack a gun or a knife maybe. Do you have any great ideas?"

I thought for a moment. "Not really, but I do have someone I trust a lot. He knows more about me than I know about myself. So maybe he can help."

It's Not Just the Ice That's Out on Embden Pond

Bruce was back living in the family compound. He and Bodine did not speak. Byron on the other hand couldn't avoid the power his brother held over him. With Bodine in North Anson picking up supplies, Byron listened to the litany of complaints that left his oldest brother's mouth. He didn't want to listen, he had his own problems. His woman Paula had complications with the birth of his son and the bills were piling up. Further she was in no shape when she did get home to be doing any cooking or cleaning. Bruce babbled on anyway. "They stole our dogs. They messed up our business. I'm facing five years in prison. Bodine won't have nothing to do with me. I… need a little sympathy here brother."

Byron simply nodded his head.

Bruce, up and pacing tripped on a toy. He swore. He picked up the toy, about to heave the little truck when suddenly struck with an idea. "You know, Paula is going to need some help around here. That woman you hired didn't even show up after the first day."

Byron gave him a shake of the head and the evil eye.

"I didn't say anything that was that bad, Byron. That woman had no sense of humor, she was useless.

Anyway forget about that. What we need is for Rhone to come back here and be a mother to her boy and help Paula."

Byron's eyes widened. "Bodine says he don't even know where she's staying."

Bruce put a hand near his mouth and whispered, "Well I know where she is and who she's with. Byron I want you to get her up here." He fingered his whiskers, "You don't need to tell her I'm back here. Tell her how much Paula needs her." The plan slowly squeezing out of him like an emerging hemorrhoid. "Get her to come here when you and Bodine are at work. Get her here, then you just let your older brother work his magic." Bruce suddenly realized who he was talking to. "Now can you remember any of what I just said?"

Byron studied that mouth. New teeth, same old Bruce. *But Paula did need help. Rhone is probably missing her boy. Bodine sure does miss her. Maybe things might work out for brother Bodine, he'd be glad for that.* Thinking all this he touched his shirt and puffed slightly. Reading his own headlines, *Byron, well he made it all happen. Guess maybe he's not the runt of this litter after all.*

He nodded then shook hands with Bruce and off he went to sharpen his saw, whistling a happy tune.

CHAPTER FORTY-TWO

Balls and Strikes

Waren surprised me on Sunday night. He had spent most of vacation week either with Henry or Daniel. I was sitting at the table putting the finishing touches on my third edit of a children's book I was sure was going to sell like gangbusters. Forty two pages with twelve illustrations from Daniel's drawings.

"Can I read this to you, for your reaction?" At that moment Rhone and Eliza arrived. I heard the car enter the drive, two doors close. Rhone and Eliza entered the kitchen. I needed to share this best seller, "Come sit down you two I'm about to unveil my literary masterpiece."

The four of us sat at the kitchen table. Rhone and Waren content to listen, Eliza following along as she looked at the pictures. When I had finished, Rhone and Waren both sung my praises. Eliza didn't say a word. "Well Eliza," Rhone asked, "this book is aimed for your age group what do you think?"

Eliza, a seven year old only knows what she knows. She looked me straight in the eye. "You have your squirrels wrong." She looked up at me. "They aren't saying what you wrote."

I raised a wrinkled brow. "Really. What do you think they are saying?"

Eliza read my body language. "Don't me mad, Miss Melody, they are just mixed up, we can fix it."

Rhone started to reprimand her daughter.

I held up my hand. "No its okay. Eliza how would you fix it?"

Innocently, Eliza studied the squirrels I had attached to the pages with a paper clip. "Can we put them all on the table like this?" She laid them out in a sequence she imagined. "Then you tell the story and I will give you the squirrel who's talking." She smiled brightly. "It's easy, we can fix it."

Well we did fix it and I learned from a seven year old. A bright, perceptive, sensitive little girl who had a gift. Now I understood what she meant when she sat with Daniel that night; they were kindred spirits. I would have to change some of the order and dialogue but it was definitely a better story.

I hugged her and fixed her a sandwich and chocolate milk. It was the least I could do. Enough surprises for tonight I thought. When Rhone and Eliza went to their room Waren sprung one more on me.

"I want to play on the baseball team."

I looked at him. I had no words.

He continued, "Henry suggested it first. We were on the shore near where he keeps his canoe. I was flinging rocks into the water, trying to get them to skim. Henry said I have a really strong arm. Then he said it was time for me to give back to the community."

I was still in the dark.

"He said I should pitch for the baseball team. He said I could have helped win a soccer championship in the fall if I had played. He said I would have been the tallest boy on the basketball team this winter. 'It is time you helped your school and community. It is time you valued yourself.' "He said that Melody, and I'm going to do it."

Well alright Waren. Of course that gave me another bright idea. I sighed.

May-day May-day

We had our first home baseball game today Wednesday, May 13, 1981. Our team is 2-0 and Waren is getting his first start on the mound. The scouting report on him is, he has a live fast ball but little else. I have no idea what that means. We are playing Garrett Schenk, a team from Anson. Waren has been wild in the three innings he has thrown in relief. Henry attended both of those games. Last night before dark he came to visit. "Waren I come bearing a new pitching delivery." Waren was immediately at attention. "Go outside and warm up your arm, throw through that tire you set up, I'll be right with you. I need to speak with Melody."

Henry beckoned me to the window overlooking the lake. "Notice the calmness of the water this evening." We both stood looking out over Embden Pond, not speaking. He turned to me, "Yet I foresee a violent storm approaching. We must prepare ourselves."

He explained. "Daniel felt he'd observed something outside your camp in the shadows several weeks ago." I looked at him. "I decided to visit the lake. Watch as the last of the ice tries to leave." His eyes crinkled. "Daniel has good night vision it seems." He nodded his head, "On my third evening I too watched a shadow person peering from your trees. It was the woodsman, DeBloise. He has new teeth, they shine in the night." He took my hand. "I believe he means to harm the mother, perhaps the daughter, and you Melody, could also be in danger."

Once more I had no words. I swallowed, thinking of the dream I had visited more than once since watching petroglyph man dance to a tune that left that wretched mouth.

"Daniel and I will be watchful. Pete is staying now with Daniel while Snowdog shadows me. If the storm moves the leaves to more than a rustle we will act."

Henry left me standing there, feeling vulnerable, I hate that feeling.

Waren threw a three hit shutout today. I asked him over the dinner table what had changed. I had watched the game but baseball is not my sport and I had other things on my mind.

"Henry told me to imagine I was skimming rocks across the water. 'Pick a spot. Turn your arm slightly sideways and watch it skip and hop.' He said that was my natural motion, I think he's right."

I had watched the team mob him and never seen him look so happy.

I put the finishing touches on the last unit in social studies I wanted to emphasize. I got the idea from what Henry told Waren about making the community proud. We are going to study citizenship and the duties and responsibilities we all share in keeping this wonderful country the special place it is.

CHAPTER FORTY-FOUR

A Last Burst of Learning

We are having cookouts at lunch time on Fridays and after home baseball and soft ball games. Darlene and The P.T.O. got three grills from Quinn Hardware in Skowhegan, at cost. One of the parents works there. Hot dogs, hamburgers and pasta salad, with popsicles for dessert three times a week till the end of the year is something the kids and parents are loving.

The Baseball team is still undefeated. The girls are 4 and 3, but if they win their last game tomorrow they make playoffs.

Once again success on the field is keeping the classroom time from bogging down. We have three weeks left of school. In the classroom we are all getting a civics lesson. We spent three days going over the Constitution and the Bill of Rights. Along the way I asked them to name their representatives to Congress, the

House and Senate. We didn't do all that well with that. But now they know.

When we got to the Bill Of Rights, only Amendment Two seemed of interest. Every boy in the class had heard of this one. The right to bear arms was something they had heard from the adults at home. It was clear in the town of Embden it would not be wise to try to legislate any gun control laws.

Outside the classroom the community was providing us opportunity to learn from the adults as well. Busloads of students spent a week alternating between sites learning how to plant trees. They witnessed the future of fish farming and farming in general. They milked cows and gathered eggs. They heard from a Veterinarian about Artificial Insemination. They watched a man brought in to trim the cattle's hooves. They were told the reason for crop rotation.

Henry spoke from the stage at the high school auditorium explaining the rivers and streams that ran through our communities. He teamed up with the Art Department whose Photography class had taken vivid pictures and turned them into slides. Students saw where streams and rivers that flowed through their towns joined and came together in the mighty Kennebec. The slides alternated between the present and the past. River drives that originated far above our towns in the Moose Head Lake region offered some historical perspective.

Our own Embden Pond got a do-over when a former employee of Camp Deveraux brought slides and told stories of what had been an important part of Embden History for forty years.

Next week we will all gather at a campground on the banks of the river in Solon and become part of a history in the making. Over three hundred students, staff, community members, and media will float down the mighty Kennebec for four miles. Learning and practicing team work along the way. NBC has been following this alternative learning project and will accompany us. This effort will air on national television.

When I signed on to teach in this little town I had no idea what wonderful ideas would take shape, blossom, and be allowed to flourish. Our Superintendent is indeed a bit of a cowboy. Yahoo.

CHAPTER FORTY-FIVE

A Simple Knock on the Door

Byron struggled with what Bruce was asking. He had put off a visit to Rhone for nearly two weeks trying to keep all Bruce had said straight in his head. While cutting wood he practiced his lines. Byron felt like the man he was working across from, Brother Bodine, deserved to know what Bruce was proposing. On the other hand if Byron brought Rhone back and it all turned out, his dream of being the hero of his own story might just come true. For his part Bodine was getting just a little tired of Byron sitting on a stump pretending to sharpen his saw all glassy eyed day after day.

"What the hell are you thinking about over there Byron, we got wood to cut, bills to pay, and pot to tend to. Or are you sneaking some of that shit into your cereal bowl in the morning? Get a move on."

Byron decided in that moment, tomorrow he'd go see Rhone.

"Bruce still bugging you about rejoining the team? It ain't gonna happen. Soons we get ahead I'm moving the hell out. He can keep the whole damn place to himself. You can come with me and the boy. Paula and your kids too."

That really decided it for Byron.

***

Rhone was just about to go hang out the sheets on this morning in late May 1981 when someone knocked.

Melody and the two kids were at school. She opened the door to Byron DeBloise, hat in hand.

"Morning Rhone, you look all good and well."

Rhone her hair up in a bun, wearing a house coat Melody had given her was in no mood for conversation. "What do you want Byron, Bodine send you? Didn't know you even knew where I was."

Byron, not the brightest but never the less not a mean man, looked down at his shoes. "Paula had some trouble having that baby. She still ain't doing to good. We sure could use some help." He looked back up beseechingly.

Rhone studied him momentarily, he resembled one of those tied up dogs begging for a scrap, "Does Bodine know you're here?"

Byron, not an able liar, glad he could speak mostly the truth. "Bodine don't know anything about this, just… just… just me."

"I suppose your brother Bruce has no idea either, that you're here?"

Again Byron could say for sure, without lying, "Bruce don't know I'm here this morning."

"But he did send you, right Byron?"

Byron squeezed the life out of his hat, he'd been caught. *Damn.*

"Come in and sit down Byron, I'll make us a cup of coffee and I'll tell you how the rest of this story goes."

When I got home from what had been an incredible day on the water it was nearly five pm. Waren was out fishing in front of the camp. Eliza's little mouth was just- a-moving as she stood beside Waren pointing at the line in the water. Rhone joined me at the window. "That little girl is opening up like a spring flower thanks to you Melody." Then she sighed. "I had a visitor this morning. Byron, you met him—the littlest warble in the bunch—anyway he came on a mission. Bruce put him up to it. So I would say it's time for me to head out. You don't need my problems."

I took her hand. "Rhone, running isn't going to do any good. Let me get in touch with Henry, he'll end this."

"I told Byron I'd be out there this weekend to talk with Bodine about the future. So I'm sure Bruce will be expecting me. I'm stalling for time Melody. That gives me three days to get gone."

"After supper, I'll send Waren for Henry. Hear him out. If you don't like the plan then you can leave, fair enough?"

The Answer Is In the Stars

Byron did just as Rhone had instructed. He told Bodine, Rhone was coming to see him this weekend. He also told Bodine not to say a word to Bruce. Rhone wanted nothing to do with Bruce and didn't want him there. Bodine listened, nodding in all the right places, but he had a question or two. "How did you know Rhone was staying with that teacher?"

Shit, thought Byron, *I ain't good at this lying business, I'd rather just be stupid.*

Byron's mouth opened and what came out was pretty nearly word for word all Bruce, then later Rhone, had told him.

"Second question, what is Bruce planning on doing to Rhone?"

Finally Byron could answer something straight out, "Gods own truth," he breathed deeply, "I don't have no idea."

"Well brother there's just one more no idea I'm going to share with you and then you're going to share that no idea with Bruce."

Byron was confused. He was told, walked through, asked to repeat, told once more; then finally the light came on. Byron smiled. He could do this.

***

Since returning, Bruce simply laid around the place. He wasn't welcome in the woods with his brothers. Paula was just beginning to be able to pick up after them all, but complained constantly. Bruce simply stated for the record a family homily. "A woman's work is never done so all the day you'll have no fun, now you'll have to pay a forfeit." Paula glared at him. Bruce chuckled, he was reminded of how his father butchered that little ditty he'd learned in the woods camps. When Bruce's mother complained about anything, his father would flub the lines then grab his wife haul her into the room separated by just a blanket and apply the forfeit. His father didn't flub the forfeit part.

Laid out on the filthy sofa, Bruce added, "Paula, if you don't want me offering up a forfeit you might want to just get'er done and shut your trap. And for the love of Christ can you shut those sticky faced leaky hoses up, I'm trying to think here."

Byron had told Bruce just what Bodine had crammed into his head. Byron felt he was believable. At least Bruce didn't ask any questions.

***

So Friday dawned with what promised to be a beautiful day. One week till school ended. Hopefully by the time Waren, and Eliza got home tonight Bruce DeBloise would be back behind bars with no hope of bailing out till the trial. I thought of how Henry had stood on that rock in the Kennebec as each raft filled with students pulled over to view the etchings. In his native leggings, beaded leather vest, a feather in a leather headband;

Henry described the meanings of the symbols. Thirty rafts took turns hearing of the history they and their families drove by on the roads each day. The whole experience left us viewing differently the richness of our area. A new sense of community pride emerged.

Henry had included Daniel in his plan. They sat this early morning at Henry's cabin drinking an herbal tea Henry had created. They moved to the steps. Several lingering stars were still visible which prompted Henry to revisit the plan as only he could visualize and verbalize. "We have been instructed to see the stars in combinations that reveal the bear, the dipper, the winged horse and so many others. If we look however at different combinations of stars other mysteries are revealed. It is looking at Rhone's problem in a different way that will send the wood cutter to his fate."

Daniel sipped his tea. The plan was re-visited. "Grandfather your wisdom keeps you young and engaged. I believe your plan will succeed."

Henry rubbed his knees, "Ah if only I could move as I once did I would have no need of this smoke screen."

CHAPTER FORTY-SEVEN

Rock, Paper, Scissors

Rhone walked on the trail leading to her former residence this Friday morning. The sun well up, new leaves and smells emerging every day from a green haze that had announced springs arrival. Little bits of color dotted the ground. Birds dashed back and forth across the rough ground that smoothed out only in winter when covered with snow. Rhone took a deep breath, she could do this. She had to do this. Bodine and Byron would be in the woods by now. Bruce would be sipping on his third cup of coffee, ragging on poor Paula. The sun was hanging at a height that signaled eleven am or so. The compound was quiet. Those damn dogs hadn't been returned. One blessing at least. She straightened her shoulders and marched right up to the door and knocked. Paula stiffened when she saw Rhone standing on the step.

"How are you feeling Paula? Byron said you had a hard delivery?"

Paula was about to answer when Bruce entered the door way.

Rhone feigned surprise and shock. "You aren't supposed to be here. Byron said you were long gone."

"Well little Miss, Byron's eyes and memory fail him from time to time." He smiled. "So either he failed to see me return or he just can't remember shit." He smiled again hoping Rhone might notice his new Ipana smile. He opened the screen, "You're looking fine, all healed and such. No hard feelings here."

Rhone could barely restrain her anger. "I'm here to see Paula, so just back off. There is a restraint order on you I'm sure you know."

Bruce put up his hands, "I'm not meaning you any harm. I would like to talk with you for a minute after you and Paula finish. Try to work some things out. Hell we're family. Bodine misses you something awful." Bruce offered up his very best hang dog look.

Rhone looked him straight in the mouth. "Those new teeth don't change the lies that exit that dirty mouth. I'll have that word with Paula then I'm out of here."

Bruce flushed, wanting to lash out but this wasn't the time. Soon though.

Rhone had her conversation about nothing with Paula, one more part of the plan. Then she began her walk back along the trail.

Bruce gave her a head start but ten minutes into the walk he saw her just up the path. He picked up his pace, breathing hard through his new teeth. Rhone heard his panting and turned to face him. Bruce lit up like a Christmas tree. He was about to unload one of his mind if I do moments when two dogs emerged from the trees with a dogs version of that little ditty leaving their mouths.

Right behind the dogs, who were circling Bruce, doing their dance, came Henry and Daniel.

Rhone spoke, "You have a nasty habit of not taking no for an answer Bruce." The dogs quieted at the command of Henry but continued to circle Bruce.

Bruce breathing deeply and sweating profusely was too frightened to move.

Henry spoke, "Do you see a future, wood cutter? This path you are traveling, beating and frightening women and children, cheating your neighbors. Growing drugs. This path ends here today."

Bruce tensed his fists. The dogs instinctively growled deep in their throats, Bruce slumped his shoulders. Daniel and Rhone watched Henry read the future.

"I can read your eyes wood cutter. You think perhaps another time." Henry took two stones from his pocket. "These stones are from the water. I have warmed them, I will see they are placed in plain sight. You will not disturb them."

Henry stepped closer. He could smell decay and a lifetime of negligence. In a motion he took Bruce's hand, "Your new teeth offer an empty smile wood cutter.

Behind them is an empty soul. There are many ways to become lost in the woods," he looked directly into Bruce's eyes, "I fear, for you there will be no way out."

Bruce wanted to remove the hand, yet he could not. The old man's grip sent a ripple of fear through him and something else, he suddenly saw his own future. He found himself nodding.

Henry removed his hand. Within a moment the two men the dogs and Rhone had disappeared. Bruce was left standing in the middle of the path, planted like one of the trees that had watched all this unfold.

When Bruce re- entered his dooryard, the three missing dogs welcomed him with the familiar yowling that Bruce realized he had missed. The dogs at least listened to him. Bruce was confused. The entire morning had been confusing. He shouted the dogs quiet. The silence, the first silence of the day really—from yapping Paula, to that bitch Rhone, to whatever that damn Indian was selling—he should maybe act and not react. Suddenly he felt better. This was his domain. He was still in charge here. Byron opened the door offering up even more good news.

Byron drove Bruce to a new woodlot. Bodine having done the negotiating for the first time used a kinder gentler approach. That's what he told Byron.

In truth it might have had something to do with the wood lot owner. Secured was a twenty acre old growth treasure, just a few miles from where they lived.

Byron shut down the engine. He pointed to his brother Bodine sitting on an enormous stump sharpening his saw. "He wants to set some things straight." That's what Bodine told Byron.

300

"I'll just sit here and sip on my coffee, he's pretty mad, you might maybe wanna listen." That's what Byron told Bruce.

Bruce, not a good listener, decided he needed to remain in charge. He would just blurt out his plan. He would leave Rhone alone, take his chances with a slick lawyer. That ought to settle his brother down.

Bodine watched his brother approach—same old body language—same old shit eating grin hiding behind plastic. *Nothing's changed.* That settled it in his mind.

Bodine held out a thermos of coffee. Bruce took it but before Bruce could warm his plastic Bodine began. "Morning Bruce, did you notice the dogs are back? Took some doing but me and Byron managed it? See this here stump I'm sitting on? There's a thousand dollars in every one of these trees." He pointed to the tree laying on the ground behind him. There's five hundred or more of these trees on this lot Bruce. I managed to convince the owner we wouldn't rape and pillage his lot." He waved his arm. "All this good fortune took place in your absence. But I'm your brother, you want back in?"

Bruce's eyes widened, he looked at the top of this bonanza a hundred feet in the air, "Bodine, I'm really sorry about what happened with Rhone and all. I'm gonna deal with all that. That's what I'm here to say"

"Well we can't fix that, not really Bruce. Not in the way you're imagining. Let's just get to work. Things may take care of themselves, who knows?" Knowing Bruce wouldn't listen he said it anyway. "These trees we're cutting are a lot bigger and more dangerous to get down. You'll want to cut an escape route in the brush." Bruce paid no attention. "Byron will show you where to start cutting. If you need any help just ask your brother. I need a new chain, I'll be back.

Waren, Eliza, and I got home shortly after four pm. At a little wooden table to the side of the front door sat Rhone flanked by Henry and Daniel. A pitcher of lemonade acted as centerpiece.

The trees to the side shaded half the table, Henry sat in full sunlight. They all waved our arrival but did not rise.

"What are we celebrating?"

"Not really celebrating just absorbing the news. Henry says it's over," offered Rhone as she beckoned her daughter to her lap. She squeezed her daughter tightly.

Knowing of the plan to confront Bruce, I asked, "So it worked, he's going to leave you alone?"

Henry with a strange light in his eyes spoke, "Yes, it is over."

He checked the sky then his watch, "It ended a short time ago."

I looked to Daniel, he widened his arms and opened his hands. "He says it's over."

Ok, I said to myself, "Well let's all celebrate then."

It was five thirty by the time we all moved from that table. Daniel offered to take Waren fishing. Rhone asked if she could borrow my car, she wanted to go buy Eliza some shorts and tee shirts for the last week of school. "My Mom is going with us. We'll be back for a late supper." Henry simply disappeared in his usual manner. As for me I needed a run. I needed to sift through beginnings and endings and what now looked like at least one person who would remain in my life for the foreseeable future.

As I tied my shoes my mother entered my thoughts. *Tied up in knots like these sneakers, tied so tight to the past that she has no future. She would simply get through it then be gone. So sad.* I closed the door, a sigh accompanying the sound of the inside lock catching. Lately I'm locking doors. Ed had been buried yesterday beside his wife. I didn't go but I'll visit the grave with Waren when school is out. With the late afternoon sun still in control for another hour, I could get in a longer run this afternoon. Thoughts of my father, directed my feet to Henry's cabin. Snow dog was sunning himself on the step, his tongue worrying an occasional fly. Henry opened the door before I could knock. "I knew you would have questions Melody, let us walk to my little stream. We can watch little sticks that have broken free and wish to explore the big water."

We gazed down from the bank lost in our own thoughts. "Have you eaten a fiddle head, Melody?"

I breathed in smells the water and the air were throwing at me on this spring evening. "Can't say I have. Though some of the kids keep telling me they are going to bring me some. They are late this year they say."

"I have found some. When you return from your run please stop in. I have fresh fish and Fiddleheads. Everyone is coming to supper."

"Thank you Henry, I will, but can you fill me in on this Bruce thing?"

"Let me suggest a route to run this evening. It is just off my little path. When you return, we will talk."

CHAPTER FORTY-NINE

Circle of Life

I entered a woods road that had in the past been well logged. I found a pace and studied the terrain. For a mile or so I jogged figuring distance by my heart rate. A logging operation on both sides of the road had claimed many acres of trees. New growth perhaps ten years in the making was covering the scars of what was called a clear cut.—I puffed up—I had learned as much as the kids during these weeks of community teaching. I dodged occasional scrub brush trying to reclaim the road but it was pretty easy going. Henry told me when it seemed this road was about to end I should look to my left. I found the break that appeared to be a foot path recently widened. Two hundred yards in on this path, a stand of timber one hundred feet high loomed on both sides as if guarding the forest. I had never seen pine trees this tall. The land was flat, un-scarred, untouched. Henry said the path was an old Indian trail that came out of the mountains to the west and one small piece of land had been claimed by his family. "If you followed the trail it to its end, you would cross what is now route sixteen. Shortly you would be on the bank of the Carrabassett River. Most of the trail is obliterated, logged over, turned to pasture, or built on. The little path you will be on is the last bit of Strongbolt history. And that too is now ending. But to good purpose."

It was darker in here. The sun resting in the upper limbs, was scoured, dispersed, filtered and evaporated. Some small vehicle had been here recently, hardly bending the grass. Why would Henry send me out here this time of day? It was a little spooky really. I stopped running. It hurt my neck to gaze so high. Tree trunks six feet in diameter standing shoulder to shoulder like a fence line turned the world greyish brown. I heard an engine and slipped into the gloom. A small Suv passed. The DeBloise brothers, Eliza's father, Bodine driving and Byron riding a fender. Bodine seemed to be talking to himself. Byron just holding on. I was reminded of Eliza talking up a storm to Waren while they fished, watching her lips move beyond the glass. I watched until the tail light came on and disappeared onto the old logging road. I decided I'd seen about enough of the woods for today so I moved back onto the path. There was leaky light still on the path, though it seemed someone had moved the clock ahead two hours. It wasn't far to the marker Henry had described, a totem pole he said. I began jogging. The path was beginning a wide sweep like a quarter moon, half way around I saw a gas can and a jacket laying across a huge stump. A pile of small logs in a little man made clearing. The earth was disturbed but not like what I had seen on the road coming in. Maybe one hundred yards ahead I could see the totem pole erected at the end of the property line. Gaily colored, standing tall. I reached it rubbed it for luck and turned around. Henry told me his property was long and narrow barely a hundred yards in width, twenty acres. Just as I started back, to my right the very top of a pine tree protruded out into the path, I didn't think much of until I heard a noise, a whimpering sound maybe. I stopped and listened. Nothing but dead air. Then I heard a sound again. It was coming from the woods. I edged my way around the crown of the tree. Curious, I made my way into inky darkness, stunted growths of bushes clawing at me. I stopped once more and listened, a chewing sound. An animal or maybe a wild game bird. *Whatever they sound like you hunter you.* I worked my way past the crown and placed my hands on the giant pine. The girth even this far from the trunk was four feet in diameter. I heard the squeaking noise again, maybe a squirrel. I caught the sight of something colored. Something lay obscured by the brush and limbs just out of my vision. The limbs reached out in all directions. I heard another sound, unrecognizable. It was pitch black in here. Suddenly my mind raced and my imagination returned me to the terror of my past dreams. This darkness didn't arise from lack of a moon or stars, yet my breath was catching. I could just recognize where limbs ended and the tangle of brush began. They seemed to be reaching for me. My ears tried to locate the sound. It had ceased. Silence surrounded me now. I sighed. I leaned into the bark. Miko touched my shoulder as he scampered the length of the trunk. I started. I quivered. It seemed I was about to encounter all my dark time demons.

A sound from a different direction startled me once again. That damn weight was on my chest, I couldn't breathe, then a voice reached me. I strained to understand. Henry was hollering to me. *Is this a dream?* I screamed.

"Melody it is alright, it's alright."

Snow dog reached me first, whining and rubbing against my legs. Even Pete arriving with his tongue hanging seemed glad to see me. Then Henry found me. He folded me into his arms. I sobbed. I sighed real loud. I couldn't speak.

Within his arms, even as he comforted me, he chuckled, *Henry being Henry.* "Snow dog insisted on a walk shortly after you left, I could hardly keep up. Pete insisted on coming as well. They brought me here.

Animals can sense when there is danger. But there is no longer danger here, Melody."

Another scuttling sound, Henry lit the sound with a flashlight. In the spotlight little Miko was echoing Henry's reassurance. *That little guy sure gets around*, I thought. I still could not speak.

"I will light your way back Melody, there is no reason to see what lies in there. I will explain over fish and Fiddleheads.

CHAPTER FIFTY

Taking Inventory

When we got back to Henry's camp, it was a full house. Rhone and Daniel were frying fish while a huge pot of fiddle heads steamed on the stove. Waren and Eliza were in Henry's lone bedroom looking at some of Henry's memorabilia. Snow dog signaled Pete and the two trotted off to do what dogs do. Nothing of substance was said until the meal was over. Henry sent Waren and Eliza out to study the stars. We four adults sat with a steaming cup of Henry's special tea in front of us, our elbows on the table, all ears.

"If you recall when we studied the stars, I might have mentioned that by studying the familiar formations in a different way, the result is a different pattern." He stopped, sipped some tea and became silent.

We waited. And waited.

Daniel finally spoke up, "Grandfather we don't all live in the heavens, can you give us mere earthlings some assistance here?"

Rhone and I laughed but nodded in agreement.

"Ok let me try again in a different way. I will use stars but they will be stars you will recognize." He winked.

We all sighed.

"When you are looking for a good result for a problem you are having and when in fact you get that result—we say the stars all lined up." Henry looked at us. He waited. And we waited.

Again it was Daniel who responded. "Yes that's true Grandfather, we do say that."

Henry smiled. "I will now attach a name to each of the stars that lined up to solve Rhone's problem. Were you aware that I knew Bodine as a boy? Well I did. I found him nearly drowned in the waters of Embden pond when he was about Waren's age. He had been fishing from a small leaky boat. The leak became worse and he panicked. He entered the water not knowing how to swim. I took him home and witnessed the father having no sympathy for the boy. He slapped him about the head and shoulders and sent him inside. He did not thank me. He muttered words I could not understand, turned and left me standing at the edge of his filthy sty."

Henry moved for a warm-up of his tea. Seated once again, he continued. "I saw the boy on occasion but we did not speak. The boy would simply nod. That was enough."

We all moved our chairs in unison, refreshing our own cups.

"When Bodine found out what had happened to you Rhone he came here to see me. He told me of the abuse that he had endured over the years and that now, his brother Bruce was continuing the family tradition. He said he could not allow his children to live like this. So Bodine is your first star Rhone, he really does care for you and his children but he has no language to show that love."

Rhone looked down, tears formed in her eyes.

"The woodlot on my land, that became the second star.

I hired Bodine and his Brother Byron, to cut it in a humane way. A selective cutting that will pay a debt I have neglected for too long." Henry studied the age spots and gnarled hands staring up at him.

He held up a third finger, "The next star was formed by the little messages that emanated from the first visit by Byron to your door Rhone. Byron was like our little squirrel Miko offering an acorn, hoping to be valued more highly—to become an Oak.

The wood cutter Bruce himself was the energy that lit that star. His callous approach to life, magnified in the way he cut wood, started a chain of events that ended here tonight."

The final star is Bodine once again, completing the circle. I told you he had no language of love, yet he loved. The only language he had observed throughout his life that brought quiet if not solace, was violence. It was love for you Rhone, and your children that sent him on this path. He thought through and executed this plan. It was when he realized you would never have him in your life that he came to me for a plan. As I said, when the star's line up."

I couldn't help myself, "Henry who is laying under that tree out there? And how did he get there and don't we need to call someone?"

"Let me finish my story, teacher, you are like Waren wanting recess. I'm nearly finished. Believe me that tree is not going anywhere." He stood then, "Even as a young man, most of this area had been cut off at least once.

My father's father however told of seeing a whole forest of trees much like what you observed on my wood lot. Men worked in teams to take these giants down. It was very dangerous work. Bruce had no experience with trees of this size and he had always been too lazy to cut brush that could afford an escape route." Henry looked serious, "Bodine welcomed his brother back to cut this lot knowing Bruce would once again be Bruce. It is the wood cutter Bruce who lies beneath the tree and he alone is responsible for his own death. He neglected to cut an escape route and when the tree started its fall he tripped and was merely slapped by a small limb. A limb that would not be fatal except for how the blow landed."

We all waited for the ax to fall, no pun intended.

"Bodine and Byron found their brother struggling for breath. The limb struck Bruce directly in the mouth. Bruce swallowed his new teeth and choked to death."

We all gasped.

"Bodine, back in the woods from getting his saw repaired found him. He and his brother came directly here, which is the real reason for my coming to find you. I did not wish for you to find him there."

"But you seemed to know it had ended earlier this afternoon Henry."

"When I took Bruce's hand on the path I felt no life. He was a dead man walking even then. Lucky guess perhaps."

Rhone bowed her head once more, I sighed, and Daniel looked at his grandfather realizing suddenly why the wood was being cut. Henry was planning a legacy for his grandson.

*****

School started on time Monday morning. Darlene couldn't wait for me to return to the kitchen for a cup of coffee. "This one's on me, Melody but only if you'll fill in the holes for me. Police cars, an ambulance and a wrecker in Embden, that's a convoy."

I told her what I knew but in a matter of fact way, I don't have Henry's story telling ability.

"Well I'm glad that's over. It is over isn't it?"

"It's over Darlene," I kidded, "over and out."

I left the kitchen just as Marie and Karen arrived, they opened their mouths. I pointed to Darlene, "She'll tell you all about it. I have some work to do. It was a busy weekend."

The kids all shared and magnified the little bit of what had reached their kitchen table. Waren remained silent on the issue.

The last four days of school is pretty much a holding tank for students and teachers alike. I appointed two of the most restless boys to collect, count and inventory text books we were done with. I sent three of the girls into the little closet off the hallway where we kept paper and all the teaching supplies from staples to glue. They would straighten sort and tally everything in there.

Students had until Wednesday to get their final report on our community learning event in for a grade. I had received just over half of them, so I knew what Wednesday and Thursday night was going to look like for myself. Some used this extra time wisely.

We cooked out at lunch and took a longer than normal time to eat.

We had a championship baseball game to play tonight in North Anson. PJ. our ace would be on the mound. I let the boys run a little practice at one thirty, the rest of us watched and kidded them from the bleachers. Waren was now the number three starter and first in as a reliever. The kids nicknamed him the fireman. Waren seemed to like that.

I picked up Henry and Daniel, stopped to get Rhone and Eliza and we made our way to Mark Emery School.

At the elementary level Baseball is a six inning game. We were the sharper dressed of the two teams, clad in baby blue uniforms with navy lettering and piping. Uniforms courtesy of an incredible Parent Teachers Organization, informally headed by our mother earth angel who always wished to remain anonymous. She was in attendance.

The first three innings the pitchers dominated. PJ had his curve working and being one of the few lefties in our league he baffled the hitters.

We were the visiting team so we batted first. In the top of the fourth Tracey hit a hard shot to left that split the fielders, Aaron followed with a walk. Two on, no outs. Troy sacrifice bunted, moving the runners along. One out. Eric hit a fly ball to right that was caught, but Tracey made it home on the throw. One- zip Embden. Two down, man on third.

Embden's coach Mr. Bown, an elementary teacher, had decided to put the fireman in to pitch in the bottom of the fourth, so Waren pinch hit for Robbie. He was hit by a pitch. He stole second on the first pitch to the next batter. Two men on, second and third, two out. The coach from Mark Emery put in a new pitcher. The kid never found the plate and we had four runs in before the inning ended with a pop up from Tracey, he batted twice in that inning.

Waren skimmed rocks over the plate from every angle. They managed a single hit in the bottom of the sixth and we won 4-0. The Embden Raiders had their first Championship Trophy.

It was nearing seven o'clock when we got back to the camp. Bodine was on the steps. He hugged Eliza and I took her inside, this was grown-up talk. I looked out toward the lake an hour later, having fed Eliza, read her a story and tucked her in. The stars were out and a good weather moon offered me two silhouettes facing each other, not touching. I went back to my kitchen table and began reading some of those reports. Thinking back to the conversation I had with old W.T.F. and recalling the three days of testing we finished at the end of April, with kids trying their hardest, I was looking forward to August and the test results.

Waren who had insisted on being dropped off at Daniels, opened the door and came to the table. "Henry pulled off some more of his magic tonight, Miss Melody."

I waited for the shoe to drop.

"He went back to his cabin when you dropped us off and showed up an hour later with a woman on his arm."

Drop the damn shoe Waren. I threw up my hands.

"He had my mother with him. She wants to meet you."

I sighed, "So one of your wishes has come true. Are you still thinking about that second wish?"

Waren nodded, "Me and Mom too, that's why she wants to meet you."

We hugged for the second time. "By the way, you pitched amazing Waren, I'm very proud of you."

I had just gotten back to my reading, just dried my eyes. Waren had gone to take a shower when the door opened, it was Rhone. She had been crying.

She pulled up a chair and let out a long sigh. *Been there,* I thought.

"Bodine wants to try again Melody. He does love me and the kids and he's not like—" she paused, "what did Henry call him, the wood cutter? Yeah Bodine's not like the wood cutter. What should I do?"

"I'm the last person you should come to about relationships, but I will say this, if it was me and it has been me in the past, follow your heart."

It was after eleven when I turned off my light. I was tired. Just three more days of school.

Today the eighth graders went to the high school for step-up day. The seniors were gone. A mock schedule was prepared that took the eighth graders from all five schools in the district through what would be a typical day in high school. The high school staff planned activities that would hopefully build team work among students who just yesterday faced each other on the field.

With the oldest students gone for the day, we all breathed a sigh of relief. We loved them and all that but they were getting pretty uppity. Tomorrow would be a field day filled with activities that was being planned by the P.T.O. So no more classroom work after today.

When the busses pulled out, we had one last little teachers meeting in Marie's room. We all sighed.

The last day of School. HURRAH!

If you think its only kids that count the last day of school among their favorite all time memories think again. Sure we'll come back in the fall ready for action but right now we need our batteries recharged. I've always said it was divine guidance that delivered vacations when we absolutely needed them most.

We had a fun day and it went off with no problems. Well one problem and one surprise, a good one. Actually two.

The problem was Evan, our bus driver custodian. It seems he finally caught on that kitchen coffee with me, Darlene as chaperone, was going to be the extent of our love life. He found some other lucky girl. Well apparently when Evan falls he falls hard. When she threw him out of her life after a month he not only landed hard, he skidded. Late last night he ended up getting caught for a DUI after breaking a window in the home of his beloved. She called the cops. They found Evan drunk and driving. Not really my problem except no one contacted the bus supervisor that we would need a sober driver this morning, Evan in jail and all. So on this last day fifteen students arrived an hour and a half late.

One good surprise happened at the end of our lunch. I could feel the stirrings of something but I had no idea. Darlene banged on a kitchen pan and every one moved to the bleachers. Earth Mother was in the background with several other parents. Gary, a team captain, highest ranking student official, called for quiet. "We have had an awesome year and bringing home a championship this week is just the tip of it. Miss Melody, you ran with us, played ball with us but most importantly taught us. Not just school stuff, life stuff. We love you and want you to have our trophy. Hopefully you stay here but if not wherever you go you will carry us all with you." PJ. Troy and Waren all carried the trophy to me.

I had no words. Tears filled my eyes and I sighed. A sigh of contentment.

The second surprise was when I pulled out of the school parking lot, headed into North Anson for some gas and ice-cream. I looked to my left as I had a habit of doing since Henry shared the secret of the stones. THEY WERE GONE!

Then I remembered what others had said. When school ends they disappear. Or could it mean something more than that.

I drove to Henry's cabin. The two dogs stood as a receiving line. I petted them both then knocked. Henry had a crinkle in his eyes as he opened the door, as if already knowing my mission. I just blurted out, "Will those pebbles be there in the fall?"

Henry looked deep into my eyes and took my hand. "The better question is, will you be here when school begins? Let's see if the stars all line up."

What a man. I simply sigh.

That night my father called. He is indeed getting married to a woman twenty five years younger than him. She wants to meet me. She is changing careers and is going to become a teacher. "Any words of advice for her Melody?"

"Yes Great Bear, tell her to let them breathe.

Good Night."

Oh and readers if you find any loose ends, just
IMAGINE!

www.ingramcontent.com/pod-product-compliance
Lightning Source LLC
Chambersburg PA
CBHW070514310726

48976CB00002BA/434